WRITERS REPUBLIC

This Is America

By Shaneque Frett

Illustrated by

Stanley Mbamalu

WRITERS REPUBLIC L.L.C.
515 Summit Ave. Unit R1
Union City, NJ 07087, USA

Website:*www.writersrepublic.com*
Hotline: *1-877-656-6838*
Email: *info@writersrepublic.com*

Ordering Information:
Quantity sales. Special discounts are available on quantity purchases by corporations, associations, and others. For details, contact the publisher at the address above.

Library of Congress Control Number: 2020950359
ISBN-13:   978-1-64620-741-1   [Paperback Edition]
                978-1-64620-742-8   [Hardback Edition]
                978-1-64620-743-5   [Digital Edition]

Rev. date: 11/12/2020

Acknowledgement

I would like to thank my sister T'Niquewa Cameron for allowing me to constantly bounce ideas off her. She is my right hand; we spend hours on the phone constantly brainstorming and every now and then greatness blooms. Her and I being mothers of all boys and this year's Black Lives Matter movement has inspired the idea for this book. For years people of color, mostly our young men, have fallen at the hands of police. Rest in heaven, Tamir Rice, George Floyd, Breonna Taylor, and Micheal Brown a few of many. We defiantly feel like this is something that is needed for our children. Thank you to my husband, Jacoi Frett, for being by my side as I pushed through this project. Stanley Mbamalu, my awesome illustrator, he really brought my vision to light it was a blast working with him. Thank you all and God bless.

Introduction

The purpose of this book is to encourage parents to discuss difficult conversations with their kids. My purpose is not to instruct your children, because there is no right or wrong answer. Every household is different and has different beliefs. Some parents feel that topics like, racism, stereotyping, profiling, hate, and police brutality are too much to expose a child to. However, society has been subjecting our children to these topics for years, and even more in recent years with the growth of social media platforms. Instead of allowing society to dictate when, how and what information your child is exposed, start in the home. You be the one to educate your children on what they need to know on these topics, so when they are faced with difficult situations they know how to respond.

Hey, my name is Dre.

This is my older brother Travis.

Travis's favorite sport was baseball. He taught me how to play. When I got good enough, I signed up for the junior league. Travis was at all my games.

One day when Travis and I were walking home from one of my baseball games, a police officer pulled up to us and jumped out his car with his gun pointing at us.

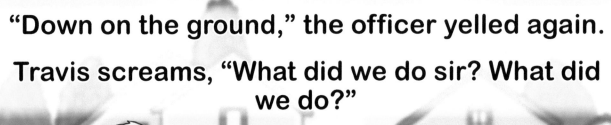

"We got a call about suspicious activity in this area. What are you doing in this neighborhood? Where are you headed?" asks the officer.

"There has to be some type of mistake sir we live in this neighborhood. We are just walking home from my brother's baseball game in the park." Travis says. "Look I can show you..."

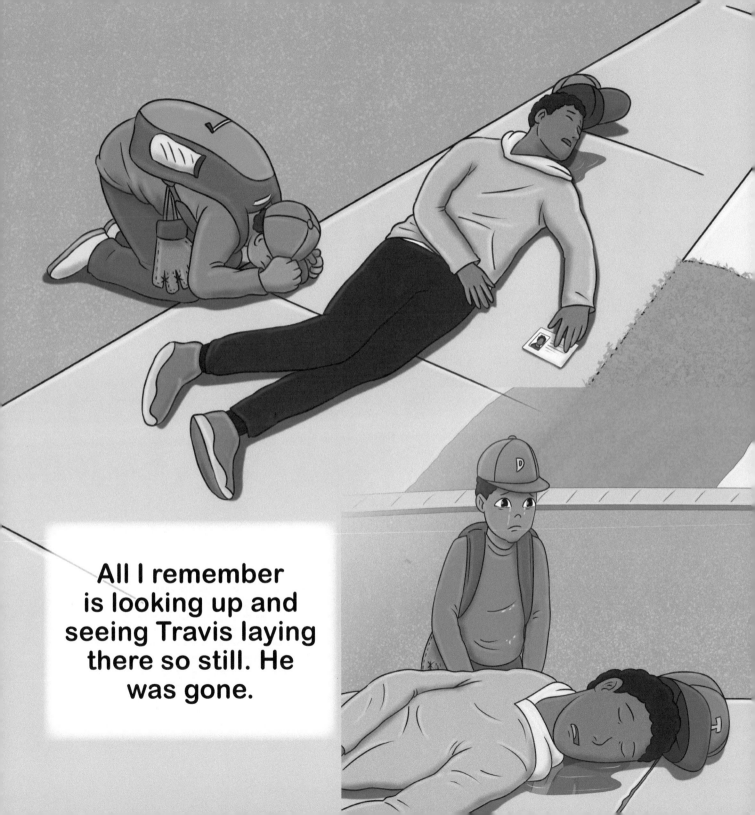

Everything happened so fast. I was confused. Later that night mom and dad talked to me about what I experienced. They explained to me that because of my skin color people may sometimes feel afraid or threatened even though we may not be doing anything wrong.

If you are like me, a person of color, then you should talk to parents about these things. What happened to my brother Travis can happen to anyone. It might sound scary, but this is the world we live in.

THIS IS AMERICA.

slavery

racism

police brutality

prejudices

discrimination

segregation

poverty

white supremacy

stereotypes

TALK WITH PARENTS

What should I do when I am approached by a police officer?

Why do you feel like the police stopped Travis and Dre?

What is hate?

What is a stereotype?

What is racism?

What is profiling?

CPSIA information can be obtained
at www.ICGtesting.com
Printed in the USA
BVHW020853021220
594474BV00046B/5

Authors: Mark Lambert
Keith Lye
Ron Taylor
Keith Wicks

Editor: Linda Moore

Art Editors: John Curnoe
Jacky Paynter

Picture Researcher: Julia Calloway

Consultant: Paula Varrow
Riddlesdown Comprehensive School

ALL COLOUR BOOK OF
SCIENCE FACTS

Our Earth · Plants and Animals · The Human Body · Science and Technology

The world around us is full of the mysteries of science. This book introduces you to a wide range of scientific topics, such as how the Earth was made, how some unusual plants feed on animals and the story of what happens to food as it passes through our digestive system, as well as some traditional science subjects such as light, sound, electricity, and some technology topics such as computers and lasers. For easy reference the topics are divided into four main sections, called Our Earth, Plants and Animals, The Human Body and Science and Technology.

Designed in self-contained double-page spreads, this is a book that you can read and enjoy from cover to cover or dip into at random. It is also a valuable reference book – the comprehensive index enables you to look up any particular topic quickly and easily. If you come across difficult words that you do not quite understand, turn to the Glossary at the back of the book. There you will find a list of difficult and important words together with a short explanation of each one.

Published by
Marshall Cavendish Books Limited
58 Old Compton Street
London W1V 5PA

© Marshall Cavendish Limited 1980 – 84

ISBN 0 85685 831 5

Printed in Italy

Contents

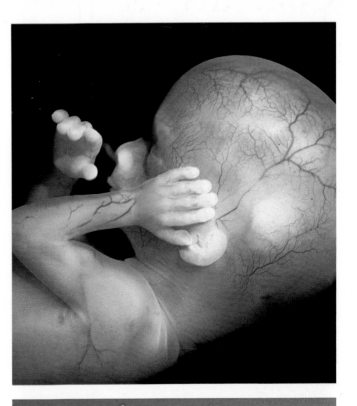

How the Earth was made

Our planet Earth is one of the nine planets which rotate around the Sun in the solar system. The Sun, a medium-sized star, is only one of millions in the Milky Way galaxy. Beyond our galaxy, the universe contains millions of other galaxies.

How was our solar system created? Scientists have put forward several theories. One theory suggests that a star once passed close to our Sun. Because of gravity, a streamer of gas and dust would have been torn from the star and the Sun. As this material rotated around the Sun, it would have collected together to form the planets, moons and other bodies in the solar system. Few scientists, however, think that this is a likely theory.

A second theory suggests that the Sun was once much bigger than it is today and that it was spinning around quickly. As it spun, it may have ejected a cloud of gas and dust, which later formed the planets. This is a

Below: Molten lava pours from a volcano at Surtsey, an island off Iceland, in 1964. In the early days of Earth history, the entire surface of the Earth was probably molten, with a temperature of more than 1000°C.

fairly new and untested theory.

The third and most popular theory is that the solar system was formed from a vast cloud of dust and gas that was drifting through space. At the centre of this cloud, the dust and gas were drawn together to form a hot mass, which became the Sun. Then the remaining material came together to form the planets.

The age of the Earth

People once thought that the Earth was formed recently. In the 1600s, a scholar, Bishop Ussher, added up all the generations of people in the Bible. He worked out that the Earth was created on 23rd October 4004 BC.

However, in the 1800s, scientists realized that the Earth must be many millions of years old. In the early 1900s, ways of measuring the ages of rocks were discovered. The oldest rocks yet found on Earth are more than 3700 million years old. But the solar system itself is much older than this. Meteors have been found that are about 4550 million years old and, recently, some Moon rocks have been dated at 4600 million years. We now believe that this is the age of the Earth.

Rocks formed in the first 900 million years of Earth history have probably been destroyed.

After it had formed, the Earth was a blazing hot planet, covered by molten rock. Huge volcanic explosions threw up lighter substances to form the thin crust. Beneath the crust lay denser substances in the mantle and the core. The core is four to five times as dense as the crust and probably consists mostly of iron and nickel.

The air around the Earth

The crust was constantly cracked and re-melted and gases were released from the rocks. These gases formed a poisonous atmosphere, containing little oxygen. Water vapour was also released from the rocks when volcanoes erupted. The water vapour formed clouds and, finally, rain fell on to the surface during great storms. As the surface cooled, water collected in hollows to form the first seas.

In these seas, chemical reactions occurred, which created the first living cells. The oldest known living things on Earth were primitive plants, about 3100 million years old. Much later in Earth history, around 1900 million

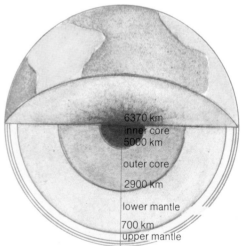

6370 km
inner core
5000 km

outer core
2900 km

lower mantle
700 km
upper mantle

THE EARTH'S INTERIOR

Above: It is about 6370 kilometres from the Earth's surface to its centre. The continental crust has a maximum thickness of 60–70 kilometres. The ocean crust, which also underlies the continents, is only about 6 kilometres thick. Beneath it is the mantle, which encloses the core. The outer core is liquid, but the inner core is solid.

years ago, advanced plants evolved. They produced life-giving oxygen, which steadily increased in the air, making it breathable. Some oxygen high up in the atmosphere was changed by the Sun's radiation into a gas called ozone. Ozone blocks out most of the Sun's harmful ultra-violet rays. Without oxygen and ozone, life on Earth would be impossible.

Right: The solar system probably formed from a vast cloud of gas and dust (1), which was drifting through space. Because of gravity, the particles were drawn together and the cloud grew smaller. Because it was rotating, the cloud was also flattened into a disc. Heavier particles were drawn together towards the centre. There they formed a large central mass (2). This extremely hot central mass developed into the Sun, while the rest of the material in the surrounding disc formed the planets (3). Today, our solar system consists of nine planets and other bodies which rotate around the Sun (4). Our Earth is the third planet from the Sun.

Below: This photograph of the Earth from space shows most of Africa and Arabia at the top. At the bottom is the icy continent of Antarctica. The oceans are partly covered by clouds.

Right: The diagram shows an edge-on view of the Milky Way galaxy. It contains millions of stars arranged in a central hub with spiral arms. Our solar system is two-thirds of the way out from the central hub. The distance across the Milky Way galaxy is about 100,000 light years. One light year is about 10 million million kilometres.

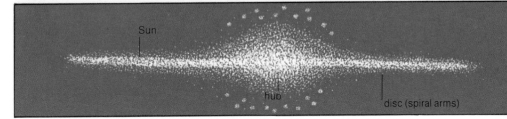

Sun

hub

disc (spiral arms)

9

The atmosphere

The atmosphere is a blanket of air surrounding the Earth. If the Earth did not have a protective atmosphere, the Sun's rays would scorch our planet during the day, and temperatures would plummet far below freezing at night.

The composition of air

By volume, dry air consists mostly of three gases: nitrogen (78.09 per cent), oxygen (20.95 per cent) and argon (0.93 per cent). The other 0.03 per cent consists of such gases as carbon dioxide, helium, hydrogen, krypton, methane, neon, ozone and xenon. The lowest layer of the atmosphere, called the *troposphere*, also contains water vapour. The amount of water vapour is quite small, varying from one to four per cent.

In some areas, dust, smoke and harmful gases enter the air from factories or from the exhaust pipes of cars. Nuclear explosions also throw radioactive particles and gases into the air. All these substances pollute the air, even when they are present in very small amounts. Air pollution is a serious hazard to health and may also damage metals and stonework. Today many countries have laws to control air pollution.

Air pressure

Clean air is invisible, tasteless and odourless, but the atmosphere weighs an estimated 5000 million million tonnes. This means that a column of air weighing about 1 tonne is pressing down on your shoulders. The effect of air pressure can be shown by pumping all the air from a can, creating a vacuum inside it. The air then presses on to the can, making it crumple and collapse. We do not notice air pressure, because the pressure inside our bodies is the same as the air pressure on the outside.

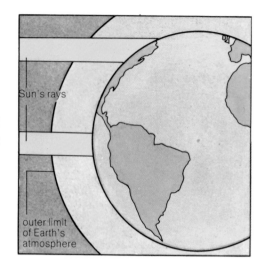

Below: A cloud of smog hangs over Santiago, a city in Chile. Smog, a word which comes from 'smoky fog', is often caused by dirt and gases poured into the air by coal fires in homes or by furnaces in factories. Another kind of smog is caused largely by car exhaust fumes. The most unpleasant effects of smog are felt when polluted air lingers for some time over the land. Industrial and car exhaust gases are usually carried away by rising air currents. But they are sometimes trapped by a process called temperature inversion. This occurs when the ground is chilled. The air near the ground then becomes colder and heavier than the warmer air above it. Hence, polluted air around ground level is trapped and cannot rise.

Above: The amount of heat that reaches the Earth's surface varies between the poles and the equator. Around the poles, the Sun's rays pass through a greater thickness of atmosphere. The atmosphere absorbs heat, so less heat reaches the surface at the poles than at the equator. Near the poles, the Sun's rays also spread over a large area, hence, the poles get less heat than tropical regions.

Below: Mountaineers often wear oxygen masks when climbing high peaks. This is because the air becomes thinner, or more rarefied, the higher one goes above sea level. Rarefied air is also a problem for athletes from low-lying countries who compete in games held in places on high plateaux.

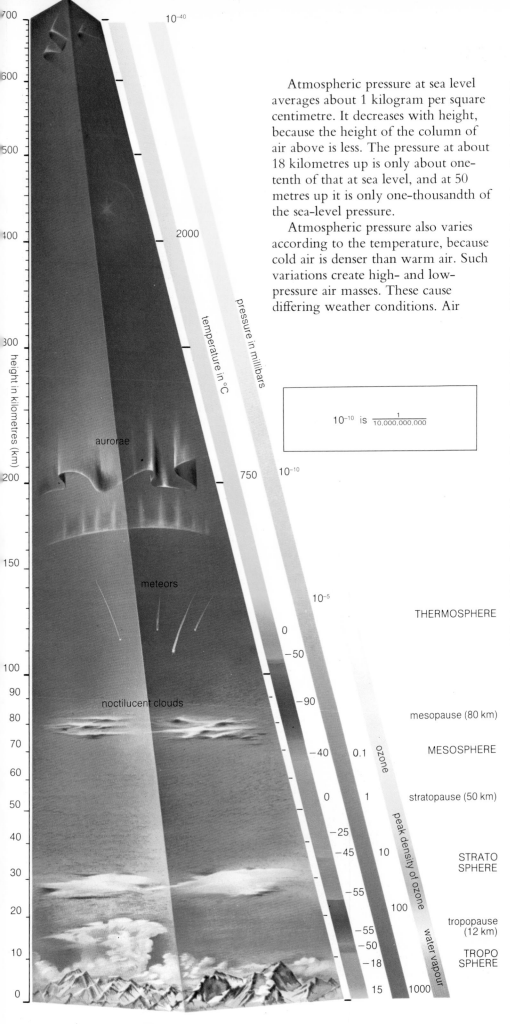

Atmospheric pressure at sea level averages about 1 kilogram per square centimetre. It decreases with height, because the height of the column of air above is less. The pressure at about 18 kilometres up is only about one-tenth of that at sea level, and at 50 metres up it is only one-thousandth of the sea-level pressure.

Atmospheric pressure also varies according to the temperature, because cold air is denser than warm air. Such variations create high- and low-pressure air masses. These cause differing weather conditions. Air pressure is measured by instruments called barometers, in units called millibars. A pressure of 1000 millibars is roughly the same as an air pressure which can support a 750-millimetre column of mercury.

Layers of the atmosphere

About 80 per cent of the mass of the atmosphere is in its lowest layer, the troposphere. On average, the troposphere is about 12 kilometres high. Its height varies from 18 kilometres above the equator to 8 kilometres over the poles.

In the troposphere, the temperature decreases with height, by roughly 7°C for every kilometre. Temperatures become stable at about −55°C at the top of the troposphere. This level is called the *tropopause*.

Above the tropopause is the *stratosphere*. Temperatures remain the same for the bottom 10 kilometres of the stratosphere. But they then rise until, at about 50 kilometres up, the *stratopause* is reached. Above this level lie the other two zones of the atmosphere, the *mesosphere* and the *thermosphere,* which are separated by the *mesopause*. The thermosphere gradually decreases in density until it fades into space.

Left: The layers of the atmosphere are the troposphere, stratosphere, mesosphere and thermosphere. The troposphere contains about 80 per cent of the air in the atmosphere, and nearly all of the water vapour. The diagram shows that temperatures fall steadily with height until they reach −55°C at the top of the troposphere, which is the tropopause. Above the tropopause is the stratosphere. Jet aircraft fly in the lower stratosphere. But the stratosphere is important because of its layer of ozone. This ozone filters out the Sun's harmful ultra-violet rays. The mesosphere, between 50 and 80 kilometres high, contains noctilucent clouds. These consist of dust from meteors which have burned up while approaching Earth. Above the mesopause is the thermosphere. This contains only 0.001 per cent of the atmosphere. Disturbances in the thermosphere, caused by streams of particles from the Sun, create glowing lights in the sky, called aurorae. Artificial satellites orbit the Earth in the thermosphere.

10^{-10} is $\frac{1}{10,000,000,000}$

Winds and weather

Winds are large-scale movements of air. The chief factor which causes air to move is heat from the Sun.

The main wind systems

The Sun's heat is most intense around the equator. There, the air is heated and rises in fast-moving upward air currents. This is because warm air is lighter (less dense) than cool air.

Because the air is rising, the air pressure at the surface is reduced. This creates a low-pressure air belt, called the *doldrums,* which extends around the Earth. Air from the north and south is sucked into the doldrums to replace the rising air. This incoming air forms the *trade winds.*

The warm rising air cools high up in the troposphere, spreads out and then flows north and south. Eventually it sinks down around latitudes 30° north and 30° south. These regions, called the *horse latitudes,* are high-pressure zones. To relieve the pressure, winds blow outwards. Some blow towards the equator in the trade winds. Others flow polewards in the *westerlies.* At the poles, the air is cold and dense. It moves away from the poles in winds called the *polar easterlies.*

Winds do not flow in a straight north–south direction. Instead, they are deflected by the rotation of the Earth. This effect is similar to what happens if you try to draw a straight line from north to south on a spinning globe. When the globe stops, you will see that you have drawn a curved line.

The world's main wind systems are shown on the map on page 13. But other factors complicate wind systems. Most important is the fact that land heats up and cools down faster than the oceans. Hence, in summer, air over tropical lands is heated faster than air over the seas. Intense heating of the land may create low-pressure air masses which draw in cooler air from the sea. Sometimes, wind directions are reversed between summer and winter; these are called *monsoons.*

Weather systems

There are two main kinds of weather systems. *Anticyclones* are high-pressure systems, in which air is descending.

They generally have stable weather conditions. *Cyclones,* or *depressions,* are low-pressure systems, where warm air rises. Depressions have changeable weather.

Depressions form in the middle latitudes, where the polar easterlies meet the warm westerlies along the so-called *polar front.* Here, the cold and warm air are mixed. Depressions are rotating air masses, with warm, low-pressure air at their centres. The cold, denser air flows around the warm air, gradually forcing it upwards and cooling it. The passage of a depression is marked by squally and rainy weather. Storms associated with depressions are called *cyclonic storms.*

Thunderstorms are other common storms. They occur when fast-rising warm air currents create cumulo-nimbus clouds (see page 14). Features of thunderstorms include thunder, lightning and heavy rain or snow.

North and south of the equator, destructive storms called hurricanes occur. These are large rotating air masses, with extremely low air pressures. Howling winds swirl around hurricanes, doing much damage.

Tornadoes are other destructive storms with even lower air pressures than hurricanes. Tornadoes are small in area, measuring less than one-half of a kilometre across, but their winds can rip trees out of the ground.

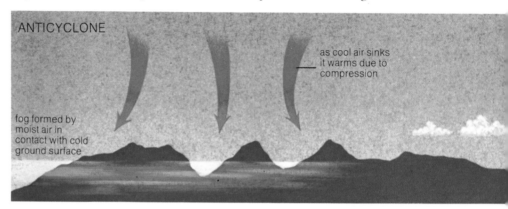

ANTICYCLONE

fog formed by moist air in contact with cold ground surface

as cool air sinks it warms due to compression

Below: A tornado in the USA. Tornadoes form when a funnel-like column of cold air sinks down from a storm cloud. Warm air rises, whirls around it and causes fierce winds.

Below right: This space photograph shows a hurricane off the coast of Cuba. The spiralling clouds show that the air is rotating rapidly around the centre, or eye, of the hurricane.

Right: The map shows the Earth's main wind belts. Trade winds are shown in brown and purple, westerlies in green, and polar easterlies in blue. Other winds, shown in red, are caused by local factors, including the unequal heating of the land and sea.

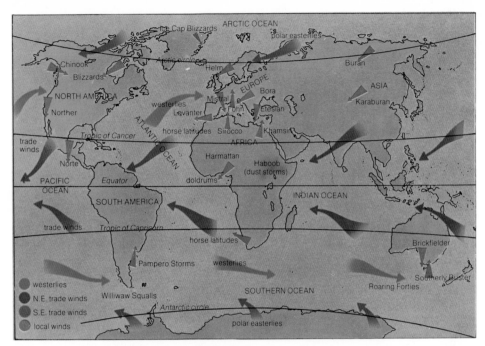

Below: Anticyclones, left, form when cool air sinks down, creating a high-pressure system, with stable weather conditions. Depressions, right, form when warm air mixes with cold air. On the left, cold air is pushing under the warm air along the cold front. As the warm air rises, cumulonimbus clouds form and heavy rain falls. On the right, warm air is forced up over the cold air along the warm front. Again, clouds form, but there is usually less rain.

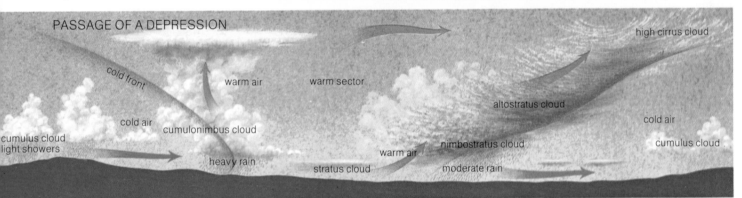

PASSAGE OF A DEPRESSION

Below right: The diagram shows how a hurricane is structured. At the centre, or eye, of the hurricane, air is sinking downwards. Here, calm weather conditions occur and there are no clouds in the sky. Around the eye, warm air is rising and storm clouds are forming. Also, the air is rotating in a spiral, creating strong, swirling winds. Winds in hurricanes may reach speeds of 300 kilometres per hour. Hurricanes form in tropical regions over the oceans. When they move over land, they leave a trail of great destruction behind them.

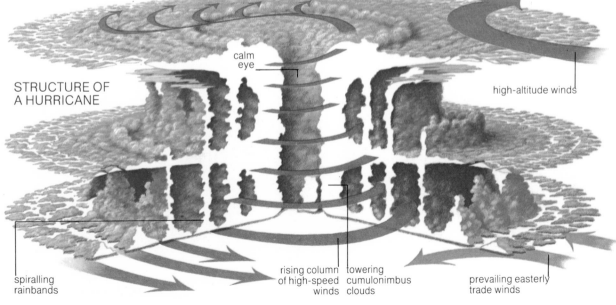

STRUCTURE OF A HURRICANE

Clouds

About 97.2 per cent of all the water in the world is in the oceans and 2.15 per cent is frozen in ice sheets and glaciers. Most of the rest is on land, either in rivers or lakes, or within the soil and rocks. Only 0.001 per cent of the world's water is airborne, but this moisture is vital for all animals and plants that live on land.

Water vapour and clouds

The Sun's heat evaporates water from the oceans. Evaporated water, or *water vapour*, is a dry, invisible substance, just like a gas. Water vapour is carried upwards into the atmosphere by rising air currents.

Warm air can hold more water vapour than cold air. In fact, the hot air over deserts may contain more water vapour than cold air over temperate regions. When air contains all the water vapour it can hold at a given temperature, called the *dew point*, it is saturated. Saturated air has a *relative humidity* of 100 per cent. Relative humidity is a measure of the amount of water vapour in air, as a percentage of the total it can contain when saturated, at that temperature.

When air with a relative humidity of 100 per cent is cooled, some water vapour must be lost by the process of

Below: The main low clouds (below 2.5 kilometres) include layered stratus, heaped cumulus, stratocumulus, nimbostratus and cumulonimbus – thunder clouds. Medium clouds are altocumulus and altostratus. High clouds (above 6 kilometres) include cirrocumulus, cirrostratus and cirrus.

Above: Cumulonimbus clouds form when warm air rises rapidly. The air is cooled and the invisible water vapour condenses into visible water droplets.

Right: Lightning consists of huge electrical sparks in clouds. Lightning heats the air, causing thunder.

Below: When the temperature of a cloud is well below freezing point, ice crystals grow into snowflakes. Near the ground, the snowflakes may melt to form sleet or rain.

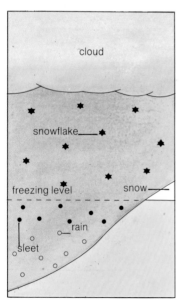

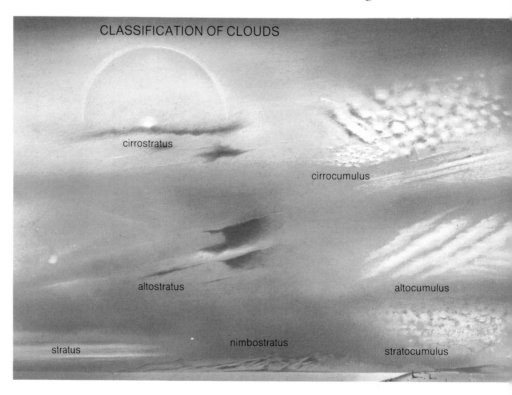

CLASSIFICATION OF CLOUDS

cirrostratus

cirrocumulus

altostratus

altocumulus

stratus

nimbostratus

stratocumulus

condensation. This means that some water vapour is turned back again into a liquid. When condensation occurs, water vapour liquefies around specks of dust or salt in the air, forming tiny but visible water droplets. A mass of these tiny droplets forms a cloud. Some clouds consist of masses of tiny ice crystals and very cold water droplets. Both are condensed at temperatures below freezing point. The water droplets may have a temperature of −15°C, but they remain liquid. However, when these *supercooled* droplets collide with ice crystals, they freeze around them.

Clouds occur in various shapes. There are two main kinds. *Cumulus* clouds are high heaps of cloud, while *stratus* clouds form in thin layers.

Precipitation

Precipitation is the general name for moisture lost from clouds. The most familiar example is rain. Rain is

formed in several ways within clouds. In warm regions, the tiny water droplets are blown around. As they move, they hit against and merge with other droplets. Finally, the droplets become so heavy that they fall to the ground as large raindrops.

In temperate regions, where the clouds are well below freezing point, the ice crystals grow as supercooled water droplets freeze around them. When the ice crystals become large, they fall downwards as snowflakes. Near the ground, they melt and become raindrops. However, if the air near the ground is cold enough, then the crystals fall as snow.

Other forms of precipitation include sleet, hail, mist, fog and frost. Sleet is a mixture of rain and snow. Hail consists of large pellets of ice. Mist and fog are masses of tiny water droplets near the ground. Frost forms when the water vapour condenses into ice crystals on chilled surfaces.

Right: Three ways in which clouds are formed. Orographic clouds form when winds rise over mountains. But as the air descends again, it is warmed, and little rain falls. Thunderclouds are formed by fast-rising air currents. Frontal clouds occur in depressions, when warm air rises over cold air.

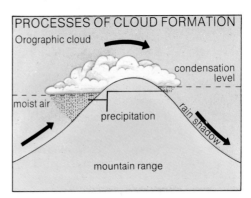

PROCESSES OF CLOUD FORMATION
Orographic cloud
condensation level
moist air
precipitation
rain shadow
mountain range

Thunder cloud
condensation level
rising air currents
hot land surface

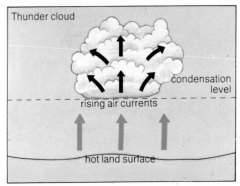

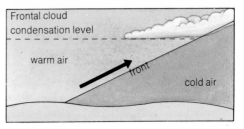

Frontal cloud
condensation level
warm air
front
cold air

cirrus
high
12 km
6 km
middle
cumulonimbus
2 km
low
cumulus
sea level

Drifting continents

If you look at a map of the Atlantic Ocean, you will see that the east side of North and South America is a similar shape to the west side of Europe and Africa. This similarity suggests that the continents were once joined together.

Studies of the ocean floor show that coastlines are not the true edges of continents. Instead, the continents are bordered by continental shelves, which are hidden by shallow seas. Recent mapping of the oceans shows that the edges of the shelves on both sides of the Atlantic fit together even better than the coastlines.

The theory of continental drift was first put forward about 70 years ago. It was supported by much evidence of similar rock structures and fossils which occur on both sides of the Atlantic. For example, fossils of an extinct reptile named *Mesosaurus* are found in South America and Africa. The simplest way to explain why these fossils occur in widely separated places was that South America and Africa must have been joined when *Mesosaurus* was living on Earth.

Moving plates

New evidence to support continental drift came to light in the 1950s and 1960s, when the oceans were studied. Most scientists now accept the theory of *plate tectonics,* which states that the Earth's crust is split, like a cracked egg, into solid plates, and that these plates are moving around.

Scientists have discovered that the rocks in the oceans are no older than about 200 million years. This makes the oceans very young compared with the continents. The youngest rocks in the oceans are near enormous mountain ranges, called *ocean ridges*. Along these ridges, new rock is constantly being added as magma wells up from the Earth's mantle. The centres of the ocean ridges are edges of plates. As the new rock is added, the plates are pushed apart, by a process called *ocean spreading*. At the top of the mantle, some rocks may be fluid, and as they move sideways, they carry the continents with them. Studies of the deepest parts of the oceans, the ocean

Right: The diagram shows part of the Earth, from the Pacific Ocean to Africa. The Earth's crust includes the continental crust (brown) and the heavier, or denser, oceanic crust (green). The crust is split into rigid plates which are slowly moving.

SOUTH AMERICAN PLATE MOVING WEST

SOUTH AMERICA

PACIFIC OCEAN

ANDES

active volcanoes fed by melting crust

Peru – Chile ocean trench

shallow earthquakes

partial melting of crust to feed volcanoes

melting crust

deepest earthquakes

continental shelf

continental slope

trenches, show that they, too, are plate edges. However, there, one plate is being forced down beneath another. The descending plate is being melted in the mantle.

Pangaea

Scientists now believe that about 200 million years ago, all the world's continents were grouped in one vast super-continent, called Pangaea. But, about 180 million years ago, Pangaea began to split up. The continents then drifted to their present positions.

Above: Surtsey, a volcanic island off Iceland, is on the mid-Atlantic ridge.

AFRICAN PLATE MOVING EAST

ATLANTIC OCEAN

mid-Atlantic ridge

AFRICA

Left: The Atlantic is split into two plates along the mid-Atlantic ridge. New rock is being added to the ridge, pushing the plates apart. Far left, a plate is being pushed under the South American plate. The descending plate is melted in the Earth's mantle.

East African rift valley

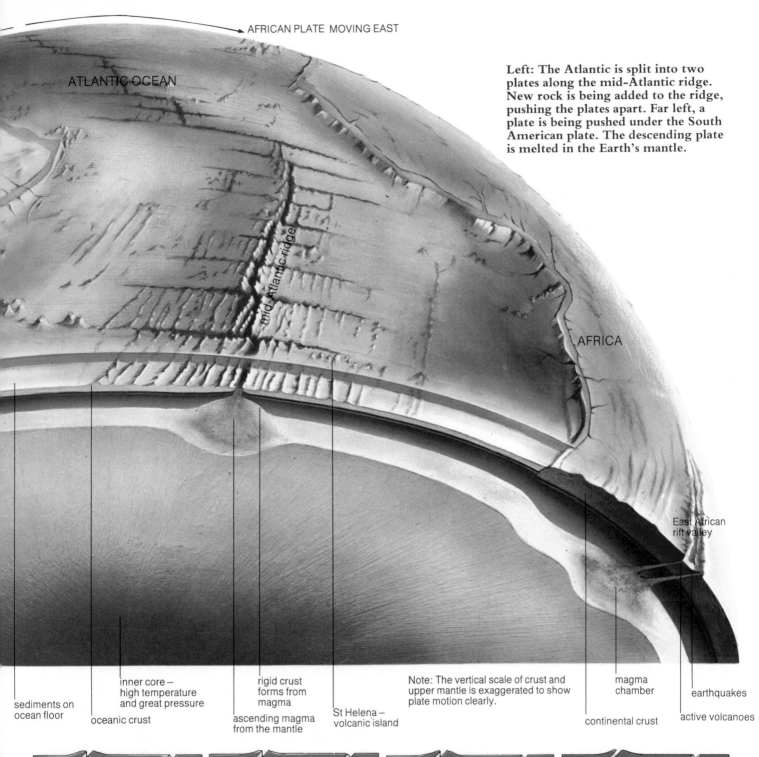

sediments on ocean floor

oceanic crust

inner core – high temperature and great pressure

ascending magma from the mantle

rigid crust forms from magma

St Helena – volcanic island

Note: The vertical scale of crust and upper mantle is exaggerated to show plate motion clearly.

continental crust

magma chamber

earthquakes

active volcanoes

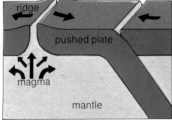
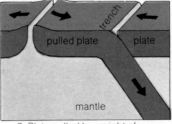
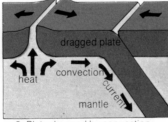
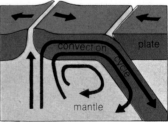

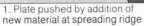

1. Plate pushed by addition of new material at spreading ridge

2. Plate pulled by weight of descending slab as it cools

3. Plate dragged by convection current in the fluid mantle

4. Plate is cooled, upper boundary of mantle convection cycle

Above: Several forces may make plates move. Diagram 1 shows magma being added to an ocean ridge. This new rock pushes the plates apart. When plates collide, one is forced beneath the other. Diagram 2 shows how the heavy descending crust may be pulling plates apart. It is also possible that parts of the upper mantle are fluid and the rocks move in convection currents(Diagram 3). Such currents may drag plates apart. Diagram 4 suggests that these currents may form continuous cycles, extending far into the mantle.

Earthquakes

Earthquakes are sudden and sometimes violent movements in the Earth's crust, which shake the land. They occur when rocks move along faults (large cracks) in the crust. Most of them occur near the edges of moving plates (see page 16).

The map on these pages shows where earthquakes have occurred around the world. Note how many of the dots are grouped in clear belts, or lines. For example, one belt winds through the Atlantic Ocean, following the centre of the mid-Atlantic ridge, a plate edge. And, in the Pacific Ocean, earthquakes also occur near the deep ocean trenches, where one plate is being pushed beneath another. Hence, the clear belts of dots on the map roughly represent plate edges.

Transform faults

A third kind of plate edge associated with earthquakes is called a *transform fault*. This is a long crack in the surface of the crust where plates move *alongside* each other.

In California, USA, there is a transform fault 960 kilometres long, called the San Andreas fault. In 1906, a sudden movement occurred along this fault. Near the city of San Francisco, the plate edges moved about 4.5 metres. This violent jerk shook the city. Many buildings collapsed and electrical short-circuits and broken gas pipes caused many fires.

Earthquake forecasting

Millions of people have died in China as a result of earthquakes. In 1556, one earthquake killed an estimated 800,000 people.

Recently, the Chinese have been searching for ways of forecasting earthquakes. Scientists have noticed that animals behave oddly before an earthquake. Others have studied strange tilts in the ground, which appear before some earthquakes. This may show that underground rocks are being twisted. Another method is to measure the amounts of a rare gas called radon in well water. This gas is usually trapped in rocks. When the rocks crack, it escapes and is dissolved in water.

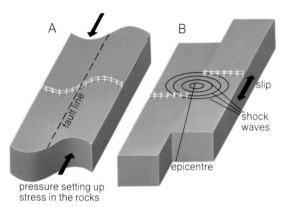

Above: Transform faults, such as the San Andreas fault in California, become jammed after an earthquake. Tension increases (A), until it is finally released in a sudden jerk (B).

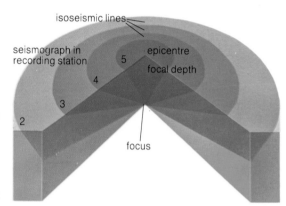

Above: The focus (point of origin) of an earthquake is underground. The point on the surface directly above the focus is called the epicentre. The distance from the focus to the epicentre is called the focal depth. Destructive earthquakes are shallow-focus, with a focal depth of less than 60 kilometres. Isoseismic lines join places which feel an equal intensity. The numbers show that the intensity is reduced away from the epicentre.

The Chinese claimed a successful earthquake forecast in 1975, when all the people of the city of Haicheng were evacuated 2 hours before the city was destroyed. But earthquake forecasting is still in its infancy.

Earthquake measurement

The point of origin of an earthquake is called the *focus*. The most destructive earthquakes are *shallow-focus*. This means that they occur near the surface.

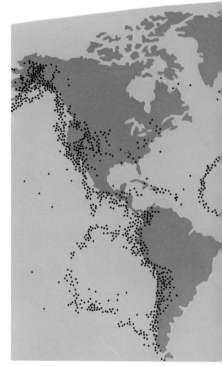

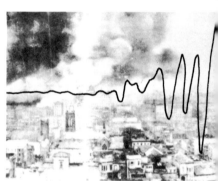

Top: The dots show places where earthquakes have occurred. Many are concentrated in belts, which mark the edges of plates in the Earth's crust.

Above: The picture shows the ruins of San Francisco after the famous earthquake of 1906. The seismograph record of the vibrations, shown on the photograph, were recorded in Albany, New York, which is 4830 kilometres away from the earthquake's focus.

Earthquakes are recorded on instruments called *seismographs*.

The strength, or magnitude, of an earthquake is measured on the Richter scale from 1 to 9. Each successive number represents a ten-fold increase in magnitude. Earthquakes of 2 on the scale are barely noticeable, but 8 on the scale represents an extremely violent tremor. The most powerful earthquake yet measured was 8.9 on the Richter scale.

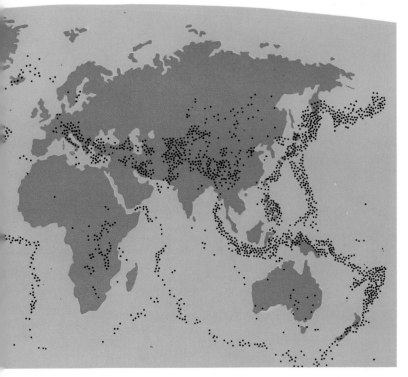

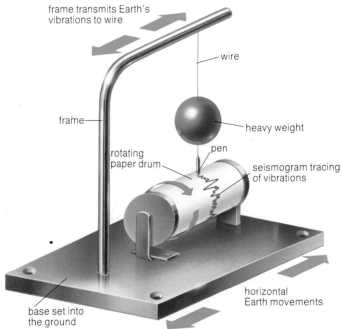

frame transmits Earth's vibrations to wire

wire

frame

heavy weight

rotating paper drum

pen

seismogram tracing of vibrations

base set into the ground

horizontal Earth movements

Above: The diagram shows a seismograph, an instrument used to detect and to record earthquakes. It consists of a spring-suspended weight, or pendulum, and a clockwork-operated rotating drum. The base is set firmly in the ground. When the ground shakes, the frame moves backwards and forwards. A pen on the weight marks all the movements on the paper around the drum.

Below: A railway line in Japan which was buckled by an earthquake in 1964.

Left: Damage costing millions of dollars was caused by an earthquake which hit Alaska in March 1964. This earthquake was one of the most severe ever recorded. It measured 8.9 on the Richter scale. The houses here were smashed by an enormous landslide, which was caused by the earthquake.

Volcanoes

Scientists have identified 500 or so *active* volcanoes, of which 20 to 30 erupt every year. When not erupting, these volcanoes are said to be *dormant* (sleeping). When volcanoes have not erupted for more than 25,000 years, they are described as *extinct*. However, many volcanoes that were thought to be extinct have suddenly erupted.

Volcanic eruptions

Volcanoes are essentially holes in the ground through which *magma* reaches the surface. Magma is hot, molten rock, containing various gases. Eruptions occur when the pressure in the magma chamber beneath the surface becomes so great that it must be released.

Sometimes, the pressure is released gently in *quiet eruptions*. These occur when the magma is runny and the gases can escape easily from it. Magma, known as *lava* on the surface, pours out from fissures or vents in long streams, which may reach speeds of up to 20 kilometres per hour. But these eruptions are not really 'quiet'. Sometimes, lava fire-fountains rise up to 500 metres into the air.

When the magna is viscous (stiff) and the volcanic gases cannot easily escape, *explosive eruptions* occur. The expanding gases shatter the magma into tiny bits of ash, or larger lumps, called bombs. The ash is thrown high into the air. In the most intense explosions, much of the original cone may be destroyed. However, most volcanoes are *intermediate* in type.

Quiet eruptions produce low, *shield* volcanoes shaped like upturned saucers. Explosive eruptions produce steep cones of ash. Intermediate volcanoes usually have cones made up of layers of ash and hardened lava.

Where volcanoes occur

Most volcanoes lie near the edges of the plates in the Earth's crust. Some rise from the oceanic ridges, where new crustal rock is being formed. For example, the volcanic island of Surtsey, which appeared off Iceland in 1963, lies on the mid-Atlantic ridge. Other volcanoes lie near plate edges where one plate is being forced into

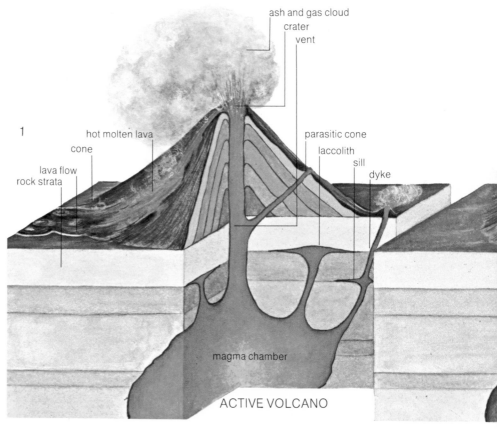

ash and gas cloud
crater
vent

hot molten lava

cone

lava flow
rock strata

1

parasitic cone
laccolith
sill
dyke

magma chamber

ACTIVE VOLCANO

Right: Krakatoa Island, Indonesia, was once a group of volcanic cones. In 1883, the largest volcanic explosion in modern times destroyed two-thirds of the island. It was heard 4700 kilometres away, and it generated high waves which drowned 36,000 people on nearby Java and Sumatra.

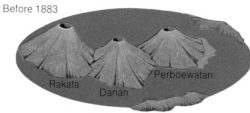

Before 1883

Rakata
Danan
Perboewatan

the mantle. The descending plate is melted, producing magma, which rises to the surface through volcanoes.

A few volcanoes, however, lie far from plate edges. They probably occur at 'hot spots' in the Earth's mantle, where radioactive heat is creating magma. This magma rises up through the overlying plate.

Forecasting eruptions

Volcanoes can cause great destruction and loss of life. In some densely-populated areas, active volcanoes are observed by scientists. The scientists check any changes in temperature and pressure in the volcanoes. They also look out for any changes in the slope of the mountain, which they measure with tiltometers. When marked changes are discovered, they issue warnings and people are evacuated.

Left: In an active volcano (1), magma rises up the vent. Magma may be exploded out as fine ash, and some may emerge as lava from the vent or from side vents (parasitic cones). Other magma is forced into surrounding rocks as dykes (sheets that cut vertically across rock strata), sills (which are parallel to rock strata) and laccoliths (domes). In an extinct volcano (2), the vent is plugged by solid lava. A lake may form in the crater. Lava plugs (3) may form hills after the cone is worn away.

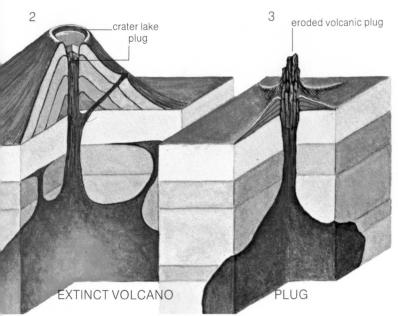

2
— crater lake
— plug

3
eroded volcanic plug

EXTINCT VOLCANO

PLUG

After 1883

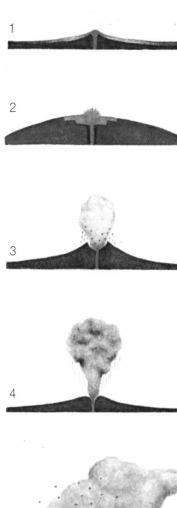

1

2

3

4

5

6

7

Right: Eruptions vary according to the pressure inside the volcano, the amount of gas in the magma, and the nature of the lava, which may be runny or viscous (stiff). Icelandic eruptions (1) are 'quiet' eruptions. The magma contains little gas and explosions do not occur, but runny lava pours from fissures (cracks) in the ground. Hawaiian eruptions (2) are also quiet. Runny lava flows from the vent and piles up in low, shield-like volcanoes. In Strombolian eruptions (3), explosive periods occur when gas in the magma shoots ash into the air. Vulcanian eruptions (4) contain more viscous magma, whose surface hardens quickly. Gas in the magma periodically explodes bits of the hardened crust into the air. Vesuvian eruptions (5) are even more explosive and huge clouds of ash rise from the vent. Peléan eruptions (6), named after Mount Pelée in Martinique, erupt clouds of hot gas and bits of magma, which roll downhill. Plinean eruptions (7), named after the Roman writer Pliny, who recorded the eruption of Vesuvius in AD 79, are the most explosive of all. There are no lava flows. Instead, the gas-filled magma is shattered into ash which rises several kilometres into the air.

Left: The Kilauea volcano in Hawaii emits fire fountains of molten magma.

Mountain building

The four main kinds of mountains are volcanoes (described on pages 20–21), fold mountains, block mountains and intrusive mountains. Most mountains were formed by forces associated with plate movements in the Earth's crust (see pages 16–17).

Fold mountains

Fold mountains form the world's most extensive ranges, including the Alps, Andes, Appalachians, Himalayas and Rockies. All these ranges were formed by plates pushing against each other.

For example, the Himalayas are a fairly recent fold mountain range. Their history begins about 180 million years ago. This was when the ancient super-continent of Pangaea began to break up (see pages 16-17). At that time, the land that forms present-day India lay a long way from Asia. It was sandwiched between south-eastern Africa and Antarctica and a huge ocean, called the Tethys Sea, lay between it and Asia. As Pangaea broke up, the Indian plate began to move away from Africa and Antarctica and to drift slowly towards Asia.

Around 50 million years ago, the Indian plate was starting to push against the Asian one. As it moved forwards, the level rock strata and sediments on the bed of the Tethys Sea were squeezed together and folded upwards into large loops. In time, the Tethys Sea vanished and the folded rocks formed the Himalayas which now join the Indian and Asian plates.

The enormous pressure between the plates greatly compressed the rocks in the Himalayas. The folding explains why fossils of sea creatures are often found near the tops of the highest mountains.

Block mountains

Pressure and tension caused by plate movements sometimes produce fractures (cracks) in rocks, forming huge faults.

Tugging movements make some blocks of land slip down along faults. Other blocks are raised up along faults, producing steep slopes called fault scarps. Such uplifted blocks of land are called block mountains.

Above: Mount Fuji, in Japan, is a volcano which last erupted in 1707. It is Japan's highest peak and towers 3776 metres above sea level. Many Japanese regard it as a sacred mountain and, every summer, pilgrims climb to the top. Volcanoes are one of the four main kinds of mountains. Diagram 1, above right, shows how the vent has cut through existing rock strata, and magma (in the forms of ash and lava) accumulates in layers to form a volcanic cone.

Below: Mighty Half Dome, in the Yosemite valley of California, is an intrusive mountain. This spectacular peak, a mountaineer's delight, consists of hard granite. It was formed from magma which cooled and solidified underground. Diagram 4, below right, shows how intrusive granite resists erosion, while the softer rocks around it are worn away.

1

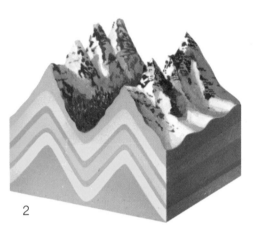

2

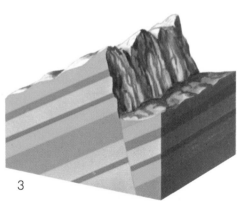

3

4

flat lying strata  symmetrical 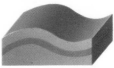 asymmetrical 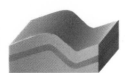 overturned 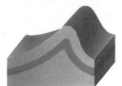 isoclinal series  recumbent

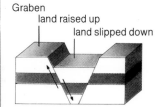

Graben
land raised up
land slipped down

Horst
land slipped down
land raised up

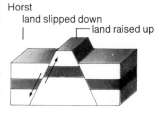

Above: The Himalayan mountains of Asia are the world's highest. The Himalayas are fold mountains, like those shown in diagram 2, left. They were formed by tremendous lateral (sideways) pressure, which squeezed up formerly level rock strata into great loops, or folds. Some kinds of folds are shown at the top of the page.

Below: The Sierra Nevadas, in the western USA, are a mountain range which was created when a block of land was pushed upwards along a fault. This produced a slope, called a fault scarp, which rises steeply above the land on the other side of the fault. Diagram 3, left, shows that when blocks of land are pushed upwards, the rocks are displaced, such that the rock strata on one side of the fault do not match with the rock strata on the other side. Such raised land areas are called block mountains.

Above right: The two diagrams show how two features called graben and horsts are formed by Earth movements. Graben, or rift valleys, are created when a block of land sinks down between two roughly parallel

Such movements occurred in eastern Africa. Huge blocks of land sank down between long faults to form the East African rift valley, the world's largest rift valley. Uplifting raised up the Ruwenzori range, a block mountain bordering the rift valley.

Intrusive mountains

The magma which comes out of volcanoes hardens into rocks called *extrusive rocks,* because the material has been *extruded,* or pushed out, on to the surface. However, much magma never

faults, creating a steep-sided trough. Horsts, or block mountains, are produced by a movement in the opposite direction, that is, when the central block is pushed upwards between the parallel faults.

reaches the surface. Instead, it is *intruded,* or is forced into, existing rock strata underground. Enormous bodies of intrusive magma, called *laccoliths* and *batholiths,* may bend overlying rock strata upwards into domes. When the magma cools, it forms such tough intrusive rocks as granite. Eventually, the softer, overlying rocks are worn away. The granite is then exposed on the surface, forming an intrusive mountain. The Black Hills of Dakota, in the USA, are an example of mountains formed in this way.

23

Rivers of ice

As mountains rise up, natural forces attack and wear them down. The wearing away of the land is called *erosion*.

There are several forces of erosion. In mountain areas, rocks are broken up by a process called *weathering*. For example, water often fills cracks in rocks during the day. At night, the water freezes. Because ice occupies more space than the same amount of water, the ice exerts pressure on the sides of the crack. Repeated freezing and thawing eventually splits the rocks apart.

In temperate regions, rivers play a major part in wearing away the land. But in cold or high mountain regions, the chief agent of erosion is ice.

The world of ice

Over two per cent of the world's water is frozen into ice. Large bodies of ice include the vast ice sheets of Antarctica and Greenland, smaller ice caps, and rivers of ice called glaciers.

Ice forms from compacted snow, called *firn,* which accumulates in high mountain basins, called *cirques*. Gradually, the air is squeezed out and the firn becomes clear blue ice. The ice spills over the lip of the cirque and flows down mountain valleys under the force of gravity. The rate at which ice moves varies. In Antarctica, the ice sheet moves by about 1 metre per year. But many mountain glaciers move 1 metre forward every day.

The end, or *snout,* of a glacier is where the rate of melting, evaporation or the breaking away of icebergs balances the rate of ice formation.

Glaciers shape the land

Loose rocks broken up by weathering fall on to the ice or become frozen within it. Rocks transported by ice are called *moraine. Ground moraine* is frozen into the base of the ice. As the ice moves, the ground moraine scrapes over the land like a giant file, forming deep U-shaped valleys. Tributary (side) valleys are not deepened to the same extent and they are left 'hanging' above the main valley. Cirques are also deepened. Where two cirques are back-to-back, the ice erodes the wall

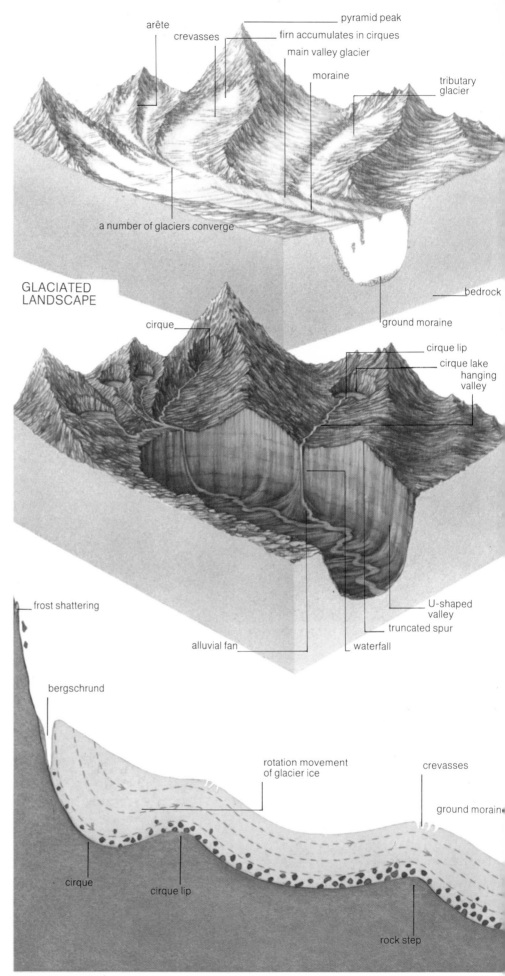

GLACIATED LANDSCAPE

DEPOSITS LEFT BY A MELTING ICE SHEET

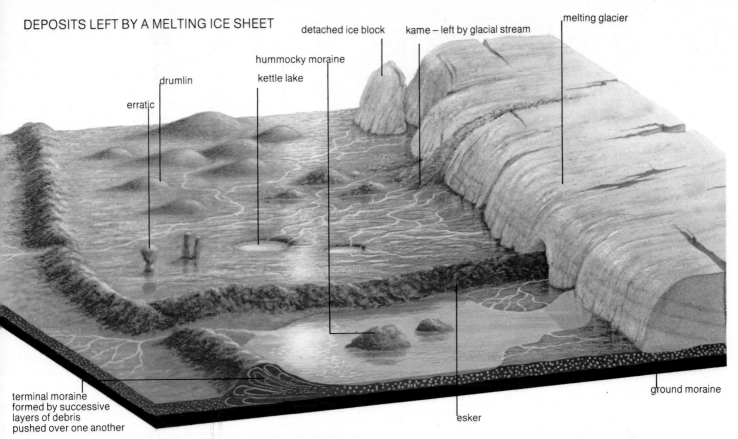

erratic · drumlin · hummocky moraine · kettle lake · detached ice block · kame – left by glacial stream · melting glacier

terminal moraine formed by successive layers of debris pushed over one another

esker

ground moraine

Left: The diagrams show a mountain region covered by snow and ice and the same region as it would look after the snow had melted. In the top diagram, glacier ice is forming from compacted snow (firn) in basins called cirques. The ice flows from the cirques into mountain valleys. Loose rocks fall on to the edges of the glaciers and some is frozen in the ice. Rocks moved by glaciers are called moraine. Tributary glaciers flow into the main valley glacier, but they lack the eroding power of the main valley glacier. The second diagram shows characteristic features of ice erosion, such as armchair-shaped cirques, pointed pyramid peaks, and knife-edged ridges, called arêtes. Some cirques contain lakes called tarns. A prominent feature is the deep U-shaped valley. Tributary valleys 'hang' above this over-deepened main valley and streams from these valleys cascade down in waterfalls. At the bottoms of waterfalls, worn rocks pile up in heaps called alluvial fans.

overdeepened hollow

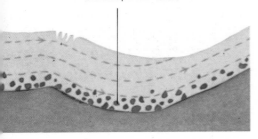

Below: Geiranger Fjord, in Norway, is a deep valley worn out by glaciers. These glaciers flowed from the Scandinavian ice sheet during the last Ice Age. The depth and steep sides of the valley testify to the power of these long-vanished glaciers. When the ice melted, the sea level rose and flooded the valley to form a long and deep sea inlet. Fjord is the name for all glaciated sea inlets.

Left: The diagram shows a section through a mountain glacier. Ice forms from snow in the cirque. The ice pulls away from the head of the cirque to form a deep crevasse, called a bergschrund. As the glacier flows over the cirque lip or rock steps, the ice is shattered and many crevasses form.

Above: Features formed from deposited moraine. The long ridge of terminal moraine represents the edge of the glacier at an earlier stage. Drumlins, erratics and hummocky moraine were also dumped by the ice, while eskers and kames were deposited by streams flowing from the melting snout of the ice. Kettle lakes occupy hollows which were formed when buried blocks of ice melted.

between them until it becomes an *arête*, a knife-edged ridge. With three or more cirques, a pyramid peak, or *horn*, is formed.

Other land features are formed when the ice drops its moraine. Some piles up in low hills called *terminal moraine*. These mark the edge of the ice at some stage in the past. *Boulder clay*, a mixture of rocks and fine 'rock flour' ground down by the moving ice, is moulded into hummocks called *drumlins*. *Erratics* are large boulders dropped by the ice. Melting ice at the snout forms streams which carry moraine away from the glacier. This water-borne moraine may pile up in winding ridges, called *eskers* or *kames*.

Such land features helped geologists to discover that large parts of the northern hemisphere were covered by ice during the last Ice Age, which ended about 12,000 years ago.

The power of the sea

On 31st January 1953, a combination of high tides and storm winds, reaching 180 kilometres per hour, raised the level of the North Sea to heights not known before. During the night, huge waves smashed many holes in the dykes (sea walls) of the Netherlands, and the sea flooded more than four per cent of the country. That same night, the coastline of East Anglia was severely battered by the waves. In one place, where the rocks consisted of loose glacial deposits, 27 metres of land were ripped away in 2 hours.

The power of the sea is, in fact, responsible for the varying coastal scenery we see around land areas. The sea has the power to erode, transport and deposit material.

Erosion by the sea

The sea can wear away the land in several ways. First, it can dissolve some rocks. Second, waves can trap air in cracks in coastal rocks. The trapped air is compressed, but when the pressure is released, the air expands explosively, making the cracks larger or breaking off lumps of rock. Third, storm waves can carry loose pebbles and rocks. When this loose material is hurled at the shore, it hollows out caves and undercuts cliffs. Finally, the restless sea rubs loose rocks against each other, wearing them down into smaller and smaller pieces. This process creates the sand and rounded pebbles we find on beaches.

Wave erosion occurs most quickly in areas where the rocks offer the least resistance. For example, bays form when softer rocks are worn back faster than nearby hard rocks, which remain as headlands. But even headlands are finally removed. This happens when waves cut caves in the sides of the headlands. The caves meet to form natural *arches*. When the arches collapse, rocky pillars, called *stacks,* are left behind on the seaward side. They, too, are eventually cut down by the pounding waves.

Transport and deposition

Waves and currents move loose sand and pebbles along coasts by *long-shore drift* (see diagram on page 27). This movement of material is interrupted when the coastline changes direction, such as at bays or river estuaries. At such places, the material is dropped and piles up in ridges called *spits*. Sometimes, spits extend right across a bay. Such spits are called *baymouth bars*. Some bars are not linked to land. Instead, the material piles up offshore in long ridges. Another kind of spit is called a *tombolo*. Tombolos link islands to the mainland, forming a natural bridge, such as Chesil Beach in Dorset, England.

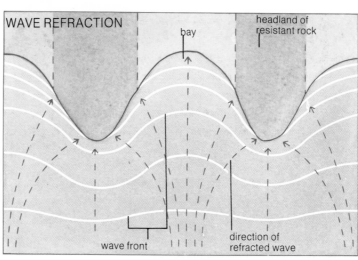

WAVE REFRACTION — bay — headland of resistant rock — wave front — direction of refracted wave

Above: The diagram shows two headlands formed from resistant rocks, enclosing a bay. The directions of the waves are shown by the arrows. As the wave front approaches land, the wave directions change according to the shape of the land, because waves tend to reach the shore roughly at right angles. The bending of wave directions is called wave refraction.

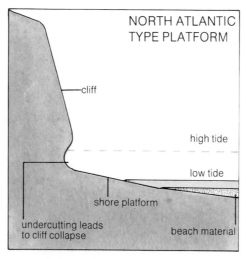

NORTH ATLANTIC TYPE PLATFORM — cliff — high tide — low tide — shore platform — undercutting leads to cliff collapse — beach material

Below left: The diagram shows a typical coastline in the North Atlantic, which is being steadily worn back by wave action. At low tide, the water level is well below the cliff. But, at high tide, the water extends right up to the cliff. Storm waves hurl loose rocks at the base of the cliff and undercut it. Finally, slabs of rock crash down and the cliff retreats.

CLIFF SCENERY — cave — bay

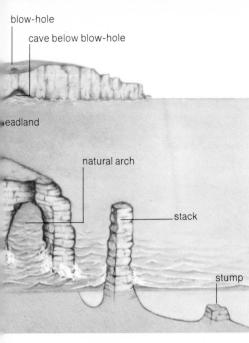

blow-hole
cave below blow-hole

eadland

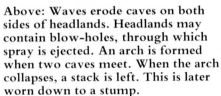

natural arch

stack

stump

Above: Waves erode caves on both sides of headlands. Headlands may contain blow-holes, through which spray is ejected. An arch is formed when two caves meet. When the arch collapses, a stack is left. This is later worn down to a stump.

Below: These natural arches are on the coast of the Algarve, in Portugal.

Above: A former island in the Scottish sea-loch Eriboll is now joined to the mainland by a low ridge of sand and shingle, called a tombolo. It consists of material worn away from another part of the coast and carried here by waves and currents. Tombolo, an Italian word, comes from the name of two land bridges, linking the former island of Monte Argentario to Italy.

Below: The process by which waves move pebbles and sand along a beach is called long-shore drift. It occurs when the wind direction and the wave front approach the beach at an angle. The advance of water up the beach, called the swash, is also at an angle. But the backwash is at right angles to the beach. Hence, material is moved up the coast in a zig-zag direction.

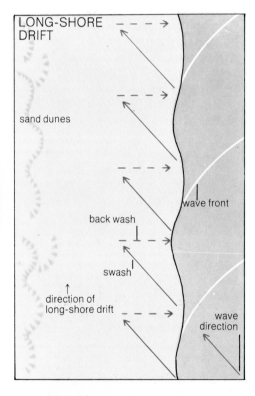

LONG-SHORE DRIFT

sand dunes

wave front

back wash

swash

direction of long-shore drift

wave direction

Left: Miami Beach in south-eastern Florida, USA, is a tourist centre with beautiful beaches. Groynes, which are low walls or jetties, have been built into the sea to protect the beach from wave erosion. The groynes trap the sand and prevent its removal by long-shore drift.

The ocean depths

The oceans cover about 71 per cent of the Earth's surface. The three main oceans are the Pacific, whose area of over 165 million square kilometres is greater than the areas of all the continents combined; the Atlantic Ocean; and the Indian Ocean. The Arctic and Antarctic oceans around the poles are really just extensions of the three main oceans.

Until recently, little was known about the ocean bed. In the last 30 years, however, mapping by echo-sounders has greatly increased our knowledge. And, since the 1930s, scientists have begun to explore the dark waters of the ocean depths in craft called bathyspheres and bathyscaphes. The record descent (10,917 metres) was made by the bathyscaphe *Trieste* in 1960.

Features of the ocean floor
The average depth of the oceans is about 3500 metres. The deepest point, in the Marianas Trench in the Pacific Ocean, is 11,033 metres below the surface. The ocean trenches are places where one plate is being pushed down beneath another (see pages 16–17).

Other plate edges in the oceans are in the centres of the oceanic ridges, where new rock is being formed from

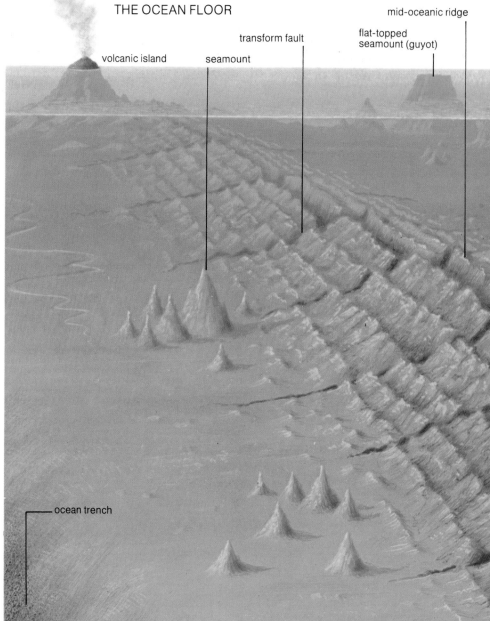

THE OCEAN FLOOR

volcanic island   seamount   transform fault   flat-topped seamount (guyot)   mid-oceanic ridge

ocean trench

Above: The ocean depths are as varied as the land. There are deep ocean trenches, seamounts, enormous oceanic ridges which contain central rift valleys, volcanic islands which rise from the ocean floor, and deep submarine (underwater) canyons, which may have been scoured out by strong muddy currents, called submarine density currents.

Left: Ocean research ships carry many instruments. This probe measures the temperatures and salinity (saltiness) of ocean water.

Right: Looking down over Tahiti, in the Pacific Ocean, our planet looks to be almost completely covered by water.

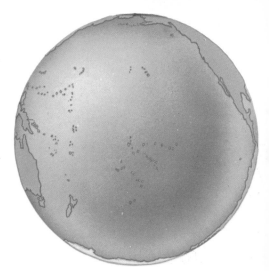

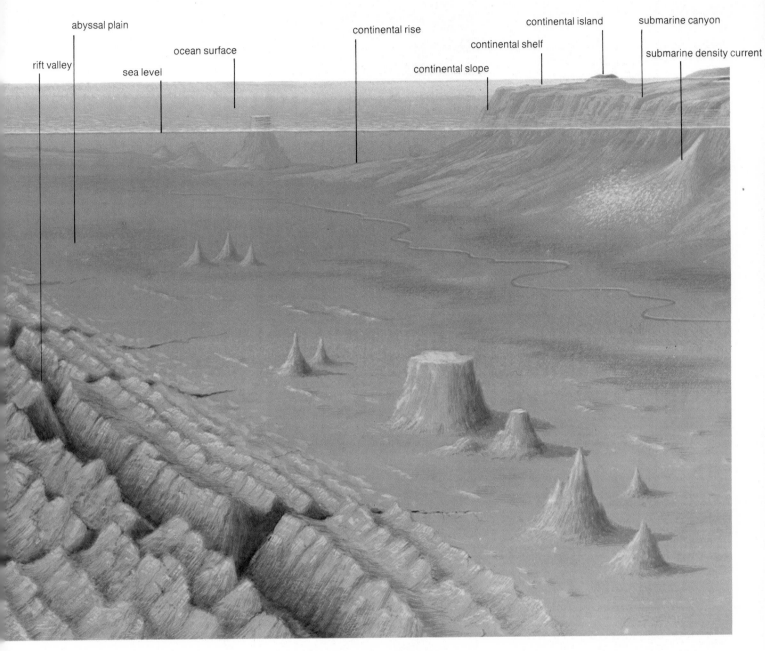

rift valley

sea level

abyssal plain

ocean surface

continental rise

continental slope

continental shelf

continental island

submarine canyon

submarine density current

Below: Echo-sounders measure the depth of water by beaming sound waves to the ocean bed and recording the time taken for their echoes to return. Seismic surveys, investigate the rock strata under the ocean bed.

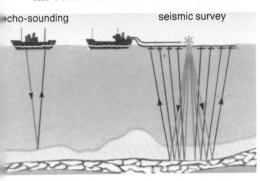

echo-sounding   seismic survey

magma in the central rift valleys. The largest oceanic ridge is in the Atlantic. It is 16,000 kilometres long and 800 kilometres wide. Its highest peak is Mount Pico in the Azores, which rises 7198 metres from the ocean floor. Beyond the ridges are flat *abyssal plains* and, in some places, *abyssal hills*.

Rising from the abyssal plains are isolated mountains called *seamounts*. The world's highest mountain, measured from its base, is Mauna Kea, a volcano on the island of Hawaii in the Pacific Ocean. Mauna Kea is 4205 metres above sea level, but another 5998 metres are hidden from view.

This gives Mauna Kea a total height of 10,203 metres.

Around most continents are gently sloping *continental shelves*. At the edge of these shelves are the steep *continental slopes*. At the bottom of these slopes are the more gently sloping *continental rises*. These are composed of sediments brought from the land by muddy underwater currents, called *submarine density currents*. Some continental slopes are cut by deep canyons, which may have been worn out by the submarine density currents, such as the one formed by the muddy water of the Zaire River in Africa.

29

The world of minerals

The Earth's crust basically consists of *elements*. These are substances which cannot be broken down into other substances by chemical means. The chief elements in the crust are oxygen and silicon, which together make up 74.32 per cent of the crust's weight; aluminium, iron, calcium, sodium, potassium and magnesium make up 24.27 per cent. Another 84 elements occur naturally in the crust, making up the other 1.41 per cent.

Minerals and rocks

Some elements, such as gold, silver and copper, sometimes occur in the crust in a pure or nearly pure state. They are minerals, called *native elements*. But most minerals are a combination of elements.

Most minerals have a definite chemical formula and are *homogeneous,* that is, any part of the mineral is the same as any other part. Halite (salt) has the formula NaCl, which means that it is a combination of equal parts of two elements, sodium (Na) and chlorine (Cl). Nearly 3000 minerals have been identified. Some of these are common rock-forming minerals, while others are rare.

Rocks consist of minerals. But rocks are *heterogeneous,* that is, the

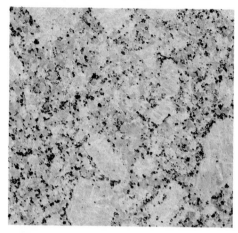

Above: Granite is a rock. It consists of several minerals.

Below: Gold is an element which occurs in a pure state as a mineral.

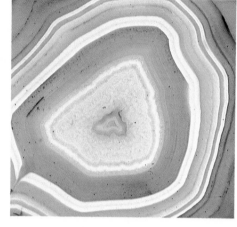

Above: Agate is a banded mineral, which is a form of chalcedony.

Below: Quartz is a common mineral, which occurs in several colours.

Right: The diagram shows places where minerals are found. When magma cools, the minerals crystallize to form such rocks as granite (1). Granite consists of such common rock-forming minerals as quartz, feldspar and mica. After granite has formed, some molten rock containing rarer minerals may be left over. These crystallize separately. Minerals also form in cavities, such as sheet-like veins and geodes (round lumps). Minerals worn from rocks may collect in river beds (2). Some minerals form when pressure, heat and gases (from the magma) metamorphose (alter) such rocks as limestone (3) and shale (4). Hydrothermal veins (5) form when hot, mineral-rich fluids are injected into existing rocks. These veins are major sources of valuable minerals. Beach deposits (6) often contain good mineral specimens. Ancient metamorphic rocks (7) may be sources of some rare minerals. Some sedimentary rocks (8), for example rock salt, consist largely of one mineral.

HOW AND WHERE MINERALS OCCUR

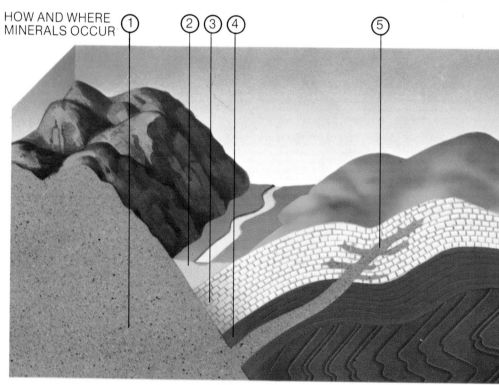

Left: Varieties of the fairly common, hard mineral corundum, shown here, include two rare and highly prized stones: the transparent red ruby and the blue sapphire. Green, violet, brown and yellow varieties also occur, but the commonest form is dull-looking. It is used as an abrasive.

Below: Crowns, sceptres and other insignia have traditionally symbolized power and status. Precious metals, such as gold and silver, and rare gemstones, especially diamonds, rubies, sapphires and emeralds, are used in the British royal insignia.

Below: Diamond, the purest form of carbon, is the hardest mineral. After skilful cutting and polishing, it reflects light, producing a play of colours, called fire.

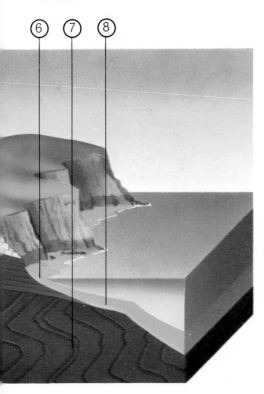

amounts of minerals in a rock vary from sample to sample. There are three kinds of rocks. *Igneous rocks* form from magma. Many *sedimentary rocks* form from fragments of other rocks, such as sandstone which forms from sand. Some are the result of chemical action, such as rock salt which forms when sea water evaporates. Others, like coal, are organic, being formed from once-living matter. *Metamorphic rocks* are rocks that have been changed by great pressure or heat or by gases released from bodies of magma.

Properties of minerals

When magma cools, most of the minerals in the mixture crystallize (form into crystals). Nearly all minerals have a definite crystal form. But in most igneous rocks, the crystals are packed together and are distorted. Well-formed crystals occur in such

places as veins and other rock cavities. Crystal forms are often used as a way of identifying minerals.

Another property of minerals is their hardness. Diamond, a form of pure carbon, is the hardest of all minerals, but you can crush talcite with your fingers. Some minerals, such as blue azurite, are always the same colour, but many others occur in several colours.

Another property is specific gravity. This is the ratio between the weight of a mineral and the weight of an equal volume of water. Other features are cleavage (the way minerals split when struck), optical properties (how they reflect, transmit or absorb light), and streak (the colour of the powdered mineral). But minerals are usually classified according to their chemical composition. Groups include oxides, silicates, sulphides, and so on.

Mineral resources

Metals play a vital part in all our lives. They were also important in the rise of civilization. About 10,000 years ago, copper became the first metal to be used to make implements. About 5000 years ago, people invented bronze, which is made from copper and tin. Bronze was important because it is harder than copper. Then, around 3300 years ago, iron came into use. This hard metal is much more common than either copper or tin. All these metals are still important today, as are other common metals such as aluminium and rare ones such as gold.

Sources of metals

Some metals occur as *native elements* (see page 30), but most are found in *mineral ores,* which are combinations of a metal with other elements. For example, iron occurs only rarely as a native element. The iron used in industry comes from such iron ores as haematite, magnetite and siderite.

Economic minerals are those that contain enough of a metal to make

Below: The map shows the distribution of important metals around the world. Some countries do not have any metals and need to import them. Although nearly 3000 minerals have been identified, only about 100 are of economic value.

mining commercially profitable. For example, although iron occurs in many minerals, commercial iron ores must contain between 30 and 60 per cent iron. But silver is a rare metal, and an economic silver ore may contain less than one per cent silver. For example, galena is a silver and lead ore; it contains nearly 87 per cent lead but only 0.5 per cent silver.

Metal ores occur in all of the three main kinds of rocks. When magma cools slowly underground to form igneous rocks, rock-forming minerals separate out to form such rocks as granite. But some of the magma remains liquid and these fluids are often rich in metals. They often squeeze into cracks in the igneous or nearby rocks, where they form *pegmatite* deposits. Finally, some *hydrothermal solutions* remain. These hot watery liquids may be even richer in minerals. They may flow through cracks in sedimentary and meta-morphic rocks, depositing mineral ores in veins and other cavities. (See the diagram on pages 30-31.)

Prospecting and mining

Prospecting was once a hit-or-miss affair. Until recently, prospectors sifted rocks in river beds looking for eroded fragments of metal ores. If they found,

Above: A prospector uses a Geiger counter to search for radioactive minerals, such as uranium.

Above right: This Kenyan African is panning river gravels, in the hope of finding traces of gold.

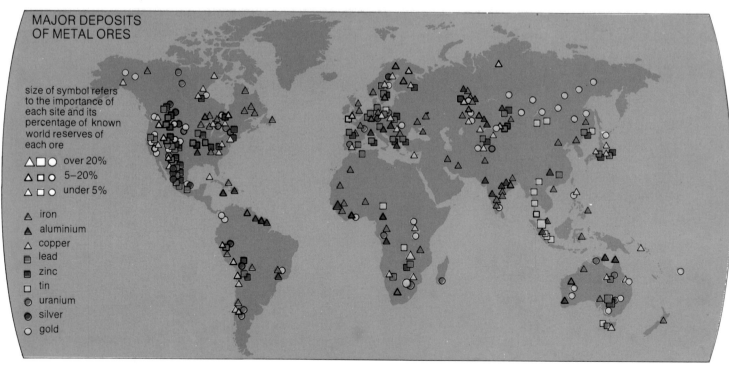

MAJOR DEPOSITS OF METAL ORES

size of symbol refers to the importance of each site and its percentage of known world reserves of each ore

△□○ over 20%
△ □ ○ 5–20%
△ □ ○ under 5%

△ iron
▲ aluminium
△ copper
▣ lead
◼ zinc
◻ tin
◍ uranium
● silver
○ gold

Above: Important metal ores include malachite (1), a copper ore. However, this beautiful green banded variety is used to make ornaments. Bauxite (2), which contains several minerals, is the only important source of the useful metal aluminium.

Above: Haematite (3) is a major iron ore. The dark red crystals of cinnabar (4) are a source of mercury.

Below: This open-cast copper mine in Queensland, Australia, also produces gold and silver as by-products.

Above: This prehistoric bronze jug was found in Cyprus. Copper was the first metal used to make implements. Bronze, made from copper and tin, is harder than copper. Its invention, about 5000 years ago, was important in the development of civilization.

say, a few grains of gold, they would then search for the vein from which the grains had come.

Today, prospectors are trained geologists. They use geological maps which show surface outcrops of rocks. From the maps, they can pinpoint areas where it would be advisable to search carefully for ores. Information also comes from seismologists about the rock structures beneath the surface. Prospecting instruments include gravimeters to record variations in rock densities; magnetometers to detect minerals with magnetic properties, such as magnetite; and Geiger counters to locate radioactive minerals, such as uranium.

Most of the world's minerals come from surface, or open-cast, mines. But underground mines reach deposits far beneath the surface.

Coal

Coal, oil and natural gas are *fossil fuels*, which were formed from the remains of once-living organisms. They are not minerals, because minerals are *inorganic* (lifeless) substances.

In the last 40 years, the importance of coal as a fuel has declined because of competition with oil and natural gas. But experts estimate that the known reserves of oil will run out in the next 30 years or so, while coal reserves will last for at least 450 years. Hence, coal may soon regain its importance. Besides being a fuel, coal has many other uses. It is used to smelt metals and to make dyes, explosives, synthetic rubber and plastics in the chemical industry.

The formation of coal

When plants die, they usually decay rapidly and the once-living matter is converted by bacteria into water, carbon dioxide and salts. The process of decay is halted when plants are buried quickly in swamps or bogs, and so the partly rotted plants pile up in layers. These layers are compacted into *carbonaceous rocks,* that is, rocks composed mostly of carbon.

The first stage in coal formation can be seen in some soggy moorlands, marshes and shallow lakes. There, the decaying plants form *peat,* a light brown substance. Peat may be cut for fuel, but first it must be dried, because up to 90 per cent of its weight is water. Dry peat contains up to 60 per cent carbon. The second stage in coal formation is *lignite* (brown coal), which is similar to peat but much more compact. It contains 60 to 75 per cent carbon when dry. It is used as a fuel and also in the chemical industry. *Bituminous,* or household, coal is hard and contains up to 90 per cent carbon. *Anthracite,* the last stage in coal formation, contains 95 per cent carbon. This shiny, black rock is clean to handle.

Right: This diagram of a typical coal mine shows the great amount of planning and costly machinery which is needed to extract coal from deep coal seams. Inset is a miner working at the coal face. But modern mining is becoming increasingly mechanized.

Above: A reconstruction of a coal-forming forest in the Carboniferous period (345 to 280 million years ago) shows the luxuriant vegetation.

fan-house, with powerful fan to extract the foul air

The top of the upcast shaft is housed in a sealed building. This ensures that the fan operates efficiently in removing used air from the whole underground area.

Other rock strata. The diagram is not to scale; these strata may be several kilometres deep.

The upcast shaft is used to bring coal, loaded in buckets called skips, to the surface.

A cut-away section through the unmined coal shows the machinery used in mining. The arrow shows the direction of mining into the coal face.

Room and pillar mining usually extracts only half the coal, leaving columns to support the roof.

underground railway

Left: Peat is the first stage in the formation of coal. In this area of Scotland, peat is forming from dead trees, heather and mosses. Dried peat is cut and used as a fuel.

Below: Soft, dark brown lignite is the second stage in coal formation.

Below centre: Bituminous coal is hard and brittle. It is a more efficient fuel than peat or lignite and is the most common coal used in homes.

Below right: Anthracite is the final stage in coal formation. It is hard, shiny and black.

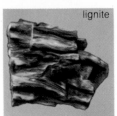
lignite

bituminous

anthracite

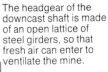

The headgear of the downcast shaft is made of an open lattice of steel girders, so that fresh air can enter to ventilate the mine.

The downcast shaft is fitted with a cage, used to convey men and equipment into and out of the mine.

coal seams

Water seepage is collected in sumps and pumped out.

conveyor belts

Above: Dark coal seams are exposed in this cliff in Antarctica. Coal has formed from the remains of ancient plants which grew in swamps. The presence of coal in Antarctica shows that this continent once had a warm climate and was situated much closer to the equator than it is today.

Most of the bituminous coal and anthracite mined today was formed around 300 million years ago. At that time, luxuriant forests with high trees, giant ferns, mosses and horsetails grew in swamps. Many of these forests were near the coast. Periodically, the swamps were submerged, and eroded material from the land, such as sand and mud, was spread over the layers of plants. Later, the land rose and forests grew again. As a result, coal *seams* or *beds* alternate with layers of other rocks. A sequence of coal seams and other rock layers is called a *coal measure*. This may be 1500 metres or more thick and contain 20 to 30 coal seams, between a few centimetres and 30 metres or more thick.

Coal mining

Some coal seams lie on or near the surface. In these, coal is removed by open-cast mining (see picture, page 158). Other seams are much deeper, and tunnels have to be cut in order to reach the coal. In most modern mines, the coal is cut by machines and hauled back from the coal face by conveyor belts.

Oil and natural gas

Oil and natural gas are fossil fuels extracted from the Earth's crust. They may occur together or separately. These fuels now supply more than half of the energy that is consumed in the modern world. And oil, besides being used to make petrol, fuel oils and lubricating oils, is also important in the chemical industry, where it is used to make such things as detergents, drugs, explosives and plastics.

However, oil and natural gas take millions of years to form, and when the reserves are used up, they cannot be replaced. Experts estimate that, at the current rate of consumption, the known reserves will run out in about 30 years time. Many nations are now reducing their consumption in order to conserve these dwindling resources.

Formation of oil and gas

Most scientists believe that oil and gas were formed from the remains of tiny animals and plants, which settled on sea and lake beds. These remains were partly changed by bacteria and then buried by thick layers of sediment. Many were buried in clays, which were compacted by pressure into rocks called *shales*. Pressure and heat also acted on the organic material, turning it into oil or gas (mainly methane). The light oil and gas were squeezed out of the shales and they flowed upwards into *permeable* rocks.

Permeable rocks may be *porous,* like sandstone, which contains tiny spaces (pores) between the grains, through which oil, gas and water can flow. Other permeable rocks, like limestone, do not have pores, but they contain many cracks through which liquids and gases can pass.

Much oil and gas, often overlying water, is found in underground reservoirs. For a large reservoir to form, the oil and gas must be trapped by *impervious rocks,* through which they cannot escape. The commonest kind of reservoir is an *anticline* (upfold), where an arched permeable rock layer is enclosed, above and below, by layers of impervious rocks. Others occur in *fault traps* or around *salt plugs* (see the diagrams at the top of this page).

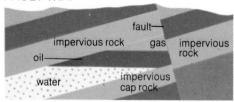

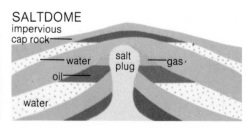

Above: Two rock structures in which oil and natural gas may be found. In the fault trap, left, the porous rock containing the gas and oil is enclosed by impervious rocks. Oil and gas may also be trapped around the tops of salt plugs, right.

Below: A diagram showing an oil production platform in the sea. Many oil fields are found in lakes or shallow seas. Inset is a diagram of an anticline (upfold). Oil and gas are trapped in the arched porous rock layer which is between two impervious layers.

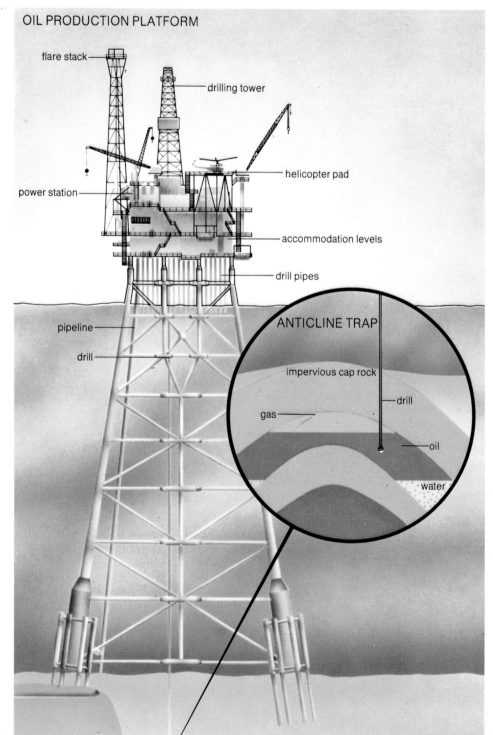

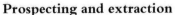

To find oil and gas, geologists must first look for promising rock structures. Underground rocks can be investigated by *seismic surveys* (see diagram, page 29). These surveys involve setting off small explosions in the ground, which generate seismic (shock) waves in the Earth's crust. By measuring the passage of the waves, the rock structures can be deduced. Other methods include aeromagnetic surveys and measurements of local variations in gravity.

When promising rock structures are found, an exploratory drilling is made. These drill-holes may reach 6000 metres or more into the ground. When a reservoir is located, the oil and gas may rise under pressure or it may have to be pumped to the surface. It is then transported to oil refineries.

Below: This drilling rig is used to discover whether oil and natural gas are below. Mud is pumped down the drill shaft to lubricate the drill bit (cutting tool). The mud may disappear, being absorbed by porous rocks. The presence of porous rocks means that oil may be present.

Above: Natural gas is burned off at an oil field in Abu Dhabi, near the Persian Gulf. The oil is extracted after the gas has been removed. The burning of gas is wasteful. It is done, however, because of the very high cost of transporting gas to markets which are long distances away.

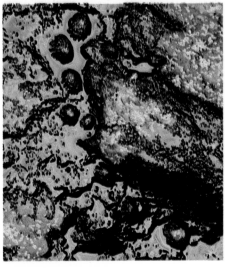

Above: A 320-kilometre-long gas pipeline conveys natural gas from an inland gasfield to a processing plant on the coast of Oman, in the Middle East. In many countries, the natural gas, which overlies large oil deposits, is burned off (see top picture) so that the oil can be easily extracted.

Above right: An oil refinery on the Isle of Grain, in south-eastern England, processes imported oil.

Right: Oil spillages from tankers have threatened the environment in recent years. Scientists have been seeking ways of controlling oil pollution and reducing its effects on marine life and coastal regions.

Records in the rocks

Fossils are evidence of ancient life on Earth, ranging from the footprints of dinosaurs to the carcasses of woolly mammoths preserved in the frozen soil of Siberia. But the soft parts of plants and animals are rarely fossilized, because they decay quickly after the organisms die.

Kinds of fossils

The most important condition for fossil formation is fast burial. This usually occurs when dead organisms are buried by mud or sand in the beds of seas, rivers and lakes. For example, when shells or other hard parts of organisms are buried, they are often dissolved away by water seeping through the sediments. This leaves hollows, or *moulds*. Moulds are often filled by minerals so that a *cast* of the original is formed. Moulds and casts are common fossils. They reveal the outer shape of the organism, but not its internal structure. Sometimes, organisms are dissolved very slowly and minerals replace the molecules of the original organism one by one. As a result, the organisms are *petrified* (turned to stone). Petrified logs even show the annual rings in the wood.

Soft organisms, such as worms or leaves, are sometimes turned into thin films of carbon, called *carbon smears*. *Trace fossils* include footprints made in soft mud which was baked hard by the Sun before being buried, eggs, animal droppings and burrows.

Insects were sometimes trapped in sticky resin from trees and they were preserved when the resin hardened into *amber*. The frozen mammoths of Siberia are extremely unusual fossils, because their flesh has been preserved. They probably drowned in swamps which later froze, preserving their bodies in a natural freezer.

Most fossils occur in sedimentary rocks, which cover three-quarters of the Earth's land area. Some distorted fossils appear in metamorphic (altered) rocks, but you will not find any fossils in igneous rocks.

The meaning of fossils

The earliest fossils date back about 3100 million years. They are fossils of

GEOLOGICAL TIME SCALE

	million years ago
Quaternary	0
	2
Tertiary	65
Cretaceous	135
Jurassic	193
Triassic	225
Permian	280
Carboniferous	345
Devonian	395
Silurian	435
Ordovician	500
Cambrian	570
Pre-Cambrian	

lobster
Crustacea

crinoid
Echinoderm

lepidodendron

brachiopod

trilobite

Left: The geological time scale shows the periods in the last 570 million years, with some typical fossils: a trilobite (an extinct arthropod); brachiopods (shellfish); a lepidodendron (a club moss); a crinoid (sea lily); and parts of a lobster.

Below: Jurassic ammonites. These extinct animals are related to squids.

38

Right: The Dinosaur National Monument, USA, contains rocks which are rich in dinosaur fossils.

Below: A fossil dinosaur skull is first coated in wet tissue paper and then covered by sacking soaked in Plaster of Paris. When the plaster has hardened, the fossil can be safely transported without fear of damage.

Left: These fossil shellfish are brachiopods. Living species number 250, but 30,000 species lived between the Cambrian and Permian periods.

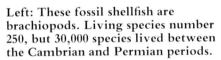

Below left: This fossil trilobite is an extinct marine arthropod. These animals probably resembled woodlice. Trilobites are common in Cambrian and Ordovician rocks. They are also found in Silurian and Devonian rocks, but they are rare in rocks of the Carboniferous and Permian periods, when they finally died out.

Below: This beautiful fossil of a teleost fish was found in Tertiary rocks in Italy.

Left: These fossilized tree trunks grew over 200 million years ago in what is now Arizona, in the USA. The trunks were buried and each molecule was replaced by minerals. As a result, the trunks were petrified, or turned to stone. Every detail of the wood is preserved in the stone fossils.

primitive plants called blue–green algae. However, fossils are extremely rare in rocks formed in Pre-Cambrian times, that is, more than 570 million years ago. This is probably because most organisms that lived in the Pre-Cambrian Period had no hard parts.

By the start of the Cambrian Period, many organisms had hard parts and so fossils occur in many of the rocks formed since then. Some fossils were formed from organisms that lived only a short time before they became extinct (died out). These fossils are useful, because they prove that rocks thousands of kilometres apart were formed at the same time. From such evidence, geologists have worked out the sequence of rocks, identifying the periods in which they were formed. Biologists have also unravelled much of the story of the evolution of life from fossil records.

PLANTS AND ANIMALS
The miracle of the cell

All living things are made up of tiny compartments called cells. The smallest animals and plants consist of single cells. Larger organisms consist of many cells.

The cells of an animal or plant all work together so that the functions of the whole organism are co-ordinated. But at the same time, each cell works on its own – like a factory in an industrial estate. The boundary of the factory is the cell wall. Animal cells have a thin flexible wall called the *plasma membrane*. Plant cells have an additional, more rigid wall. In a living plant cell this wall is mostly composed of a material called *cellulose*.

The contents of the cell consist of the *cytoplasm* and the *nucleus*. The nucleus is the central controller of the cell – the factory computer. It issues the instructions that tell the other parts of the cell what to do. The cytoplasm is a colourless or white-ish watery fluid containing chemicals and several structures called *organelles*. The chemicals are used by the organelles in their work. For example, sugar and dissolved oxygen are present. These are used by organelles called *mitochondria* in a process called respiration. Chemical changes take place in the mitochondria and they release carbon dioxide and energy, the latter being used by the rest of the cell. Thus the mitochondria are the powerhouses of the cell – the factory generators.

Like any other factory the cell has a product – in this case *proteins*. These are built up from chemicals called *amino acids*. The instructions for making proteins come from a substance called *chromatin* in the nucleus. This sends out chemical messages containing instructions for collecting up amino acids and linking them together to form proteins.

In the cytoplasm there are granular structures called *ribosomes*. Some of these are attached to a folded membrane called the *endoplasmic reticulum*. Proteins are made on these ribosomes. Some proteins are used for growth or repair. Others are special chemicals called *enzymes*, which are essential aids to many of the chemical reactions that take place in a cell.

The cell factory also has to export substances to other cells and to get rid of its waste products. Certain chemicals can go straight through the plasma membrane. Others have to be actively transported across by special carrier chemicals. Chemicals with large molecules are packaged up by the *golgi apparatus* and then transported through the membrane.

The waste disposers of the cell are the *lysosomes*. These take in waste matter and break it down. Then they are expelled from the cell.

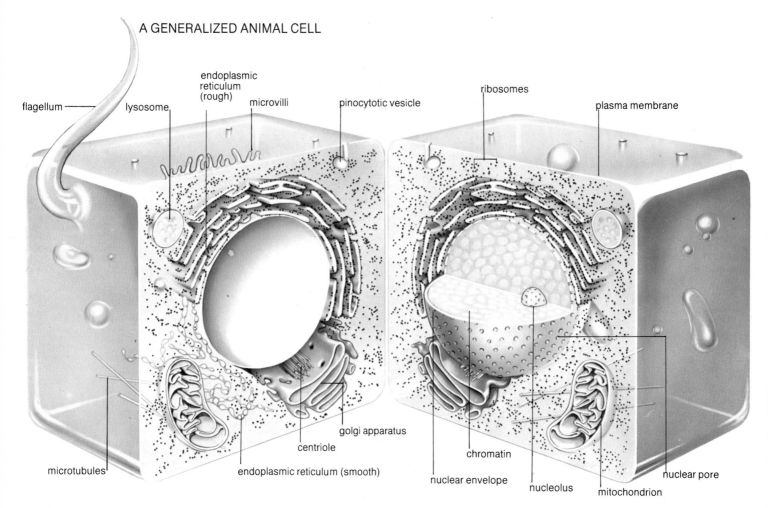

A GENERALIZED ANIMAL CELL

flagellum — lysosome — endoplasmic reticulum (rough) — microvilli — pinocytotic vesicle — ribosomes — plasma membrane — microtubules — endoplasmic reticulum (smooth) — centriole — golgi apparatus — chromatin — nuclear envelope — nucleolus — mitochondrion — nuclear pore

PINOCYTOSIS (CELL DRINKING)

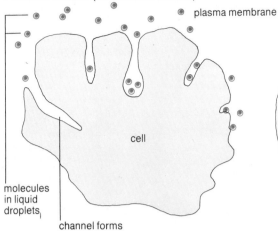

plasma membrane

droplets enclosed in vacuole inside cell

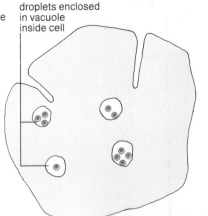

molecules in liquid droplets

channel forms

cell

PHAGOCYTOSIS (CELL EATING)

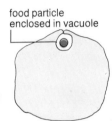

food particle

finger-like projections (pseudopodia) form

food particle enclosed in vacuole

cell

Left: Cell drinking. Cells that can do this form a small channel which expands into a sac called a pinocytotic vesicle. Water is taken into the cell, trapped inside the vesicle.

Below left: Cell eating. Some cells, such as an *Amoeba*, can take in solid food particles. Each particle is surrounded and enclosed in a food vacuole, where it is digested.

Below: A single-celled organism called *Euglena*. The dark brown nucleus and green chloroplasts can be seen.

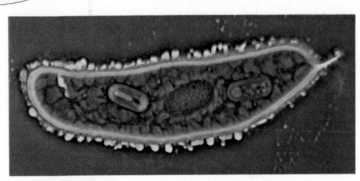

Left: A diagram showing the structures, or organelles, that can form part of an animal cell. The nucleus contains a granular substance called chromatin, which is the material that gives coded instructions to the rest of the cell. The nucleolus is a dense body in the nucleus that makes ribosomes. Coded instructions and ribosomes pass out through the nuclear envelope. This membrane connects up with the folded membrane called the endoplasmic reticulum, which connects in some cells with outfoldings of the plasma membrane, called microvilli. The cell's energy is supplied by the mitochondria, exports are handled by the golgi apparatus and waste products are dealt with by the lysosomes. The centriole is concerned with cell division. Some animal cells have flagella. Others have cilia, which are similar structures but shorter.

Right: Four different kinds of cell seen under a microscope. 1. Epithelial cells from part of a mammal's small intestine. 2. Human blood cells. The nuclei are stained red in this picture. Red blood cells have no nuclei and so appear grey. The larger white blood cells appear dark red because their nuclei are stained red. 3. The epidermal (skin) cells of a Box leaf, showing the stomata (see page 48). 4. A cross-section of part of the stem of a lime tree, showing the water-carrying xylem cells (stained red).

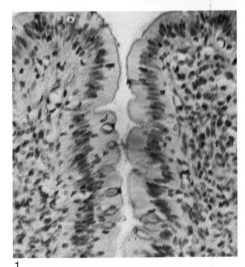

1

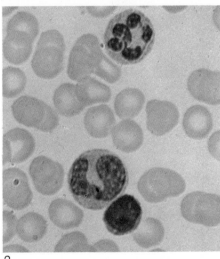

2

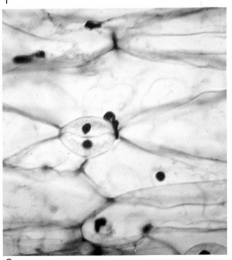

3

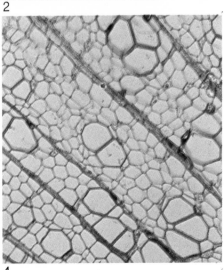

4

Smallest and simplest plants

The earliest evidence that we have for the existence of life on Earth comes from fossils found in rocks 3100 million years old. At that time, it seems there were bacteria and simple plants called *blue–green algae*.

Bacteria and blue–green algae still exist today. The main difference between them and other living things is that their cells do not contain nuclei. The chromatin (see page 40) floats freely in the cytoplasm. But blue–green algae contain *chlorophyll* and can therefore make their own food (see page 48). And it was from the blue–green algae that the more advanced forms of algae evolved about 1500 million years ago.

The term 'algae' covers about 20,000 species of plants that range from microscopic, single-celled organisms to giant seaweeds. However, these very different plants have two main things in common. First, they are all very simple plants without roots, stems or leaves. Second, they do not have the complicated plumbing systems found in more advanced plants. Therefore they have to live in water or in damp places.

There are many types of single-celled algae. Many of them are green in colour. *Chlorella* forms a green scum on ponds and *Pleurococcus* gives a green tinge to the bark of trees. Some of them, such as *Chlamydomonas* and *Euglena,* have whip-like organs called flagella, which they use for swimming.

Diatoms are golden-brown, single-celled algae that are very common in the sea and in fresh water. A diatom has a shell instead of a cell wall. The shell is in two parts, one of which fits over the other like a pill-box lid.

There are also golden and yellow-green algae. Many of them can be found, together with microscopic animals, in plankton, which forms the food of a large number of sea animals.

More advanced kinds of algae consist of many cells. *Volvox* is a colonial type that consists of a hollow ball of chlamydomonas-like cells. *Spirogyra* is a filamentous alga, so called because it is made up of a long thread, or filament, of cells. It may form thick, green mats in ponds.

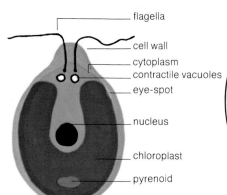

Above: The single-celled alga *Chlamydomonas*. **It has a large cup-shaped chloroplast and a pyrenoid, which is used to store starch. The contractile vacuoles get rid of water.**

flagella
cell wall
cytoplasm
contractile vacuoles
eye-spot
nucleus
chloroplast
pyrenoid

Above: The asexual reproduction of *Chlamydomonas.* **The cell simply divides into 2, 4, 8 or 16 parts, which emerge as new individuals, identical to the original cell.**

The most familiar algae are the seaweeds. These are many-celled algae in which the cells are built up into a large plant body that can be seen without the aid of a microscope. Sea lettuce is a common green alga found between the tide marks. Red seaweeds are generally found in deeper waters and many have delicate and beautiful structures. Brown seaweeds include the largest algae of all – the wracks and kelps. Bladderwrack, so called because of the air-filled bladders that help to keep the fronds upright in the water, is a common shore weed. The largest giant kelp has long, leathery fronds up to 200 metres long.

Many algae are useful to man. Some seaweeds are used to make animal foods and some can be eaten by humans. Some single-celled algae are used in the treatment of sewage. Substances extracted from algae are used to make such things as tooth-paste, tyres, ice-cream and paint.

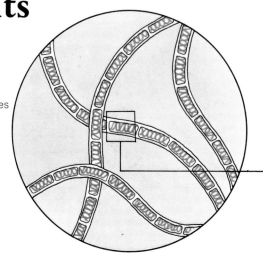

Below: The sexual reproduction of *Chlamydomonas*. **The cell divides into sex cells. Two sex cells fuse to form a zygospore, which divides to form new individuals.**

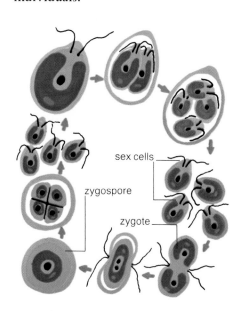

sex cells
zygospore
zygote

Below: The Bladderwrack (*Fucus vesiculosus***) is a common seaweed. The air-filled bladders keep the fronds of the seaweed floating upright in the water.**

Left: The filamentous green alga *Spirogyra*, as seen through a low-power microscope. The filaments consist of long chains of cells.

Below: A single *Spirogyra* cell. The chloroplast forms a flat ribbon that spirals round the inner edge of the cell. It is dotted with many pyrenoids – structures that store starch. The vacuole is a space filled with a watery fluid. It contains nutrients taken in from the water that surrounds the plant.

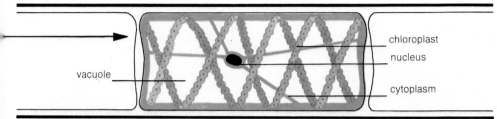

vacuole — chloroplast

nucleus

cytoplasm

Above: A red algae with its filaments arranged in feather-like shapes. Most red algae are found in deep water, but a few can be seen between the tide marks.

Right: Different types of seaweed on a seashore in Britain.

Below: A green seaweed growing in warm, tropical waters.

Right: The sexual reproduction of *Spirogyra*. 1. An adult filament. Two of these come to lie alongside each other. 2. The filaments touch and their cell walls begin to form small tube-like outgrowths. 3. A tube forms between two cells of the adjacent filaments. 4. The contents of the cells in one filament form a green mass – the male sex cell. The contents of the cells in the opposite filament form a female sex cell. 5. The male sex cell begins to move through the tube. 6. The sex cells fuse to form a zygote. This develops a hard, black coat and becomes a zygospore. The hard coat can withstand extreme conditions, such as cold and lack of water. 7. The filament breaks down and the zygospore is released. Eventually, when conditions are right, it will germinate to form a new filament.

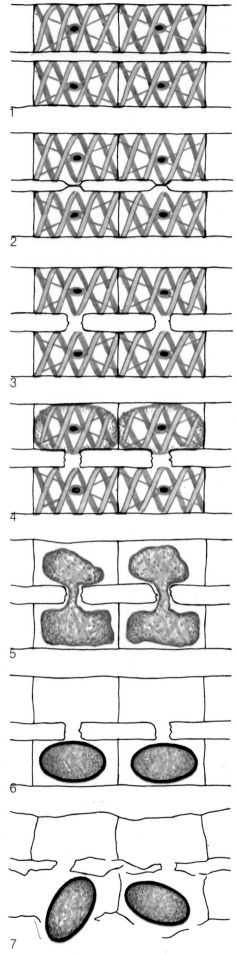

Tallest and oldest plants

There are many unusual and spectacular plants in the world. But there is one group of plants that holds several records. These are the conifers – so called because they produce their seeds in cones. The world's oldest, tallest and most massive trees are all conifers.

Most conifers are easy to recognize by their long, needle-shaped leaves. Nearly all conifers are *evergreen* trees or shrubs. However, the term 'evergreen' does not mean that the leaves never die. Instead, each leaf lives for 3 or 4 years and leaves are being shed all the time. As a result the conifer always has a large number of living leaves.

The conifers include the pines, redwoods, firs, cedars, spruces and larches. Most of them grow in the northern hemisphere and there is a broad band of coniferous forest that stretches round the world just below the Arctic circle.

The most familiar conifers are probably the pines. They have separate male and female cones and the large female cones hang downwards. Some pines are planted by foresters for their timber. Pine is a soft wood and is used for making paper, furniture, telegraph poles and fence posts. The most important timber trees are the White Pine and the Scots Pine. This group also contains the world's oldest living trees. The Bristlecone Pine is a short, mountain tree that looks rather twisted and malformed. Some specimens are reckoned to be over 4500 years old.

The redwoods are the largest trees in the world. The Coast Redwood, which is found in California, USA, often grows to a height of over 75 metres. The tallest living tree is a Coast Redwood, 111.6 metres high.

The Giant Redwood, also called the Giant Sequoia, Wellingtonia or California Big Tree, is the most massive of the world's trees. The largest specimen, named 'General Sherman', is over 83 metres high and measures more than 24 metres around the base of its trunk. The redwoods are also extremely old. Coast Redwoods often live for over 1800

Above: Bristlecone Pines, the world's oldest living trees, in the White Mountains of California. The oldest ever recorded was 4900 years old. The oldest living specimen, known as Methuselah, is 4600 years old.

Left: These spruces have needle-like leaves and light-brown cones with many closely packed scales.

years and scientists estimate that Giant Redwoods are capable of living for over 6000 years – even longer than Bristlecone Pines.

Firs are also tall trees and some are grown for their timber. There are 35 species found all over the northern hemisphere and they have tough, upright cones.

The Douglas Fir is not in fact a true fir and is sometimes called the Douglas Spruce or Douglas Pine. Its timber is much used. There is an unproven claim that the tallest tree that ever lived was a Douglas Fir felled in 1895.

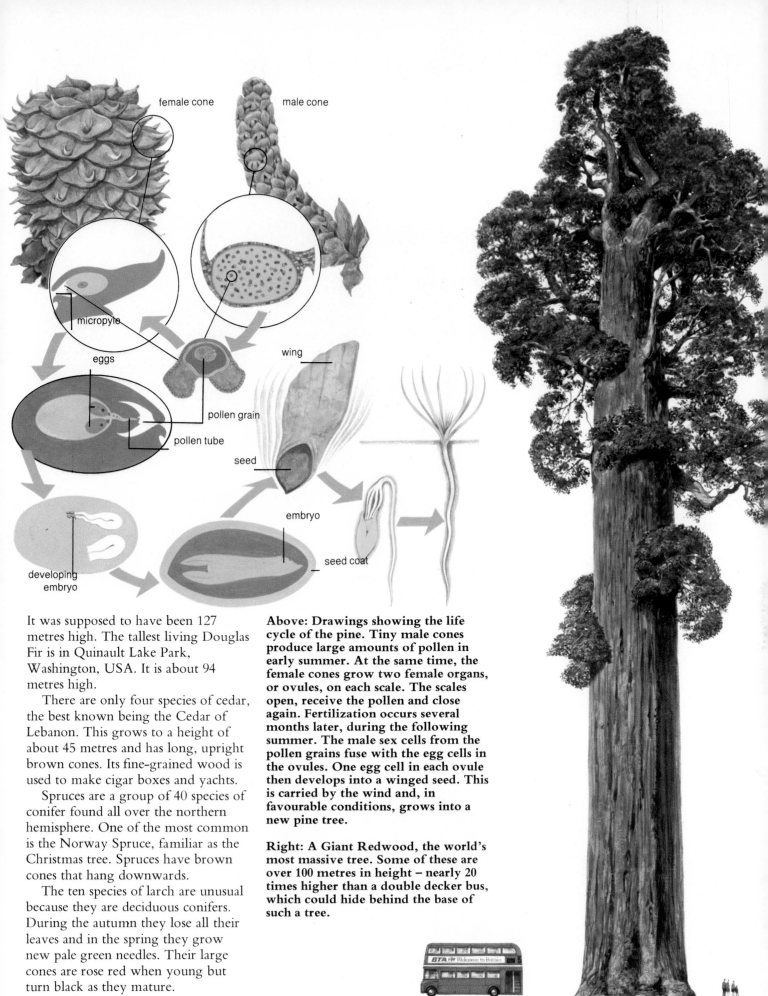

female cone

male cone

micropyle

eggs

pollen grain

pollen tube

wing

seed

embryo

seed coat

developing
embryo

It was supposed to have been 127 metres high. The tallest living Douglas Fir is in Quinault Lake Park, Washington, USA. It is about 94 metres high.

There are only four species of cedar, the best known being the Cedar of Lebanon. This grows to a height of about 45 metres and has long, upright brown cones. Its fine-grained wood is used to make cigar boxes and yachts.

Spruces are a group of 40 species of conifer found all over the northern hemisphere. One of the most common is the Norway Spruce, familiar as the Christmas tree. Spruces have brown cones that hang downwards.

The ten species of larch are unusual because they are deciduous conifers. During the autumn they lose all their leaves and in the spring they grow new pale green needles. Their large cones are rose red when young but turn black as they mature.

Above: Drawings showing the life cycle of the pine. Tiny male cones produce large amounts of pollen in early summer. At the same time, the female cones grow two female organs, or ovules, on each scale. The scales open, receive the pollen and close again. Fertilization occurs several months later, during the following summer. The male sex cells from the pollen grains fuse with the egg cells in the ovules. One egg cell in each ovule then develops into a winged seed. This is carried by the wind and, in favourable conditions, grows into a new pine tree.

Right: A Giant Redwood, the world's most massive tree. Some of these are over 100 metres in height – nearly 20 times higher than a double decker bus, which could hide behind the base of such a tree.

The colourful world of flowers

The flowering plants are the most successful plants in the world. No other plant group contains such a variety of form. Such very different plants as grasses, orchids, trees and cacti are all flowering plants; and there are very few places in the world where flowering plants do not grow.

The secret of the success of flowering plants lies in the flowers themselves. These are the most efficient reproductive systems in the plant kingdom. To help in the process of reproduction, flowering plants have enlisted the aid of other agents – chiefly insects and wind, but occasionally mammals and birds.

The outer parts of a flower consist of the petals, which are often brightly coloured, and the sepals, which are generally green. The centre of the flower contains the sex organs. The male organs are the *stamens*. At the ends of these are small bags of pollen called *anthers*. The female parts of the flower consist of an ovary, containing one or more *ovules,* and a long style, at the end of which is a *stigma.*

Pollination is the process by which grains of pollen are transferred from an anther to a stigma. After pollination has occurred, a pollen grain produces a long tube, which grows down the style into the ovule. There, a male cell from the pollen grain fertilizes the egg cell. The ovule then develops into a seed.

Below: Violas have attractive, insect-pollinated flowers. Self-pollination is prevented by a flap that covers the stigma.

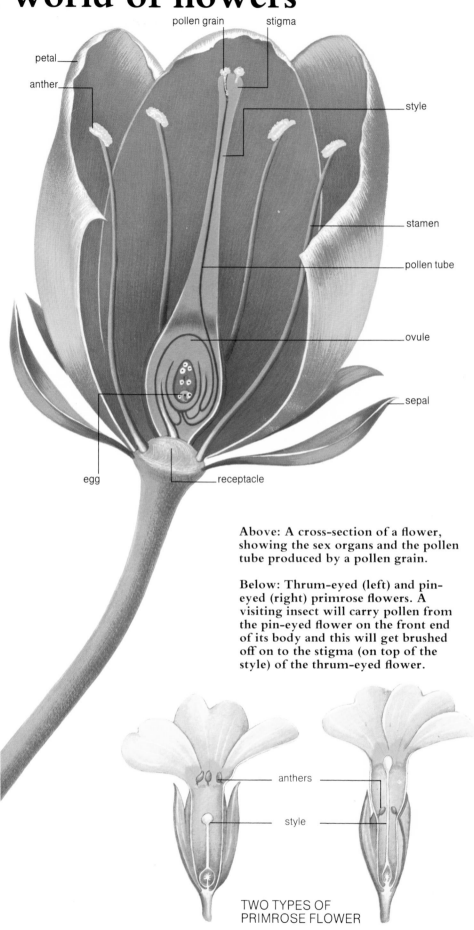

Above: A cross-section of a flower, showing the sex organs and the pollen tube produced by a pollen grain.

Below: Thrum-eyed (left) and pin-eyed (right) primrose flowers. A visiting insect will carry pollen from the pin-eyed flower on the front end of its body and this will get brushed off on to the stigma (on top of the style) of the thrum-eyed flower.

TWO TYPES OF
PRIMROSE FLOWER

46

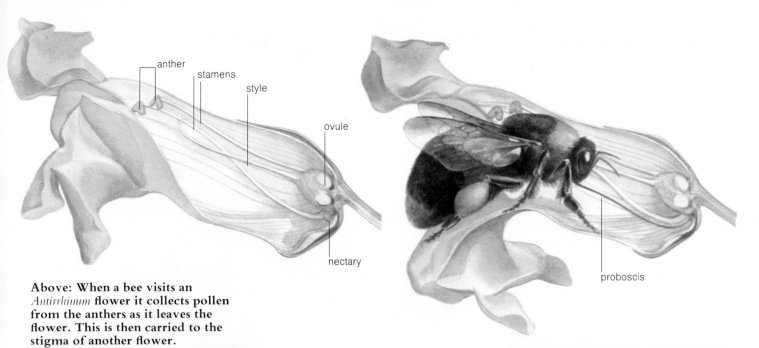

anther
stamens
style
ovule
nectary
proboscis

Above: When a bee visits an *Antirrhinum* flower it collects pollen from the anthers as it leaves the flower. This is then carried to the stigma of another flower.

Above: A type of bee orchid. One of its petals resembles a female bee and this attracts males, which pollinate the flower.

Below: Bees visiting the flower of an arum lily, attracted by the scent produced by the spike.

The strongest and healthiest plants are produced by *cross-pollination*, in which pollen is transferred from the anthers of one plant to the stigma of another. Many flowers, therefore, have ways of preventing *self-pollination* (transfer of pollen from the anthers to the stigma of the same flower).

Insect-pollinated plants have brightly coloured flowers to attract the insects. They also produce nectar, which insects, particularly bees, collect for food. When an insect reaches a flower it may be guided to the nectar by special markings, such as lines or dots. While drinking the nectar, the insect becomes dusted with pollen and may deposit pollen from another flower on the stigma.

Many insect-pollinated flowers have ingenious ways of ensuring cross-pollination. In some the anthers and stigma ripen at different times. In others there may be a complicated system of flaps that only allows an insect to enter in a particular way.

Wind-pollinated plants, such as grasses, do not have brightly coloured flowers as they do not need to attract insects. However, they produce large quantities of light pollen that is carried by the wind to the feathery stigmas of other flowers. In order to ensure cross-pollination, some plants have separate male and female flowers. Alder and hazel trees have separate male and female catkins, which are bunches of tiny flowers.

Above: A cactus is a type of flowering plant that stores water in its swollen stem. This allows it to live in dry conditions.

Below: A beech tree has separate male and female flowers – the male flowers are those with bunches of stamens.

47

How plants work

The body of a plant is divided into roots, stem and leaves. Each of these parts has particular functions, which are the same in nearly all plants. However, their shape and size vary considerably, depending on such factors as the age of the plant and where it lives.

The roots have two functions. First, they anchor the plant and help to prevent the soil from being blown away. Second, they take in water from the soil. A typical root system begins with a *primary root,* which is attached to the base of the stem. This divides into a number of *secondary roots,* which branch repeatedly. Water is taken up by the finest branches, the *root hairs,* which are only one cell thick.

Some plants, such as grasses, have no primary roots; instead they have a mass of fibrous roots just below the

Below: A typical flowering plant, with roots, stem and leaves.

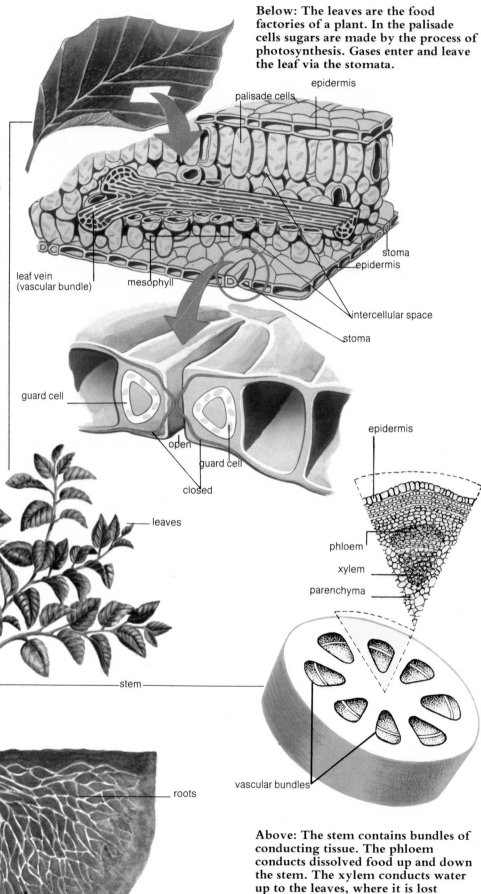

Below: The leaves are the food factories of a plant. In the palisade cells sugars are made by the process of photosynthesis. Gases enter and leave the leaf via the stomata.

epidermis
palisade cells
leaf vein (vascular bundle)
mesophyll
stoma
epidermis
intercellular space
stoma

guard cell
open
guard cell
closed

leaves

stem

roots

epidermis
phloem
xylem
parenchyma

vascular bundles

Above: The stem contains bundles of conducting tissue. The phloem conducts dissolved food up and down the stem. The xylem conducts water up to the leaves, where it is lost through the stomata.

48

soil surface. The roots of other plants penetrate deeper. The large primary roots, or *tap roots,* of thistles and dandelions reach deep into the soil.

The stem also has two functions. First, it supports the leaves and flowers. Small plants have green stems and the support is provided by stiffening cells inside the stem. Large plants develop wood to give extra support and they become covered in bark for protection.

The stem's second function is to transport water up to the leaves and food materials to all parts of the plant. Water is conducted through a plumbing system of tubular cells called the *xylem.* Food materials are carried in a tissue called the *phloem.*

The leaves have the most important function of all. Without their work no life would exist. This is because leaves make food for the plant, which in turn may be eaten by animals.

Plants make food by using energy from sunlight in a process called *photosynthesis.* Inside the cells of leaves are organelles (see page 40) called *chloroplasts.* These contain a green pigment called *chlorophyll,* which is the chemical that enables photosynthesis to take place. It converts light energy into chemical energy. This allows carbon dioxide, which the plant takes from the air, to react with water to form sugar (food). At the same time oxygen is formed and released into the air.

The sugar is then either stored as starch or used immediately in a process called *respiration* (breathing) to

Below: In summer the leaves of a deciduous tree are green, due to the green chlorophyll pigment they contain. In autumn the tree withdraws the chlorophyll from its leaves,

leaving them coloured yellow or brown (due to the presence of other pigments – xanthophylls and carotenes – that were masked by the green chlorophyll in summer).

Above: The underside of the leaf of a *Tradescantia* **plant, showing the stomata, each with two guard cells.**

Right: If a plant cannot get enough water from the soil, it wilts. This is due to the fact that the cells of the stem and leaves collapse. Normally, when there is enough water available, the cells contain sufficient water to keep them rigid.

Below: The roots of a plant have tiny root hairs that collect up water from the soil.

create energy for other processes that take place in the cells of the plant. During respiration, oxygen from the air is used to chemically break down the sugar, releasing carbon dioxide and energy.

The gases (oxygen and carbon dioxide) that are taken in and released during respiration enter and leave the leaf through tiny holes in its under-surface, called *stomata* (singular: *stoma*). Stomata also play an important part in a process called *transpiration.*

Transpiration is the evaporation of water from the stomata. It has two main purposes. First, it helps to keep the plant cool on hot days. The stomata can be opened or closed to control the rate at which water is lost by transpiration. Second, it draws water up from the roots, and the water contains minerals that are essential to the plant.

Plants that cheat

Most plants do their own work and live fairly independent lives. They have chlorophyll in their leaves and thus make their own food. Their roots draw water and minerals from the soil and they support themselves.

But some plants do not have any chlorophyll; they rely on others to provide their food. Some plants have no roots; they tap others to get water and minerals. And a number of plants rely on others to support them. Such plants can be called 'cheats'.

Fungi are a large group of plants, all of which lack chlorophyll. They feed by means of a mass of tiny threads called the *mycelium,* which they use to get food in one of two ways. Some fungi, called *saprophytes,* live on decaying plant or animal material. Other fungi, known as *parasites,* live on other plants or on animals. They take food directly from their hosts and give nothing back in return. In fact, the host is often seriously harmed and may eventually be killed by the parasite.

There are many examples of both types of fungus. Pin moulds are saprophytes that live on stale bread and other foods. Potato Blight is a parasite that can destroy potato crops. But the most familiar fungi are the mushrooms and toadstools. Actually, a toadstool is only the spore-producing fruiting body of the fungus. The mycelium remains hidden in the soil or in the wood of a tree.

Many toadstool-producing fungi are saprophytes, for example the Field Mushroom, and some are parasites, for example the Honey Fungus. But there are also a number that live with other plants in a relationship that is mutually beneficial to both partners and harms neither of them. This method of living together is called *symbiosis.* The roots of some fungi become entangled with the roots of certain trees to form structures called *mycorrhizas.* The fungus benefits by taking sugar from the roots and the tree gains a larger surface area over which water can be absorbed.

A number of other plants are also parasites. For example, the Common Mistletoe is a partial parasite of apple

Below: Some of the many hundreds of fruiting bodies of fungi.
Hygrophorus obrusseus **is a toadstool that grows in fields during the summer.** *Clavulinopsis corniculata* **produces a branching fruiting body during the summer and autumn. The spores are produced all over the surface. The toadstool of** *Hygrophorus puniceus* **grows**

in fields and besides roads in the autumn. The fruiting body of *Bovista nigrescens* **can be found in fields at any time of year. When it ripens it splits open to reveal a purplish mass of spores. The Common Field Mushroom,** *Agaricus campestris,* **is the most popular of the edible fungi. It grows in fields in late summer and**

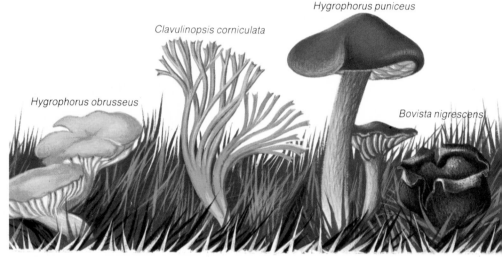

Clavulinopsis corniculata

Hygrophorus puniceus

Hygrophorus obrusseus

Bovista nigrescens

Below: The Honeysuckle is a climber. It does not need to grow its own supporting stem and so saves energy for other purposes. This one has climbed a young fir tree and has severely restricted the growth of the fir's upper branches. Eventually the fir tree may be completely overwhelmed.

Below: Epiphytes are plants that grow in the branches of other trees without harming them in any way. In this case the epiphyte is a lichen (a plant partnership between an alga and a fungus) that has produced an enormous growth in the branches of a beech tree. It is thus able to get plenty of light.

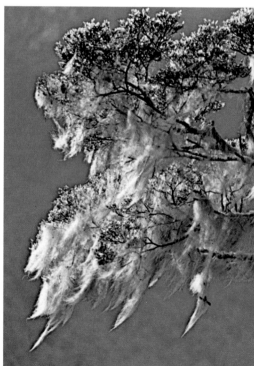

Fistulina hepatica
(Beefsteak Fungus)

Grifola gigantea

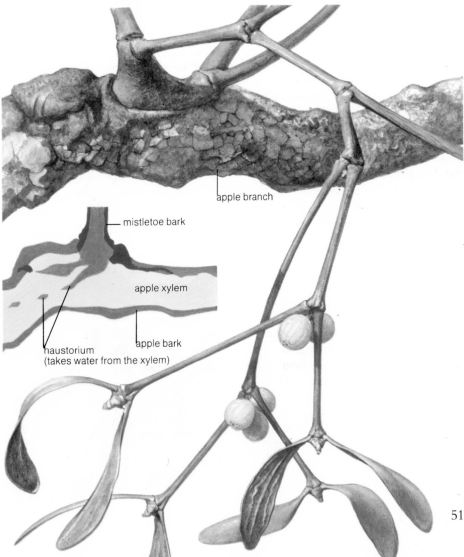

autumn. **The Shaggy Ink Cap,** *Coprinus comatus,* **is another edible toadstool that can be found in fields in summer and early autumn. The Beefsteak Fungus,** *Fistulina hepatica,* **is also edible, but rather sour. This fungus and** *Grifola gigantea,* **which grows at the base of certain trees, produce their spores inside pores instead of gills.**

Coprinus comatus
(Shaggy Ink Cap)

Agaricus campestris
(Field Mushroom)

Right: Mistletoe is a partial parasite of apple trees. It makes its own food by photosynthesis, but takes water from the xylem of the tree, through a growth called a haustorium. The white berries, which are eaten by birds, contain seeds. These stick to the birds' beaks, are wiped off on other trees and germinate there.

trees, and Dodder is a total parasite of several plants, including clover, nettles, gorse and heather.

Climbing and rambling plants cheat in another way. Most plants put a lot of energy into growing strong stems, so that they can reach upwards towards the light. Climbers, on the other hand, use other plants for support, thus saving energy. Various methods are used for climbing. Some plants, such as Honeysuckle and Bindweed, twine round their supports. Others, such as the Sweet Pea, use tendrils for grasping. Ivy has roots that can grow into the bark of a tree.

Some plants do not even bother to climb towards the light. They live all the time high up in the branches of trees. Such plants are called epiphytes. They get their water and food from dead material trapped in the branches. Epiphytes include mosses, ferns and lichens, which are symbiotic associations of fungi and algae.

apple branch

mistletoe bark

apple xylem

apple bark

haustorium
(takes water from the xylem)

51

Carnivorous plants

It is a well-known law of nature that animals eat plants for food. Therefore it may seem strange that some plants have become adapted for eating animals. But plants that live in peat bogs have problems in getting all the food they need, and some of them have evolved into the killers of the plant world.

Carnivorous plants use several methods of trapping prey. Perhaps the best known is the spectacular Venus's Fly Trap. The traps, formed at the ends of the leaves, consist of two lobes fringed with spikes. Insects are attracted by nectar produced round the edges of the lobes. On the inner surface of each lobe there are three trigger hairs. If a raindrop or very small insect touches one hair, the trap remains open. But if an insect large enough to be useful to the plant touches two of the hairs, the lobes close inwards and the two fringes of spikes interlock. The insect is thus held inside the trap and is digested by chemicals called enzymes produced by glands on the surface of each lobe.

A pitcher plant is a tropical carnivorous plant that has jug-like traps containing a watery digestive fluid. There are several types of pitcher plant and they form their traps in various ways. In *Nepenthes* the pitcher

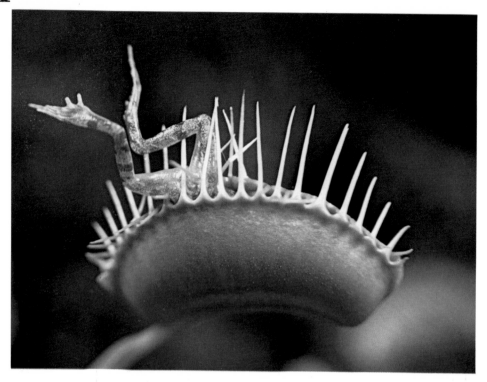

Below: A fly in danger of losing its life at the mouth of a North American pitcher plant. The downward-pointing hairs on the lid of the plant prevent the fly from climbing upwards. Below these is a region of shorter hairs followed by a smooth, slippery area. If the fly descends any farther it will not be able to climb out and will eventually lose its grip and fall into the liquid at the bottom. There it will drown and be digested.

Above: An unwary frog has triggered off this Venus's Fly Trap, providing the plant with an unusual meal. Although these plants are designed to catch insects, anything that touches two of the trigger hairs will cause the trap to close.

Below: An unlucky fly trapped on the leaf of a sundew. The drops of sticky fluid on the tips of the leaf tentacles prevent the fly from escaping.

is formed from the tip of the leaf mid-rib. Many species of *Nepenthes* are epiphytes (see page 51). *Sarracenia* species form their pitchers from whole leaves that grow up from the swampy ground.

Often, the mouth of a pitcher plant is sheltered by a lid. Insects may be attracted by bright colours, nectar or both. Inside the rim of the pitcher the surface is slippery, and some species have downward-pointing hairs. As a result the insect cannot grip the surface, falls into the fluid below and drowns. The fluid contains enzymes which digest the insect.

The bladderworts have ingenious underwater traps that work by suction. Each trap is a bladder with a trap-door at one end. The trap-door is surrounded by hairs that guide the prey towards it. On the door itself there are trigger hairs. When the prey touches these the trap-door flies open and water rushes in, carrying the prey with it. The trap-door closes again and the trap is reset by glands that pump water out of the bladder through its wall. The prey is digested by enzymes.

Another group of carnivorous plants work in the same way as sticky fly-paper. For example, the leaves of a sundew have long tentacles that exude a sticky substance at their tips. When an insect lands on a leaf it is caught in this substance. Other tentacles then bend over to hold the insect down even more firmly. It is then digested by enzymes produced by glands on the surface of the leaf.

Butterworts are so-named because of the sticky butter-coloured substance with which their leaves are covered. It is produced by small, hair-like glands and glues insects down while they are being digested.

Above: The pink butterwort has a rosette of sticky leaves close to the ground. Insects that land on the leaves are caught and digested.

Right: The bladderwort has underwater branches that carry the bladders. Each bladder is a suction trap. Water is pumped out and then any movement of the trigger hairs causes the trap-door to fly open, sucking in water and small animals.

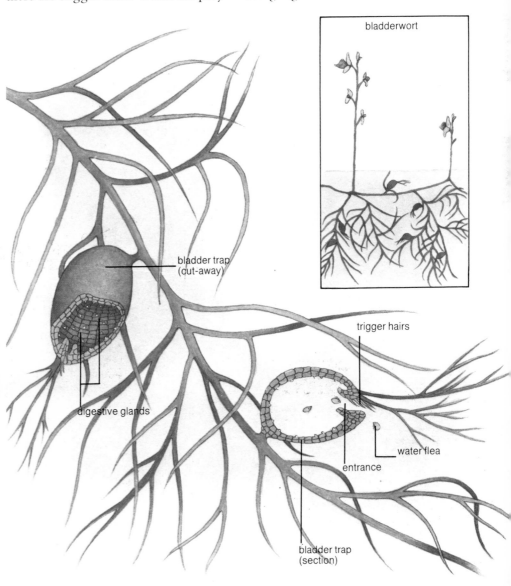

bladderwort

bladder trap (cut-away)

digestive glands

trigger hairs

entrance

bladder trap (section)

water flea

Smallest and simplest animals

All over the world, wherever there is water, food and oxygen there are tiny single-celled animals. Most of them can only be seen through a microscope and few are more than 1 millimetre across. They belong to a group known as the *Protozoa,* which means 'first animals', because the first kind of animal life that appeared on Earth over 3000 million years ago was probably the single-celled animals. Today there are over 30,000 living species of Protozoa.

The Protozoa are divided into four main groups: the flagellates, the rhizopods, the ciliates and the sporozoans or spore-formers. A flagellate has one or more whip-like organs, which are used to propel the animal through the water. Flagellates include many free-living types. Others have symbiotic (mutually advantageous) relationships with other animals. For example,

Euglena

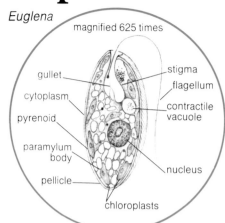

magnified 625 times

gullet
stigma
flagellum
cytoplasm
contractile vacuole
pyrenoid
paramylum body
nucleus
pellicle
chloroplasts

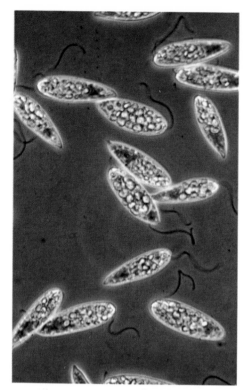

Above and right: *Euglena* is a green flagellate. Its chloroplasts indicate that it is a plant, but it has several animal features, such as movement and the ability to take in and use foods not made by photosynthesis. The stigma, or eye-spot, is sensitive to light and *Euglena* tends to move towards light. Contractile vacuoles control *Euglena's* water content and paramylum granules are a form of storage compound.

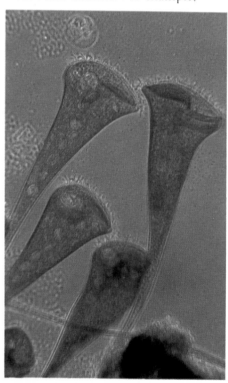

Stentor feeding

Stentor – showing green colouration

Sporozoan
magnified 4000 times

paired organelles
mitochondrion
pellicle
nucleus
cytoplasm
contractile fibrils

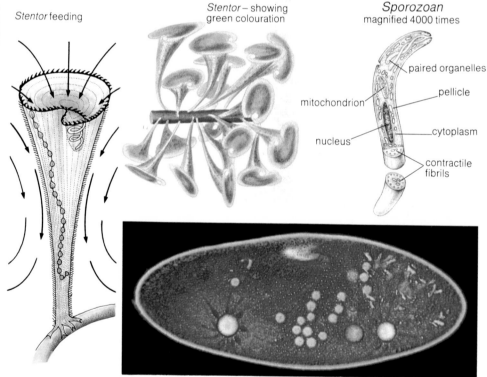

Above: *Stentor* is a large ciliate that is capable of changing its shape and of taking avoiding action when danger threatens. However, it only occasionally uses its cilia for swimming. When it feeds, bands of cilia cause currents of water that carry food particles to flow into its gullet. *Stentor* sometimes appears green because it is giving shelter to a green

alga called *Zoochlorella,* which provides *Stentor* with extra food and oxygen.

Above right: A sporozoite, just one of the stages in the life cycle of a sporozoan. The sporozoite of *Plasmodium,* the malaria parasite, is the stage that the mosquito injects into humans. Malaria is an unpleasant disease common in tropical areas.

Above and right: *Paramecium* is a common ciliate. It uses its covering of cilia for both movement and feeding. Its two contractile vacuoles control the water content of the cell. Its two nuclei have different functions. The macronucleus controls feeding and other activities of the cell, and the micronucleus controls the process of reproduction.

Amoeba

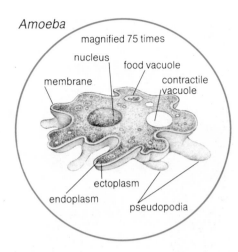

magnified 75 times

nucleus

food vacuole

membrane

contractile vacuole

ectoplasm

endoplasm

pseudopodia

Above: *Amoeba* **is a rhizopod.**

Right: *Paramecium* **moves in a corkscrew fashion through the water by causing waves of beating cilia to pass down its body.** *Euglena* **also moves in a corkscrew fashion. It thrashes its flagellum in such a way that it is drawn through the water.** *Amoeba* **moves by putting out a 'false foot' or pseudopodium.**

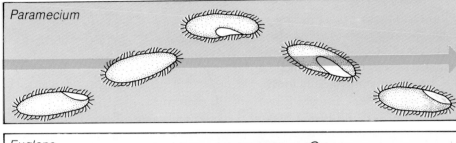

Paramecium

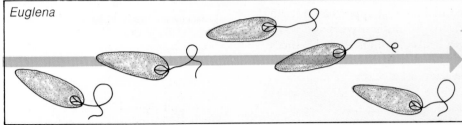

Euglena

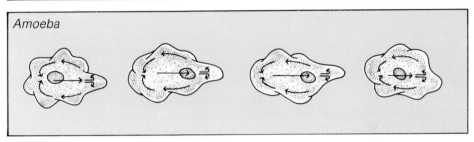

Amoeba

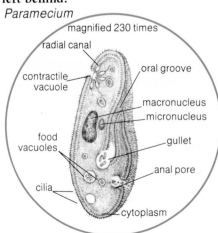
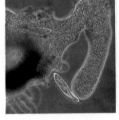
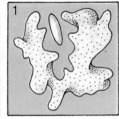
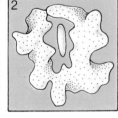
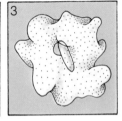
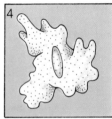
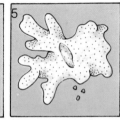

Above: *Amoeba* **feeds by engulfing its prey, in this case a** *Paramecium*. **1. The** *Amoeba* **puts out two pseudopodia. 2. The pseudopodia are extended all around the prey. 3. The prey is totally engulfed in a food vacuole inside the** *Amoeba*. **4. The prey may struggle for a while, until all the oxygen is used up. 5. The prey is digested inside the food vacuole and indigestible remains are left behind.**

Paramecium

magnified 230 times

radial canal

contractile vacuole

oral groove

macronucleus

micronucleus

food vacuoles

gullet

anal pore

cilia

cytoplasm

Trichonympha lives in the gut of a termite and helps it to digest cellulose, which it cannot do by itself. Other flagellates are parasites and may cause disease. For example, *Trypanosoma* causes sleeping sickness in humans.

One group of flagellates illustrates the difficulty of distinguishing between some single-celled plants and animals. Flagellates such as *Chlamydomonas*, *Euglena* and *Volvox* are generally claimed by botanists as being Algae (see page 42) because they contain chlorophyll. But they move by using their flagella and so zoologists often claim that they are Protozoa. In addition, *Euglena* can, under certain conditions, give up making its own food by photosynthesis (see page 49) and feed in an animal-like manner by taking in food from outside its body.

The rhizopods include the well-known *Amoeba*. This simple animal moves by flowing. Its body is like a

bag of jelly, from which it puts out temporary extensions called pseudopodia ('false feet'). But most rhizopods have a more complicated structure. For example, radiolarians have skeletons composed of radiating spikes.

The ciliates are animals that, at least during some part of their lives, are covered in rows of tiny bristles called cilia. These are used for movement and for feeding. For example, *Paramecium* 'rows' itself rapidly through the water. *Stentor* on the other hand is attached by a stalk and uses its cilia to create currents of water from which it removes food particles.

The sporozoans are the smallest of the Protozoa and they are all parasites. They go through a number of stages during their lives and at some point produce large numbers of spores. Some sporozoans are the cause of unpleasant diseases. For example, *Plasmodium* causes malaria in humans.

The shell-makers

Snails and their relatives belong to a highly successful group of animals called the molluscs. One of the reasons for their success is that most of them have hard external shells to protect them from predators.

The three main classes of molluscs are the *gastropods* (snails, limpets and slugs), the *bivalves* (oysters, mussels, cockles, clams and scallops) and the *cephalopods* (cuttlefishes, squids and octopuses). At first glance it is difficult to see the relationship between a snail, an oyster and a squid. But they all have the same basic body plan, consisting of a head, foot and body. In each case this body plan has been modified (adapted) to suit a particular way of life.

Snails are a familiar sight in the garden. But most gastropods live in water – some in fresh water and many in the sea. Limpets, periwinkles and topshells are a common sight at low

Below: Sea slugs are gastropods that do not have shells. They are often brightly coloured. The structures on the back of this species are modified gills and they also contain stinging cells taken from jellyfish that the sea slug has eaten.

tide and in warm seas there are large gastropods such as cowries and abalones.

A limpet moves by a rippling action of its large foot. At the front the head has sensitive tentacles for finding food and the mouth has a kind of rasping tongue, called a radula, for scraping up algae. The soft body is contained in the top part of the shell.

Periwinkles and many other coiled snails have the advantage of being able to withdraw into their shells and close the entrance with a lid-like flap or operculum. Many snails eat plants, but some, such as the Common Dog Whelk, are carnivores.

Slugs and sea slugs have either very small shells or none at all. The advantage of this is that they can squeeze through narrow passages and burrow for prey. They protect themselves by camouflage and by producing an unpleasant-tasting slime. Some are brightly coloured as a warning to predators.

Bivalves have shells formed from two valves hinged together. They feed by drawing in currents of water and filtering out the food particles. The head is very small and the foot is often large and muscular.

A burrowing bivalve, such as a cockle, clam or razor shell, uses its foot to pull itself down into the sand or mud. Some burrowers can even bore into wood or rock, using their shells as grinding tools. Oysters cement themselves to rock. Mussels attach themselves by threads. Scallops swim by rapidly opening and closing their shell valves.

Among the cephalopods only one, a primitive animal called *Nautilus,* has an external shell. Cuttlefishes and squids have internal shells, and octopuses have no shell.

Cephalopods are the most intelligent of all the invertebrates (animals without backbones). They have large heads which are surrounded by tentacles. The tentacles are a modification of the mollusc foot and are used for feeding. Squids and cuttlefishes have ten tentacles and octopuses have eight. They all have suckers for catching prey.

Above: A giant pond snail laying a string of eggs wrapped in mucus. Pond snails are hermaphrodite – that is they have both male and female sex organs. They are also pulmonates, which means that instead of gills they breathe through lungs and often rise to the surface to gulp air.

Below: The shell of a Mediterranean gastropod called *Murex*.

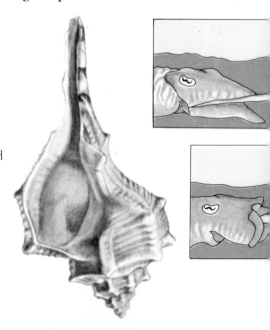

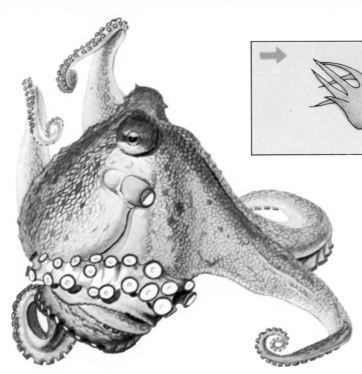

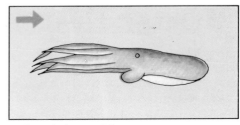

Left and above: The common octopus spends much of its time crawling around on the sea bed, catching its prey with its eight suckered tentacles. But it can swim, and in an emergency uses its funnel (which can be seen in the centre of the drawing, far left) to produce a jet of water. Like the squid and cuttlefish it can also produce an inky 'smoke-screen'.

Below: An oyster forms a pearl to protect itself against parasites and foreign particles. The mantle secretes a pearly material, which builds up round the invader in layers.

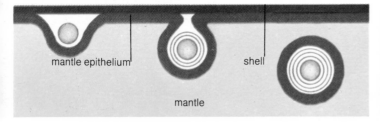

mantle epithelium

shell

mantle

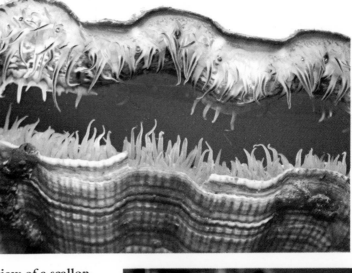

Below left: A cuttlefish lies in wait in the sand (top). It catches small animals by shooting out a pair of suckered tentacles (bottom).

Below right: A cuttlefish swims by using undulating movements of its fins. When alarmed it moves rapidly backwards by producing a jet of water from its funnel. It also releases an inky liquid as a sort of 'smoke-screen'.

Above: A close-up view of a scallop, showing the mantle, which is fringed with tentacles, and a number of pearl-like eyes.

Right: Mussels feed by creating a current of water that passes into a tube called the inhalent siphon. Inside, the food is filtered out and the water leaves via another tube called the exhalent siphon.

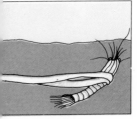

Butterflies and moths

Butterflies and moths are the most admired and collected of all insects, largely because of their bright colours and attractive appearance. They make up a group called the *Lepidoptera*, a name which means 'scaly winged', and there are over 120,000 species.

It is not always easy to distinguish between a butterfly and a moth. However, there are some general rules. Most moths fly at night, whereas most butterflies are daytime fliers. Many butterflies fold their wings vertically over their backs when at rest. Moths either fold them along their backs or keep them outstretched.

One of the fascinating things about butterflies and moths is their life cycle. They do not hatch out of their eggs as miniature winged insects, but go through two very different stages before reaching adulthood.

· When the egg hatches, a caterpillar emerges. This is basically a feeding and growing machine. The parent took care to lay the egg near or on a plentiful food supply. The caterpillar has powerful jaws, which it uses almost constantly to chew up plant material. As it grows, its outer skin often becomes too small. Then the caterpillar grows another skin underneath and just slips out of its old skin.

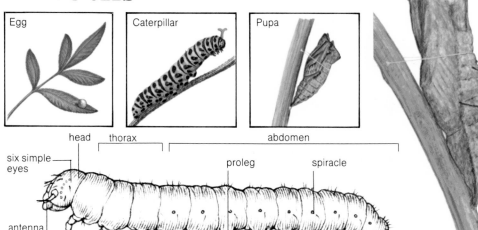

Top: The four stages in the life cycle of a Swallowtail Butterfly – egg, caterpillar, pupa (chrysalis) and adult (newly emerged from its chrysalis).

Above: A drawing showing the main features of a caterpillar. The important walking legs are the fleshy prolegs. The caterpillar breathes through its spiracles.

Below left: The Puss Moth caterpillar rears up when alarmed to show off its brightly coloured markings. This startles would-be predators.

Below: Two ways in which caterpillars move; A, by using the prolegs; B, by looping movements.

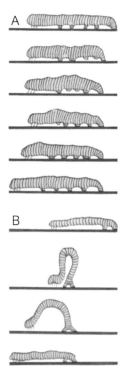

Adult

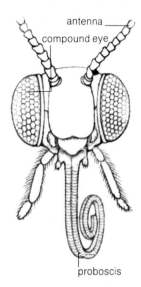
antenna
compound eye
proboscis

Left: A Scarlet-windowed moth disguises itself as a red leaf. The line across its wings looks like the middle line of a leaf.

Below left: Three ways of avoiding being eaten. A sudden display of spots that resemble mammal eyes will startle a predator away by bluff (1, 2). The Bee Hawk Moth (3) and the Lunar Hornet Moth (4) mimic stinging insects and so predators avoid them. The white variety of the Peppered Moth (5) is camouflaged on the bark of a tree. In smoke-blackened industrial areas, however, the black variety (6) is better camouflaged.

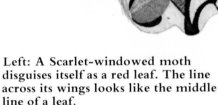

Below: A Privet Hawk Moth.

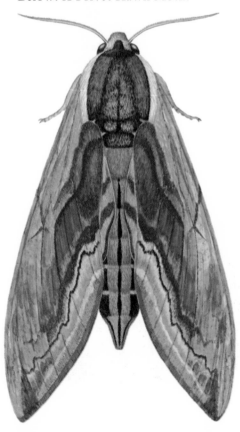

When the caterpillar reaches full size, it attaches itself to a suitable place by means of silken threads. Then again, it slips out of its skin. But this time a harder, differently shaped skin appears underneath. This is the *pupa,* or *chrysalis.* For some time the pupa remains still, apparently at rest. But inside there is much activity. All the organs of the caterpillar break down to form a kind of chemical soup. This is then used to nourish small groups of cells, which grow into new adult organs.

When this process, known as *metamorphosis,* is complete, the adult emerges from its pupa. At first its wings are crumpled and damp. They are expanded by forcing blood into the veins.

The adult's purpose is to find a mate and reproduce. In doing this it uses up much energy. A butterfly or moth therefore often drinks nectar, sucking it up through its proboscis. After mating, the female lays her eggs and the cycle begins again.

The colours of butterflies and moths all have a purpose. Members of the same species recognize each other by their colours. Patterns and drab colours are often used as camouflage, and bright colours may be a warning to predators that the species is unpleasant. Many butterflies and moths use the technique of suddenly exposing bright markings to startle and confuse predators. Others mimic (copy) the colours of distasteful types so that predators will avoid them.

Above left: The head of a butterfly or moth. Its compound eyes give it excellent vision and its proboscis is used for its only method of feeding – drinking nectar from flowers.

Above: A Convolvulus Hawk Moth feeding from tobacco flowers. It has an extremely long proboscis, which it can aim accurately into the flowers. The kink in the proboscis allows it to feed from flowers at any angle.

Below: A Monarch Butterfly has distinctive markings to warn predators that it is unpleasant to eat. Having once or twice made the mistake of trying this species, a predator will avoid others thereafter.

Social insects

Most insects lead solitary lives. They hunt or forage for themselves and their 'social life' is very limited. But some bees, some wasps, ants and termites live together in organized communities. Each community is made up of several different types of individuals, known as *castes*, who perform different tasks. And all the individuals work together for the good of the community as a whole.

The head of a Honeybee colony is the queen, whose main task is to lay eggs. Sterile females, called *workers*, make a nest of vertical wax sheets, or combs. Each comb is covered on both sides with hexagonal cells. The queen lays eggs in some of the cells and the eggs hatch into grubs. Still inside the cells, the grubs develop into pupae and then into adult workers.

During the first two weeks of its life, a worker tends and feeds the grubs. The next week is spent building and repairing the nest and converting nectar into honey. Finally, it leaves the nest to collect pollen and nectar.

New queens and fertile males, or *drones*, are produced in late summer. The first new queen to emerge usually kills the others and flies off to mate with a drone. When she returns, the old queen either dies or flies away with a number of workers to begin a new colony. In the winter the whole colony hibernates (sleeps) in the nest.

A wasp nest is built of paper, made by chewing up wood. The nest is started by the queen, but after the first workers emerge they take over this task. The colony only lasts for a year. When the new queens are produced, they fly off and mate with males. Then the first frosts kill all but the new queens, who sleep during the winter.

Ant nests may usually be found underground, in tree stumps or hanging in trees. But they do not have

Above: The larva of a queen Garden Black Ant being tended by two workers. Ants are amazingly strong and can move objects several times their own size. Garden Black Ants are commonly found under logs and stones or in the walls of buildings.

Below and left: A section through the nest of a Common Wasp. The nest is begun in the spring by a queen that has hibernated during the winter. She builds a few cells in which she lays eggs. When the first workers hatch, they take over the nest-building and by the end of the summer the nest may be up to 23 centimetres in diameter and contain 5000 wasps. The queen lays eggs in every cell and these hatch into larvae, which are fed by the workers. Still inside their cells, the larvae pupate (see inset) and finally emerge as adults. During the early summer, the workers' job is to catch and chew up insects to feed the larvae. But in the late summer the queen stops laying eggs. With nothing left to do, the workers look for sweeter foods and thus become a nuisance in kitchens and at picnics. In the autumn when the frosts come, all except the new queens die.

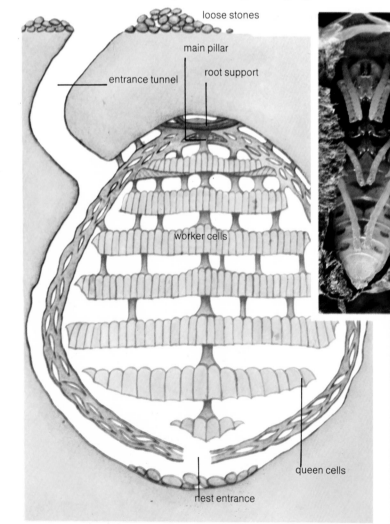

loose stones

main pillar

entrance tunnel

root support

worker cells

queen cells

nest entrance

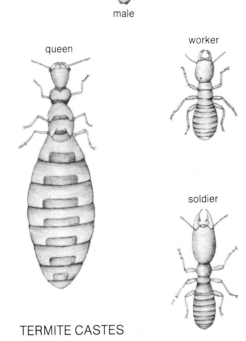

male

queen

worker

soldier

Far right: There are four castes of termites (top) – the queen, king, workers and soldiers. The queen only lays eggs and the king fertilizes them. The soldiers guard the nest. At certain times of the year winged males and females develop, fly off and begin new colonies. The workers tend the nest and feed the soldiers and the king and queen. At night they go out foraging for food (centre). The shapes of termite nests vary according to the species. Some are pyramidal (bottom); others may be tall and thin – sometimes over twice the height of a man. Inside the nest is a network of passages and chambers. The outer passages are constructed to keep air circulating through the nest.

Right: A swarm of Honey Bees. An old queen has left her nest with a swarm of workers. They will build a new nest and start a new colony.

Below: A Honey Bee with its pollen baskets full of pollen. This will be stored in special cells in the nest.

the cells found in bee and wasp nests. There may be more than one queen and, as well as workers, some species have soldiers, who guard the nest.

Ants eat a variety of foods. Some are carnivores; others eat sap or seeds. Leaf-cutter ants grow their own food. They cut pieces of leaf, chew them up and store them in special chambers. They eat the fungus that grows on the chewed leaves. Some ants 'herd' aphids like cattle. They eat the sugary honeydew that the aphids produce.

A termite colony is ruled by a king as well as a queen. The workers are all young termites. There are both males and females, but most of them never grow into adults. However, some develop into soldiers and some grow into winged adults. These fly off, mate and form new colonies. Some termites build their nests underground. Others make huge mounds with a network of tunnels and chambers inside.

TERMITE CASTES

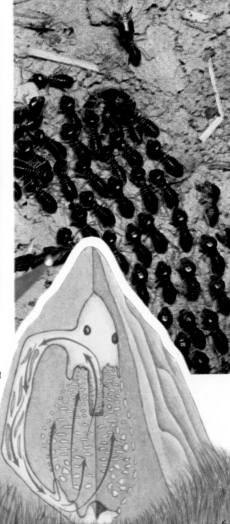

termite nest

61

The web-makers

Insects, spiders and scorpions appeared on land about 400 million years ago. The first insects were wingless and could easily be caught by the spiders and scorpions. But then insects developed the ability to fly and for about 100 million years, until the arrival of the birds, they ruled the air. But soon they were not safe even in the air. Spiders developed the art of building webs – deadly traps for unwary insects.

Spiders are sometimes thought of as insects. But in fact they belong to a different group known as the *arachnids*. All insects have six legs, whereas all spiders and scorpions have eight. Spiders do not have antennae and their bodies are divided into two parts.

Spiders that construct webs do so by using structures called *spinnerets*. Inside a spinneret, silk glands produce a liquid which is then forced out through a tiny hole. When it meets the air it hardens to form the silk. The webs of some spiders, such as garden spiders, are sticky, and insects that fly into such a web are held until the spider can reach them. The web of a house spider, on the other hand, is not sticky. The spider waits for an insect to land on its web and then rushes out and seizes it.

Not all spiders make webs, and silk is used for a number of other purposes. The trap-door spider digs a burrow, lines it with silk and covers it with a silken lid with pieces of leaf woven in for camouflage. When an insect comes near the burrow the spider rushes out and grabs it.

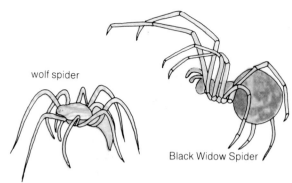

bird-eating spider

wolf spider

Black Widow Spider

Above: A bird-eating spider, a wolf spider and a Black Widow Spider. Bird-eating spiders may be up to 20 centimetres across. The many species of wolf spider include the tarantulas of southern Europe. The Black Widow has the most harmful venom, but its bite is rarely fatal.

Below left: The head of a wolf spider showing its fangs and six of its eight eyes. The spider uses its fangs to inject poison into its prey, which is soon paralysed or killed.

Below : A female wolf spider carrying her young on her back.

Below left: A yellow crab spider camouflaged on a flower. It lies in wait, motionless, until an unwary insect visits the flower. Then it pounces. Crab spiders get their name from the shape of their body and the fact that they scuttle sideways on their long, curved legs. There are many species, each one coloured so that it is disguised on a flower, leaf or dead vegetation.

Below: A tarantula. Many spiders have been called tarantulas, including the bird-eating spiders of South America. But the name strictly belongs to about 12 species of European wolf spiders. The name is derived from the town of Taranto in southern Italy. Here the people are said to have performed a dance called the tarantelle to counteract the effects of the poison.

trap-door spider

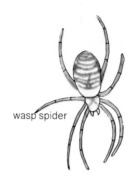
wasp spider

Above: A jumping spider leaps onto its prey from several centimetres away. A trap-door spider hides in a burrow, which has a lid camouflaged with leaves and moss. On the underside are two small holes which the spider uses to hold the lid down firmly. Some trap-door spiders use interlocking teeth on the lid and the rim of the burrow. When an insect ventures too near, the spider rushes out and seizes it.

Above and right: Wasp spiders get their name from their yellow and black markings.

A jumping spider uses a silk thread as an anchor line, in case it misses its target when jumping. Some spiders use long silk lines as parachutes and may be blown long distances by the wind. Silk is also used for wrapping prey and enclosing eggs in a cocoon.

Some spiders trap their prey without the use of silk. Jumping spiders leap on to their victims from several centimetres away. Crab spiders lie in wait, often disguising themselves as part of the surroundings, such as a bird-dropping or the centre of a flower. Wolf spiders catch their prey by simply chasing after it.

Spiders feed mostly on insects, although some of the larger ones sometimes catch birds and small mammals. After the victim has been caught, the spider first paralyses or kills it by injecting venom through two hollow fangs. Spiders use the same technique to defend themselves. Most are harmless, but some, such as the Black Widow Spider of America, are extremely poisonous. When the prey has been immobilized, the spider injects it with digestive juices. Spiders cannot take in solid food and therefore feed on the partly digested contents of their victims' bodies.

Mating can be an unpleasant event for a male spider. The female is often much larger and may attack anything that moves. Therefore the male must approach cautiously and take care to identify himself. Some males present a female with a dead fly and then mate while she is eating it. Some females eat the male anyway after mating.

Above: The characteristic web of a garden spider.

Below left: The rear end of a spider showing the three pairs of spinnerets from which silk is produced. The size of the opening decides the quality and strength of the silk.

Below right: Stages in the building of a web. First, the spider constructs a bridge line, followed by a Y-shape underneath. Then a second, inner bridge line is added, followed by a system of spoke-like supporting threads and a central spiral that strengthens the web. Finally, the spider spins a spiral of sticky thread. The web is completed with a signal thread that connects with the spider's retreat and tells the spider when an insect is struggling in the web.

spinnerets

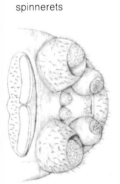
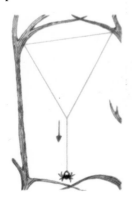
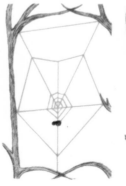
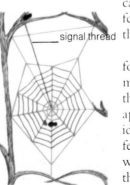

signal thread

Lampreys, sharks and rays

The earliest forms of life on Earth were all invertebrates (animals without backbones). Then, about 500 million years ago, the first vertebrates appeared. They resembled modern fishes in many ways but they had no jaws. They probably fed by shovelling up mud and filtering out the food particles. By about 350 million years ago they were extinct, but their modern descendants are the lampreys and hagfishes, which also have no jaws.

Lampreys are eel-like animals. They have no scales and their bodies are covered in a protective slime. The mouth of a lamprey is surrounded by a sucker, which is equipped with rows of hooked teeth. The lamprey is a parasite. It fastens itself on to a host fish and feeds on its body tissue and blood. However, the host is not normally killed. Some lampreys live in the sea, only returning to fresh water in order to breed. Others live permanently in streams and rivers.

Hagfishes live in the sea, buried in mud or sand. They feed on worms and dead or dying fishes.

Sharks and rays belong to a group of fishes known as cartilagenous fishes. Their skeletons are made of cartilage. The main advantage of this is that cartilage is lighter than bone. Unlike bony fishes, sharks and rays have no swim bladder (see page 66) and so cannot 'float' in the water. In most cases they sink to the bottom unless they keep swimming. Their skins are covered in thousands of tiny, pointed scales. In the mouth these scales are larger and form rows of teeth.

Sharks include the dogfishes. These are small, scavenging fish that spend most of their time on the sea bed. Some sharks feed on plankton, but the most notorious are the hunters, such as the Great White Shark and Great Blue Shark. Sharks have poor eyesight and generally find their prey by scent or sound. Sometimes they will attack human bathers, but this is not because of any particularly anti-human feeling. It is more probably due to the fact that the dangling legs of a bather appear to the short-sighted shark to be a fish in distress and therefore easy prey.

Right: A sea lamprey clings on to its host fish by means of a powerful sucker armed with hooks. Its grip is so strong that the fish is unable to dislodge it.

Below: A lamprey's tongue (in the centre of the sucker) is armed with two larger teeth, which are used to rasp a hole in the host fish's flesh. The lamprey feeds on blood and the host may die from loss of blood.

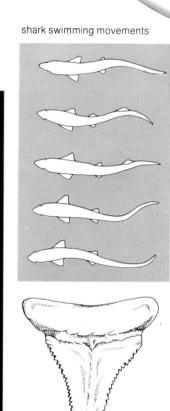

shark swimming movements

tooth of a Great White Shark

64

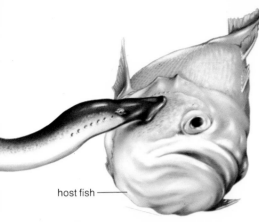

host fish

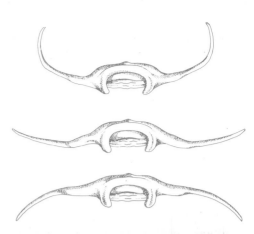

Right and below right: The giant manta ray, sometimes known as a devil fish, flaps its way through the water using its enormous pectoral fins as wings. Although mantas reach 2 tonnes in weight, with a wingspan of 7 metres, they are completely harmless. They feed solely on plankton (see page 67), gathering it into their wide mouths as they swim. Sometimes mantas leap right out of the water, landing with a loud slap.

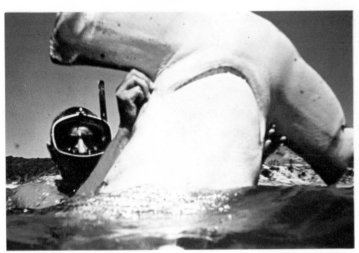

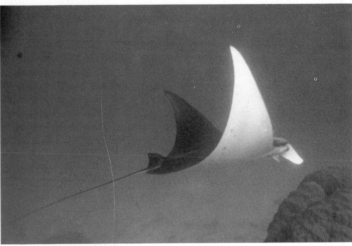

Left: A shark swims through the water by sideways movements of its body (top). The tail is constructed so that it tends to lift in the water, but the head is prevented from diving by its flattened shape. The Great White Shark (bottom) is the fiercest of all the sharks. It kills large animals, such as dolphins, seals and sealions, but its reputation as a 'man-eater' is probably due to its size and its large, fierce-looking teeth (centre).

Above left: A Hammerhead Shark. No one really knows the reason for the extraordinary shape of its head. Its nostrils are placed on the ends of its snout, and this may help it to locate the source of odours.

Below: A Blue-spotted Stingray. This species may grow to 2 metres in length. Its whip-like tail carries a sharp spine with a poison gland at the base. This is used to stun its prey.

Although rays and skates are very different in appearance to sharks, they are actually quite closely related. But instead of being long and streamlined, their bodies are flattened. The large pectoral fins and the flat sides of the body form 'wings', which they use to glide gracefully and swiftly through the water.

Most rays feed on shrimps, crabs and shellfish, which they crush with their powerful jaws. Sawfishes have long, blade-like snouts with teeth along each side. This saw is mainly for digging up shellfish, although it can be used to kill fish.

Rays are generally white underneath and patterned on top. Their flat shape and patterns help them to remain undetected on the sea bed. However, some rays have more aggressive methods of defence.

An electric ray has two electric organs on the side of its head. These can produce up to 200 volts, and they may be used to capture prey. The ray wraps its fins around its victim and stuns it with an electric shock.

A stringray has a poisonous spine at the tip of its tail. A jab from this sting is painful and often serious.

Masters of the oceans

All life began in the world's seas and many successful groups of animals have evolved there – for example, the crabs and lobsters, the squids and octopuses and the sea urchins and starfish. But none of these has equalled the success of the bony fishes. This enormous and varied group of animals has completely mastered the art of living in water. Bony fishes can be found in all parts of the oceans and even in freshwater rivers and lakes.

Several things have contributed to the success of bony fishes. One of the most important of these is the fact that they have a *swim bladder*. This is an air-filled sac inside the body, which helps the fish to maintain the correct buoyancy for it to 'float' in the water.

Another important feature of bony fishes is the skeleton. This is made up of thousands of tiny bones, and a number of these form the jaws. Unlike sharks and rays, whose mouths are on the underside of their bodies, the jaws of bony fishes project forwards and are able not only to bite but also to nibble. As a result, bony fishes have adapted to a variety of feeding habits.

Bony fishes first appeared about 400 million years ago. They evolved into two groups. The *lobe-fins,* so-called because their fins were large and fleshy, eventually became extinct except for the lungfishes and the coelacanths.

The majority of bony fishes are *ray-fins,* so-called because their delicate fins are supported by a number of slender bones, or rays. Many bony fishes have long, streamlined bodies and swim by flexing their bodies from side to side, using their tails as propellers. They use their fins as control surfaces. For example, the pectoral (shoulder) fins are used for steering and braking. Some very specialized fishes, however, use their fins in other ways. When swimming slowly, wrasse row themselves along using their pectoral fins as oars. Flying fishes gather speed underwater and then launch themselves above the surface. Using their pectoral fins as wings, they can glide over long distances.

Most bony fishes reproduce in the same way. The female lays eggs, which are then fertilized by the male.

Right: Fish get their oxygen from the water. They do this by causing water to pass over their gills, which are delicate organs with a plentiful blood supply near the surface. Dissolved oxygen passes into the blood.

water in

gills gill cover

water out

gill filament

gill arch

gill filaments

gill arch

Above: A Dragon Fish (also called a Lion Fish or Zebra Fish), one of the many scorpion fishes. It has 17 poison spines which it uses for defence. Its stripes make it hard to see in the seaweed in which it lives.

Sargasso Sea

Above: Eels migrate from both North America and Europe to the Sargasso Sea in order to spawn, after which they die. The newly hatched young take about a year to reach America and three years to reach Europe.

Above: One of the many brightly coloured angelfishes. The colouring helps members of the same species recognize each other.

Below: A plaice, one of the flatfishes.

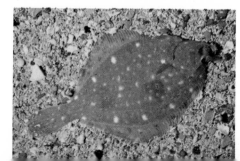

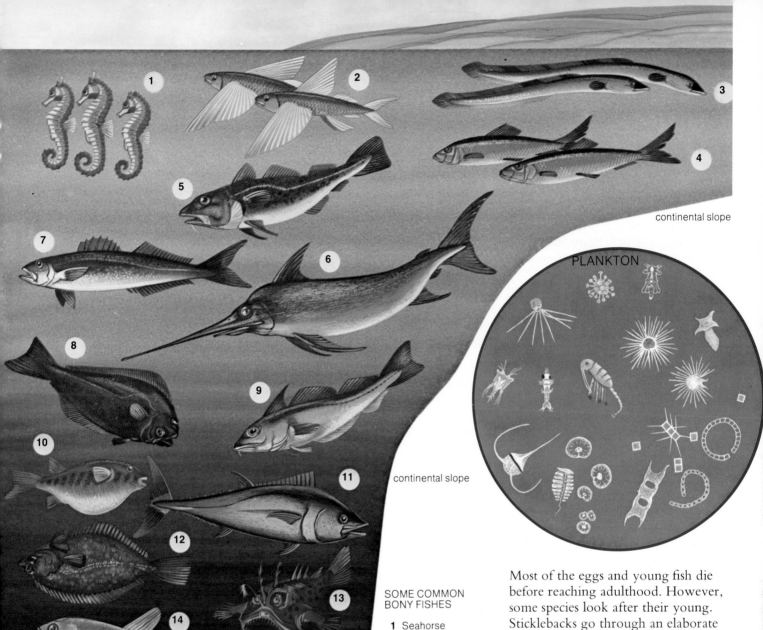

continental slope

PLANKTON

continental slope

SOME COMMON BONY FISHES

1 Seahorse
2 Flying Fish
3 Common Eel
4 Herring
5 Cod
6 Swordfish
7 Blue Fish
8 Halibut
9 Haddock
10 Puffer Fish
11 Tuna
12 Flounder
13 Anglerfish
14 Bristlemouth
15 Hatchet Fish
16 Lantern Fish
17 Deepsea Stalkeye

Most of the eggs and young fish die before reaching adulthood. However, some species look after their young. Sticklebacks go through an elaborate courtship and then the male tends the eggs in a nest. A male seahorse keeps the eggs in a brood pouch until they hatch. Mouthbrooders keep their eggs and young inside their mouths.

Some species travel long distances to breed. Salmon spend most of their time in the sea. But they migrate up rivers, to shallow inland streams in order to breed. Eels migrate from fresh water to the sea.

Bony fishes have adapted to many different lifestyles and this is shown by their enormous variety of shape and colour. Some are carnivores and actively hunt smaller fishes. For this they need to be streamlined, fast swimmers. Many of the smaller fishes can dart through the water to escape predators. Others have methods of defence such as camouflage, warning colours, flattened shapes, armour, electric organs and poison spines.

Above right: The plankton that drifts in the sea contains microscopic plants, such as diatoms, and tiny animals, such as shrimp-like copepods, and many kinds of larvae and eggs.

Left: Few creatures live at the bottom of the oceans, so prey is scarce. Thus some deep sea fishes have developed methods of swallowing very large prey. This species does so by pulling its head back and swinging its lower jaw forwards.

67

Living on land and in water

About 350 million years ago the first land vertebrates (animals with backbones) appeared. These were the amphibians – animals capable of living both on land and in water.

Amphibians evolved from a group of lobe-finned bony fishes. No one knows for certain exactly how or why they evolved. But it is possible that young lobe-fins began to use their fleshy fins to haul themselves out of the water. Their motive would have been to escape from predators. But on land they would have discovered a plentiful food supply of insects and insect grubs. They could breathe on land using a simple lung. Thus they had no reason to want to return to the water and every reason to remain on land where they were safe. Their descendants acquired limbs instead of lobed fins and gradually became more and more adapted to life on land.

However, amphibians are not true land animals because they all, to some extent, depend on water or wet conditions. They have moist skins and many of them have to take in oxygen through their skin. Some amphibians live in water permanently and most of the others need water to breed.

There are three modern groups of amphibians. The caecilians are tropical, worm-like creatures that have lost their limbs and spend most of their time burrowing underground. The frogs and toads have developed powerful hind limbs for jumping. The newts and salamanders, closest in appearance to the early amphibians, have four walking legs and a long body with a tail.

Frogs and toads are found all over

Above right: A pair of Common Frogs mating. The male grasps the female firmly and fertilizes her eggs as she lays them. A mass of frog-spawn can be seen in the background.

Right: Stages in the development of a frog. A newly hatched tadpole has external gills for breathing and suckers for clinging to plants. Soon, eyes, mouth, internal gills and, later, limbs develop as shown.

Below: A West African Hairy Frog.

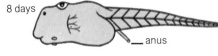

tadpoles

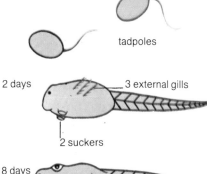

2 days — 3 external gills

2 suckers

8 days — anus

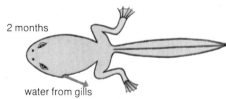

water to internal gills

1 month — flap covering internal gills

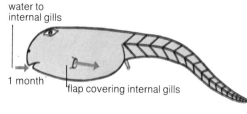

2 months

water from gills

3 months

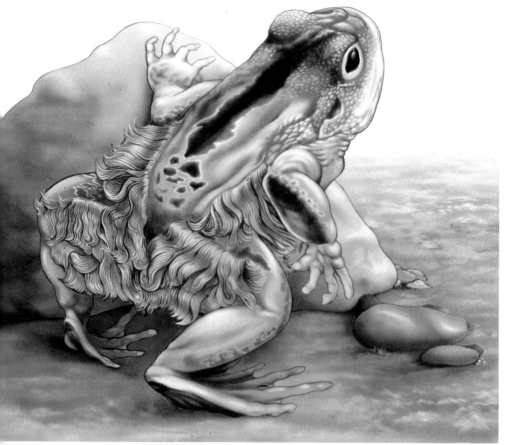

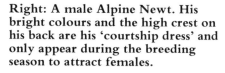

Right: A male Alpine Newt. His bright colours and the high crest on his back are his 'courtship dress' and only appear during the breeding season to attract females.

Above left: A South American toad calling to attract a mate. The large inflatable sac amplifies the sounds he produces. Every species of frog and toad produces its own particular call.

Above right: A Fire Salamander, so called because it was once thought to be able to withstand fire. The colours are a warning to predators that this salamander produces an unpleasant poison. Unlike most amphibians this species gives birth to live young.

Right: A South American caecilian. This creature looks like a worm and moves like a snake, but it is a blind, legless amphibian.

Above: Pyrenean Mountain Salamanders mating. As with frogs, the male clasps the female firmly, but in this case the eggs are fertilized inside the female.

the world, living in swamps, marshes, and even in trees and deserts. However, they nearly all return to water to breed. The female lays her eggs and the male immediately fertilizes them. They are then left unattended while the young develop into tadpoles. When they hatch out, the tadpoles have a tail, suckers and feathery gills. Gradually, each tadpole undergoes a complete change, or *metamorphosis*. The feathery gills disappear, legs develop and the tail shortens. Finally the young frog emerges from the water.

Some frogs and toads do not return to water to breed. Asian tree frogs build foam nests in trees. The eggs develop inside the foam and when the tadpoles hatch out they drop into the water below. The male Midwife Toad carries the fertilized eggs around with him. When they are about to hatch, he places them in water.

Newts and salamanders are mostly found in the northern hemisphere. Many live among damp leaves or under stones. Others live in caves, trees or permanently in water. Mating may take place on land or in water. The eggs are fertilized inside the female and then usually laid underwater on the leaves of plants. The tadpoles look very much like the adults, except for their feathery gills. Some salamanders, such as the Mudpuppy and the Axolotl, keep their tadpole features all their lives and become capable of breeding without undergoing metamorphosis.

The reptiles

Between 225 and 65 million years ago, reptiles dominated the land. There were several reasons for their success. Unlike amphibians, they developed waterproof skins so that they did not lose moisture and dry up. They also evolved efficient lungs for breathing. But perhaps the most important difference between the reptiles and the amphibians was that the reptiles began producing tough, shelled eggs that did not have to be laid in water.

About 65 million years ago something happened that ended the rule of the reptiles. No one knows exactly what it was, but as a result, only four groups of reptiles survive today, together with the birds and mammals, which are descendants of two other reptile groups.

The smallest of the modern reptile groups contains only one member, the Tuatara. It is the only survivor of a group that existed 200 million years ago. The Tuatara only survives in New Zealand, where it is protected.

The tortoises and turtles, which belong to another reptile group, have also changed little over the last 200 million years. Their bodies are enclosed and protected by a hard shell made of bony plates. Tortoises are land animals, as were the ancestors of the group. But turtles have returned to the water and developed paddle-shaped limbs for swimming. Tortoises and turtles lay their eggs on land, usually burying them in earth or sand. The eggs are then left to hatch out by themselves.

Above: A flying lizard, called a Flying Dragon, from south-east Asia.

Right: Lizards move by wave-like movements of the body. Their legs help to push them along.

Above: A South African chameleon clambering along a twig. A chameleon can change its colours to match its surroundings. It uses its long sticky tongue to catch insects.

Above right: A terrapin in its pond.

Below left: An Indian Star Tortoise. Tortoises have changed little over millions of years.

Below: A Spectacled Caiman, so called because of the spectacle-like ridge across its snout. Caimans are found in South America. This species grows to about 2 metres in length.

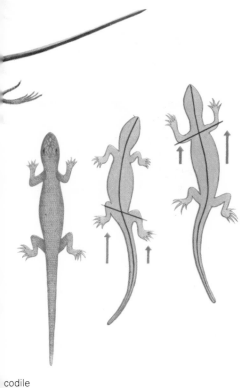

codile

gator

Crocodiles are another group of reptiles, which live in swamps in tropical countries. The group includes true crocodiles, alligators, caimans and gavials (also called gharials). They have long snouts and their nostrils and eyes are raised to allow them to float just beneath the surface of the water. Crocodiles lay their eggs in mounds and they are guarded by the female.

The lizards and snakes are the largest group of reptiles, numbering over 5500 species. There are many types of lizard, ranging from the tiny geckos, which can climb up any surface, to the 3-metre-long Komodo Dragon of Indonesia. Most lizards walk on four legs, but some can run on their hind legs and a few burrowing types have no legs at all.

Snakes are probably descended from legless lizards. There are two types of snake. A constrictor, such as a python, throws coils around its prey and suffocates it. A biting snake strikes with its fangs. Many snakes also inject venom through their fangs. All snakes swallow their prey whole. The upper and lower halves of the jaw move apart to allow the prey to pass into the snake's body.

Most lizards and snakes lay eggs and some even protect them until they are hatched. But a few keep their eggs inside them until they hatch, and give birth to active young.

Above: In a crocodile the fourth tooth from the front on the lower jaw is visible when the mouth is closed. In an alligator this tooth fits into a pit in the upper jaw.

Below: An egg-eating snake swallows a whole egg by temporarily dislocating its jaws. The egg is broken by muscles inside, and the pieces of eggshell are regurgitated.

Above: A King Cobra, the world's largest poisonous snake (up to 5 metres long), threatens by rearing up and displaying its hood. It feeds mostly on other snakes.

Above: Sand Snakes hatching out.

Below: Diagrams to show how a snake moves along a burrow. It presses itself against the sides and the waves pass down its body.

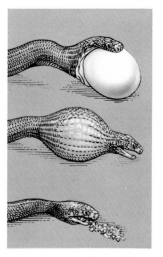

The world of birds

On any day of the year bird-watchers can be found peering through binoculars. And many people spend much of their time studying or just looking at birds. The fascination of birds is due to their immense variety of form, colour, habit and behaviour.

The birds evolved about 150 million years ago from a group of reptiles that developed feathers instead of scales and began to use their fore-limbs as wings for flying. The main advantages of flight were to escape from predators and to exploit new sources of food, such as flying insects.

Birds also developed the ability to control the temperature of their bodies – that is, they became what we call 'warm blooded' – and thus were able to be more energetic than reptiles. Flight and warm-bloodedness have since made the birds one of the most successful groups of animals in the world. They even outnumber the mammals, the only other warm-blooded animals. There are 8500 species of birds and only 4200 species of mammals.

The demands of flight – wings, feathers, a light body and powerful flight muscles (see page 74) – mean that all birds are similar in appearance. There is less variety of form than in the mammals. Nevertheless, birds have adapted to a wide range of lifestyles.

A bird's way of life is generally shown by the position of its eyes, the form of its feet and the shape of its beak. For example, owls, which hunt small mammals at night, have large, forward-pointing eyes, talons for grasping their prey and hooked beaks for tearing flesh. On the other hand, a woodcock has eyes on either side of its head. It can therefore watch for predators in all directions while it probes for worms with its long beak.

Other birds have feet adapted for perching, climbing, running, wading or swimming and their beaks may be specially adapted for eating foods such as insects, seeds, plants, fish or shellfish. For example, avocets use their long, upturned beaks to skim insects from the surface of mud or water and a swift catches insects in mid-flight with its wide, gaping beak.

Like reptiles, birds lay eggs. But their behaviour before and after egg-laying is usually more complicated. Many male birds establish their rights over territories by calling or by displaying special plumage. Their feathers are often more colourful than those of the females, and they are used in displays to attract a female. Many birds have elaborate courtship rituals before mating.

In most cases the eggs are laid in a nest. Again, types of nest vary considerably. Some birds use very simple nests on the ground. Others build more elaborate nests, made from such materials as grass, twigs and mud, in trees and hedges. Some birds use old nests, such as holes in tree trunks previously made by woodpeckers.

After the eggs hatch, the young birds are cared for by the parents until they are ready to leave the nest.

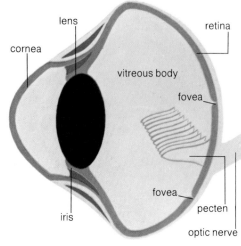

Above left: A chick hatching out. It has a horny point, or egg tooth, on its beak, which it uses to crack open the shell.

Above: A diagram of a bird's eye. Most birds rely on acute sight to catch their prey. A bird's retina is very sensitive, the most sensitive parts being the foveas. The function of the pecten (which is only found in birds) is uncertain, but it may help a bird detect distant objects.

Right: A Lappet-faced Vulture feeding on a carcass. Vultures perform useful work in clearing up dead animal remains.

Below: During courtship, Great Crested Grebes perform a series of elaborate rituals. In the 'discovery' ritual, one bird approaches the other in a shallow underwater dive and rises up into a penguin-like stance. In the 'penguin dance', the two birds face each other with beaks full of weed and sway from side to side.

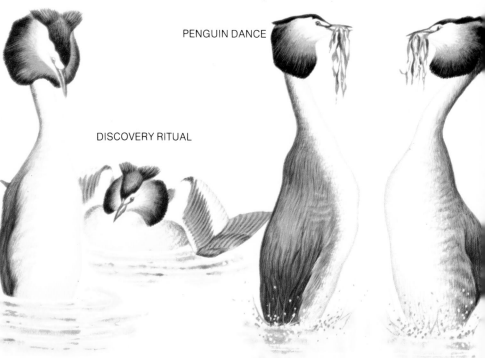

PENGUIN DANCE

DISCOVERY RITUAL

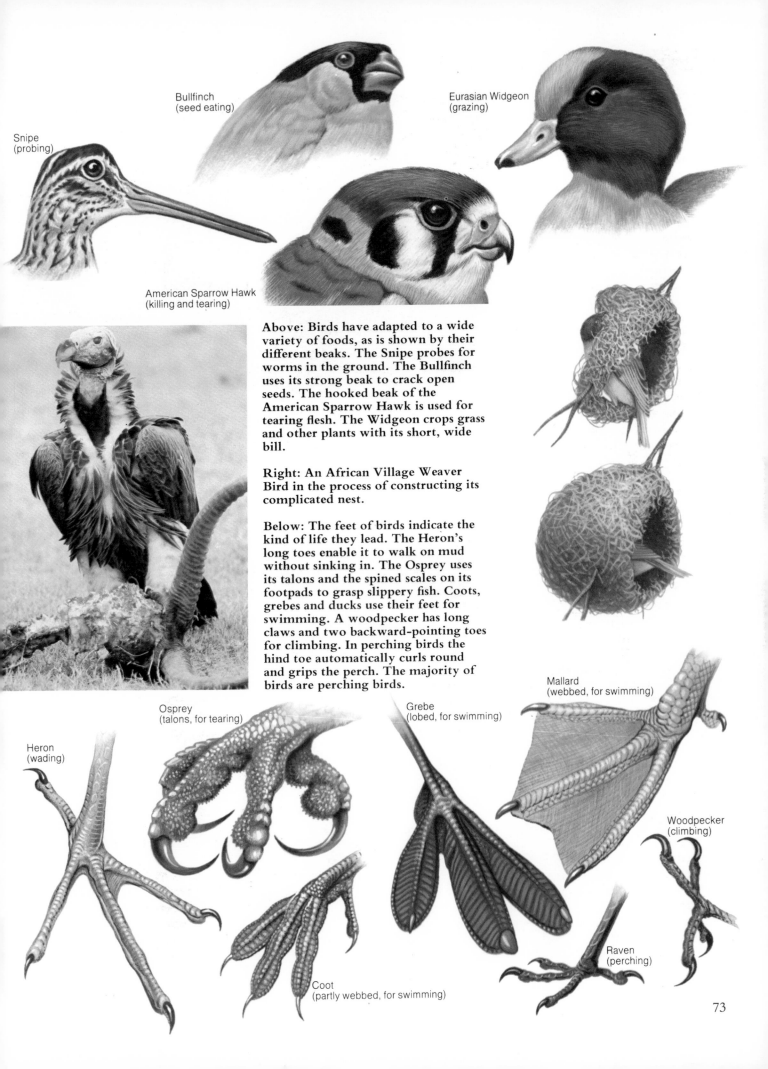

Snipe
(probing)

Bullfinch
(seed eating)

Eurasian Widgeon
(grazing)

American Sparrow Hawk
(killing and tearing)

Above: Birds have adapted to a wide variety of foods, as is shown by their different beaks. The Snipe probes for worms in the ground. The Bullfinch uses its strong beak to crack open seeds. The hooked beak of the American Sparrow Hawk is used for tearing flesh. The Widgeon crops grass and other plants with its short, wide bill.

Right: An African Village Weaver Bird in the process of constructing its complicated nest.

Below: The feet of birds indicate the kind of life they lead. The Heron's long toes enable it to walk on mud without sinking in. The Osprey uses its talons and the spined scales on its footpads to grasp slippery fish. Coots, grebes and ducks use their feet for swimming. A woodpecker has long claws and two backward-pointing toes for climbing. In perching birds the hind toe automatically curls round and grips the perch. The majority of birds are perching birds.

Heron
(wading)

Osprey
(talons, for tearing)

Grebe
(lobed, for swimming)

Mallard
(webbed, for swimming)

Woodpecker
(climbing)

Coot
(partly webbed, for swimming)

Raven
(perching)

How birds fly

For centuries men have dreamed of being able to fly. At first, people thought they had only to copy the birds. Some were so determined to get airborne that they made wings from wood and feathers, strapped them to their arms, and jumped from tall buildings. But despite frantically flapping their make-shift wings, all of them fell to their deaths.

Only in recent years have people realised that they cannot hope to fly just by copying birds. The reason is simple. A human being is not designed to fly. A bird is designed for little else.

The key to being able to fly is to produce enough upward force – scientists call it *lift* – to overcome the downward force of your weight. Because birds are very light they do not need much lift to get into the air. By comparison, human beings are very heavy. They can only produce enough lift by building aircraft with large wings and powerful engines.

How do birds produce the lift they need? Everyone knows that birds fly by flapping their wings. But the flapping itself is a very complicated movement. If we could watch a bird's wing slowed down, we would see that it is really two movements in one. The bird pushes its wing down and forwards at the same time.

By pushing its wings forward, the bird produces the lift it needs to stay in the air. To understand how this happens we need to look at the shape of a bird's wing. Seen sideways on, the upper surface is gently curved. The lower surface is more or less flat. As the bird pushes its wing forward, air is forced to rush over and under the wing. But because the upper part is curved the air has further to travel and moves more quickly. The air passing under the wing travels more slowly. The difference in the way the air moves produces an overall upward force – the all-important lift.

The downward part of the wing movement does not add any lift. It produces instead the force that propels the bird through the air. Together these two movements – down and forward – make the miracle of bird flight possible.

Above: A Saw-whet Owl about to pounce upon an unsuspecting mouse. Special soft plumage allows an owl to fly silently through the air as it hunts its prey by night.

Below: Bird flight is achieved by the arrangement of the feathers on the wing, which is a modified arm and hand. Each feather is held together by tiny hooks, or barbules.

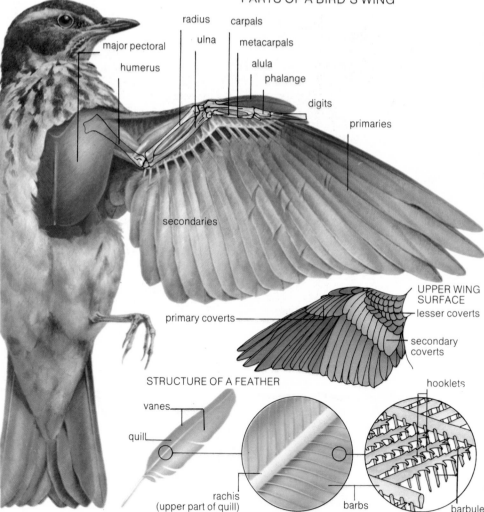

PARTS OF A BIRD'S WING

major pectoral
humerus
radius
ulna
carpals
metacarpals
alula
phalange
digits
primaries
secondaries
primary coverts

UPPER WING SURFACE
lesser coverts
secondary coverts

STRUCTURE OF A FEATHER
vanes
quill
rachis (upper part of quill)
barbs
hooklets
barbule

74

A bird needs more than specially shaped wings to fly. Even for a bird, flying is hard work. It needs a powerful heart and strong chest muscles to flap its wings. For lightness a bird has hollow bones. But to stand up to the strains of flying they contain tiny cross-pieces. These act like the struts of a bridge to strengthen the bones. Wings are also as light as possible. They are made of a small framework of bones covered in light, streamlined feathers.

Different birds have different shaped wings because they need to fly in different ways. A high-speed flier has thin swept-back wings, whereas those of a heavy soaring bird, such as a vulture, are much broader.

Above: A Crimson Rosella about to land on a tree trunk. Its wings are angled to reduce speed and its claws are outstretched to grasp the tree trunk.

Above: A Blue Tit caught in mid-flight at the bottom of its down-stroke. The primary feathers at the wing tips provide propulsion and the secondary feathers provide lift.

Left: The way in which a bird flies can be deduced from the shape of its wings. Birds that soar have broad wings with slots at the tips to control turbulence. Gliding birds have long, thin wings, and fast flyers have swept-back parts at the ends. A Hawk must be extremely manoeuvrable and so has short broad wings and long tapered primary feathers. Some woodland birds need to be able to take off rapidly. They have short broad wings, strongly curved to increase lift, and long tails to help them manoeuvre between the branches.

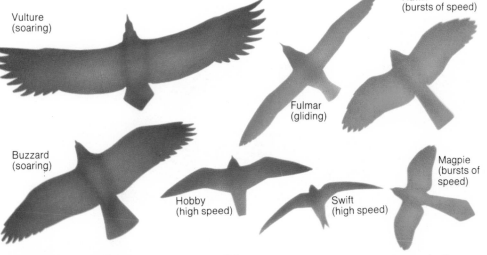

Vulture (soaring)

Hawk (bursts of speed)

Fulmar (gliding)

Buzzard (soaring)

Magpie (bursts of speed)

Hobby (high speed)

Swift (high speed)

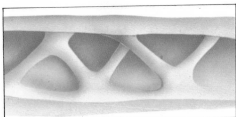

SECTION THROUGH A WING BONE

Left: A bird's wing bones are hollow and reinforced with struts.

Below: A hummingbird can hover in one place because its wings are connected to its shoulders by swivel joints. Its wings tilt so that air is always forced downwards.

Right: A Hermit Hummingbird.

Long-distance travellers

Each autumn you can see flocks of birds getting ready to fly south. In spring they return to build their nests and raise their young. Why do they fly away for the winter? Where do they go? How do they find their way?

The reason for these migrations dates back to the Ice Ages. As the ice sheets retreated farther and farther north, birds began to extend their ranges, moving into new areas in which they could breed. However, each winter the cold weather forced them to return to warmer areas in the south, where there was plenty of food.

Today there are large numbers of birds that migrate, and many of them still return to the areas where they lived during the Ice Ages. Many of them are insect-eaters. Swallows, swifts and martins travel thousands of kilometres to their winter feeding

MAJOR MIGRATION ROUTES

Pintail Duck

Ruby-throated
Humming Bird

grounds in the tropics. Many Arctic species, such as ducks and waders, travel south to the northern temperate regions for the winter. The greatest distance is covered by the Arctic Tern. It breeds in the Arctic and then migrates to the Antarctic, a distance of about 17,000 kilometres.

Before migrating, a bird stores up energy in the form of fat. Some birds break their journeys into a number of stages, stopping frequently to feed and build up energy for the next stage. Others may travel very long distances. Greenland Wheatears are believed to travel direct to northern Spain, a distance of about 3000 kilometres across the ocean. Many birds, such as warblers, travel north in the spring to escape from the tropical heat of Africa. They cross the Sahara desert and the Mediterranean Sea in one exhausting, non-stop journey. It takes about 60 hours, and at the end of such a journey a bird has lost about one-third of its body weight.

The study of ringed birds has helped scientists to establish the routes of some migratory birds. In addition, certain places are well known as feeding areas, resting places or crossings. But most routes are still known only approximately.

We do know, however, that birds navigate with remarkable accuracy. Many swallows return to the same nest each year. Even young swallows, with no previous experience, return to the district in which they were hatched.

Birds appear to have an inborn sense of direction. Experiments have shown that they probably navigate by the Sun and the stars. They seem to have some kind of instinctive memory that tells them what the position of the Sun or stars should be in relation to the direction in which they are travelling. To do this they must have a kind of built in 'biological clock', so that they can allow for the movement of the Sun and stars every 24 hours. However, we know very little of how these navigational skills actually work.

Below: The Greylag Goose, the ancestor of the domestic goose, breeds in central and northern Europe and migrates to southern and western Europe and Africa for the winter.

Above: A flock of migrating Knots. These birds are members of the sandpiper family. They breed within the Arctic circle in North America, Greenland and the USSR, and in winter they fly south. Many make long journeys as far as southern Africa, New Zealand and Australia.

Left: A map showing the routes of some migrating birds. Central and southern Africa are popular wintering areas for many European birds.

Right: An Arctic tern. This bird undertakes one of the longest migrations. It breeds in the Arctic and then migrates to the Antarctic, thus enjoying the summers of both hemispheres. It also sees more daylight than any other animal, because for 8 months of the year it lives in regions of constant daylight.

Mammals with pouches

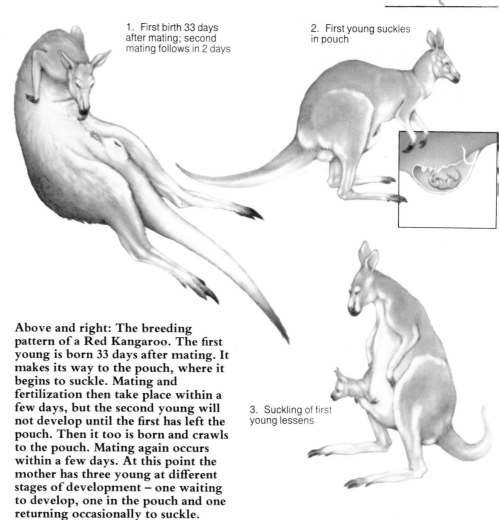

About 100 million years ago the first mammals appeared on Earth. Very soon there were three distinct groups – the *monotremes* (egg-laying mammals), *marsupials* (mammals with pouches) and true mammals, or *placentals*.

Today the placentals are the most successful group. Of the monotremes, only six species remain (the Duck-billed Platypus and five spiny anteaters, or echidnas). And the marsupials are largely confined to Australasia. This is probably because they could not compete with the placentals in the rest of the world. But Australasia became separated from the other continents (see page 17) before the placental mammals arrived. So the marsupials in Australasia, who had no competitors, still survive today.

There are also a few marsupials in other areas. The opossums and rat opossums are found in South America, which was once joined to Australasia. And the Common Opossum has actually spread northwards into the USA and Canada. It lives in forests, feeding on insects and small mammals.

The most important characteristic of marsupials is that they have no placenta. In placental mammals this is an organ used to nourish the young as they develop in the womb. A young marsupial, however, is nourished by the yolk of the egg. This soon runs out and so the young is born at an early stage of development. The parent then keeps the young in its pouch, where it suckles and continues to grow.

Probably the best known marsupials are the kangaroos and wallabies, which move by leaping on their hind legs. The long, heavy tail of a kangaroo is used for balancing and as a rudder to help in turning at high speed. Large kangaroos can travel at speeds of up to 40 kilometres an hour. They are grazing animals, equivalent to placental plant-eaters such as deer and cattle in other parts of the world.

Many other marsupials have their equivalents among the placentals. Bandicoots are burrowing marsupials that live similar lives to rabbits, although they eat insects and roots. The carnivorous Tasmanian Devil

1. First birth 33 days after mating; second mating follows in 2 days

2. First young suckles in pouch

3. Suckling of first young lessens

Above and right: The breeding pattern of a Red Kangaroo. The first young is born 33 days after mating. It makes its way to the pouch, where it begins to suckle. Mating and fertilization then take place within a few days, but the second young will not develop until the first has left the pouch. Then it too is born and crawls to the pouch. Mating again occurs within a few days. At this point the mother has three young at different stages of development – one waiting to develop, one in the pouch and one returning occasionally to suckle.

resembles the European Wolverine, the Pouched Mouse resembles other mice, and the Wombat is a rodent-like marsupial.

Some marsupials have an even closer likeness to their placental counterparts. The Thylacine, a carnivore now thought to be extinct, looked very much like a placental wolf. Flying phalangers have membranes of skin stretched between their front and hind limbs and are almost identical to flying squirrels. The marsupial mole has evolved many of the same features as placental moles.

Other marsupials do not have obvious placental counterparts. The Koala Bear lives a solitary life in the forests of Eucalyptus trees, where it feeds on the leaves. The Cuscus is a strange animal with a grasping tail. It moves slowly through the trees, eating leaves and insects.

Top: The powerful hind legs and long, slender feet of a kangaroo enable it to move rapidly in a series of jumps – sometimes over 9 metres.

4. Second birth after first young has left pouch (about 7 months after second mating)

5. Second young suckles in pouch and first young returns to suckle occasionally

Above left: An American Opossum, out foraging with her young clinging to her back. Young opossums remain in the pouch for about 10 weeks and then the whole family sleeps huddled together in the nest. Opossums are the only marsupials found in South America; and only one, the Virginia Opossum, has spread into North America.

Above: A Koala Bear, one of the best-known marsupials, feeding on eucalyptus leaves. At one point Koalas were in danger of being wiped out by hunters, who wanted their furs. Fortunately, they are now protected by law.

Left: A Brush Wallaby with twins in its pouch. Marsupials normally produce only one young at a time, so twins are an unusual sight. The picture is also unusual for another reason – the animals shown here are albinos. This means that their bodies lack the pigments (colouring substances) normally present in the eyes, skin and hair, so their fur appears white instead of brown.

Right: A young Long-nosed Bandicoot climbs into its mother's pouch. Bandicoots are burrowing animals and their pouches open to the rear to prevent them from filling with soil. They are shy, nocturnal animals that live in most parts of Australia. They feed mainly on roots and insects.

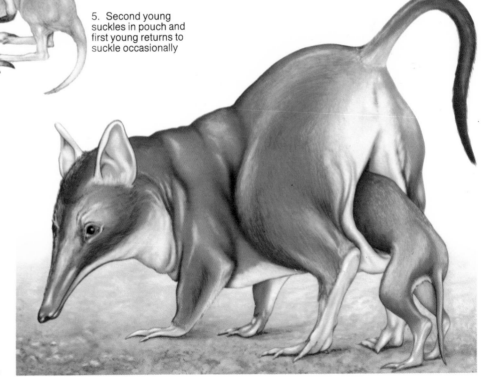

The big cats

The cats are the most impressive of all carnivorous mammals. Even the domestic cat, with its agility and independence, commands our respect. And the Lion has been known for many years as the 'king of the jungle'.

The group known as the big cats includes the Tiger, Leopard, Jaguar, Lion and Cheetah. There are several factors that distinguish these animals from the smaller cats. Big cats can roar, the pupils of their eyes are large and round, and when purring they have to pause in order to breathe. Small cats, on the other hand, cannot roar, their pupils are vertical slits, and they can purr almost continuously.

At one time there were big cats in nearly all parts of the world. But the arrival of humans reduced the areas in which they could hunt successfully. More recently, big cats have been killed for their skins and some of them are now in danger of extinction.

Most big cats are solitary animals, except in the mating season. They live and hunt alone, usually at night, and a single animal may require a large territory. A Tiger, the largest of the big cats, is thought to need at least 26 square kilometres of living space and may range over 650 square kilometres. Today the eight races of Tiger are confined to Asia. There they prey on large mammals, such as deer, wild boar and even baby elephants.

Leopards are more widespread, being found in Africa as well as Asia. They are good tree-climbers and prey on all kinds of mammals, from rats and hedgehogs to gazelles and zebras.

The Jaguar is the only big cat to have reached the Americas. There it feeds on peccaries (wild pigs) and other small animals, including fish. However, its highly prized spotted fur has made it a target for hunters. The Jaguar is no longer found in North America, and in South America it is an endangered species.

Lions are unusual in that they are *not* solitary animals. They live together in *prides*. A typical pride may contain from six to 30 animals, including one or two adult males and a number of females and their young. The males look after the pride, driving away any young males that attempt to take over, but they do not hunt. This duty is performed by the lionesses, who work together, stalking, driving or lying in ambush. They hunt during the day, preying on animals that live in herds, such as zebras, wildebeest and waterbuck. At one time there were Lions in Europe, but today they are only found in Africa, south of the Sahara desert, and parts of India.

The Cheetah also hunts by day but is unlike other big cats in that it cannot roar. Also, it is the only cat that cannot retract its claws. However, the Cheetah is the fastest land animal in the world. It stalks or moves slowly towards its prey and then rushes at it from a few metres away.

Cheetahs are found in Africa and Asia and they prey on small antelopes, such as gazelles.

Above: A pride of lions and cubs feeding on a zebra kill. Only the lionesses take part in the hunt; they co-operate together by encircling a herd of grazing animals. At the right moment a victim is selected, separated from the herd and brought down.

Left: Tigers are the largest of the big cats, weighing up to 200 kilograms. They were once widespread but today seven of the eight races are endangered. Unlike other big cats, Tigers are strong swimmers.

Above: The Cheetah is the fastest land animal in the world and can run at speeds of up to 100 kilometres per hour. However, it can only do this for short periods, and if it fails to catch its prey within a few hundred metres, it has to stop, exhausted.

Right: Leopards are good climbers. They often lie in wait in trees and drop down on unsuspecting prey as it passes below. A Leopard may carry its prey, sometimes heavier than itself, up into a tree and store it in a fork between two branches.

Below: Lions spend much of their time sleeping, as shown here. A meal every few days is usually sufficient and they have nothing to fear from any other animal, except Man. The cubs remain with the pride for 2–3 years. The young males and some of the females are then expelled. These males wander around in groups, hunting and becoming more powerful. Eventually they will take over another pride.

Giants of the land

'Elephants have right of way' announce the signs in Queen Elizabeth National Park, Uganda. This instruction is more for the protection of the motorists than the elephants. There is not much that will stop the largest living animal in the world from going where it pleases!

There are two species of elephant alive today, the African and the Indian Elephant. The most noticeable difference between them is that the African Elephant has much larger ears. This is because it lives mainly in open savanna, where its large, flapping ears help to keep it cool. Indian Elephants, on the other hand, live in forests and spend most of their time in shade, so they do not need such large ears.

In general, the African Elephant is the larger of the two species. It grows to about 3.5 metres in height at the shoulder and may weigh over 6 tonnes. The Indian Elephant rarely exceeds 3 metres in height and weighs less than 5 tonnes.

The most familiar features of an elephant are its trunk and tusks. The trunk is actually a combination of the animal's nose and upper lip. It is an efficient scent-detecting organ and is used to grasp vegetation, which is

passed to the mouth, and to suck up water, which is squirted either into the mouth or over the animal's back. The trunk is very sensitive and can pick up an object as small as an aspirin tablet. The tusks, which are in fact two long teeth, are used as weapons and to dig for water in times of drought.

Elephants eat enormous quantities of food. A normal diet includes 180 litres of water and 230 kilograms of vegetation each day. In addition, African Elephants will push down small trees to reach the top leaves. Thus in the limited area of a game reserve, the elephant population has to be kept down by culling (shooting selected animals) to prevent the loss of vegetation becoming serious.

The courtship between a bull and cow elephant is affectionate and may go on for days or weeks. After mating, their relationship continues for about 10 months. The cow then appears to realize that she is pregnant and the bull's place is taken over by a female companion, or 'auntie'. The birth takes place about 12 months later, well hidden in a dense thicket, and the mother and 'auntie' continue to protect the calf for several years.

Elephants are renowned for their

intelligence. Members of a herd cooperate not only in protecting the young but also in giving aid to wounded elephants. There are also stories of elephants remembering acts of kindness performed by humans. Trained Indian Elephants are used to handle timber in India and Borneo. They learn the meaning of a number of foot signals and words of command and they have a particularly close relationship with their riders.

Above: An African Elephant grazing on the savanna. Its large ears help to keep it cool in the hot sun.

Left: An African Elephant cow charging. Cows with calves are always more dangerous, but unless an animal is really provoked, the charge is usually just a threat; the elephant will generally stop or veer away.

Below: The structure of an elephant herd. The main part of the herd consists of cows, calves and immature males and females. Mature bulls stand apart and the oldest often lead solitary lives.

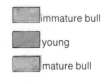

immature bull

young

mature bull

mature cow

immature cow

Above left: An African Elephant enjoying a dust bath. Elephants often have favourite dusting places and the process helps to keep their skin in good condition and free of parasites. Mud baths are also popular.

Above left: An Indian Elephant bathing in the water of a river. Elephants spend a considerable amount of time hosing themselves down and obviously enjoy doing so; it keeps them cool and clean.

Below: A small group of elephants leaving a water-hole. The adults of a herd cooperate in looking after and protecting the young, and sometimes a kindergarten is formed, looked after by one or two cows.

Above: An Indian Elephant at work. Indian Elephants are generally easier to train than African elephants. They are mostly used in the timber industry, where a trained elephant will lift, push, carry, haul and manoeuvre large tree trunks at the command of its rider. An elephant's working life is from the age of 20 to about 55 years.

Giants of the sea

The largest living animal in the world is the Blue Whale, which may reach 33.5 metres in length and weigh over 170 tonnes. This giant creature is probably the biggest the world has ever seen.

Despite their appearance, whales are not fishes. They belong to a group of mammals whose ancestors moved from the land to the sea long ago. Like other mammals, they are air-breathing, warm-blooded animals that give birth to well-developed young, which they suckle. But whales are superbly adapted to life in the oceans. They breathe through nostrils on top of their heads, their bodies are streamlined, their forelimbs have become flippers and their hind limbs have become become powerful, horizontal tails. To keep them warm they have a layer of blubber, or fat, which may be up to 40 centimetres thick in some whales.

Although whales are air-breathing animals, they do not survive for long if they are stranded on a beach. This is because their tremendous weight prevents them expanding their lungs.

In water, however, a whale can breathe easily, and one of its remarkable features is the length of time it can remain underwater between breaths. There are several special mechanisms that help it to do this. For example, it renews about nine-tenths of the air in its lungs with each breath (humans only renew about a quarter). Thus it starts with plenty of fresh air. In addition, its heartbeat slows down when it dives and oxygen is directed only to the essential organs, such as the brain.

Whales are divided into two main groups, toothed whales and baleen whales. The toothed whales include the dolphins and porpoises, which are carnivores that feed mostly on fish. The most ferocious dolphin is the Killer Whale, which eats fish, seals and even other whales.

Dolphins are extremely acrobatic animals. They communicate with each other in a language that consists of clicks, whistles and grunts. Like many other whales they navigate by a kind of sonar; they emit pulses of ultrasonic

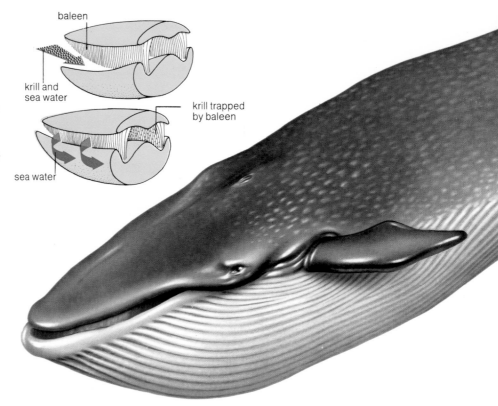

sound and listen to the echoes reflected by nearby objects.

The largest toothed whale is the Sperm Whale, which grows up to 20 metres in length and weighs about 50 tonnes. It feeds mainly on cuttlefish and squids – even giant squids over 10 metres long! It can dive to a depth of 1000 metres and may remain submerged for up to 90 minutes.

The baleen whales feed in an entirely different way. Inside their mouths they have plates of whalebone, or baleen, which are used to filter shrimp-like animals called krill from the water. A baleen whale may eat several tonnes of krill during a single feeding session. Baleen whales are the largest whales; they include the right whales and the rorquals, such as the Blue Whale and Humpback Whale.

Whales used to be common, but in the last 100 years their numbers have been greatly reduced by whaling.

Top: A baleen whale feeds on krill (tiny shrimp-like animals). The whale swims through a shoal of krill, sucking water into its mouth. The mouth closes and the tongue forces the water out between the baleen plates, leaving the krill inside.

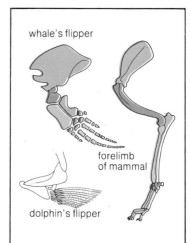

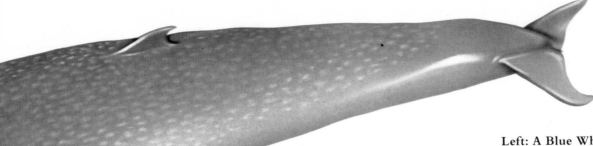

Left: A Blue Whale, the largest animal that ever lived, is about 25 times heavier than an elephant.

Left: The flippers of whales and dolphins can be compared to a mammal's forelimbs.

Below: Whaling has become a vast and very efficient industry – too efficient from the whale's point of view! Many whales have been killed in recent years and as a result whale populations have been drastically reduced. A factory ship can process a 100-tonne carcass in less than an hour and can handle 12 whales a day. Despite the fact that many of the most endangered whales are now protected, there is some doubt as to whether their populations will recover. In July 1979, the International Whaling Commission banned the use of factory ships for all except the Mincke Whale, but it remains to be seen whether or not this ban will be effective.

Above: Dolphins appear to be the most intelligent sea mammals. They seem to have a sophisticated form of communication and scientists are attempting to interpret their language. They enjoy playing, but unlike other mammals, whose play has a purpose, they appear to play just for the fun of it and enjoy performing in aquaria.

Above: The birth of a dolphin. Scenes like these can only be observed in an aquarium. The young dolphin is born tail first. The mother then noses her young to the surface, where it takes its first breath.

Below: A black and white dolphin skimming over the waves off the coast of Argentina.

Monkeys

People often find monkeys appealing, probably because of their many human-like characteristics. In fact, they are distantly related to us; monkeys, apes and man all belong to the same group of mammals – the *primates*.

The majority of monkeys live in tropical forests. They eat fruits, eggs, insects and sometimes small frogs and lizards. They are expert climbers and move from tree to tree with ease.

There are two main groups – New World monkeys and Old World monkeys. The terms 'New World' and 'Old World' are used by scientists to divide the world into two parts, each containing different kinds of animals. The New World consists of the Americas, and the Old World includes Europe, Asia and Africa.

The New World monkeys appear to have evolved separately from Old World monkeys and apes for about 50 million years. As a result, they have several distinctive features. Their noses are broad and flat, and their nostrils are far apart and tend to open to the side. In general, their limbs are more slender and many of them have long, grasping tails. Old World monkeys, on the other hand, have nostrils which are closer together and which open to the front, and none of them have grasping tails.

New World monkeys are found in the tropical forests of South America. Capuchins, which are typical New World monkeys, live high in the trees and descend only occasionally to drink. They live in small families, each of which occupies a definite territory. Like other monkeys, capuchins use their delicate fingers to groom themselves and each other.

Marmosets are the smallest of all monkeys. Unlike other monkeys, they have claws on their hands and feet and they move around the trees in a squirrel-like way.

Right: The Mandrill is one of the most distinctive monkeys because of its bright coloured face-markings, which are repeated around the sex organs. The purpose of these markings is uncertain. Some zoologists have suggested that being coloured so brightly at both ends baffles and frightens predators. But it is more likely that the males use their coloured sex organs as a threat display to other males and that this is reinforced by the coloured face. Mandrills live in the forests of parts of central Africa. They grow to about 80 centimetres long.

dominant males
other adult males
young males and females
adult females
babies

Above: The structure of a baboon troop on the move. The dominant males remain in the centre with the females. When danger threatens, the whole troop closes up together.

Right: When a male baboon yawns, he is not tired. Instead, he is showing his formidable teeth to other males, to threaten them and to indicate his high social standing.

Far left: A Spider Monkey, the most agile of the New World monkeys, moves through the trees using its tail as a fifth limb.

Left: Two of the many guenons of Africa. The bearded De Brazza's Monkey (top) lives in the shorter trees of the forest and the Green Vervet Monkey (bottom) lives on the forest floor.

Below: A Squirrel Monkey is only 25 centimetres long, with a 40-centimetre tail. These animals live in large bands of 500 or more.

Other New World monkeys include the agile spider monkeys, the Saki, which looks like a little old man, the strange, red-faced Uakari and the noisy howler monkeys, whose cries can be heard up to 3 kilometres away. The gentle Woolly Monkey is popular in zoos and the Night Monkey is the only nocturnal monkey in the world.

The Old World monkeys include the baboons, Mandrills and macaques. Unlike most other monkeys, baboons and mandrills spend most of their time on the ground and only return to the trees at night, so that they are out of the reach of predators.

Most macaques live in Asia, but the Barbary Ape, so called because like the apes it has no tail, is found in North Africa and Gibraltar. Another well-known macaque is the Rhesus Monkey, which has been used in medical research. The rhesus factor is a characteristic of its blood that is also found in humans.

Other Old World monkeys include the colourful guenons of Africa, the leaf-eating colobus monkeys and the long-nosed Proboscis Monkey.

The great apes

Except for man, the apes are the most advanced primates. About 20 million years ago man and the apes had a common ancestor, and apes are therefore our nearest living relatives.

There are nine species of apes altogether. These include six species of gibbon, the Orang-utan, the Gorilla and the Chimpanzee. Gibbons are the smallest and most agile apes. They have some of the characteristics of Old World monkeys and are classified in a group by themselves. The remaining three apes are known as the great apes.

Orang-utans are found only in the forests of Borneo and Sumatra. They have many human-like characteristics – in Malay, Orang-utan means 'old man of the woods'. These fruit-eating apes can move rapidly when necessary, but most of the time they climb lazily among the treetops. At night an Orang-utan makes a temporary nest of branches and twigs in the fork of a tree and covers it with a roof of large leaves to keep off the rain.

The face of a female Orang-utan is naked, but a male grows a bright orange moustache and beard. Both sexes have a pouch underneath the throat, but the male's is larger and he uses it to make fierce roaring noises.

Gorillas have unjustly earned a reputation for being savage monsters. In fact, they are gentle, shy animals that are more likely to move quietly away at the first sign of danger. When severely provoked, a Gorilla may show aggression by rearing up and beating its chest. But if the intruder stands still the Gorilla will usually not attack.

Gorillas are found only in Africa. There are two lowland populations and one mountain population. But despite slight differences between them, zoologists agree that they all belong to the same species. They live in troops, each led by a dominant male, which can generally be recognized by its silver-grey back. The rest of the troop consists of a few younger males and several females and their young. Gorillas spend most of their time on the ground, eating leaves and fruit. At night an adult Gorilla sleeps on a bed of leaves.

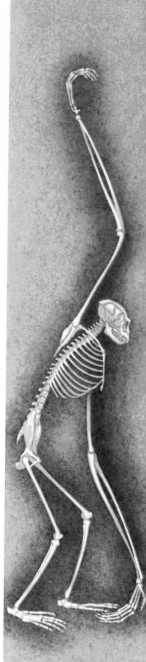

Top: A Lar Gibbon hangs nonchalantly from a tree in Borneo.

Above and below: A Mountain Gorilla, the race of Gorilla that is most in danger of extinction. Films such as *King Kong* **show the Gorilla as a ferocious beast, but it is really shy and gentle. The most it will do when disturbed is to threaten. Some of the typical threat displays of a male Gorilla are shown below.**

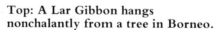

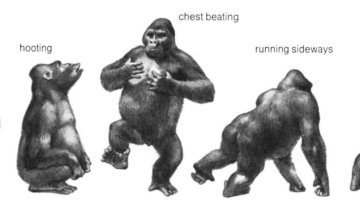

hooting   chest beating   running sideways   uprooting plants

88

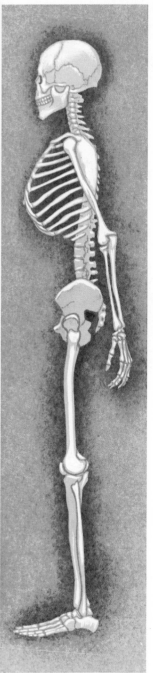

excitement

fear

elation

sadness

Chimpanzees are generally regarded as man's closest ape relatives. Their complex behaviour has been extensively studied and they are certainly highly intelligent. Sometimes they use sticks and stones as tools or weapons. They learn quickly and are able to work out fairly complicated problems. In the wild, they communicate with each other using a wide range of calls and signs.

Chimpanzees are found in equatorial Africa. They are highly social animals and live in large troops consisting of males and females of all ages. Within a troop there is a heirarchy that is understood and respected by all the members. Chimpanzees eat a variety of foods, including fruit and insects.

Above left: A mother Orang-utan and her young on a vine in Borneo. An Orang-utan has a marvellous sense of balance and can walk upright along a branch with great ease. Orang-utans are also intelligent animals, perhaps even more intelligent than Chimpanzees. Sadly, however, they are becoming rare, partly because Man is destroying the forests in which they live.

Above: The skeleton of a gibbon (left) compared with that of a man (right). About 40 million years ago, apes and Man had a common ancestor. But over the years, apes developed separately from Man. Apes such as gibbons lived in forests and spent most of their time high in the trees, swinging from branch to branch. They therefore needed a light skeleton with thin bones and long arms. Man, on the other hand, began to walk upright on the ground and he learnt to use tools. His skeleton is therefore much sturdier and stronger, to support his body. He also has a much larger skull surrounding his larger brain – this indicates his greater intelligence. Despite these differences, you can see that the two skeletons have a similar structure.

Above and right: The Chimpanzee is Man's closest ape relative. One of its important social activities is grooming. A mother grooms her young (right) for some time, increasing the bond between them. Adults also spend time grooming each other. Chimpanzees have the ability to use tools, such as twigs, to obtain their food. They eat mainly fruit, leaves and insects. They can stand and walk in a semi-upright position and they are quite enthusiastic about painting. In fact they are highly intelligent. However, they should not be compared too closely with Man. For example, a Chimpanzee's facial expressions (above) are totally different. When a Chimpanzee appears to us to be grinning, it is in fact showing fear.

THE HUMAN BODY
How we see

Of all our senses, we rely most on that of sight, or vision. Our eyes tell us most about the world we live in.

Blind people are at a great disadvantage compared with sighted people, even those whose sight is not very good. In order to move around safely, a person who is nearly or completely blind needs to use the keen sight of a specially trained guide dog. But a person whose vision is merely poor can usually get around quite well with the aid of spectacles.

But what is sight? To see something, you need eyes, but you also need a brain. Light from the outside enters your eyes, which then send messages about the light to your brain. These messages are carried from eye to brain by the *optic nerves*.

As with your other senses, it is really your brain that recognizes the nerve messages, that knows what you are looking at. Without your brain, your eyes would be like cameras taking photographs without anyone being there to look at them!

Right: A cut-away diagram of the human eye. As in a camera, the lens focuses light; but the eye lens is flexible. Small muscles adjust its shape so that, normally, light patterns always focus exactly on the retina. The optic nerve carries messages about these light patterns to the brain. This is how we see.

Below: An eye in close-up. You can see that the front coverings of the eyeball are quite transparent, to let in light. Eyelashes shade the eye from glare and protect it from dust and grit. The eyelids sweep the eye clean and tears keep it moist.

How the eye works

In some ways, the human eye does resemble a small ball-shaped camera. It fits into the eye socket of the skull, where it is swivelled about by six small muscles. At the front of the eye is a transparent lens, through which light passes. Light rays are bent by the lens so that they focus at the back of the eye, on a layer called the *retina*. This layer is rather like the photographic film in a camera. When light from an object is focused on it, it forms an image of the object.

But unlike a photograph, the image on the retina is only a *temporary* one. You can easily test this. If you stare at a bright light, such as that from an electric lamp, then close your eyes, you see at first a bright, coloured image. This retina image soon fades. Because the retina quickly returns to normal, it can soon form another image. In this way, you can see one thing after another.

In the retina are special cells which are sensitive to light. These are the

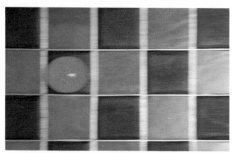
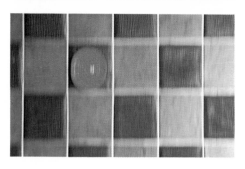

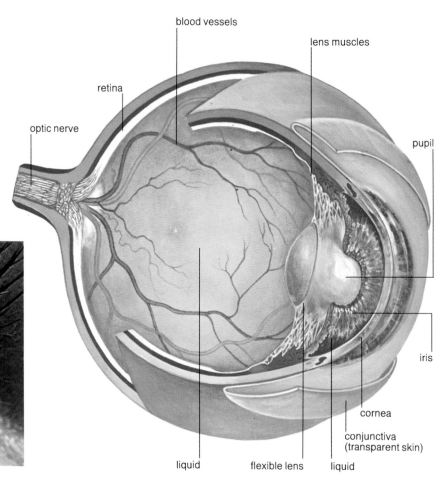

blood vessels

lens muscles

retina

optic nerve

pupil

iris

cornea

conjunctiva (transparent skin)

liquid

flexible lens

liquid

90

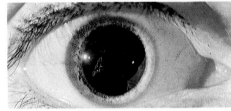

Left: A common form of poor eyesight is called astigmatism. This is caused by the transparent cornea of the eye being the wrong shape. As light enters the eye, the mis-shapen cornea refracts (bends) the light so that it is not correctly focused on the retina. The pictures show a red counter on a chequer board, as seen normally (top), and as seen with two kinds of astigmatism.

Above: An eye with a wide-open pupil, and another (left) with a contracted pupil. The pupil is a hole formed by the iris (see also the cut-away diagram). The iris opens in dim light, to make a wider pupil that lets in more light; in bright light, it contracts to make a smaller pupil.

Below: The eyes of a hunting falcon are among the world's keenest.

cells which form images and which pass on messages to the optic nerves and the brain. These cells are of two kinds, called *rods* and *cones*.

Rods are sensitive only to the amount of light – its intensity. They enable us to see in black, grey and white. Cones are sensitive to coloured light and enable us to see colours. You may have noticed how colours seem to disappear as light fades in the evening. This is because rods are more sensitive than cones, so in dim light you see only in black and different shades of grey.

Sight defects

Eyesight can be poor in a number of ways, some of which are shown by the diagrams. Often, the eye lens focuses wrongly, so that images do not fall exactly on the retina. As we grow older, the lens may become stiff, so that it cannot change shape to re-focus light. In this way, most older people become naturally far-sighted, and need to wear spectacles for reading.

Below: Two kinds of sight defect – near and far sight. Normally the eye lens adjusts its shape so that it always focuses an image of the object on the retina. We then see the object clearly. But if the lens focuses light in front of or behind the retina, we see a blurred image. In far sight, the image is focused behind the retina. Nearby objects look blurred and we need spectacles for such tasks as reading. In near sight, distant objects look blurred. We then need spectacles for such tasks as driving a car. The lenses of spectacles focus light through the eye lens so that images fall exactly on the retina.

Near sight

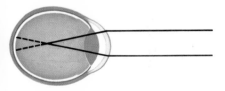

Near sight
corrected with spectacles

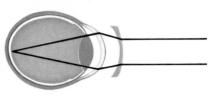

Far sight

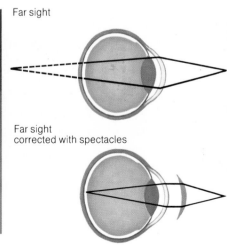

Far sight
corrected with spectacles

How we hear

We hear by means of sound waves. Usually these waves are movements of air, which travel from whatever makes a sound to our ears. However, if we are swimming underwater, sound waves are carried by water.

Sound cannot travel in outer space because nothing is there to carry the sound waves. An astronaut on a space walk therefore needs a radio intercom to talk to his fellow crew members.

The human ear is divided into three parts – the *outer, middle* and *inner ear.* What we usually call the ear is really only its outermost part. The outer ear consists of the familiar flap of flesh, together with the tube that leads from this to the *ear-drum.*

Beyond the ear-drum, inside the head, is the middle ear. This is a continuation of the ear tube, which contains three small bones. The first of these is connected to the ear-drum, and all three bones connect together.

Deep inside the head is the inner ear. The last of the three small bones connects, in a rather complicated way, with a coiled part of the inner ear called the *cochlea.*

How the ear works

When sound waves reach our ears, they are collected by the outer ear, which acts like a funnel. The sound waves cause the ear-drum, which is stretched tightly like a drumskin, to vibrate.

The ear-drum passes on these vibrations to a series of small bones of the middle ear. The last of these passes the vibrations on to the cochlea, in the middle ear.

Like the rest of the inner ear, the cochlea is filled with a watery liquid. It also contains a thin membrane, which lies along the coils of the cochlea. When the liquid and the membrane vibrate, they cause nerves to send messages about the vibrations to the brain. When we say that we hear a sound, this is what we mean.

We hear a difference between high-pitched and low-pitched sounds because these affect different parts of the cochlear membrane. High-pitched sounds cause vibrations at the base of the cochlea. Lower-pitched, or deeper,

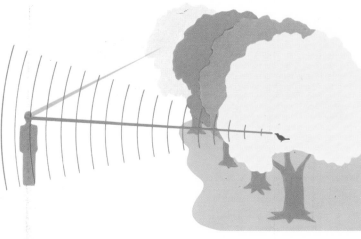

Above: The man hears the bird singing but cannot tell exactly where the sound is coming from until he moves his head.

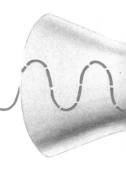

sounds cause vibrations farther along the cochlea.

Other parts of the ear

Besides the parts already described, the inner ear also contains *semicircular canals.* These are concerned not with hearing but with our sense of balance.

The *Eustachian tube* connects the inner ear with the throat. If it becomes blocked, air pressure builds up in the inner ear. This is why a bad cold, which can block the tube, may affect our hearing.

Above right: The diagram shows how we hear a sound, such as that from a bell. The sound wave, which is a movement of air, first passes up the ear canal. Then the sound wave causes a number of connecting movements to take place inside the ear. First, the ear-drum vibrates. In turn this causes the movement of three small ear bones (these movements are shown by the smaller diagram). The movements are then passed on to the cochlea, inside which they finally reach many small nerve endings, which lead to the large auditory nerve. This sends an electrical signal to the brain – and we hear the sound.

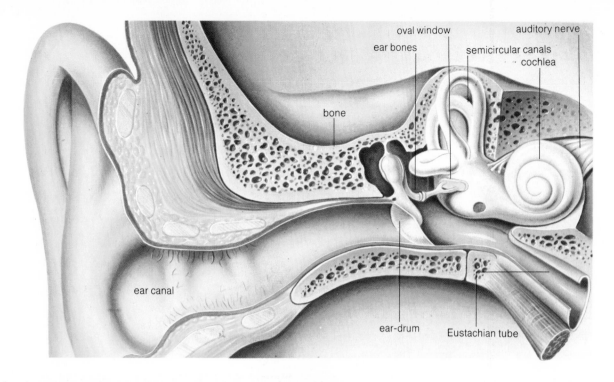

ear canal

bone

oval window
ear bones
auditory nerve
semicircular canals
cochlea

ear-drum

Eustachian tube

Above: All we can see of the ear from outside is the familiar fleshy flap. But the ear actually extends deep into the head. The inner ear connects with the brain via the auditory nerve, and the middle ear connects with the throat via the Eustachian tube.

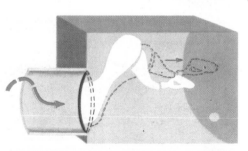

sound wave

ear canal

outer ear

ear-drum

middle ear

ear bones

cochlea

bone

pressure wave

inner ear

Below: The loudness of sounds is measured on a scale of units called decibels. The bottom of this scale, 0 decibels, is fixed as the faintest sound that can be heard by the human ear. There is no top to the scale, but we cannot listen to sounds of more than about 100 decibels without pain. Very much louder sounds, such as those of explosions, can burst our eardrums!

Movement
of ear bones

45
conversation
60
crowd
30
75
vacuum cleaner
refrigerator
90
pneumatic drill
15
leaves rustling
NOISE CHART
120
painful sound
QUIET LOUD
VERY QUIET VERY LOUD
0 decibels

93

Taste, smell and touch

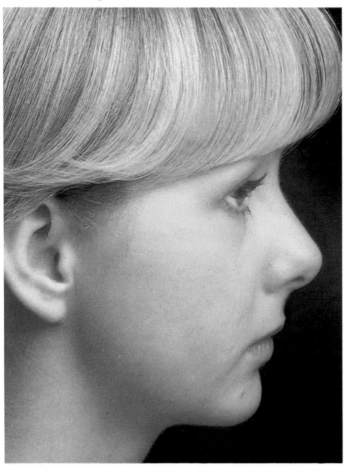

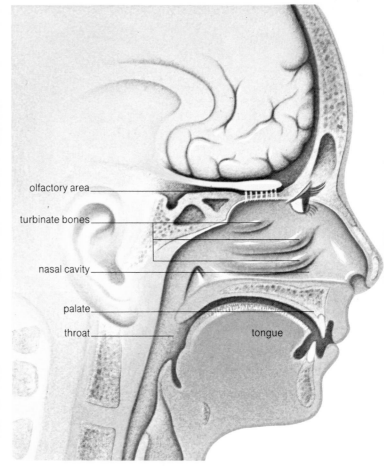

olfactory area

turbinate bones

nasal cavity

palate

throat

tongue

Taste and smell are senses that are linked together. For example, when you taste food, part of your enjoyment comes from your sense of smell. This is shown to be true when you get a bad cold. Then, your nose becomes blocked up and meals are not so enjoyable, because without smell you cannot appreciate the full flavour of the food.

By means of the senses of taste and smell we are able to detect chemical substances, such as those in food and drink, or those in the air we breathe. For this reason, taste and smell are known as the *chemical senses*.

To many animals the sense of smell is much more important even than to ourselves. Wolves, for example, find their food largely by smell. Their sense of smell is far more acute than ours.

Even so, we are able to detect the odours of very small amounts of some chemical substances. These include pleasant-smelling substances such as perfumes, and unpleasant ones such as the odour of rotten eggs! We can

smell such substances even when they are present only as one part in many million parts of air. Also, we can detect very many different kinds of smells.

By comparison, our sense of taste is very crude. We can taste substances only when these are present in our food or drink in fairly large amounts, usually more than one part in a thousand. And we know only four different kinds of taste: bitter, salt, sweet and sour. The varied flavours of foods are really combinations of these four tastes with many different odours.

We detect odours by means of many millions of tiny nerve endings. These are situated high up in the lining of the nose. They send messages to the brain about odours. The part of the brain that receives these messages is called the *olfactory lobe,* and the main nerve that carries them there is called the *olfactory nerve.*

We detect tastes with small nerve endings called *taste buds.* We each have about 10,000 of these, situated all over

Above: A cross-section of the girl's head shows her organs of smell and taste. When she breathes air in through her nose, it passes around the turbinate bones and so comes into close contact with the moist membranes of her nasal cavity. These contain millions of nerve endings, which send messages about odours to her brain.

the tongue and on other parts of the mouth and throat.

The linings of the nose, mouth and throat are all very moist. This helps us to smell and taste, because chemical substances dissolve in the moisture, so reaching the sensitive nerve endings.

Touch and pain
When any part of your body touches something, you feel a sensation. This is your sense of touch.

Some parts of your body are more sensitive to touch than others. For example, your fingertips are very sensitive. You use your fingers for all kinds of delicate work. By contrast, your buttocks are not nearly so

94

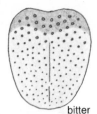
bitter

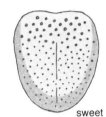
sweet

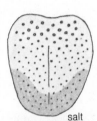
salt

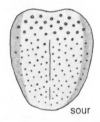
sour

Left: The main organ of taste is the tongue, which is covered with small nerve endings called taste buds. Four different areas of the tongue are sensitive to the four different tastes – bitter, sweet, salt and sour. The food we eat has many different flavours, because each taste is associated with a mixture of different odours.

Right: The diagram shows how tastes, detected by the mouth and tongue, are combined with odours, detected in the nasal cavity. Air breathed in passes not only around the nasal cavity, but also upwards from the mouth into this cavity. The nerve endings in these areas then send messages to the brain.

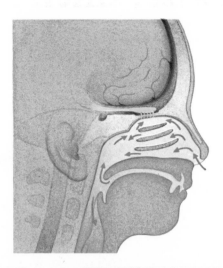

sensitive. For this reason, if you need an injection, the doctor may give you this in your buttocks.

Parts of the skin which are very sensitive to touch contain many nerve endings, and parts which are less sensitive contain fewer nerve endings. These nerve endings are not all alike, because the sense of touch is really several senses. With the nerve endings in your skin, you also feel pain, tickling, itching, heat and cold.

Touch messages often bring us comfort, as when we lie snug and warm in bed. Pain messages help to protect us against harm. The message 'Hot' makes us draw away from a hot object quickly and automatically.

Above left: Someone who is blind will usually develop an extra-keen sense of touch. This is vital for reading braille, which consists of a series of tiny raised dots.

Above right: A tea-taster judges the quality of tea by its aroma and its taste. For this work he needs highly developed senses of taste and smell.

Below: Our skin contains a number of different types of nerve endings, three of which are shown. Commonest of all are free nerve endings, which carry messages about pain to the brain. End bulbs tell the brain about pressure and cold, and corpuscles about pressure and heat. The diagram on page 108 shows where these nerve endings are found in the skin.

free nerve ending (pain)

end bulb (cold)

corpuscle (heat)

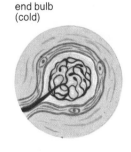

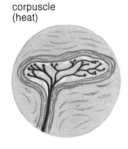

The body's framework

Your body needs its bony skeleton as a hard, firm support for its other, softer parts. For the same reason, most other kinds of animals also have a skeleton, although this may be very different from the human skeleton.

An insect or a crab, for example, has a hard skeleton on the outside of its body, not on the inside. A jellyfish is one kind of animal that has no skeleton at all. It spends its life floating in water, so its soft jelly-like body does not need much support.

When you walk, run or jump, your muscles stretch and relax. Even violent stretching does not dislodge them from their proper place, because they are firmly attached at both ends to the bones of your skeleton.

Your skeleton also serves as a framework protecting your soft, inner organs. Your ribs, for example, surround your heart, lungs and many other soft parts, like a protective cage.

Bones and joints

Your skeleton, like those of all other large land animals, is made of bone. From outside, bones feel smooth and hard. Inside, however, they are softer and spongy.

The spongy core of a bone is called its *marrow*. This is red or yellow in colour because it contains many blood cells and fatty cells. In fact, the bone marrow is a main place for the manufacture of blood cells.

The hard surface of bone is covered with a thin but tough membrane. Both the outside and the inside of a bone receive nourishment through many small blood vessels, and bones also contain many nerves.

Unlike your own bones, those of a newborn baby are quite soft. As the baby grows, its bones become harder. Also, a baby has more bones than an adult, but during growth some of them fuse (join) together. An adult normally has 206 bones. The longest of these is the femur, the bone of the upper leg or thigh. The smallest are the tiny ear bones, or ossicles.

As we grow up, the femur and other long bones of our legs and arms grow longer. They reach their full length in our late teens – the end of

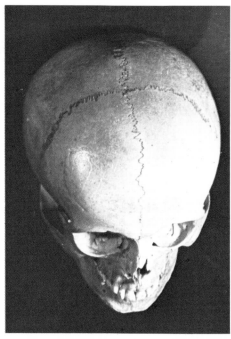

puberty. After that time, we normally do not grow any taller.

The place where one bone connects with another is called a *joint*. Some joints, such as those of the wrist and knee, are very movable. (Can you think of two more very movable joints?) Others, such as the joints between the many bones of the backbone, are less movable. Yet other joints, such as those between the bones of the skull, do not move at all.

Between the bones of a joint are one or more layers of *cartilage* (gristle). Cartilage prevents the bones grating against one another. It is thickest between the joints of the backbone. Here, it forms pads called *discs*. If one of these discs becomes dislodged, it may cause severe pain. This is known as a slipped disc. Movable joints, particularly those of the elbow and knee, also contain a liquid which oils the joint and so helps it to move smoothly and easily.

Broken bones

If we break a bone, we call this a *fracture*. Some fractures are much more serious than others, because the broken bone-ends injure blood vessels and nerves. Fractures are treated by keeping the broken parts still inside a plaster cast. Usually, the broken bones then knit together well.

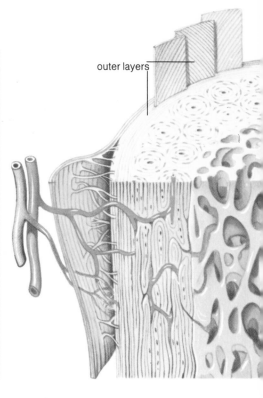

outer layers

Above left: The strong bones at the top of the skull protect the brain from shocks. In a newborn baby, these bones have not yet fused together to form the joints visible in the picture. This allows the baby's soft head bones to move about slightly, as the baby is being born.

Above: A section of a long bone, showing its complex but very strong structure. This is a honeycomb-like network of hard bone material. The Haversian canals carry many small blood vessels. Nearer the centre is the extremely strong bone of the marrow. Blood cells are made in the marrow.

Below: A cross-section of the head of the femur, the longest bone in the body. This fits into a socket in the hip joint, and has to withstand great pressures as the body moves.

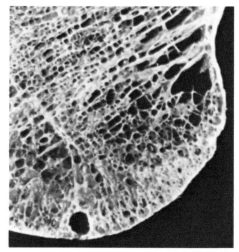

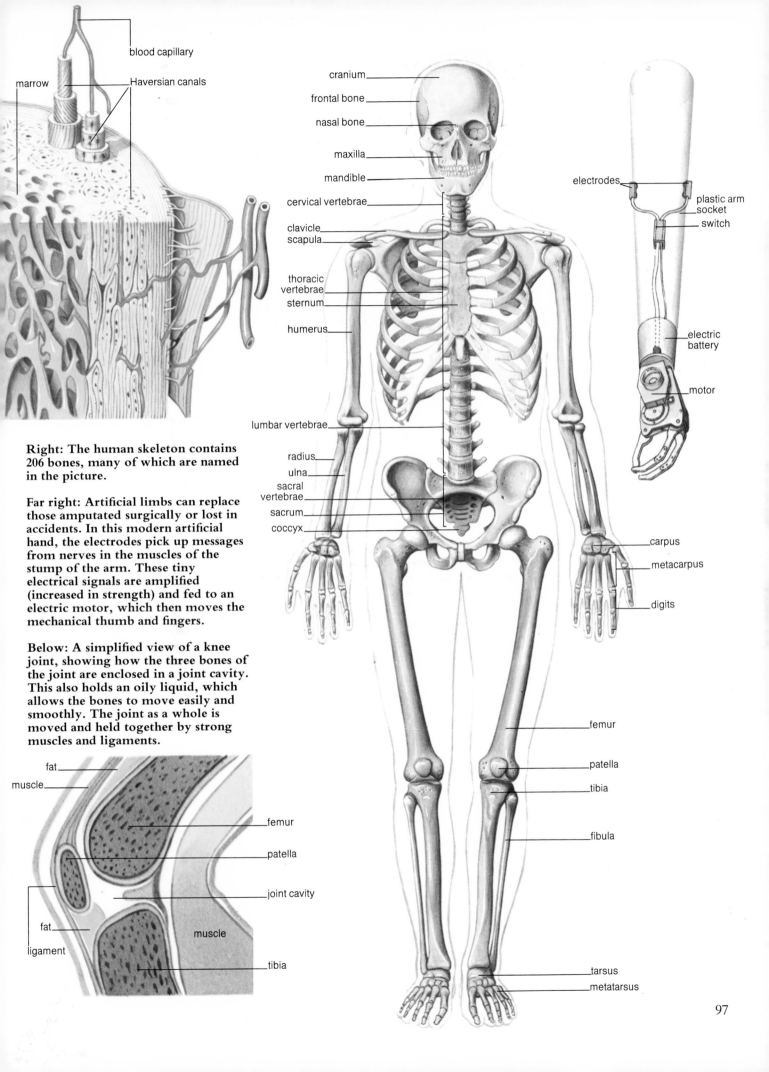

blood capillary

marrow

Haversian canals

cranium

frontal bone

nasal bone

maxilla

mandible

cervical vertebrae

clavicle
scapula

thoracic
vertebrae

sternum

humerus

lumbar vertebrae

radius

ulna

sacral
vertebrae

sacrum

coccyx

electrodes

plastic arm
socket

switch

electric
battery

motor

carpus

metacarpus

digits

femur

patella

tibia

fibula

tarsus

metatarsus

Right: The human skeleton contains 206 bones, many of which are named in the picture.

Far right: Artificial limbs can replace those amputated surgically or lost in accidents. In this modern artificial hand, the electrodes pick up messages from nerves in the muscles of the stump of the arm. These tiny electrical signals are amplified (increased in strength) and fed to an electric motor, which then moves the mechanical thumb and fingers.

Below: A simplified view of a knee joint, showing how the three bones of the joint are enclosed in a joint cavity. This also holds an oily liquid, which allows the bones to move easily and smoothly. The joint as a whole is moved and held together by strong muscles and ligaments.

fat

muscle

femur

patella

joint cavity

fat

muscle

ligament

tibia

97

Muscles and movement

Our muscles enable us to make movements. Even the very smallest movement, such as the closing of an eyelid, requires the use of one or more muscles. The pictures show how the main muscles are arranged on the body, and the various movements they control.

All these large muscles are called *skeletal muscles,* because they are attached at each end to the bones of the skeleton. You can see that in general these muscles are shaped like a spindle. They are thickest in the middle and taper off towards the ends, where they are attached.

Each skeletal muscle is tightly enclosed by a thin, but tough bag of tissue. Where this tapers off at the ends of the muscle, it becomes very tough indeed, like a strong rope. These tough, white ends are called *tendons* or *sinews.* They are what actually connects a skeletal muscle to bones.

Although they are so tough, tendons can sometimes be damaged, as when a runner injures the Achilles tendon of his lower leg. In this case, the runner must rest until the tendon heals – he is hardly able to walk without the use of his calf muscle.

How muscles work

When our skeletal muscles produce movements of our body, they do so by pulling – but never pushing – on the bones to which they are attached.

For this reason, the large muscles of our arms and legs act in pairs. One muscle *contracts,* or shortens, to move the limb, while the other muscle *relaxes,* or gets longer (see diagram). In other body movements, such as bending and twisting movements of the trunk, many muscles may be used.

Different types of muscle

Everyone is familiar with skeletal muscle (the kind described so far). It is the red meat of the animal body seen in butchers' shops. This type of muscle makes up nearly half of our body weight (if we are not too fat!).

However, there are two other kinds of muscle in our bodies, although they are not nearly so familiar. One kind is *smooth muscle* which causes movements

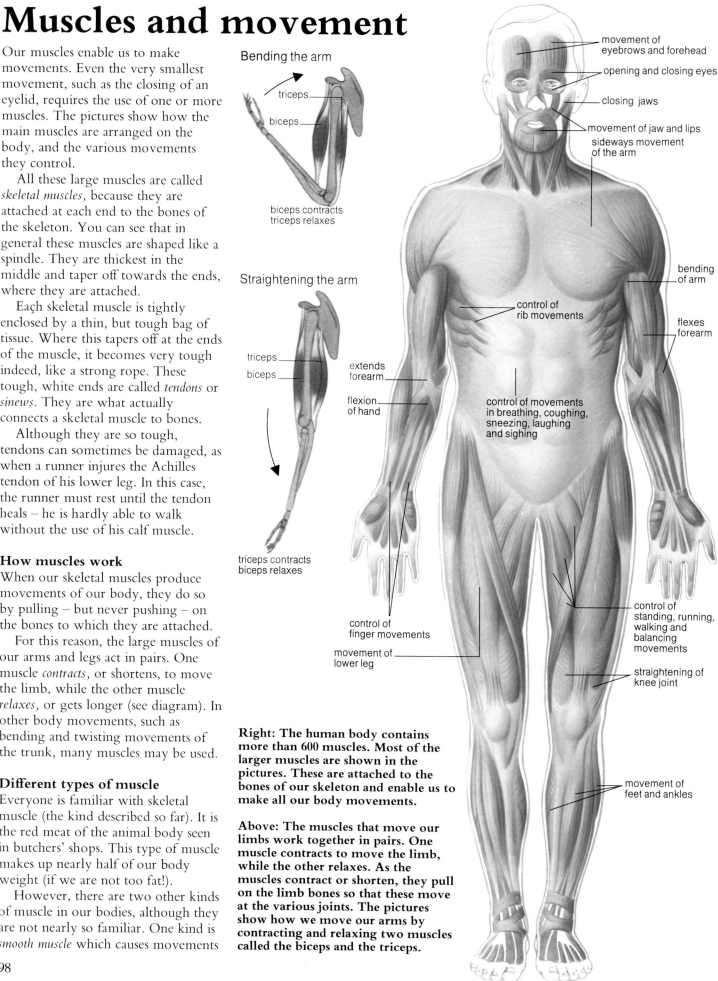

Bending the arm

triceps

biceps

biceps contracts
triceps relaxes

Straightening the arm

triceps

biceps

extends
forearm

flexion
of hand

triceps contracts
biceps relaxes

control of
finger movements

movement of
lower leg

movement of
eyebrows and forehead

opening and closing eyes

closing jaws

movement of jaw and lips
sideways movement
of the arm

bending
of arm

flexes
forearm

control of
rib movements

control of movements
in breathing, coughing,
sneezing, laughing
and sighing

control of
standing, running,
walking and
balancing
movements

straightening of
knee joint

movement of
feet and ankles

Right: The human body contains more than 600 muscles. Most of the larger muscles are shown in the pictures. These are attached to the bones of our skeleton and enable us to make all our body movements.

Above: The muscles that move our limbs work together in pairs. One muscle contracts to move the limb, while the other relaxes. As the muscles contract or shorten, they pull on the limb bones so that these move at the various joints. The pictures show how we move our arms by contracting and relaxing two muscles called the biceps and the triceps.

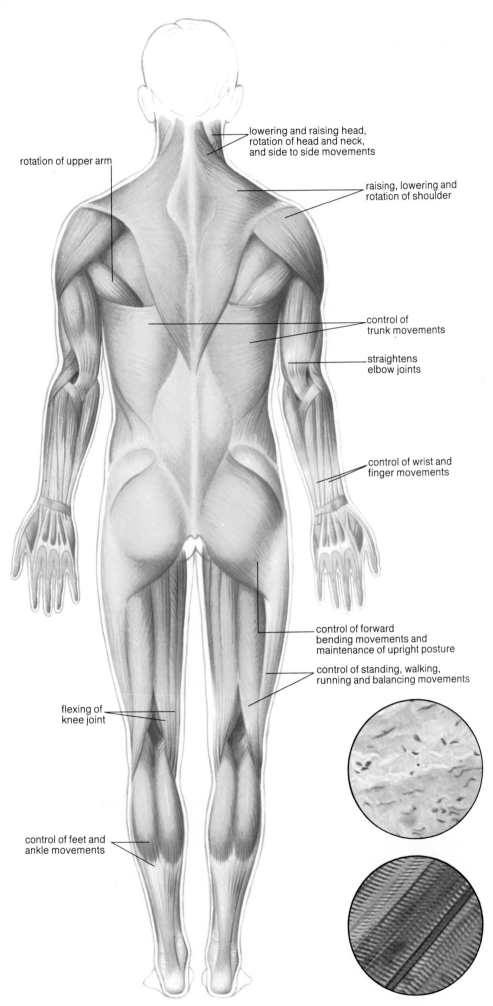

rotation of upper arm

lowering and raising head,
rotation of head and neck,
and side to side movements

raising, lowering and
rotation of shoulder

control of
trunk movements

straightens
elbow joints

control of wrist and
finger movements

control of forward
bending movements and
maintenance of upright posture

control of standing, walking,
running and balancing movements

flexing of
knee joint

control of feet and
ankle movements

of such inner parts as the stomach, intestines and pulsating arteries. The third type is found only in the heart, and is called *cardiac* or *heart muscle*.

Control of muscles

When you decide to move, your brain sends nerve messages to your skeletal muscles. These then contract or relax so that the movement is made.

The smooth muscles of your inner organs are also 'told' by nerve messages when to act. But you do not first decide to make their movements. Your arteries continue to pulsate, and your stomach to contract and relax, without you ever having to think about them.

Heart muscle, smooth muscle and their nerves act automatically. They are like the automatic pilot which keeps a plane flying steadily, while the pilot relaxes.

Above: By special training, such as weight-lifting, an athlete or muscleman can develop his muscles to a remarkable size and strength.

Left: The two small circles show the appearance of muscle when it is magnified under a microscope. The lower picture shows skeletal muscle, the kind shown in the pictures of the body. When magnified, this skeletal muscle has a striped appearance. The upper picture shows the type of muscle that causes movements of our internal organs. This does not have a striped appearance, and so is known as smooth muscle.

Blood and circulation

Blood serves many purposes in our bodies. It carries nourishment to living tissues in all parts of the body and takes away waste substances from the tissues. It also carries hormones, the chemical messengers of the body (see pages 106–7). Other important substances in the blood are antibodies, which fight infections in the body.

You can see already that blood is a complicated mixture. Besides the substances named, blood contains several types of living cells. Most familiar are the *red blood cells,* which give blood its red colour. They carry oxygen from the air we breathe, as nourishment for the tissues. They also carry away carbon dioxide waste from the tissues, back to the lungs, where we breathe it out.

Blood has a smaller number of *white blood cells.* These help protect the body against infections. Some white cells make protective antibodies. Others move about in the blood, swallowing up any harmful foreign matter, such as infectious bacteria.

Blood cells and other particles are carried in the liquid part of blood, which is called blood *plasma.* When separated from the red and white cells, it is an almost colourless liquid.

The plasma contains many dissolved materials. These include food substances that nourish tissues. They are made from the food that we eat. Also dissolved in the plasma are food wastes from the tissues. These are carried by the blood to the kidneys, which filter them out of the body as urine.

Finally, blood contains many substances which enable the blood to clot and to seal up wounds until these are healed.

The circulation system

Blood flows to all parts of the body in a system of tubes called *blood vessels.* The diagrams show the body's main blood vessels, the *arteries* and *veins.*

Arteries and veins are connected by many smaller blood vessels, to make a system in which blood flows continuously around the body. This is called the blood circulation system. From the diagram, you can see how

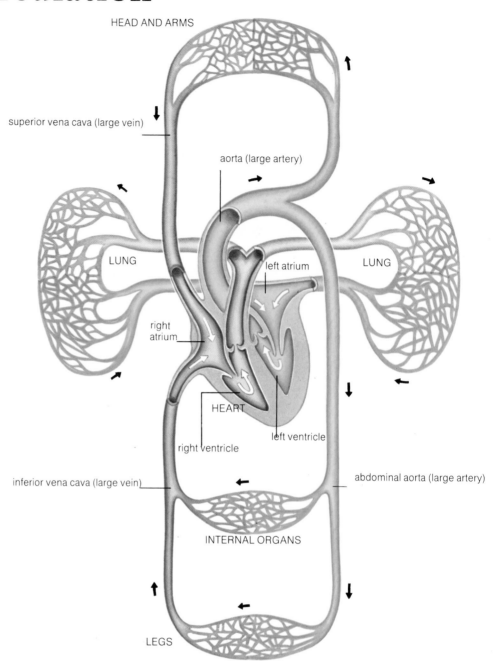

blood is pumped from the heart to the lungs, to gather oxygen. The blood, which is now bright red because of the oxygen, returns to the heart and is pumped out again, through arteries, to all other parts of the body.

Having given up its nourishment to the tissues, the blood flows back in the veins to the heart. It is now darker in colour because it contains carbon dioxide instead of oxygen.

When this dark blood reaches the heart, it is pumped again to the lungs. Here, it gives up its waste carbon dioxide and gathers a new supply of nourishing oxygen.

Above: The diagram shows how blood circulates around the body. Bright red blood, rich in oxygen, is pumped by the heart into arteries. These branch and get smaller as they carry oxygen to tissues in various parts of the body. As tiny capillaries, they link up with equally tiny veins. The veins carry dark red blood (shown blue), containing waste carbon dioxide, away from the tissues. The veins merge to form larger veins which eventually lead blood back to the heart. The heart pumps this dark blood to the lungs, where it gives up its waste carbon dioxide and takes in more oxygen. The bright red blood then returns to the heart, to be pumped once again around the body.

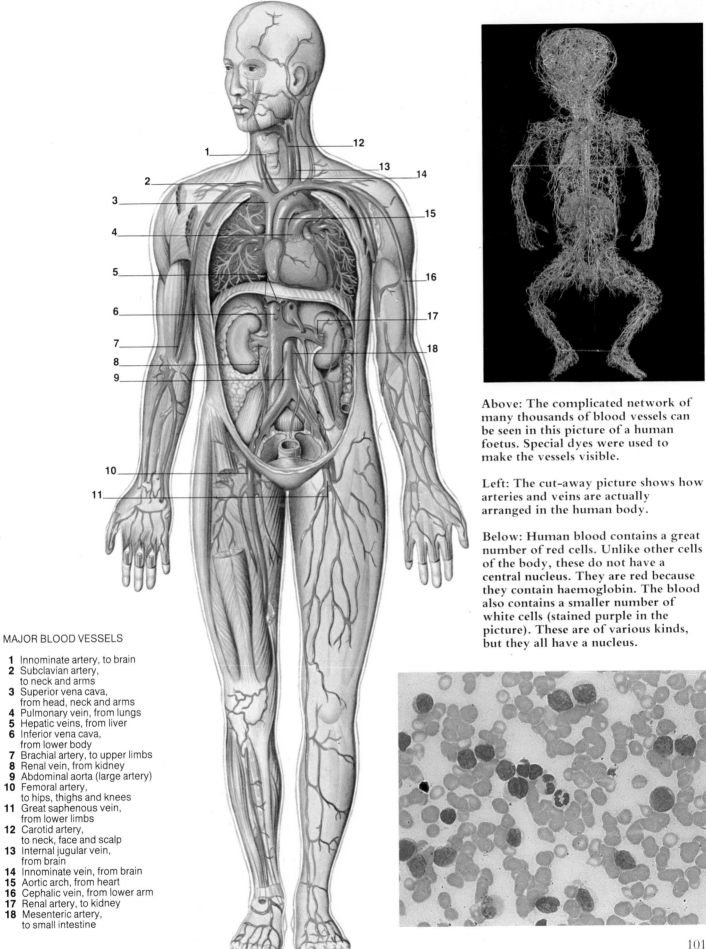

Above: The complicated network of many thousands of blood vessels can be seen in this picture of a human foetus. Special dyes were used to make the vessels visible.

Left: The cut-away picture shows how arteries and veins are actually arranged in the human body.

Below: Human blood contains a great number of red cells. Unlike other cells of the body, these do not have a central nucleus. They are red because they contain haemoglobin. The blood also contains a smaller number of white cells (stained purple in the picture). These are of various kinds, but they all have a nucleus.

MAJOR BLOOD VESSELS

1 Innominate artery, to brain
2 Subclavian artery,
 to neck and arms
3 Superior vena cava,
 from head, neck and arms
4 Pulmonary vein, from lungs
5 Hepatic veins, from liver
6 Inferior vena cava,
 from lower body
7 Brachial artery, to upper limbs
8 Renal vein, from kidney
9 Abdominal aorta (large artery)
10 Femoral artery,
 to hips, thighs and knees
11 Great saphenous vein,
 from lower limbs
12 Carotid artery,
 to neck, face and scalp
13 Internal jugular vein,
 from brain
14 Innominate vein, from brain
15 Aortic arch, from heart
16 Cephalic vein, from lower arm
17 Renal artery, to kidney
18 Mesenteric artery,
 to small intestine

101

The heart

As mentioned on page 101, your heart is the organ that pumps blood around your body. It is a very remarkable pump, because it must keep working, day and night without pause, for as long as you live.

This means that your heart pumps a truly enormous amount of blood during your lifetime. Each day of your life, it pumps blood around your body more than 1000 times. If you live to be 70 years old, then your heart will have pumped altogether at least 200 million litres of blood. This is a lot of work for an organ not much bigger than a fist!

How the heart works

The heart is a hollow organ made of muscle. It lies between the lungs, on the left side of the chest. It pumps blood by making squeezing movements, which cause the blood to spurt at high pressure into arteries.

You can feel this pumping action by taking your pulse. On your inner wrist, an artery comes near the surface. If you gently lay your fingers on this artery, you can easily feel the blood spurting through it.

But your heart is not a simple pump. It is really two pumps close together, separated by a thick wall of muscle called the *septum*.

The pump to the right of the septum pumps blood to your lungs.

Left: A cut-away picture of the heart. This shows the four pumping chambers of the heart, the right and left ventricle and the right and left atrium. It also shows the valves which connect each atrium with its ventricle, and the blood vessels which lead out from and into these chambers.

Bottom: Four diagrams describing the pumping action of the heart.
1. The right atrium fills with dark blood from the body. The left atrium fills with bright red blood from the lungs.
2. The right atrium contracts, pumping blood into the right ventricle. The left atrium contracts, pumping blood into the left ventricle.
3. The right ventricle contracts, pumping dark blood out to the lungs. (Notice how the valves are open or closed.) The left ventricle contracts, pumping bright red blood out to the rest of the body.
4. The ventricles relax after their pumping action. They are now ready once again to receive blood, as in 2.

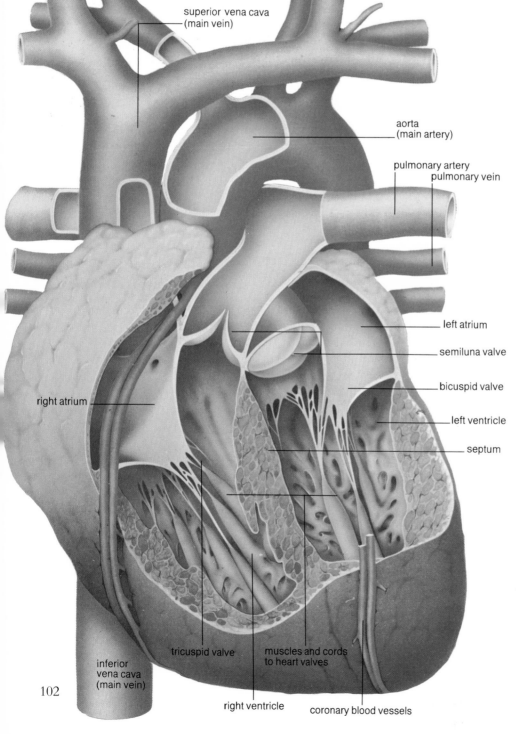

superior vena cava
(main vein)

aorta
(main artery)

pulmonary artery
pulmonary vein

left atrium

semiluna valve

bicuspid valve

left ventricle

septum

right atrium

tricuspid valve

muscles and cords
to heart valves

inferior
vena cava
(main vein)

right ventricle

coronary blood vessels

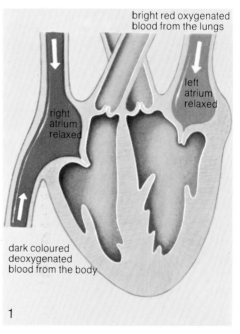

bright red oxygenated
blood from the lungs

left
atrium
relaxed

right
atrium
relaxed

dark coloured
deoxygenated
blood from the body

1

This blood leaves the right pump by an artery called the *pulmonary,* or lung, *artery.* Blood refreshed with oxygen from your lungs then returns to your heart, but to its *left* pump, through the *pulmonary vein.*

The left pump is the stronger of the two, with thicker muscle. When it contracts, it pumps refreshed blood at high pressure into a large artery called the *aorta.* From the aorta blood travels to smaller and smaller arteries in your body (as shown on pages 100–101).

When blood has passed around your body it returns to the right pump of your heart through two large veins, each called a *vena cava.* This blood has given up its oxygen to the tissues of the body, and has collected from them waste carbon dioxide.

But the blood is now back where it started, and is ready to be pumped again to your lungs to be refreshed with more oxygen.

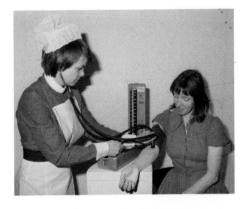

Above: A girl has her blood pressure taken as a check on fitness. First, a rubber bag is wound firmly around her arm. This bag is connected to an air pump and also to a mercury manometer which measures air pressure inside the bag. The pressure is raised until the pulse in the artery just stops. This can easily be detected by feeling for the pulse near the girl's wrist or listening with a stethoscope, as shown. The pressure is slightly released, and a blood pressure reading is taken as soon as the blood is heard to flow again. This is the systolic, or highest, blood pressure. By deflating the bag further, another, lower blood pressure, the diastolic pressure, can also be measured.

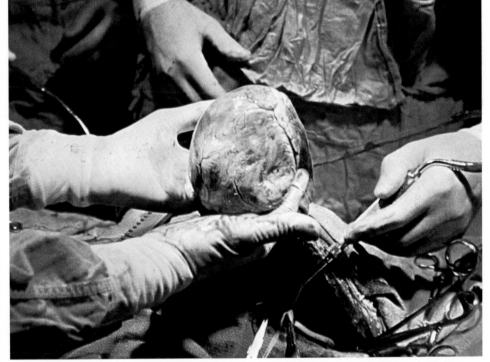

Left: A heart operation in progress. The surgeon has removed the patient's heart outside his body. The patient is connected to a heart–lung machine which takes over the pumping of the blood. This allows the surgeon to perform such delicate operations as replacing diseased heart valves.

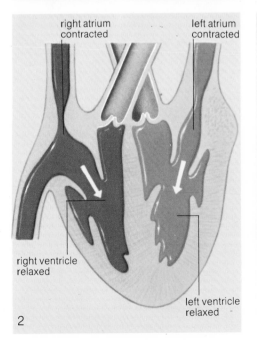

right atrium contracted   left atrium contracted

right ventricle relaxed

left ventricle relaxed

2

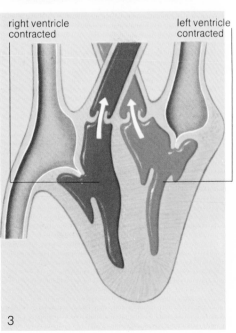

right ventricle contracted   left ventricle contracted

3

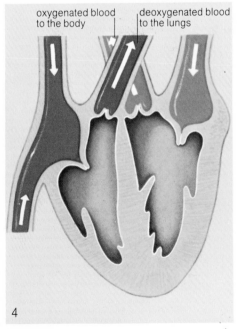

oxygenated blood to the body   deoxygenated blood to the lungs

4

The brain

You use your brain to make any movement or to think any thought. It is the headquarters, or control centre, of your whole body. It sends messages to, and receives messages from, all parts of your body, to control the body's actions.

These messages are carried by nerves and also by chemical messengers in the blood called hormones (see pages 106–7). Your brain controls both nerves and hormones.

Besides your conscious actions – the ones that you think about – your brain also controls many unconscious actions and movements. For example, it controls your balance, the rate at which your heart beats, and the movements of your digestive system. You do not have to think about any of these. They are all controlled automatically by your brain.

A delicate computer

The pictures show the shape and size of the human brain. This delicate control centre is protected, on the outside, by the strong skull bones.

Inside the skull, the brain is further protected by a tough skin and also by a liquid that surrounds the brain, acting as a shock absorber. This skin and the liquid also cover the spinal cord, with all its vital nerve cells, which descends from the brain down the inside of the backbone.

Below: Various views of the human brain show its size and general shape. Most of its surface is seen as the cerebral hemispheres. Because they are so deeply folded or fissured, they have a very large area. Into them are packed a vast number of nerve cells and an even greater number of connections between nerve cells. The cerebral hemispheres control all our thoughts, sensations and conscious actions.

Bottom left: This picture shows the brain in more detail. The cut-away parts are concerned with unconscious, or automatic, control of the body. For example, the cerebellum controls movements of the body without us having to think about them.

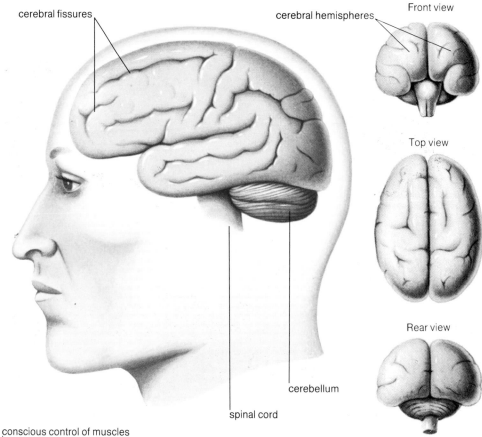

cerebral fissures

cerebral hemispheres

Front view

Top view

Rear view

cerebellum

spinal cord

The brain itself is made entirely of nerve cells, which are connected together in a very complicated way. The brain has a huge number of these cells – about 10,000 million!

Often, the brain is compared to a computer. But although so small, the human brain is far more complex than even the largest computer and can perform many more tasks.

Control parts of the brain

Different parts of the brain have different control tasks. All the higher tasks (those that you consciously perform) are controlled by the deeply wrinkled outer parts.

These outer layers of nerve cells control all your thoughts, feelings and

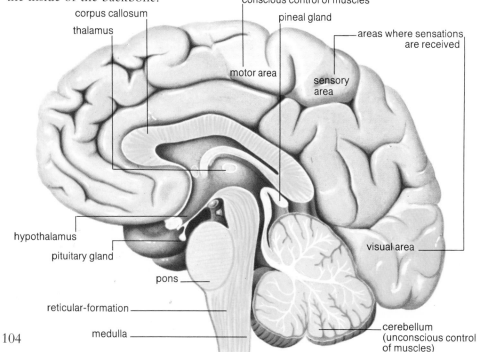

conscious control of muscles

pineal gland

corpus callosum

thalamus

areas where sensations are received

motor area

sensory area

hypothalamus

pituitary gland

pons

reticular-formation

visual area

medulla

cerebellum (unconscious control of muscles)

104

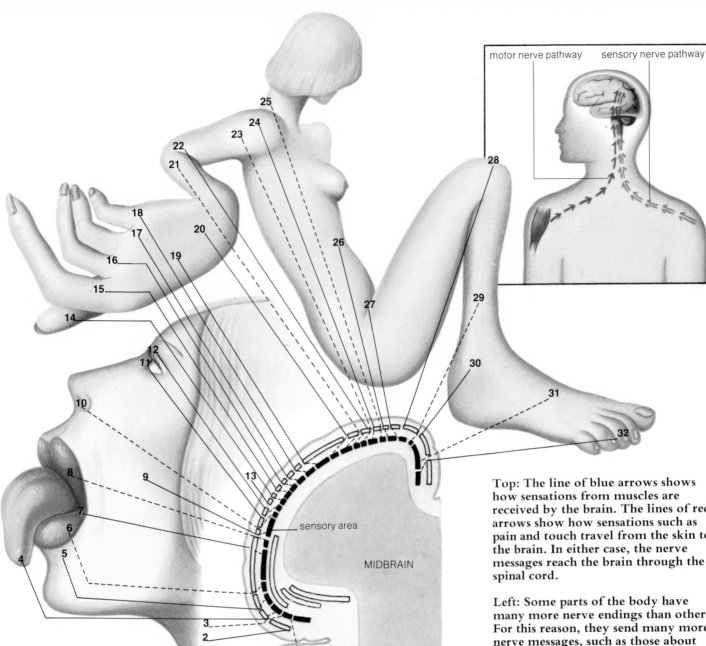

Top: The line of blue arrows shows how sensations from muscles are received by the brain. The lines of red arrows show how sensations such as pain and touch travel from the skin to the brain. In either case, the nerve messages reach the brain through the spinal cord.

Left: Some parts of the body have many more nerve endings than others. For this reason, they send many more nerve messages, such as those about pain and touch, to the brain. The picture shows the face and body with parts equal in size to the number of nerve messages that they can send to the brain. Different parts are numbered, and lines from them show where their messages are received by the brain.

1 abdomen	20 wrist
2 and 3 throat	21 fore-arm
4 tongue	22 elbow
5 teeth and gums	23 arm
6–8 lips	24 shoulder
9 face	25 neck and head
10 nose	26 trunk
11 eye and eyelid	27 hip
12 brow	28 knee
13 neck	29 leg
14 thumb	30 ankle
15–18 fingers	31 foot
19 hand	32 toes

Left: The electrodes fitted to this man's head detect the electrical messages in his brain.

sensations. Different areas of these outer layers receive messages from your senses and send instructions to your muscles.

Deeper inside the brain are the parts that control the body automatically. These parts control such things as body temperature and breathing.

Low down at the back of the brain is a distinct part called the *cerebellum*. This part controls balance, by automatically co-ordinating the action of one muscle with another.

Normally, you do not have to think about balance. Of course, if you try to walk a tightrope, you will have to think hard about it! In this case, conscious and unconscious parts of your brain act together.

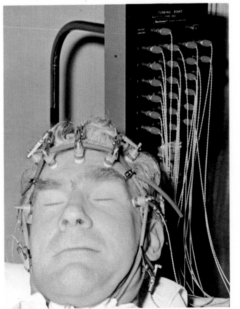

Control systems of the body

On pages 104–5, we saw that to control the body, the brain receives and sends out many messages, and that these can be carried by nerves.

Such important messages as those from the eyes, ears and other sense organs travel quickly along nerves to reach the brain. When you wish to make a movement, your brain sends out orders to your muscles. These orders are also nerve messages.

But what is a nerve message? Nerve cells have long, wire-like parts called *axons* that, like metal wires, can conduct electricity. In fact, a nerve message is a very small electric current, travelling along the axon of a nerve cell.

Nerves are spread over all parts of the body. They extend from the brain to the spinal cord, and from there make many other connections within the body. Taken all together, brain and nerves are called the *nervous system*.

The nervous system has two parts. One part controls thoughts, feelings, sensations and limb movements – all the activities of which you are conscious.

The other part of the nervous system controls the many activities of internal organs such as the heart, blood vessels, stomach and various glands. This kind of control is unconscious – you do not have to think about it.

Control by hormones

Messages travel very fast in the nerves, to and from the brain and spinal cord. But other control messages travel more slowly in the body, and have a more lasting effect. These are the hormone messages. They control changes that take place over a long period of time, such as growth.

Hormones are often called chemical messengers. They are made by special glands, called *endocrine glands*. You can see from the picture where these glands are located in the body.

When hormones leave the endocrine glands, they pass into the bloodstream, and are carried to many internal organs. Some of these organs are themselves endocrine glands, and make further hormones.

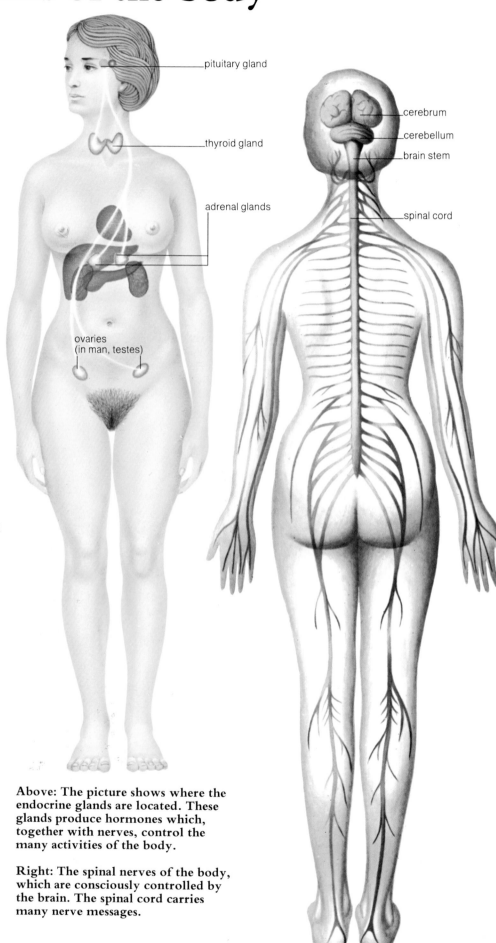

pituitary gland

thyroid gland

adrenal glands

ovaries
(in man, testes)

cerebrum

cerebellum

brain stem

spinal cord

Above: The picture shows where the endocrine glands are located. These glands produce hormones which, together with nerves, control the many activities of the body.

Right: The spinal nerves of the body, which are consciously controlled by the brain. The spinal cord carries many nerve messages.

106

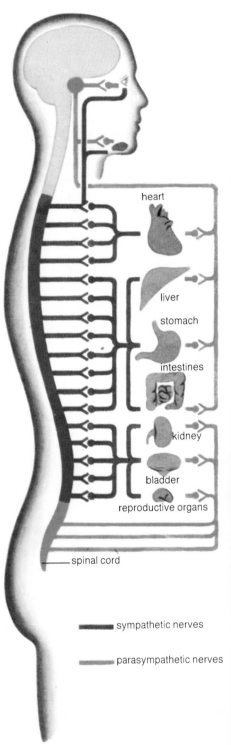

heart

liver

stomach

intestines

kidney

bladder

reproductive organs

spinal cord

— sympathetic nerves

— parasympathetic nerves

Above: Many nerves are not consciously controlled. They act automatically, controlling the glands and muscles of our internal organs. There are two sets of such nerves, sympathetic and parasympathetic nerves. Their action is opposite. For example, one sympathetic nerve closes a valve in the stomach, and one parasympathetic nerve opens it again.

Of all the endocrine glands, the pituitary is perhaps the most powerful. Indirectly, it controls all the other endocrine glands. But the pituitary itself is controlled by the brain.

Doctors sometimes prescribe extra hormones as medicines, and many women take a hormone fertility pill.

Double control
You can see that many parts of our bodies are controlled both by nerves and by hormones. This double control is very subtle and varied.

Brain, nerves and hormones, all acting together, account for our complex human behaviour.

Below: A slight tap below the kneecap causes the girl's lower leg to twitch rapidly upwards as shown. She cannot prevent this movement by thinking 'I shan't do it'. The movement is caused by messages to her muscles carried quite automatically by her nerves. Such movements are called reflex actions.

Above: A very young baby does not yet have good control over its muscles. For example, its arms and legs tend to wave about in a rather uncontrolled way. All the same, small babies are already very alert, and respond to many sights and sounds. As the baby gets older it will soon learn muscle control.

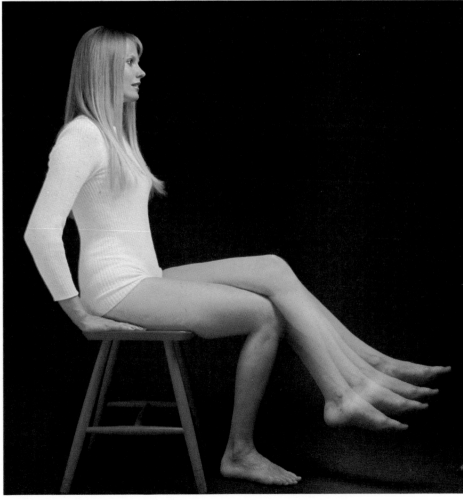

Skin

Your skin is the outermost part of your body. It covers all surface areas of your body, even your eyeballs. These, however, are covered with skin so thin that it is quite transparent – you can see through it clearly.

Over most other parts of your body, skin is much thicker. It is thickest of all on the parts where it is most likely to be worn away, such as on the soles of your feet.

Skin really consists of several layers. Of these, you usually see only the outermost surface layer. This is made of dead, flattened skin cells, which regularly flake away from your body. Normally you do not lose your protective outermost layer, because skin cells are being replaced all the time. They form in the deepest layer and are pushed upwards as new cells from underneath. Near the surface, they die, harden and become flattened, to make a protective surface.

What else does skin do?

Skin is also protective in another important way. It keeps out harmful microbes from the body. If for any reason such microbes do manage to get past the skin into the body, they can cause serious infections. More often, however, they cause only a pimple or a boil.

Skin is also the main organ by which the body keeps its temperature steady. On a hot day your body needs to lose heat. Many tiny blood vessels in your skin lose heat to the outside, so cooling your body. This cooling is also helped by the evaporation of sweat from your skin.

On a cold day your body needs to keep all its heat. The tiny blood vessels in exposed parts of your skin are shut off, so that they cannot lose heat. Also, the hairs of your skin help to keep in heat by trapping air which acts like a blanket, keeping out cold. Fatty cells, deep down in the skin, also help to keep out cold.

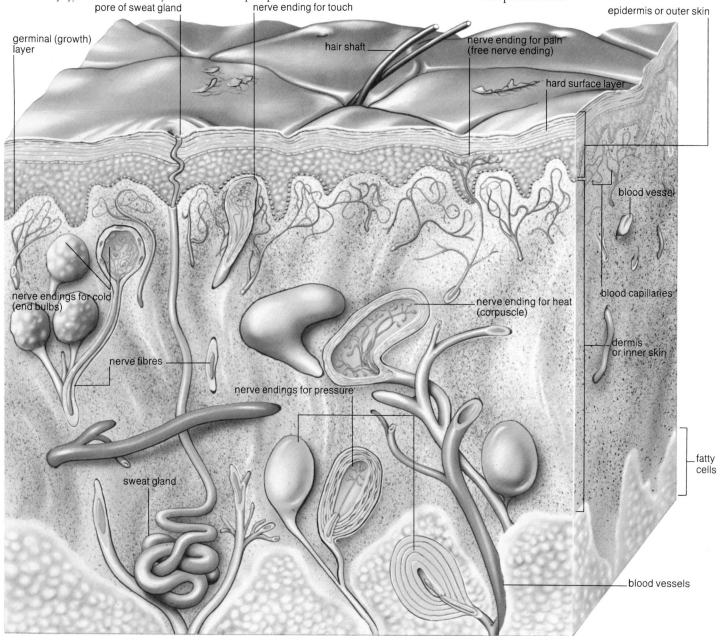

germinal (growth) layer

pore of sweat gland

nerve ending for touch

hair shaft

nerve ending for pain (free nerve ending)

epidermis or outer skin

hard surface layer

blood vessel

blood capillaries

nerve endings for cold (end bulbs)

nerve ending for heat (corpuscle)

nerve fibres

dermis or inner skin

nerve endings for pressure

sweat gland

fatty cells

blood vessels

Finally, through the skin your body can get rid of many of its wastes. These are mostly dissolved in sweat and so evaporate away from the body, or are removed when you bathe.

Nerves and glands

There are many nerve endings and glands in the skin. The nerve endings enable us to feel heat, cold, touch and pain. Besides sweat glands, skin contains other glands which make an oil that keeps the skin supple.

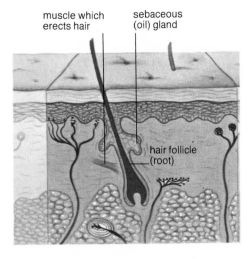

muscle which erects hair

sebaceous (oil) gland

hair follicle (root)

Left: A section of the human skin showing how a hair is rooted. The hair root, or follicle, is supplied by a gland with an oily substance called sebum. Often in adolescence, too much of this sebum is produced, so that it blocks the follicle. This will lead to the formation of a blackhead or a pimple, as shown below:
1. The follicle is blocked. Bacteria begin to grow in the sebum.
2. The hair dies and a blackhead forms.
3. The bacteria multiply and cause inflammation – a pimple.

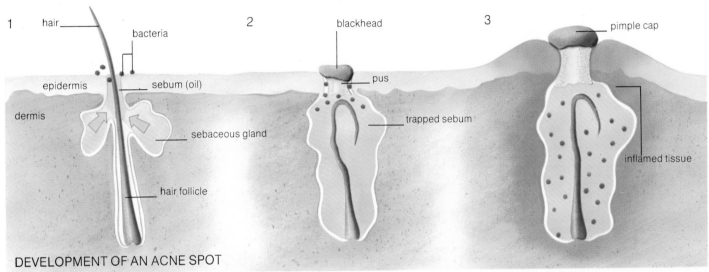

1
hair
bacteria
epidermis
sebum (oil)
dermis
sebaceous gland
hair follicle

2
blackhead
pus
trapped sebum

3
pimple cap
inflamed tissue

DEVELOPMENT OF AN ACNE SPOT

Left: A section through skin, magnified to show its many details. The outer skin, or epidermis, consists of cells produced by a bottom layer called the germinal layer. These cells flatten and die as they near the surface. They form a hard, non-living layer that protects the living cells beneath. The lower skin, or dermis, is much thicker. It contains many blood vessels, glands and nerve endings.

Right: In old age, skin loses its elastic quality (its 'springiness'). At the same time, the body may shrink slightly because it loses much of its fat. This causes the inelastic skin to form many wrinkles.

Below: A fingertip has a skin pattern which is different for every person. This is why fingerprints are so valuable in the detection of crime.

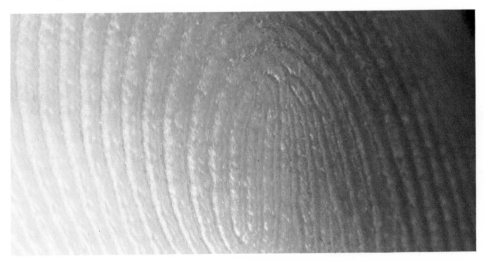

Lungs and breathing

To get oxygen, which is essential for life, you breathe air into your lungs. Oxygen from the air passes from your lungs into your blood. It is carried by the blood to all the living cells of your body. Inside living cells, oxygen is used for breaking down foods to provide energy for the body. This energy-releasing process is called *respiration*.

The air that you breathe out contains more carbon dioxide gas than the air you breathe in. This carbon dioxide is a waste substance made by the living cells of your body. Like oxygen, carbon dioxide is carried by the blood – but towards, not away from, the lungs. When the carbon dioxide reaches the lungs, it passes out of the blood into the lungs.

You can see that respiration both nourishes the body and helps it to get rid of its wastes.

How you breathe

When you breathe in, air travels from your nose, mouth and throat down your windpipe, or *trachea*. The trachea

Below: The main parts of the human respiratory (breathing) system. Air breathed in is moistened and warmed in the mouth, nose and throat before passing down the trachea to the lungs.

branches into two. Each branch is called a *bronchus*, and carries air to one of your lungs.

Your lungs lie in the upper part of your chest. They are spongy bags of tissue, protected behind the bony cage of your ribs. Both lungs are enclosed, inside the ribs, by a larger, airtight bag of tissue.

When you expand the muscles of your chest, to breathe in, this increases the volume inside the airtight bag, and so also increases the volume of your lungs, making air rush into them.

When you contract the muscles of your chest, to breathe out, this decreases the volume of the airtight bag, and also that of your lungs, forcing air out of them.

Inside a lung

To understand how a lung works, we must look at it in closer and closer detail, as shown by the pictures.

Soon after entering a lung, a bronchus branches many times, to make a system of tubes resembling the branches and twigs of a tree. When magnified, this 'twig' is seen to end in many tiny air bags, or *air sacs,* which are bunched together like grapes.

Air breathed into the lungs travels right through the bronchial tree to

reach all of the many thousands of air sacs.

Each air sac is surrounded by the smallest kind of blood vessels, called *capillaries*. These capillaries extend both from arteries carrying blood rich in oxygen, and from veins carrying blood loaded with carbon dioxide.

The walls of both air sacs and capillaries are so thin that gases can easily pass through them. In this way, oxygen passes from the lungs into the blood, and carbon dioxide passes from the blood into the lungs, and so out of the body.

air in   air out

lung
rib cage
diaphragm

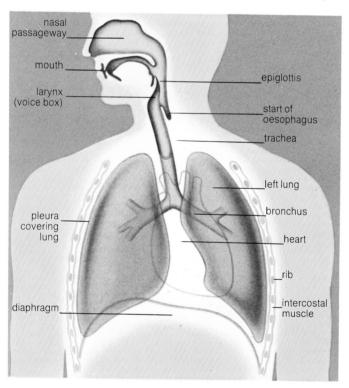

nasal passageway
mouth
larynx (voice box)
epiglottis
start of oesophagus
trachea
left lung
bronchus
heart
rib
intercostal muscle
pleura covering lung
diaphragm

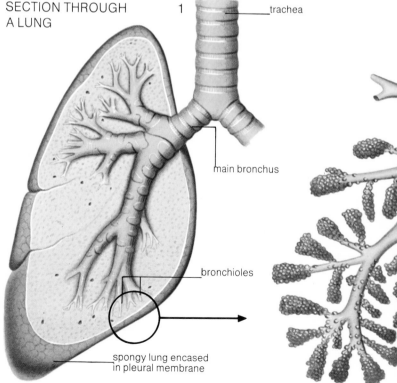

SECTION THROUGH A LUNG

1   trachea

main bronchus

bronchioles

spongy lung encased in pleural membrane

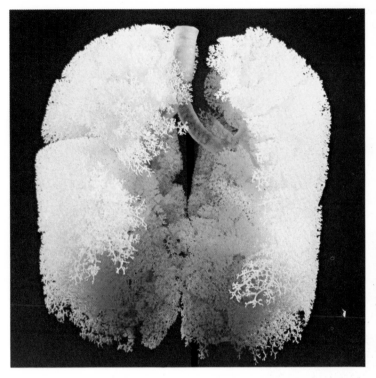

Above left: Breathing movements are controlled by muscle action. During breathing in, muscles raise the rib cage, and the diaphragm draws down. This increases the size of the chest space, and so draws air into the lungs. During breathing out, the opposite happens. Muscles lower the rib cage and the diaphragm rises. This decreases the size of the chest space, so that air is expelled from the lungs.

Above left: This exact model of a pair of lungs was made by pumping a plastic material into the lungs, then dissolving away all the tissue with chemicals. The model shows how the lungs are made up of air tubes which branch repeatedly and get smaller and smaller, until they form a texture resembling that of a bath sponge. There are about 300 million tiny air sacs at the ends of the branches.

Above: This athlete is undergoing a wind test, which will measure his fitness and the efficiency of his breathing.

Below: To understand how a lung works, it is necessary to look at it in greater and greater detail, as shown by the diagrams. (Also, see the text for more details of the 'inside story' of a lung.)

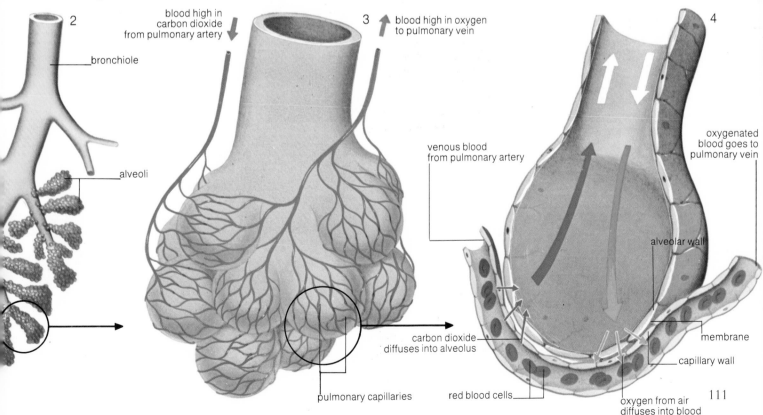

2

bronchiole

alveoli

blood high in carbon dioxide from pulmonary artery

3

blood high in oxygen to pulmonary vein

pulmonary capillaries

4

venous blood from pulmonary artery

oxygenated blood goes to pulmonary vein

alveolar wall

carbon dioxide diffuses into alveolus

red blood cells

membrane

capillary wall

oxygen from air diffuses into blood

111

Stabbers, slicers and grinders

With their teeth, animals bite and chew up their food. The teeth of a meat–eater, such as a Lion, are mainly sharp weapons for stabbing and slicing. The teeth of a grass–eater, such as a cow, are mainly large grinders for breaking up fibrous vegetable food. Human beings eat both meat and vegetables, and so have teeth for stabbing, slicing and grinding food.

As a very small baby, you did not need teeth because your main food was milk. But inside your gums, teeth were already present, waiting to *erupt*, or grow out, from your gums.

These first teeth were your *milk teeth*. They begin to erupt when you are about 6 months old, enabling you to start eating more solid foods. But when you are about 6 years old, they start to fall out again, leaving gaps.

These gaps are gradually filled as your *adult teeth* start to grow. But whereas you had only 20 milk teeth, your adult teeth number 32 in all. You can keep these teeth for the rest of your life – but only if you look after them well!

Different kinds of teeth

Adults, if they have lost none of their teeth, have 16 in the upper jaw and 16 similar teeth in the lower jaw.

Of the 16 teeth in each jaw, four at the front are slicers, also called *incisors*. Behind these are a pair (one on each side) of long, pointed stabbers, also called *canines*.

Farther back still are two pairs of grinders, also known as *premolars*. At the very back of the jaw are three pairs of grinders called *molars*. The last pair of these, known as *wisdom teeth,* usually erupt much later than all the others. In some people, they appear only in old age, when all other teeth may be absent!

Structure of a tooth

A tooth can stab, slice or grind even the toughest food by means of its very hard, outermost layer. This layer, called the *enamel,* is the hardest substance in the body – harder even than bone.

Beneath the enamel is a thick layer of another solid, but not so hard,

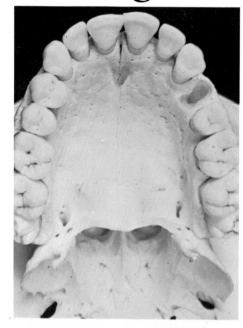

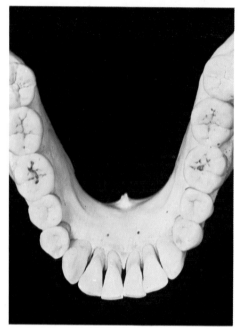

substance called *dentine*. Deeper still, at the centre of the tooth, is the soft tooth pulp. This contains blood vessels to nourish the living tooth. It also contains nerves – which soon tell you if you have tooth decay!

A tooth is held firmly in the gums by one, two or three roots. These have a hard, outer layer which resembles bone.

The diagram on page 113 shows how decay begins when bacteria get through the enamel into the pulp, and how it becomes very painful when a tooth abcess forms.

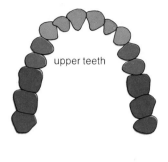

upper teeth

lower teeth

■ incisors (slicing)
■ canines (stabbing and tearing)
■ premolars (grinding)
■ molars (grinding)

Above and left: A full set of human teeth, showing the shapes of the eight incisors or slicers; the four canines or stabbers; and the eight premolars and 12 molars, all grinders.

Below: The diagram shows how you should brush your teeth, in order to remove food particles that collect between them. If you allow food to stay between your teeth, bacteria will grow in the food, to make acid which eats holes in your teeth. Other bacteria can then enter your teeth and cause decay.

Above right: The perfect teeth of this Giriama man are the result of his low-sugar diet.

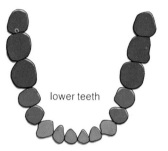

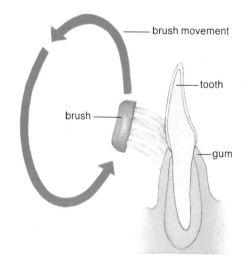

brush movement

tooth

brush

gum

112

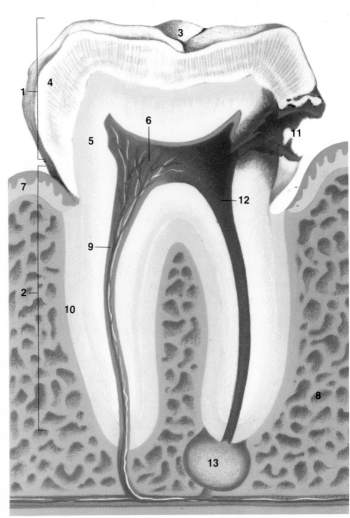

Below: Too much sugary food quickly leads to tooth decay, unless teeth are brushed regularly.

Below centre: Decayed or broken teeth are often crowned with gold.

Below right: If teeth are not properly brushed, dental plaque will form on them. Plaque contains the bacteria that cause tooth decay.

Above right: A molar tooth, cut away to show its inner and outer parts. This tooth is held in the jaw by two roots, although some molars have three. At the base of one root is a painful abcess (13), causing toothache. This has arisen from infection by bacteria, which have penetrated the tooth where it is decayed near the gum (11). The abcess is very painful because it lies near the path of a nerve (9). The names of the different parts of a tooth are given by the numbers.

1 crown
2 roots
3 cusp
4 enamel
5 dentine
6 pulp
7 gum
8 jawbone
9 nerve and blood vessels
10 cement
11 tooth decay
12 spread of decay into pulp
13 abcess

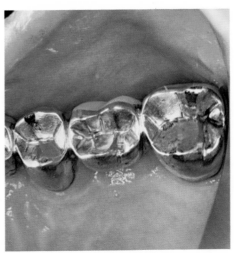

Digestion

You need food for energy and growth. Before your body can use food for these purposes, the food must first be broken down into simpler substances. This breaking–down process is called digestion.

Digestion takes place in a long passage, or tube, called the *alimentary canal* (alimentary means 'nourishing'). This tube starts at the mouth, continues to the stomach and intestines, and ends at the anus.

You begin to digest your food as soon as you have put it into your mouth. By chewing the food, you break it down into smaller pieces. The chewed food becomes mixed with your saliva, which makes it slippery and so still easier to swallow.

Right and below: The diagrams show what happens to food after it has been chewed and swallowed. A ball of food, moistened with saliva, passes down a tube called the oesophagus, until it reaches the stomach. There, the food is partly broken down or digested, before passing on to the small intestine, where digestion is completed. The fully digested food is absorbed into the blood through villi in the walls of the small intestine. Undigested material passes on to the large intestine, where most of the water in the undigested material is absorbed into the body. The waste material, called faeces, is expelled from the body through the anus.

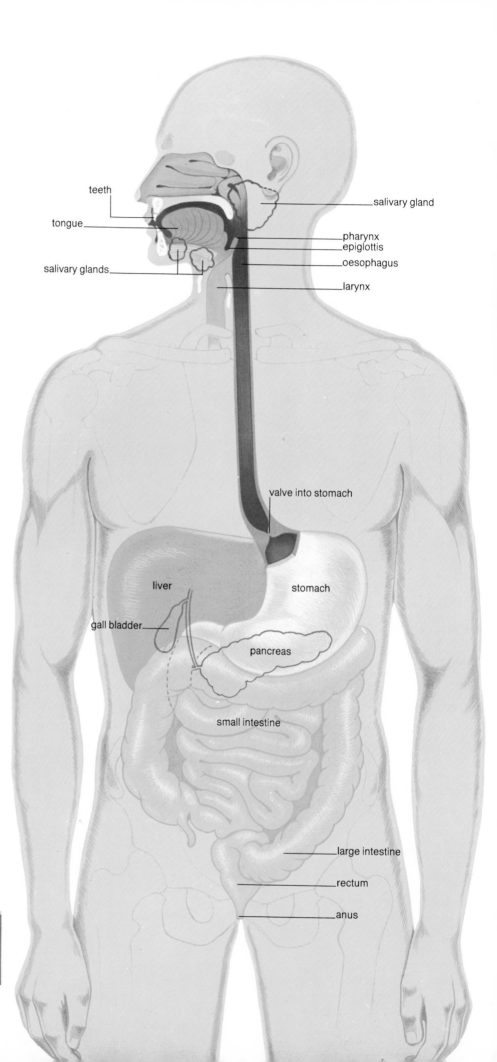

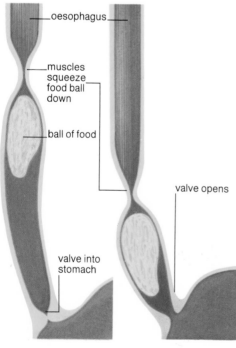

114

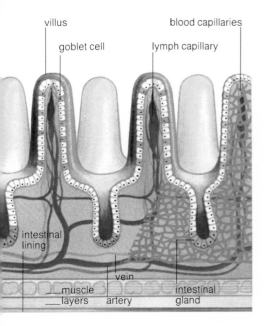

villus · goblet cell · blood capillaries · lymph capillary · intestinal lining · vein · muscle layers · artery · intestinal gland

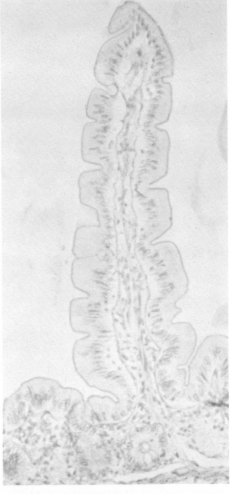

Above and right: Tiny finger-like projections called villi absorb digested food into the bloodstream. The photograph (right) shows a single villus greatly magnified.

Below: These astronauts are in weightless conditions. Even the one who is upside down can eat and drink quite satisfactorily. This is because food and drink, even when weightless, are pushed, by muscles, through the alimentary canal.

Saliva helps to break down the food chemically into simpler substances. It contains an enzyme that begins to break down starchy substances in the food, such as those in potatoes.

Your body contains many other enzymes, including several which help to break down food farther down in the alimentary canal.

In the stomach

When you swallow food, it passes down a narrow tube called the *oesophagus*, into the stomach. Muscles of the oesophagus squeeze the food down automatically. This type of squeezing movement also occurs in other parts of the alimentary canal.

The stomach is a bag which holds food while it is further digested. Glands in the lining of the stomach make an acid, a slimy substance called mucus and juices that contain more enzymes.

The stomach's muscles enable it to make churning movements, which mix up the food thoroughly with the stomach juices. At this stage, the food has become a liquid mass called *chyme*.

In the intestine

Chyme passes out of the stomach into the small intestine, where it is digested still further by more enzymes. These are made by glands in the intestine itself and also in the *pancreas*.

In the small intestine most food is finally broken down into substances that can pass into the cells of the body. These substances are absorbed into the bloodstream through small finger-like projections called *villi*. They are then carried by the blood to parts of the body where they are needed for energy and growth.

Fatty foods, however, are finally broken down in a rather different way, by a substance called *bile*, made in the gall bladder. Bile and special enzymes break down fat into droplets so small that they can pass into the villi and so into the bloodstream.

Most food substances have now been absorbed. In the large intestine, water from food is absorbed into the body. At the anus, undigested substances are passed out of the body.

115

How a baby develops

A baby begins to develop inside its mother when two cells come together. One cell, the *egg,* is made inside the mother's *ovaries.* The other cell, the *sperm,* is made inside the father's *testes.* Sperm and egg come together after the mother and father have made love.

Millions of sperms are released into the mother's womb, but only a few hundred survive to swim up to the egg. Then a part of one sperm, its nucleus, penetrates (passes through) the surface of the egg and combines with the egg nucleus. So the fertilized egg, as it is called, is partly mother and partly father.

After an egg has been fertilized by a sperm, no other sperm can penetrate it. But if the mother's ovaries release two eggs instead of one, two different sperms can fertilize these two eggs at the same time. In this case, the mother will eventually give birth to *unlike twins,* which may be two brothers, two sisters, or a brother and a sister.

Cells multiply

When an egg is fertilized, it is situated just outside the mother's ovaries, inside a tube. This tube leads to the mother's *uterus,* or *womb,* in which the baby will develop.

As the fertilized egg passes down the tube, it divides, first into two cells, then four, and so on, until a hollow ball of cells is formed. This is the beginning of the baby's body.

Sometimes, however, when the fertilized egg first divides, its cells may separate. This can form two sets of cells, each of which develops into a ball of cells. Later the mother gives birth to *identical twins* – two identical brothers or sisters.

Life in the womb

The ball of cells travels on to the womb, which is a pear-shaped bag with a thick lining which has many blood vessels. It sinks into this lining, which at first supplies it with nourishment.

Two weeks after fertilization, the *embryo,* as it is called, has grown to be about 1 centimetre wide and has become enclosed in a small, liquid-filled membrane bag. At this stage, the

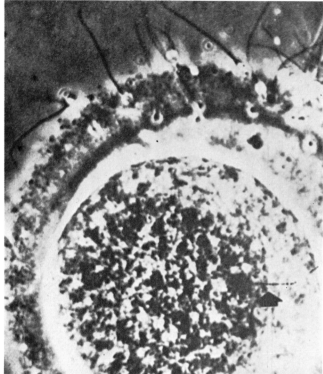

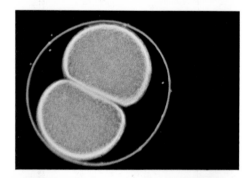

1

1½ months

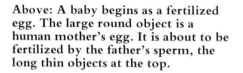

Above: A baby begins as a fertilized egg. The large round object is a human mother's egg. It is about to be fertilized by the father's sperm, the long thin objects at the top.

Right: After fertilization, an egg divides, first into two, then four, then many cells, until it has formed an embryo.

embryo looks more like a small fat fish than a baby.

At 2 months after fertilization, however, it has developed human features and limbs, even though it is still only about 2.5 centimetres long. By this time an organ called the *placenta* has grown to feed the embryo. It supplies food and oxygen from the mother's blood, through a tube which leads to the tiny baby's navel.

After 3 months, finger and toe nails and hair begin to grow. The developing baby, now called a *foetus,* is about 7 centimetres long. At this time, the mother first notices that her abdomen is starting to swell.

Nourished by the placenta, the unborn baby continues to grow in its mother's womb. After 7 months, it is fully formed enough to be born, but this usually does not happen until the ninth month (see pages 118–9).

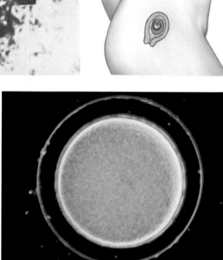

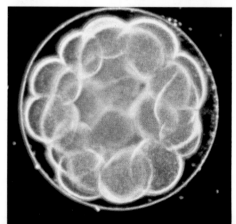

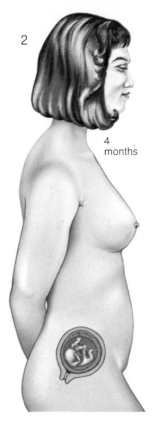 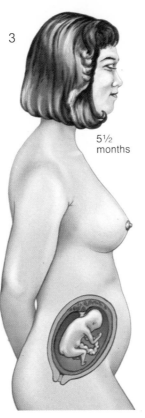 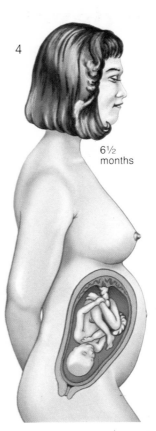 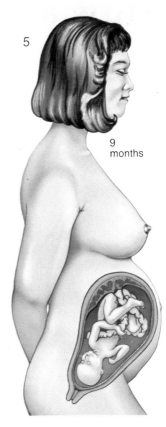

2 4 months

3 5½ months

4 6½ months

5 9 months

Above: Five stages in the development of a baby during its 9 months inside the mother's womb. In its first weeks of life the tiny creature, called at this stage the embryo, is too undeveloped to move around much. Later on, the larger foetus takes up several positions in the womb. At about 7 months the unborn baby settles into its final position, usually head down.

Below left: The embryo in the womb, after 40 days. This is the same stage of development as stage 1 shown above. Already the embryo is beginning to take on the typical shape of a human being, although such features as its ears, eyes, hair and nails have not yet developed fully. The embryo gets its oxygen and food from the placenta, which is supplied by its mother's

blood. The developing baby floats in the amniotic fluid trapped in the womb. As the baby grows, the womb expands to hold it.

Below: For several months before it is born, a baby will make active movements. In its last month in the womb, these will include thumb-sucking, as shown in the picture.

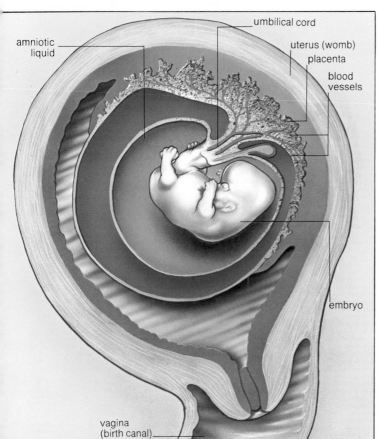

amniotic liquid

umbilical cord

uterus (womb)

placenta

blood vessels

embryo

vagina (birth canal)

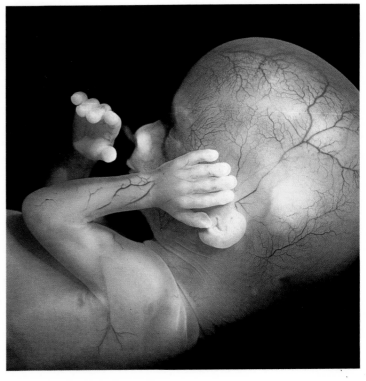

Birth of a baby

After 9 months in its mother's womb, a baby is ready to be born. But for several months the baby has shown that it is already living an active life.

Its mother feels the baby moving around inside her womb – quite often the baby gives little kicks. It also sucks its thumb and makes facial expressions, such as that of crying. Of course, an unborn baby never actually cries or utters any other sound, because it does not yet breathe air.

At 9 months the baby has grown to be about 45 centimetres long, and it weighs about 3 kilograms. It now fills up the womb and is too big to move around much. The baby settles down into the position from which it will be born. Normally this is head downwards, although some babies are born bottom-first. As the baby settles down, it drops lower in its mother's abdomen. Because the baby now presses less on her lungs, she feels the settling down as 'lightening'.

Labour

When a woman is giving birth to a baby, she is said to be in labour. This is an accurate word, because a woman has to work very hard indeed to give birth to her baby.

The baby is born through a passage called the *birth canal*, leading from the womb to outside the mother's body. The womb, which has grown in size with the baby, has powerful muscles which contract to push the baby out through the birth canal.

The mother may have felt these womb contractions for many months, but now they become very regular, and so powerful that they cause labour pains, which can be very severe.

As the baby is pushed forwards and downwards, the opening, or neck, of the womb gets wider and wider to allow the head through. At this time, the membrane bag which surrounds the baby often breaks, releasing the liquid in which the baby has floated during its life in the womb.

The birth canal lies between the bones of the mother's pelvis. As the baby is forced through this bony space, and out between its mother's legs, it has to turn its head so that the

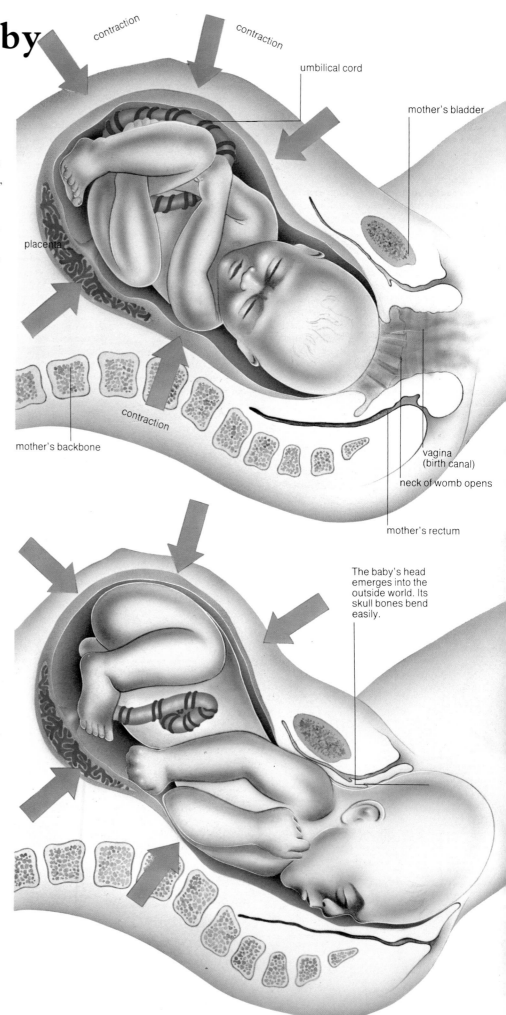

contraction

contraction

umbilical cord

mother's bladder

placenta

mother's backbone

contraction

vagina (birth canal)

neck of womb opens

mother's rectum

The baby's head emerges into the outside world. Its skull bones bend easily.

Left: The top diagram shows a baby about to be born. It has settled into its final head-down position low in its mother's abdomen. Its head is held and guided between her pelvic bones. The neck of her womb has opened ready for the baby's head to be pushed through. This pushing is done by the muscles of the womb. Their contractions have now become powerful and regular. The mother feels these contractions as 'labour pains'. In the lower diagram the baby is being born. Shortly before this stage of birth, the membraneous bag surrounding the baby would have burst under the pressure, releasing the watery liquid in which the baby had floated. This is called 'the breaking of the waters'. Now the baby's head is firmly thrust out of the womb and vagina into the outside world. The soft, unjoined bones of the skull bend easily as they pass along the birth canal. Soon, the baby will have emerged completely. Its umbilical cord will then be cut and tied off. The

process of birth will end when the placenta (or afterbirth) is delivered, a short while later.

Below left: For this mother and her baby, the great moment of birth has arrived. You can see from the mother's expression that giving birth is exhausting work. The baby's head has appeared, and the surgeon's hand is helping to guide the head and the rest of the baby's body, as the baby enters the outside world.

Below right: The newly-born baby is held up by its feet to be measured and weighed. A wrist band identifies the baby – who otherwise might get mixed up with some other baby born at about the same time in the hospital! The baby's umbilical cord, which carried its food and oxygen during its life in the womb, has been cut, and the cut end has been taped over temporarily. Soon, the stump of the cord will wither away, to form the baby's navel.

head (the widest part) can slip through the opening.

Luckily for the baby, its skull bones are still quite soft, and so can change shape easily. A newborn's skull is often lengthened, and its eyelids bruised, by its forceful entry into the outside world.

The baby now takes its first breath – although it may need a slap on the bottom to make it do so. Then, it utters its first sound – a healthy yell! As breath enters its lungs, the baby changes colour from white-ish to pink-ish. Soon, it will take its first meal at its mother's breast. But first it is cut free from its old food line – the tube (called the umbilical cord) leading to the placenta.

The last stage of its mother's labour is when she delivers, or gives birth to, the placenta. This happens about 20 minutes after the baby is born.

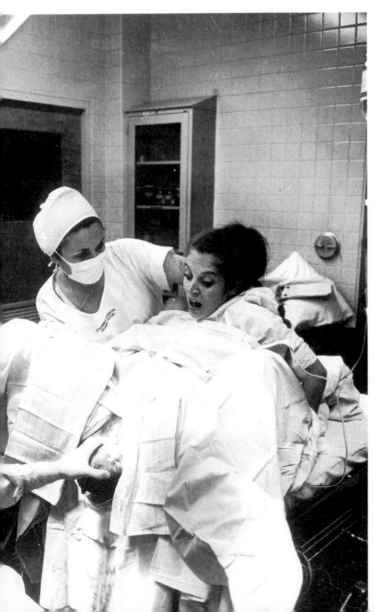

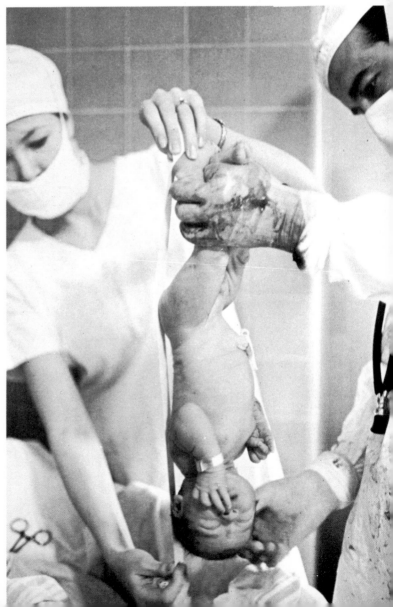

Fuel for living

You need food both for growth and for energy. In growth, food provides body weight. As a young person, you need food to provide the extra weight of your fast-growing body.

As an adult, you will have stopped growing up. But some parts of your body will continue to grow, as parts become used up. For example, dead skin cells are always being shed from the skin surface as new cells form underneath (see pages 108–9), and food provides all the substances needed for this new skin.

Both grown-up and growing-up persons need food for energy. This energy is used mainly by the muscles. You know that when you walk, run and jump, you use energy. All these activities use your skeletal muscles.

But you also use energy for such purposes as eating, digesting food and keeping warm. These activities use the smooth muscles of your digestive tube and your blood vessels.

High- and low-energy foods

Some foods provide more energy than others. High-energy foods include those having lots of fat or oil, such as butter, cream cheese, sausages, bacon and peanuts. Other high-energy foods are those with lots of starch or sugar, such as biscuits, bread, and currants.

Look for these foods in the table. You will see that all of them have a high energy value, measured in Calories. A Calorie is the amount of energy needed to heat up 1 litre of water by 1 degree Centigrade. It is the unit always used to measure the energy value of foods.

You need high-energy foods when you are exercising or doing hard physical work. Then, your body uses up these foods. But if you live a rather lazy life, without much exercise, then fatty, starchy and sweet foods (including sweets!) will make you overweight. Instead of 'burning up' these foods, your body turns them into fat.

You will then need to go on a diet. This need not be unpleasant, because you can still choose from a wide range of foods – those that are low-energy foods. Look for these in the table.

Right: The Calories shown in the table are units of heat – a form of energy. In the muscles, food energy is partly turned into heat.

Below: Whether you can be considered too fat, too thin or just right, depends on your physical body type. If you are an endomorph type, you will be naturally plump and may easily become overweight, or obese. If you are a mesomorph, you will tend to turn more of your food into muscles. But if you are an ectomorph, you will probably remain skinny. Most people are a mixture of these extreme body types.

ENERGY VALUE OF SOME COMMON FOODS	Calories in 100 grams of food
Bread and flour	
White bread	253
Wholemeal bread	241
Wheatgerm bread	237
White flour	348
Toast	299
Other cereal foods	
Rye crispbreads	318
Cream crackers	557
Cornflakes	365
Boiled rice	122
Sweet foods	
Mixed sweet biscuits	496
Plain chocolate	544
Milk chocolate	578
Honey	288
Jam	262
Marmalade	261
Sugar – white demerara	394
Ice cream	192
Black treacle	257
Fats and oils	
Butter	793
Margarine	793
Lard	894
Olive oil	899
Suet	894
Dairy produce	
Cheddar cheese	412
Cream cheese	813
Milk	65
Sweetened condensed whole milk	322
Egg	158
Double cream	449
Single cream	189
Meat and fish	
Fried back bacon	597
Grilled beef steak	304
Grilled lamb chop – lean and fat	500
Fried pork sausage	369
Fried sheep's kidney	199
Fried calf's liver	262
Roast beef – lean and fat	385
Roast lamb – lean and fat	292
Roast pork – lean and fat	455
Steamed cod	82
Fried cod	140
Soused herring	189
Grilled kipper	108
Salmon, canned	133
Fruit and vegetables	
Eating apples	45
Bananas	76
Grapes	60
Pears	41
Oranges	35
Dates	248
Dried sultanas, raisins, currants	248
Baked beans	92
Fresh peas – boiled	49
Dried peas – boiled	100
Boiled cabbage	8
Boiled potatoes	79
Potato crisps	559
Potato chips	236
Miscellaneous	
Peanuts	586
Cocoa	446

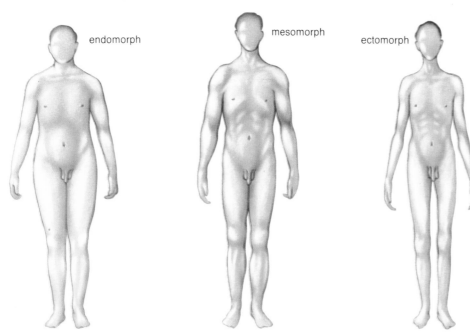

endomorph　　　mesomorph　　　ectomorph

Above: The small child's badly swollen stomach is caused by malnutrition, that is, too little of the right kinds of food.

Above right: Items of food in the type of well-balanced diet most people eat in advanced western countries.

Below: The graph shows how different physical activities need different amounts of energy. Cycling, for example, uses more energy than walking. For this reason a cyclist in a long-distance race will frequently take drinks of a fast-energy food, such as glucose. This gives him extra energy, to help him make sudden sprints.

They include fish (boiled or steamed) and many fruits and vegetables. You can eat lots of these without putting on weight.

Why do people get fat?

Some people put on weight much more easily than others. They always have to be careful what foods they eat. Other people are less likely to get fat on a normal diet, but they over-eat when they are feeling bored or depressed. Since these people usually do not take enough exercise, they too often get fat.

Too much body fat is harmful, causing disease of the heart and blood vessels. Too little of the right kinds of food can also be harmful. For example, lack of vitamins can cause unpleasant diseases.

Left: Rice with, and without, its coating or husk. The husk contains a vitamin that prevents beri-beri, an unpleasant disease which is common in poor countries.

Below: Daniel Lambert, a famous fat man of the 18th century.

ENERGY EXPENDITURE
WITH VARIOUS ACTIVITIES

walking up stairs — 900

skiing — 800

— 700

— 600

swimming — 500

cycling — 400

dancing

gardening — 300

sweeping — 200

walking slowly

— 100

sitting   standing

lying down

Calories expended per hour — 0

Keeping fit

Pages 120–21 showed that by taking enough exercise, you can avoid getting fat or overweight. This is one important way in which exercise is good for your health.

Exercise also keeps your muscles in good working order. This not only makes you strong, but because muscles are attached to bones, it also helps to keep your skeleton properly balanced. Good posture, while sitting, standing and walking, is also very important. Many older people have trouble with their joints. This can be caused, at least in part, by lack of exercise and poor posture earlier in life – bad habits that often last a lifetime.

Right: Some differences between a fit and an unfit person. The unfit person can suffer from the following: drooping head caused by poor posture (1); rounded shoulders and back pain (2); weak chest and lungs (3), also made worse by bad posture; weak heart and hardened arteries (4), which often come with age; 'middle-age spread' (5), made worse by a poorly balanced diet; weak limb muscles (6); stiff joints (7); and flat feet (8), common in overweight persons.

Below: Cross country running is a good way to keep fit. It develops leg and chest muscles and exercises the leg, arm and shoulder joints.

Types of exercise

We take exercise mainly in two ways. First, we can join in team sports and athletics. Second, we are usually obliged to attend school gym lessons for a certain part of each week, to take exercise with the rest of the class.

Adults also play sports, and they may go to keep-fit classes regularly to exercise their muscles. Or, they may prefer to take exercise by themselves, as when they jog, swim or do press-ups at regular intervals.

Another type of exercise now popular among adults is yoga. This is a posture form of exercise which keeps muscles and various other parts of the body in good balance. Yoga also teaches good breathing, which is important to health, and calmness of mind which is also important.

Exercise with care

For a healthy life, sufficient exercise is always necessary. However, it is also possible for exercise to cause injuries.

If you exercise too violently, as when running and jumping, you can pull a muscle or strain or dislocate a joint. Similar injuries can happen when you play team sports. One example is tennis elbow, a type of joint strain that is common among professional tennis players.

Soccer players, who often receive kicks, may suffer injuries to the knee joint which have to be mended by a surgical operation. Rugby players may even get kicked in the head, face or neck, receiving injuries which usually require a few stitches, but which may be much more serious.

In general, the younger and fitter you are, the less you have to worry about most of these injuries. In middle age, most people become less active and get somewhat heavier, slower and stiffer. This makes them liable to more permanent injury when they exercise unwisely.

Tips for a healthier life

A long and healthy life is made more likely by several things. A well-balanced diet, with plenty of the right foods, is important. So too is regular exercise, although this need not be very strenuous, particularly if you are already physically active in your everyday life.

To keep healthy, you must also avoid poisoning your body by smoking tobacco or taking other harmful drugs. Too much wine, spirits and beer can also be harmful.

Finally, a calm and happy mind is always healthier than a worried one.

Left: A runner's body uses up energy in many different ways.
1. His skin gives off heat. This is partly radiated away, and partly evaporated away with his sweat.
2. His face reddens because small blood vessels (capillaries) in his skin get wider, so bringing more blood near the surface of his body.
3. He breathes more deeply – up to 12 times the amount of air he needs while resting. This supplies his blood with the extra oxygen needed for 'burning up' more food in his tissues.
4. His heartbeat speeds up, to pump more blood around his body.
5. His muscles use up more food and oxygen. If they get short of either, he
is in trouble with cramps.
6. Some of his energy needs can be supplied by his liver, which contains a store of a quick-energy food.

Below: The dive-off at the start of a swimming race. These competing swimmers will be exercising violently throughout their race. For most people, swimming is a gentler form of exercise. It can develop many muscles of the body without overstraining any one of them.

Below right: For those who wish to take their daily exercise at home, a keep-fit machine, such as this bicycle, may be the answer.

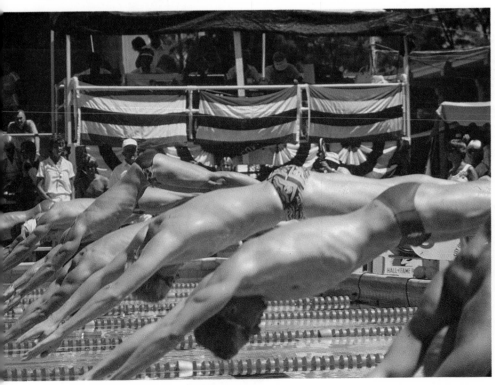

Sleep and other body rhythms

Each day of your life may seem different from the one before. No day repeats itself exactly – even when you are bored! But in many ways, processes in your body are repeated over and over again, throughout your life. That is to say, your body works in *rhythms*.

Some of these rhythms are so obvious that you do not think about them. For example, your heart beats regularly and more or less steadily. This is one of the faster rhythms of your body.

Other fast rhythms are those of your brain. These less familiar rhythms take the form of small electrical signals or brain waves. They can be measured on an EEG machine.

Much slower body rhythms are those which happen in a 24-hour cycle, as you wake and sleep. These are called *circadian* rhythms, after Latin words for 'cycle' and 'day'. Sleep itself is one such rhythm. So too is the temperature of your body and the activity of several of your glands. These all vary regularly in the 24-hour cycle of day and night.

Below: The scalp of this girl is connected by electrodes to an EEG machine. This machine records the electrical waves made by the girl's brain as she drowses and sleeps. Examples of these brain waves are shown on the right.

Your circadian rhythms can be upset when you take a long plane journey. This is usually known as jet lag. For example, you may take off at breakfast time, travel for 8 hours, and land, thousands of miles away, before lunch time! Your body does not know what time it is, and you may find that you fall asleep before bed time or feel hungry in the middle of the night.

The longest of body rhythms are concerned with sex and reproduction. When a girl reaches puberty, her body begins to prepare itself for bearing children. Among the first signs of this is *menstruation,* or loss of blood from the womb, which happens regularly about once every 4 weeks. This long rhythm will continue, except when she is pregnant, until middle age, when she becomes infertile.

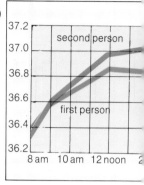

VARIATION IN TEMPERATURE (°C)

Above right: The body's temperature rhythm is one example of a circadian rhythm. Actual body temperatures vary slightly from person to person.

Below left: At all times your brain has an electrical activity. These brain waves, which can be recorded by an EEG machine, change as you pass from wakefulness to sleep.

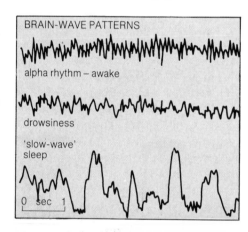

BRAIN-WAVE PATTERNS

alpha rhythm – awake

drowsiness

'slow-wave' sleep

0 sec 1

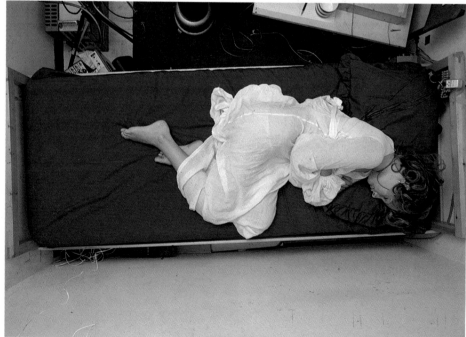

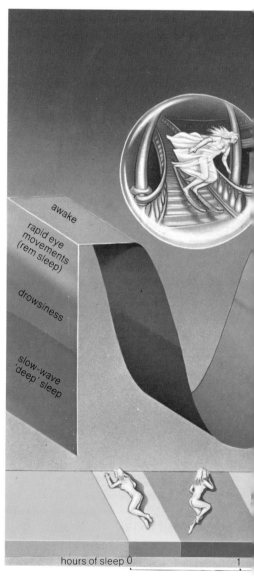

awake

rapid eye movements (rem sleep)

drowsiness

slow-wave 'deep' sleep

hours of sleep 0   1

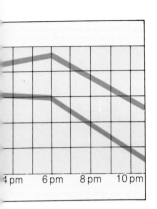

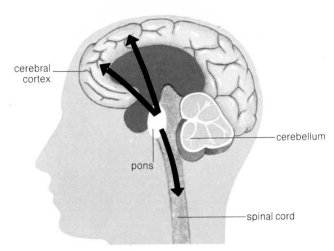

cerebral cortex

cerebellum

pons

spinal cord

Sleep and dreams

When you are asleep, your brain shows several types of rhythm. As you close your eyes, your brain waves settle down into a regular, fast rhythm, called *alpha waves*.

As you sink deeper into sleep, this fast rhythm changes to slower, less regular waves. Later still, your brain waves become fast again, and at the same time, your eyes make rapid movements. If you are woken up at this time, you will nearly always remember having a dream.

Why do we sleep, and why do we need to dream? The answers to these questions are not known exactly. If a person is deprived of sleep, he soon becomes ill. We seem to need sleep and dreams as vital 'time off' from the busy lives we lead while awake.

Above: While you sleep, nerve messages are sent out by a part of your brain called the pons. Some of these messages are carried to higher parts of your brain, where they help to produce dreams. Other messages are carried to your muscles. These prevent the muscles from carrying out the physical movements of your dreams.

Below: Your sleep gets regularly deeper and shallower. During the shallow periods, your closed eyes make rapid movements. If you are woken at these times, you always remember having a dream. Sometimes, as when you have a nightmare, you wake yourself up. During vivid dreams, your heart rate and blood pressure rise, and your brain waves also change.

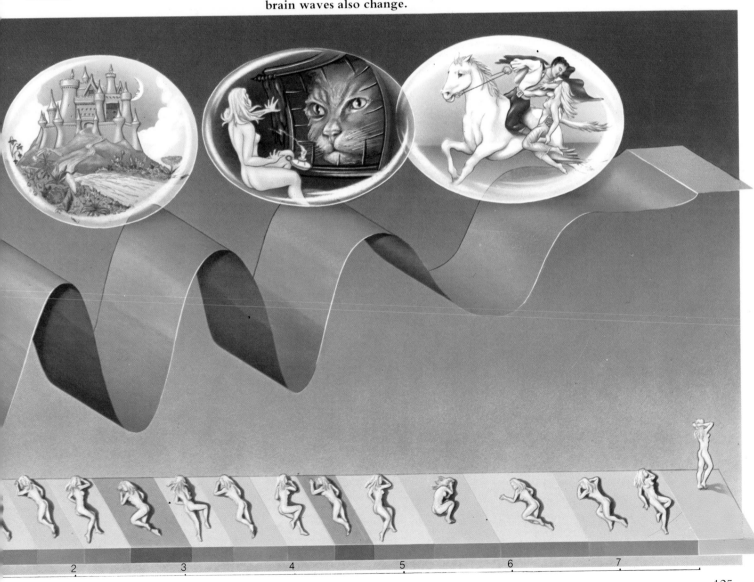

125

Elements, atoms and molecules

Everything around us is made up of particles called *atoms*. These are so tiny that a line of 50 million atoms side by side would be only about 1 centimetre long. Atoms themselves consist of even smaller particles called *neutrons*, *protons* and *electrons*. All the physical and chemical properties of a substance are determined by the structure of its atoms and the way they are combined and arranged within the material.

Any substance made up from atoms all containing the same number of protons is called an *element*. The number of protons in each atom is known as the *atomic number* of the element. This differs from one element to another. Atomic numbers range from 1 (hydrogen) to over 100. Carbon, for example, has an atomic number of 6, oxygen 8, and lead 82.

Protons have a positive electric charge. Electrons, however, have an equal, but opposite (negative) charge. Neutrons have no charge at all. As a normal atom has equal numbers of protons and electrons, their charges cancel exactly, so no overall charge can be detected. A substance can become charged only if the balance of protons and electrons is upset.

Although the atoms of any element all contain the same number of protons, different numbers of neutrons are usually present. In natural carbon, for example, most of the atoms contain six neutrons. But just over one per cent of the atoms each contain seven neutrons. These different atomic forms are called *isotopes*. The isotopes of an element all have the same chemical properties, although some of their physical properties differ.

The *mass number* of an atom is the total number of protons and neutrons it contains. Scientists use this number when referring to a particular isotope. Hence, the common natural isotope of carbon, which contains six protons and six neutrons, is known as carbon-12. And the rarer natural isotope, which contains an extra neutron, is called carbon-13. Besides the natural isotopes, various artificial isotopes can be produced by nuclear reactions – that is, reactions involving changes in the nucleus, or centre, of an atom. The

Right: A hydrogen atom has a nucleus of one proton, with one electron orbiting around it. Unlike other atoms, it has no neutrons in its nucleus. It is the smallest and simplest of all atoms.

Far right: In a neon atom, ten electrons orbit a nucleus of ten protons and ten neutrons. Two electrons move in an inner zone, or 'shell', and eight in an outer shell.

Below: Helium (left) has two protons, two neutrons and two electrons. Lithium-7 (right), an isotope of lithium, has three protons, four neutrons and three electrons.

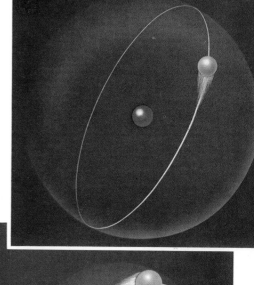

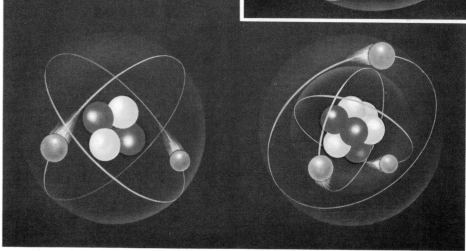

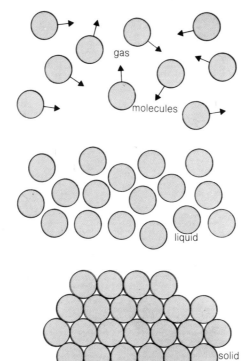

Left: The physical state of a substance depends on the kinetic energy (energy of movement) of its atoms or molecules. In a solid, the particles have low energy, and vibrate about fixed positions. In liquids, the particles have sufficient energy to move away from one another. This enables the liquid to change shape and hence to flow. Gases consist of high-energy particles that move about almost freely. So a gas will fill the whole space containing it.

gas

molecules

liquid

solid

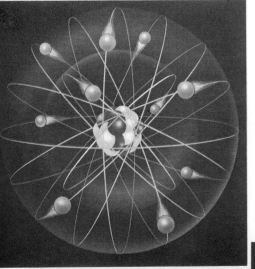

isotopes carbon-10, carbon-11, carbon-14 and carbon-15 can be produced in this way.

As its name implies, the mass number of an atom is an indication of its mass. For protons and neutrons are approximately equal in mass, while electrons are so light in comparison that they need not be included in the count. Whereas the mass number of an atom is always a whole number, the *atomic weight* of an element is not. The latter is the average mass number of a known mixture of isotopes, normally the mixture found in nature. Because natural carbon contains mostly carbon-12 atoms, with just a small proportion of carbon-13, the exact atomic weight of carbon works out to be 12.011.

Atoms usually occur in combinations called *molecules*. A hydrogen molecule, for example, consists of two hydrogen atoms joined together. Chemists represent such a molecule by the formula H_2. *Compounds* are substances whose molecules contain atoms of different elements. The compound water (H_2O) consists of hydrogen and oxygen.

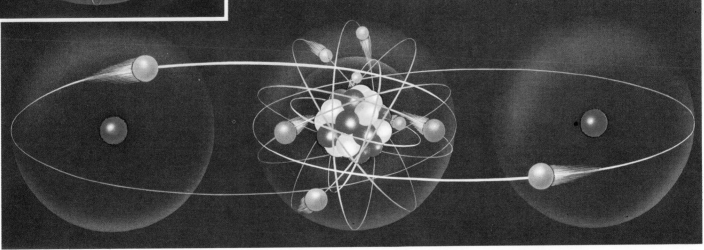

Right: Atoms of different elements can combine to form various compounds. Each of the compounds shown here consists of two or more of the elements shown on the far right of the diagram.

Below: Both diamond and graphite are forms of the element carbon. Although differing in physical properties, both give rise to the same chemical compounds. The two forms are called allotropes.

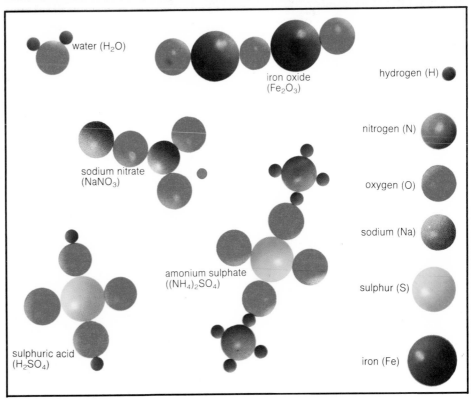

water (H_2O)

iron oxide (Fe_2O_3)

hydrogen (H)

nitrogen (N)

oxygen (O)

sodium nitrate ($NaNO_3$)

sodium (Na)

amonium sulphate ((NH_4)$_2SO_4$)

sulphur (S)

sulphuric acid (H_2SO_4)

iron (Fe)

What is electricity?

Thunder and lightning terrified people in ancient times. For the blinding flashes and powerful explosions seemed to be a warning that the gods were angry. But we now know that there is a simple explanation – electricity. Clouds sometimes become charged with electricity. This may flow to the ground, or to another cloud, as a giant spark. The fierce heat produced by the flash (lightning) causes nearby air to expand with explosive violence (thunder).

All the objects around us are made up of tiny particles called atoms (see pages 126–7). Each atom consists of smaller particles called neutrons, protons and electrons. Neutrons have no electrical charge, whereas protons and electrons have charges that are equal in strength, but opposite in effect. Normally, each atom contains an equal number of electrons and protons. So their charges cancel out and have no overall effect. However, if the balance of electrons and protons in an object is upset, then the object will show signs of being charged. To identify the two different kinds of charge, we say that electrons are negatively charged and protons are positively charged. Hence, an object with a negative charge is one that has

an excess of electrons. And a positively charged object has an excess of protons.

A rubber balloon can be charged simply by rubbing it with a piece of wool. When this is done, atoms in the rubber gain electrons from the wool. As a result, the balloon becomes negatively charged and the wool acquires a positive charge. Oppositely charged objects attract each other. So the wool will attract the balloon. But bodies with similar charges repel each other. This is why, if two balloons are charged in the same way, they will tend to move apart. One thing that all charged bodies have in common is that they will attract light, uncharged objects. For example, removing a long-playing record from its plastic cover charges it and causes it to attract nearby dust.

Under suitable conditions, a

Below left: Two uncharged, hanging metal balls (1) force each other apart when they are given strong, similar charges (2 and 3). Unlike charges force them together (4).

Below right: Ribbed glass insulators support high-voltage cables, preventing current flowing down the pylon. Hanging loops join one section of cable to the next.

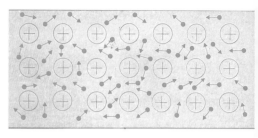

Above and below: In a metal, electrons normally move at random (above). But, when a voltage is applied across the metal (below), the electrons drift to the positively charged end. This flow is called an electric current.

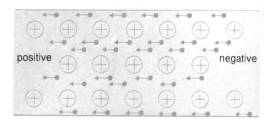

Above right: Lightning flashes are huge sparks produced by charged clouds. The sparks jump from the clouds to the ground (as here), or from one cloud to another.

Right: A plastic sheet was given a strong electric charge by firing electrons at it. Connecting the charged plastic to the ground caused this feathery spark pattern.

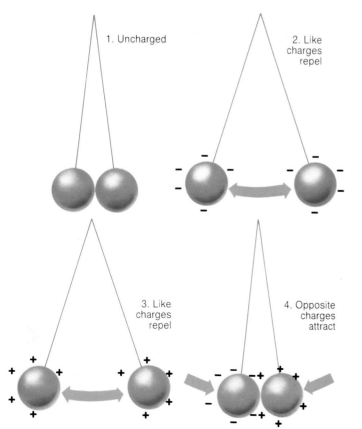

1. Uncharged

2. Like charges repel

3. Like charges repel

4. Opposite charges attract

Above: In a Wimshurst machine, glass discs are charged by friction. The charge is stored in capacitors.

charged body can retain its charge for ever. Because the electricity stays where it is, it is referred to as *static*. And the study of electricity in this state is called *electrostatics*.

In the 1700s, many scientists designed machines that produced electricity by rubbing one material against another. The electric charge obtained was often high enough to give a severe shock or cause a spectacular spark. Thus began the study of current electricity – electricity in motion. But a major problem prevented much progress being made. It took some time to build up a powerful charge on an object. And the whole charge would then be used up in a tiny fraction of a second to make one spark. However, some strange experiments by an Italian called Luigi Galvani led to a major breakthrough. Galvani experimented with dead frogs and found that he could make their legs twitch by touching them with two different metals. This discovery led directly to the invention of the electric cell, which could supply a steady current over a long period of time.

Portable electricity

Why do frogs' legs twitch when touched with two different metals? On discovering this effect in 1786, Galvani assumed that frogs contained electricity. For it was well known that electricity could make muscles move. Galvani's theory was wrong, but another Italian, Alessandro Volta, discovered the right answer in the 1790s. Electricity could be produced by a combination of two different metals and a solution that would conduct electricity. In Galvani's experiments, the frogs' legs had provided sufficient moisture. But Volta showed that a salt solution was more effective. Using one copper and one zinc disc, separated by a piece of cloth moistened in the solution, Volta made the first electric cell. This produced only a weak current. But he found he could obtain a stronger current by stacking several cells in a pile. Volta's pile formed the first practical battery – a source of portable electricity.

Since Volta's time, many different types of electric cell have been invented. But the basic principle of

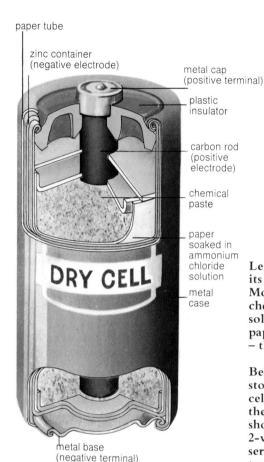

paper tube

zinc container (negative electrode)

metal cap (positive terminal)

plastic insulator

carbon rod (positive electrode)

chemical paste

paper soaked in ammonium chloride solution

metal case

DRY CELL

metal base (negative terminal)

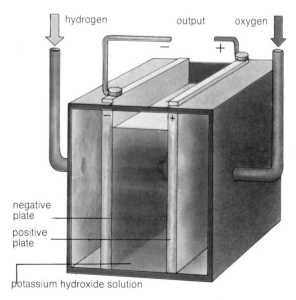

Left: A 'dry' cell is not really dry, but its liquid chemicals cannot be spilt. Most of the cell is filled with a damp, chemical paste. And the electrolyte solution is held in a layer of absorbent paper. Dry batteries are primary cells – they cannot be recharged.

Below left: An accumulator, or storage battery, contains secondary cells – cells that can be recharged after they have run down. The accumulator shown is a car battery containing six 2-volt cells. They are connected in series to produce 12 volts across the terminals.

Below: Like ordinary cells, the fuel cell converts chemical energy into electricity. But the fuel cell does not run down, for it has a constant supply of fuel. In the fuel cell shown, electricity is generated when oxygen and hydrogen fuel react with potassium hydroxide.

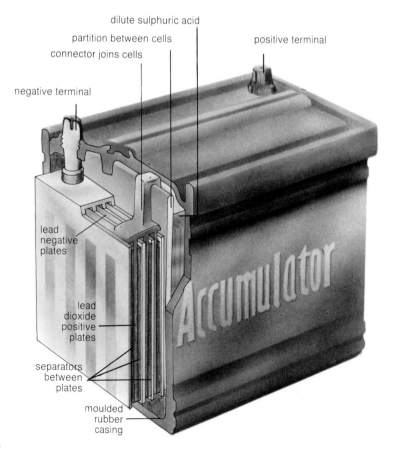

dilute sulphuric acid

partition between cells

connector joins cells

positive terminal

negative terminal

lead negative plates

lead dioxide positive plates

separators between plates

moulded rubber casing

Accumulator

hydrogen

output

oxygen

negative plate

positive plate

potassium hydroxide solution

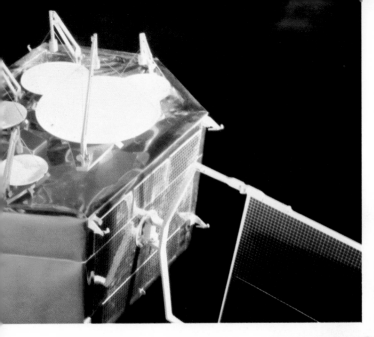

Above: A model of the European Orbital Test Satellite. The two wing-like structures are made up of solar panels. These are special batteries containing numerous tiny photoelectric cells. The cells convert the energy of sunlight into electricity, which is used to power the satellite's electrical and electronic equipment. The solar panels are mounted on adjustable frames that automatically turn towards the Sun. This ensures that the photoelectric cells receive maximum sunlight and, therefore, provide adequate electrical power for the satellite.

Below: The rate at which a faulty heart pumps blood can be regulated by an electronic pacemaker, which is implanted in the patient's chest. It generates electrical pulses that are used to stimulate the heart muscles. The pacemaker shown here is powered by five tiny, long-life mercury cells.

Above: In the future, most cars may run on electricity, like the experimental model shown above. Its electric motor is powered by a battery of fuel cells mounted under the bonnet.

Left: The tiny cells in this watch powers a circuit called a crystal oscillator. The oscillator generates accurately timed electrical signals that are used to control the watch movement.

operation is the same in each case. Current is made to flow between two *electrodes* composed of different materials. Separating the electrodes is a solution called the *electrolyte*. Even so-called 'dry' cells contain liquid in the form of a paste. When the two electrodes are connected together by a wire or other electrical conductor, reactions take place at the electrodes. In one electrode, a surplus of electrons is produced. These flow through the circuit, from one electrode to the other, as a current.

When a cell is in use, the reactions that take place in it gradually change the nature of the electrolyte. Eventually the cell 'runs out' and can no longer supply a useful current. In the case of *primary cells,* the only remedy is to replace them. But *secondary cells* can be recharged. By connecting them to a suitable mains unit, electricity is passed through them for a period of several hours. This has the effect of reversing the chemical reactions that have taken place during use. As a result, the electrolyte is gradually restored to its original state.

When this process has been completed, the cell is ready for use once more.

Secondary cells are also known as storage cells or *accumulators*. A typical car battery consists of six such cells connected together. The car's generator normally keeps the battery well charged while the car is moving along. But sometimes the battery may need overnight charging from a special mains unit.

Most car batteries are of the lead–acid type. They have electrodes of lead and lead dioxide in an electrolyte of dilute sulphuric acid. Some portable electrical equipment, such as flashguns and razors, contains small nickel–cadmium storage cells. One electrode consists of nickel compounds, while the other is made of cadmium. The electrolyte is an alkali called potassium hydroxide. Equipment powered by these nickel–cadmium cells often has a tiny built-in mains unit. This makes recharging simple. If the device is left connected to the mains overnight, by morning the cells will be fully charged and ready to use once more.

Electricity and magnetism

Soon after the electric cell had been invented, many interesting discoveries were made about electricity. For having a source of steady current available, scientists were able to carry out many new experiments. The most important of these discoveries was *electromagnetism* – the production of magnetism by an electric current. This led directly to the invention of the electric motor, generator and transformer – three important devices in the modern world.

Electromagnetism was discovered by chance in 1819 by a Danish physicist called Hans Christian Oersted. He was, at the time, demonstrating that a wire carrying a strong current becomes hot. Each time he switched on the current, he found that a nearby compass needle deflected from the north–south direction.

Hearing of Oersted's discovery, others investigated the strange effect and found ways of increasing the magnetism produced by an electric

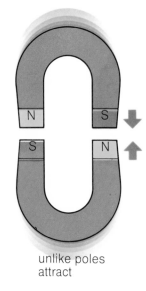

unlike poles attract

Above: Lines of magnetic force can be revealed by sprinkling iron filings around magnets. The bar magnet (right) and electromagnet (left) produce similar patterns.

Below: Powerful electromagnets are used to lift heavy loads of iron or steel. The magnet shown here is suspended from a crane and can lift loads weighing up to 2 tonnes.

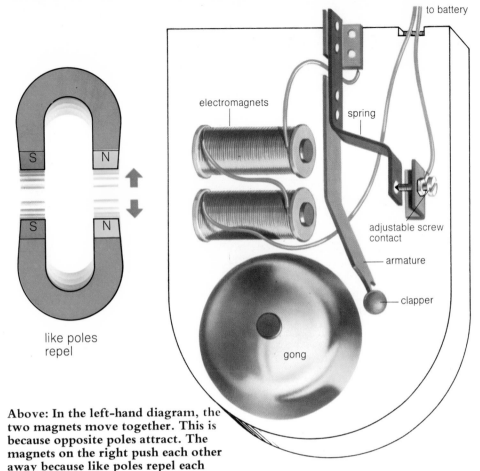

electromagnets

spring

to battery

adjustable screw contact

armature

clapper

gong

S N

S N

like poles repel

Above: In the left-hand diagram, the two magnets move together. This is because opposite poles attract. The magnets on the right push each other away because like poles repel each other.

Above right: The diagram shows how an electric bell works. Current flows through the electromagnets via the contact and spring. The electromagnets attract the armature, so that the clapper strikes the gong. The spring no longer touches the contact. So the current ceases, and the armature returns to its former position. The whole process repeats rapidly, causing continuous ringing.

Below: Electricity can be induced in a coil by moving a magnet through it (left). In a transformer (right), current in one coil magnetizes the core and induces electricity in a second coil.

current. A loop of wire was found to be much more effective than a straight wire, and two loops were even better than one. Coils with numerous turns were then constructed, and the magnetic effect was further increased by winding the coils on bars of soft iron. By the 1820s, electromagnets capable of lifting loads of over 1 tonne had been built.

As Oersted discovered when his compass needle deflected, electricity can cause movement. In 1821, an English scientist called Michael Faraday found a way of using

electricity to cause *continuous* movement. In fact, he had invented the first electric motor. Ten years later, he demonstrated the opposite effect – how movement could produce electricity. Moving a permanent magnet near a coil caused a current to flow through the wire. This discovery led to the development of powerful electricity generators.

Today, the principles of electromagnetism are used in many devices. For example, in the *dynamic* microphone, sound waves make a coil vibrate near a magnet. Any relative movement between a coil and a magnet generates electricity. In the microphone, the movement corresponds to the sound waves being picked up. Hence the current generated is a replica (copy) of the sound waves.

The electric signals from a microphone can be amplified (strengthened) and then reproduced as sound by a loudspeaker. They can also be recorded on magnetic tape. In a tape recorder, the amplified signals are passed through an electromagnet called the tape head. As the signals fed to the head vary, the magnetism of the head varies too. A tape, coated with a substance that can be magnetized, passes the head at constant speed. As a result, it acquires a magnetic pattern corresponding to the sound waves picked up by the microphone. On replaying the tape, its varying magnetization generates corresponding electrical signals in the tape head. These signals are amplified and then reproduced on a loudspeaker.

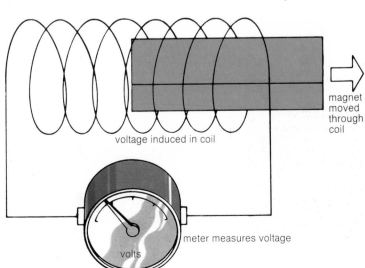

voltage induced in coil

magnet moved through coil

meter measures voltage

volts

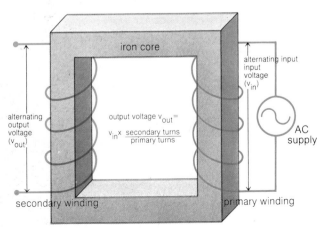

iron core

alternating input voltage (v_{in})

alternating output voltage (v_{out})

output voltage $v_{out} =$

$v_{in} \times \dfrac{\text{secondary turns}}{\text{primary turns}}$

AC supply

secondary winding

primary winding

What is light?

We are able to see an object when it emits (gives out) light, reflects light or modifies (changes) light passing through it. The Sun is a giant light source – you can see it because it emits light. But you are reading this book by means of the light reflected from its pages. Many different colours can be seen in the illustrations. This means that the apparently colourless light falling on the book must, in fact, contain all these colours. Otherwise the book could not reflect them. Further evidence that white light is a mixture of colours can be seen when looking at stained glass windows lit from behind by the Sun. Each colour is produced by a stain that allows light of that colour to pass through easily. Other colours are mainly absorbed. This property of absorption determines the character of colouring agents. Red dye, ink or paint, for example, absorbs most light except red.

The first person to discover how colours are produced was the English scientist Sir Isaac Newton. In the

1660s, he found that a glass prism could split up a beam of sunlight into a band of colours. He called this band the *spectrum* of light.

A prism bends light rays passing through it. But it bends different colours by different amounts. This is why the various colours present in white light are separated from one another on passing through a prism. As Newton discovered, a second prism can be arranged to bend the coloured rays back to form a single beam of white light again.

Another device that *refracts,* or bends, light is the lens. But lenses have curved surfaces and are generally designed to form images or to concentrate beams of light. The magnifying glass, for example, is a simple lens used to form an enlarged image of a nearby object.

The nature of light

Light is a form of energy consisting of electrical and magnetic vibrations. These can travel as waves through any transparent medium, including empty space. Some other forms of energy, such as radio waves and ultra-violet waves, are electromagnetic too. They travel through space at the same speed as light. But, in other ways, they have quite different properties.

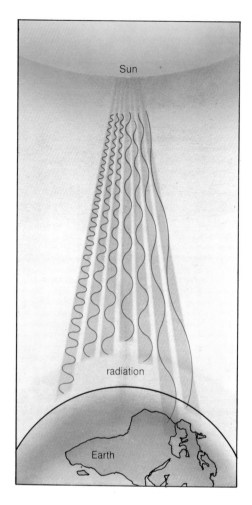

Below left: A glass prism splits a beam of white light into its coloured components.

Below: The diagram shows how each colour is bent by a different amount.

Below: When a smooth surface reflects light (1), the angle of reflection equals the angle of incidence. A rough surface scatters light (2). Light is refracted (bent) on entering and leaving a glass block (3).

Right: A rainbow is formed when raindrops split sunlight into a spectrum of colours. The colours of the rainbow are red, orange, yellow, green, blue, indigo and violet.

134

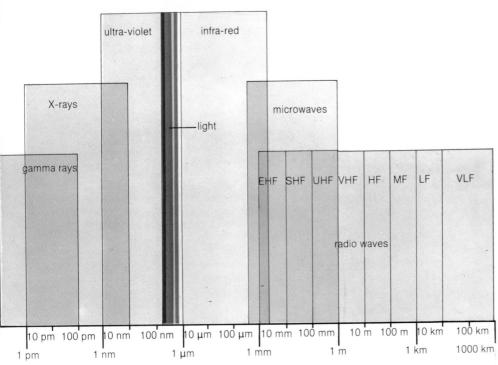

ultra-violet
infra-red
X-rays
light
microwaves
gamma rays
EHF SHF UHF VHF HF MF LF VLF
radio waves

| 10 pm | 100 pm | 10 nm | 100 nm | 10 μm | 100 μm | 10 mm | 100 mm | 10 m | 100 m | 10 km | 100 km |
| 1 pm | | 1 nm | | 1 μm | | 1 mm | | 1 m | | 1 km | 1000 km |

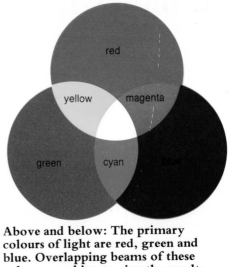

red
yellow   magenta
green   cyan   blue

Above and below: The primary colours of light are red, green and blue. Overlapping beams of these colours combine to give the results shown above. Below are shown the results of mixing paints of the primary pigment colours – magenta, cyan and yellow. (These are sometimes wrongly referred to as red, blue and yellow.)

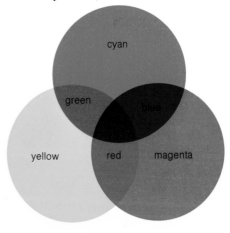

cyan
green   blue
yellow   red   magenta

Above left: The Sun emits energy in the form of waves. These include gamma rays, X-rays, ultra-violet rays, visible light, infra-red (heat) radiation and radio waves. They are all forms of electromagnetic radiation, which travels through space at just under 300,000 kilometres per second. The basic difference between these forms of radiation is in their wavelength – the distance between the start of one wave and the next. Without heat and light from the Sun there would be no life on Earth. But most of the harmful radiation from the Sun is filtered out by the atmosphere.

Above: The whole range of electromagnetic waves is called the electromagnetic spectrum. The spectrum of light occupies just one small part of the electromagnetic spectrum, but it is the only part we can see. The diagram shows the wavelengths of various types of radiation. The wavelengths are expressed in fractions and multiples of one metre (m).

One picometre	(pm)	$= 1/10^{12}$	metre
One nanometre	(nm)	$= 1/10^{9}$	metre
One micrometre	(μm)	$= 1/10^{6}$	metre
One millimetre	(mm)	$= 1/10^{3}$	metre
One kilometre	(km)	$= 10^{3}$	metres

The main difference between the various kinds of electromagnetic waves is their *wavelength*. This is the distance between the start of one wave and the next. Wavelength depends on *frequency* – the rate at which the waves are produced. For if they are emitted extremely quickly, they will follow close behind one another. In other words, a high frequency corresponds to a short wavelength, and vice versa.

In the visible spectrum, the red rays have the lowest frequency, while the violet rays have the highest frequency. Intermediate frequencies correspond to other distinctive colours, such as blue and yellow. But it can be misleading to associate a definite frequency with any observed colour. Yellow, for example, may be produced by a single frequency, or by a mixture of those corresponding to red and green.

Microscopes and telescopes

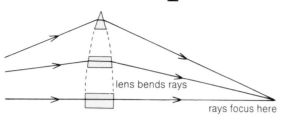
lens bends rays

rays focus here

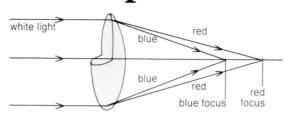
white light

blue

red

blue

red

blue focus

red focus

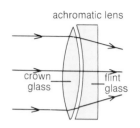
achromatic lens

crown glass

flint glass

Lenses

The fact that a curved, transparent object can be used to magnify must have been discovered soon after the invention of glass. For a round glass container filled with water produces an enlarged (although distorted) image of an object placed behind it. In this way, the curved body of water acts as a crude lens. More convenient magnifying lenses were later made from solid lumps of glass with polished curved surfaces. These were specially shaped in order to minimize distortion. Besides producing enlarged images of objects close to it, the magnifying glass could also bring the Sun's rays to a focus. This enabled it to be used as a burning glass for making fire. Focusing the heat rays on to flammable material soon produced a flame.

Both these properties are due to the fact that light bends when it passes from one type of transparent substance to another, unless it strikes the new substance exactly at right-angles to its

surface. A line drawn at right-angles to a surface is called a *normal*. Light travelling from air to glass bends towards the normal. And, on passing from glass to air, it bends away from the normal. This simple rule enables us to work out the paths of light rays through lenses so that we can see how images are formed.

The magnifying glass has two convex (bulging) surfaces and is an example of a simple *converging* lens. This means that it can bend light rays

Far right: A compound microscope with twin eyepieces to reduce eyestrain. Rotating the turret changes the objective lens and alters the magnification.

Right: The refracting telescope has an objective lens. The reflecting telescope uses a concave mirror instead. A plane mirror reflects the rays into the eyepiece.

Below: A terrestrial telescope with a cut-away diagram showing the path of light rays passing through its various parts.

Above: A convex lens acts as a series of prisms (left). Rays passing through the lens are bent unless they strike the surface at right-angles. The point at which the rays come together is called the focus. Like a prism, a lens bends different colours by different amounts (centre). So the two colours focus at different points. This is why many simple lenses produce unwanted colour fringes. In the 'achromatic' lens (right), a second lens component eliminates fringing by bending the coloured rays and causing them to recombine with each other.

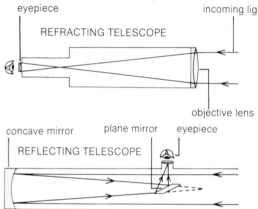
eyepiece

incoming light

REFRACTING TELESCOPE

objective lens

concave mirror

plane mirror

eyepiece

REFLECTING TELESCOPE

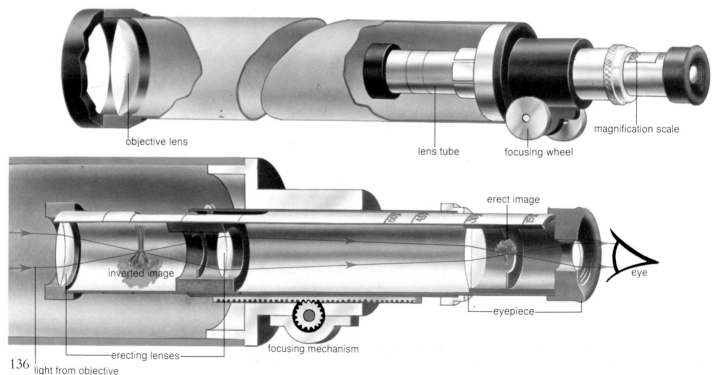
objective lens

lens tube

focusing wheel

magnification scale

erect image

eye

inverted image

eyepiece

erecting lenses

focusing mechanism

light from objective

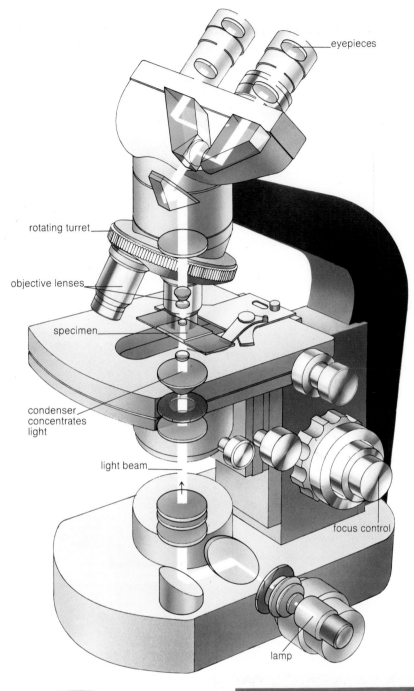

eyepieces

rotating turret

objective lenses

specimen

condenser
concentrates
light

light beam

focus control

lamp

together so that they meet at a point. A lens with concave (hollowed) surfaces has the opposite effect. It spreads rays out and is described as *diverging*. Other lenses may have one flat and one curved surface, or one convex and one concave surface. But they can all be put into the categories 'converging' or 'diverging'. Various combinations of lenses are used in microscopes, telescopes and other optical instruments.

Microscopes

Scientists refer to the magnifying glass as a simple microscope. Although a useful device, it cannot produce great magnification without distortion. Compound microscopes use two lenses, or sets of lenses, and are capable of much higher magnification. In its simplest form, the compound microscope consists of two converging lenses mounted a short distance apart. Their separation can be adjusted in order to bring the specimen being studied into sharp focus. The lens nearest the specimen is called the *objective,* and the lens nearest the eye is called the ocular, or *eyepiece*. The objective forms an enlarged image of the specimen, and this image is further enlarged by the eyepiece. Many compound microscopes are fitted with several objectives on a rotating mount called a *turret*. Each objective provides a different amount of magnification. The turret is turned until the required objective is positioned over the specimen.

Telescopes

A pair of converging lenses can be used to form a simple *refracting* telescope. The image produced will be inverted, but this does not matter when looking at the stars or planets. However, for general use, an upright image is required. In some telescopes, extra lenses are used to make the final image upright. Another method is to use a diverging lens for the eyepiece. A *reflecting* telescope has a curved mirror instead of an objective lens.

Left: Microscopic algae, and the equipment used to photograph them.

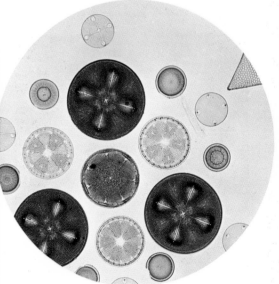

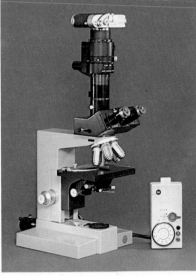

Instant pictures

In most cameras, a lens forms an image on a film coated with light-sensitive chemicals. After exposure, the film has to be developed and fixed. These processes make the recorded images visible and permanent. Some film produces transparencies for use in a viewer or projector. Other films produce negatives – images in which the dark and light areas are reversed. These are used to make prints. This stage again reverses the light values, so that they are correct in the final pictures. Most people have their films developed and printed by one of the large firms specializing in this work. So there is usually a delay of at least a day before the photographs are available. But users of Polaroid cameras can see their pictures within seconds, as rapid automatic processing is carried out immediately after each picture is taken.

Instant-print photography was invented by Dr Edwin Land of the Polaroid Corporation, and it became generally available in 1947. Land's camera worked like any other, but the film was quite different. This was supplied as separate sheets in a pack, which also contained the developing and fixing agents and the printing paper. The prints appeared within 1 minute. Today's Polaroid cameras produce black-and-white prints in about 15 seconds.

With ordinary film, exposure to light causes chemical changes to take place in the film's coating of silver salts. On development to the negative stage, the changed regions show up as dark patches. Unexposed silver salts are then dissolved away by the fixer, so that the film is no longer sensitive to light. In the Polaroid process, the unexposed silver salts are transferred to the print material, where they are used to form an image. Thus the regions of the film corresponding to darkness form a dark image. So an ordinary (positive) print is produced without using the negative image formed on the film. (With some film packs, the negatives can be retained for the production of further prints on ordinary photographic paper.)

In the simplest black-and-white Polaroid system, a sheet of film is pulled out of the camera after exposure. With it comes a sheet of printing paper. Removing these from the camera bursts a sachet of mixed developer and fixer. Rollers in the camera spread the solutions over the film and paper, causing processing to start. Exposed silver salts in the film are quickly converted to a negative image by the developer. So they are unaffected by the fixer, which dissolves only the exposed salts. These are deposited on the paper, which is almost in contact with the film, and soon form an image.

The colour Polaroid process, although more complicated, works in a similar way.

Below: After removal from the camera, a Polaroid colour print develops automatically. Within minutes, the image acquires full density and colour.

Bottom left: Coloured rays show the path of light through a Polaroid SX-70 camera. A mirror on the left reflects the rays onto the film.

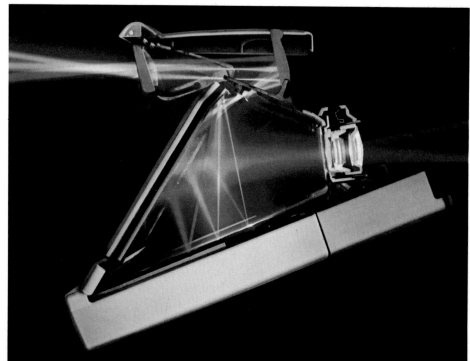

Right: An undeveloped print emerges from a Polaroid SX-70 camera. The print passes out between two rollers, turned by an electric motor. Pressure from the rollers bursts a pod of alkaline solution. This spreads through the paper and activates a developer already present. A thin battery in the film pack provides power for the motor.

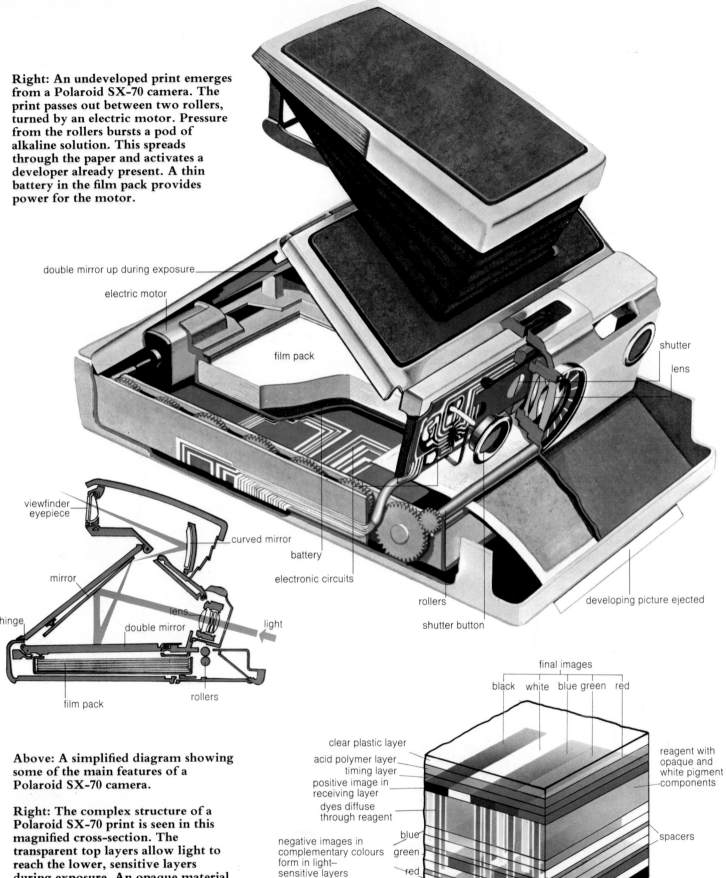

double mirror up during exposure

electric motor

film pack

shutter

lens

viewfinder eyepiece

curved mirror

battery

electronic circuits

mirror

hinge

lens

double mirror

light

film pack

rollers

rollers

shutter button

developing picture ejected

Above: A simplified diagram showing some of the main features of a Polaroid SX-70 camera.

Right: The complex structure of a Polaroid SX-70 print is seen in this magnified cross-section. The transparent top layers allow light to reach the lower, sensitive layers during exposure. An opaque material spreads to protect these light-sensitive layers during development. An alkali activates developing agents, which produce three separate colour negative images. Unused dyes diffuse through the opaque layer and form a single, positive image above it.

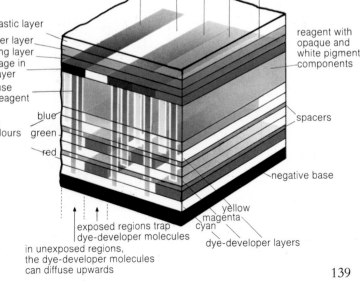

final images

black   white   blue   green   red

clear plastic layer

acid polymer layer

timing layer

positive image in receiving layer

dyes diffuse through reagent

reagent with opaque and white pigment components

negative images in complementary colours form in light–sensitive layers

blue

green

red

spacers

negative base

yellow

magenta

cyan

dye-developer layers

exposed regions trap dye-developer molecules

in unexposed regions, the dye-developer molecules can diffuse upwards

139

What is sound?

Sound, like many other kinds of energy, travels in the form of waves. Heat, light and radio waves are different types of electromagnetic radiation that can travel through empty space. But sound needs a *medium* (substance) through which to travel. We hear sounds by means of vibrations that pass through the air around us.

Any source of sound, such as a voice or a musical instrument, produces vibrations. For example, plucking a guitar string tuned to the note middle C makes it vibrate 256 times per second. This rate, called the *frequency* of the vibration, is written as

Right: A sound wave can be represented by a graph showing how the intensity (strength) varies with time. The graphs here represent sounds of three frequencies. At a frequency of 20 hertz (20 cycles per second), one complete wave occurs in 1/20 second. At a frequency of 50 hertz, there are two and a half waves and, at 100 hertz, five waves in this same period.

Below left: Sound from one tuning fork causes an identical one to vibrate too.

Below right: Sound waves in a tube set up permanent 'standing wave' patterns. Powder settles at the nodes – points of zero vibration.

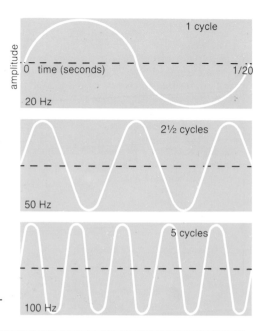

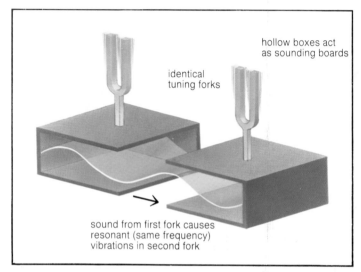

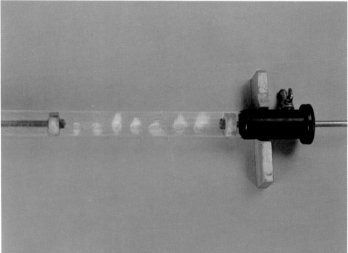

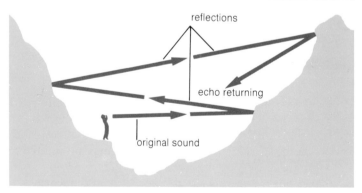

Above: Sound is reflected by large, hard surfaces. The reflected sound reaches the ear later than the direct sound, as it has farther to travel. So it gives rise to an echo.

Left: A new tractor undergoes special safety tests to check that its noise level is not excessive. The tests are carried out in a special chamber – a room lined with blocks of sound-absorbent material.

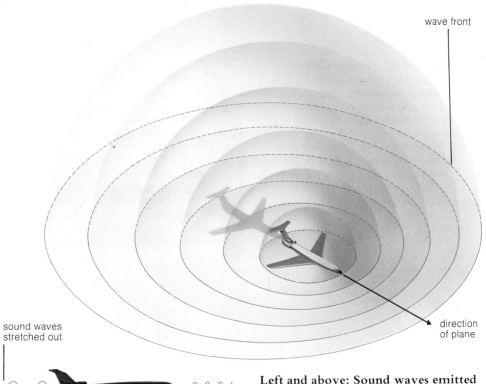

wave front

sound waves stretched out

actual frequency of plane's sound

sound waves compressed

direction of plane

Left and above: Sound waves emitted by a plane are compressed in front of it and stretched out behind. This makes the pitch sound higher when a plane is approaching, and lower when it is moving away (Doppler effect).

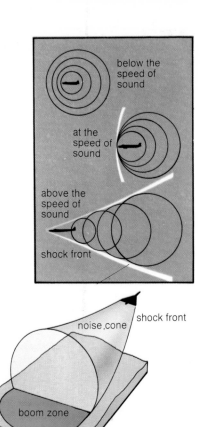

below the speed of sound

at the speed of sound

above the speed of sound

shock front

noise cone

shock front

boom zone

Above: The faster an aircraft travels, the more it compresses the air in front of it. An aircraft moving at the speed of sound builds up a high-pressure disturbance called a shock front. Alarming bangs called sonic booms are heard within the boom zone as the shock front passes over the ground. Sometimes the shock causes windows to shatter.

Left: Concorde, the Anglo–French supersonic airliner, can reach a speed of 2400 kilometres per hour. This is known as Mach 2, which means twice the speed of sound.

256 cycles per second (c/s) or 256 hertz (Hz). (The hertz is a unit equal to 1 cycle per second.) The vibrating string makes the surrounding air vibrate at the same frequency. And the vibrating air makes our ear-drums vibrate too. Our hearing mechanism converts these vibrations into electric signals that our brain interprets as sounds (see page 92 for more information on hearing).

Vibrations in the air will give rise to the sensation of sound only if their frequency falls within certain limits. For a person with extremely good hearing, this range extends from about 20 hertz to nearly 20,000 hertz. But it varies from person to person. And the

ear's sensitivity to high-frequency sounds decreases as the person gets older. Hence, a high-pitched whistle may be audible to a child, but not to its parents.

Frequencies above the range audible to humans are described as *ultrasonic*, meaning 'beyond sound'. But even ultrasonic vibrations may be audible to some animals. Dogs, for example, can be called by means of a 'silent' whistle. This works like an ordinary whistle, but produces ultrasonic vibrations.

Sound travels at different speeds through different materials. In air at 0°C, the speed of sound is nearly 1200 kilometres per hour. When a source

emits sound, the surrounding air is alternatively compressed and then rarified (stretched out). These disturbances spread out from the source, rather like the ripples formed when a stone is dropped into water. In both cases, the medium itself does not move bodily. It merely transmits the disturbances by vibrating. Whereas ripples on water are the result of an up-and-down movement, sound is transmitted by means of vibrations that occur along its direction of travel. However, sound can be represented by various wave-like graphs showing, for example, how the air pressure varies with time.

Musical instruments

Anything capable of making the air vibrate at an audible frequency can be used as a musical instrument. Many instruments have stretched strings that vibrate if struck, plucked or bowed. In wind instruments, the player makes a column of air vibrate, often using a thin reed in the mouthpiece.

However the vibrations are produced, it is their frequency that determines the pitch of the note. On a piano, for example, the lowest note has a frequency of 27.5 hertz and is known as bottom A. At the other end of the keyboard is top C, with a frequency of 4186 hertz. Notes of different frequencies are obtained by using strings of different length, thickness and tension. A short, fine, tight string vibrates much faster than one that is long, thick and slack. Small hammers strike the strings to make them vibrate when the keys are pressed. Guitars and violins have few strings, but each one can be made to vibrate at various frequencies. This is usually done by pressing the string against a fingerboard, thus restricting the length free to vibrate.

In a slide trombone, the column of air in the curved tube is set in vibration when the musician blows through the mouthpiece. Moving the slider of the instrument alters the length of the vibrating column. This has the same result as altering the effective length of a guitar or violin string. If the length of the column is decreased, the frequency of the vibrations increases, resulting in a note of higher pitch. In a trumpet, the length of the vibrating air column can be altered by means of three valves. And, with both these wind instruments, different notes can be produced also by blowing into the mouthpiece in different ways.

When we talk of a note of a certain frequency, we mean that this is the main, or *fundamental*, frequency present. But other frequencies, called *harmonics,* are normally present too. These are lower in amplitude (strength) than the fundamental, and higher in frequency. Harmonics occur because several different kinds of vibrations are set up when an instrument is played. For example, when a string vibrates, it produces a

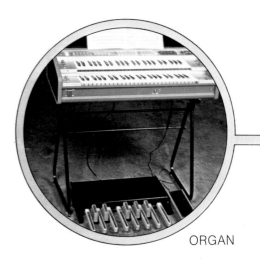

ORGAN

BASSOON

fundamental 1

2nd harmonic

3rd harmonic

4th harmonic

6th harmonic

2

whole string vibrates at fundamental frequency

string

'stopped' halfway vibrates at twice the frequency

3

string vibrating at fundamental and second harmonic

a 4

b

c = a + b

addition of fundamental and second harmonic waves

142

**Left: 1. A stretched string can vibrate in many ways. As the ends are fixed, these are nodes (points of no vibration). The string may vibrate simply, with one antinode (point of maximum vibration) between the two nodes. This type of vibration produces a note called the fundamental. More complex vibrations, with more nodes and antinodes, give rise to sounds called harmonics. These are higher in frequency than the fundamental.
2. Halving the length of a string doubles the frequency of its fundamental note. Its pitch rises by one octave on the musical scale.
3. In practice, a vibrating string**

**produces a fundamental and several harmonic frequencies. For simplicity, only the fundamental and second harmonic are shown here.
4. Fundamental (a) and second harmonic (b) combined give a complex sound wave (c).**

Above right: The frequency ranges covered by a variety of musical instruments.

Below right: A synthesizer for generating electronic music.

Below: Vibration patterns in the air column of a wind instrument.

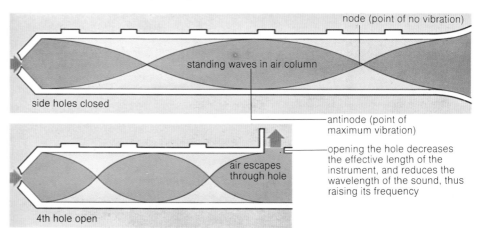

node (point of no vibration)

standing waves in air column

side holes closed

antinode (point of maximum vibration)

air escapes through hole

4th hole open

opening the hole decreases the effective length of the instrument, and reduces the wavelength of the sound, thus raising its frequency

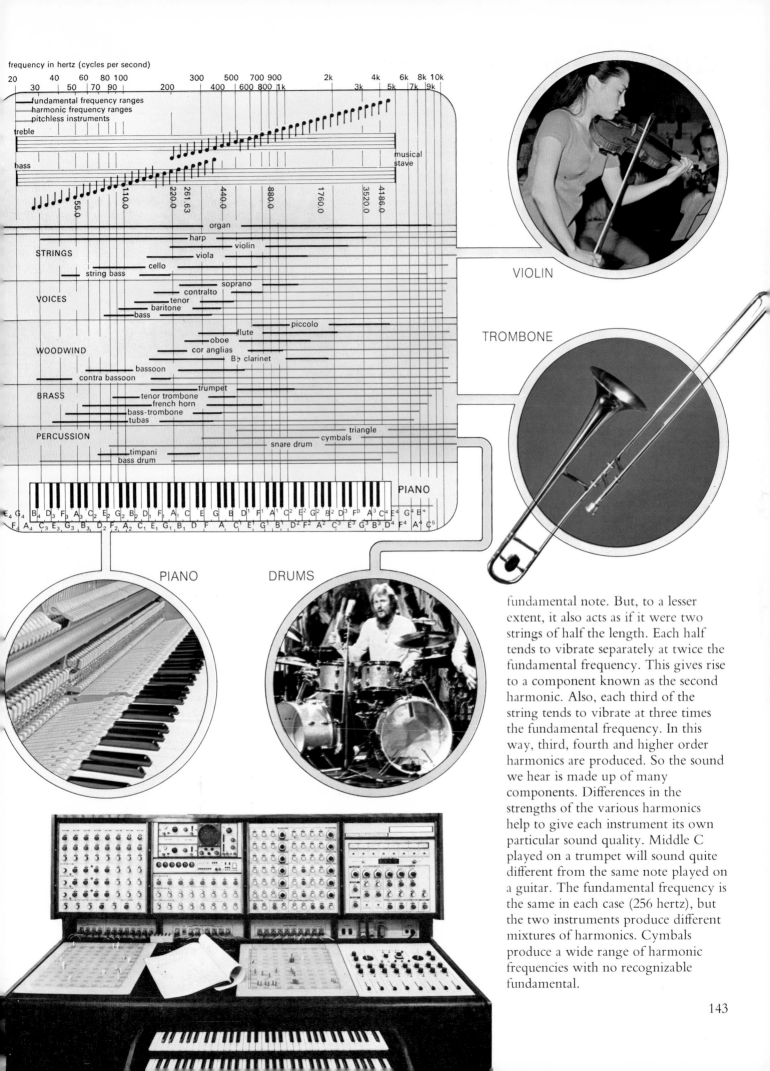

fundamental note. But, to a lesser extent, it also acts as if it were two strings of half the length. Each half tends to vibrate separately at twice the fundamental frequency. This gives rise to a component known as the second harmonic. Also, each third of the string tends to vibrate at three times the fundamental frequency. In this way, third, fourth and higher order harmonics are produced. So the sound we hear is made up of many components. Differences in the strengths of the various harmonics help to give each instrument its own particular sound quality. Middle C played on a trumpet will sound quite different from the same note played on a guitar. The fundamental frequency is the same in each case (256 hertz), but the two instruments produce different mixtures of harmonics. Cymbals produce a wide range of harmonic frequencies with no recognizable fundamental.

143

Measuring time

For thousands of years, man has used the Sun, Moon and stars as natural time-keepers. A year is the time taken for the Earth to orbit the Sun. Throughout this period, different stars become visible in the sky, and the weather undergoes seasonal changes. These regular cycles of events enabled ancient civilizations to associate the appearance of certain stars with the approach of a new season. The changing phases of the Moon provided the basis on which the year was divided into months. But the most important of all astronomical events has always been the Earth's rotation on its axis. This makes the Sun appear to rise and set, and thus marks the passing of each day.

The ancient Egyptians found a way of using the movement of the Sun across the sky to divide the day into smaller periods of time. Their invention, called a shadow clock, or sundial, consisted of a rod placed upright in the ground. As the Sun moved round, it caused the shadow of the rod to change length and position throughout the day. The moving shadow passed over a scale marked on the ground. This enabled the time of day to be seen immediately. Another time-keeping device used by the Egyptians was the clepsydra, or water clock. In its simplest form, this was a vessel containing water, which leaked slowly from a hole in the bottom. The water level indicated the time on a scale marked down the inside of the container.

The sandglass used the trickling of sand through a narrow-waisted glass container to indicate the passing of a fixed period of time. This device is still used in some kitchens as a 3-minute timer for boiling eggs. Originally, the sandglass was used for timing longer periods, often a half-hour. A candle with notches marking off the hours was once widely used for time-keeping, but it tended to be rather inaccurate. Variations in the wax, the length of wick, or in the draught could affect the rate of burning.

Purely mechanical clocks first appeared around 1300 in Europe. They were driven by means of a

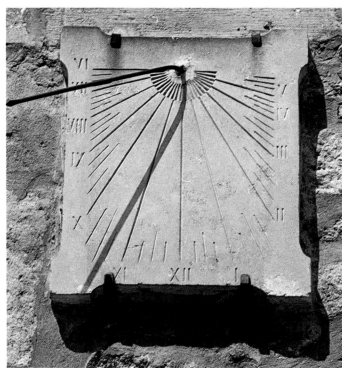

Above: A rod called a gnomon casts a shadow on the face of the sundial. The engraved Roman numerals indicate the time of day.

falling weight. This was attached to a rope coiled around a cylinder. As the weight descended, it pulled the rope and turned the cylinder. A device called an *escapement* was used to control the speed at which the cylinder turned. The escapement consisted of a bar that rocked to and fro to interrupt the rotation of a toothed wheel. Spring-driven clocks were introduced in the 1400s. A major improvement came in the 1650s, when Christiaan Huygens discovered how to use a pendulum to regulate the rocking of the escapement, thus making clocks more accurate. Some 20 years later, Huygens invented the hairspring and balance-wheel system of regulation as an alternative to the pendulum. It then became possible to make fairly reliable watches and portable clocks.

Recent developments in the field of microelectronics have led to the production of watches accurate to within a few seconds per month. Many show the day and date and have alarm and stop-watch facilities. Some watches even indicate the day in a choice of several languages.

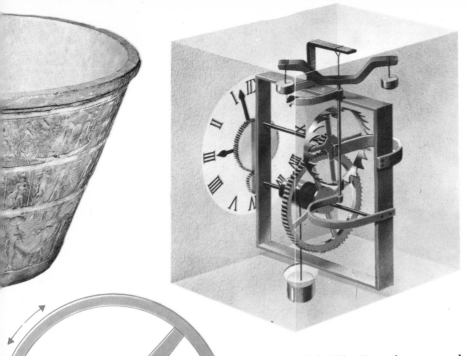

Above left: The Egyptian water clock was simply a container with a hole in the bottom. As water slowly leaked through the hole, the level in the container indicated the time that had elapsed.

Above: A falling weight drives this model of an early mechanical clock. Two weights at the top swing back and forth to regulate the mechanism.

Left: The to-and-fro movements of a balance wheel control a lever escapement. The rocking pallets allow the escape wheel to turn tooth by tooth.

Far left: Galileo's pendulum escapement mechanism of the 1580s.

Above: A clock at the old observatory in Greenwich, England, displays Greenwich Mean Time on its 24-hour dial. This is the local time on the line of 0° longitude, which passes through the observatory. Greenwich Mean Time is also Western Europe's standard time.

Below left: The interior of a mechanical watch, showing the high-precision cog wheels and other parts. The balance wheel and speed adjustment lever are at the bottom.

Below: This electronic digital watch generates accurate timing pulses and counts them. The count is usually displayed in figures as hours and minutes (this one is switched off).

balance wheel

pallets

escape wheel

What is energy?

To a scientist, energy means the ability to do work, such as lifting a weight. In everyday conversation, people often use the word 'power' to mean the same as energy. But power is actually the *rate* at which work is done or energy used up.

Energy can take many forms including mechanical, chemical, electrical, radiant and nuclear energy. Radiant energy includes heat, light, radio waves and other forms of radiation in the electromagnetic spectrum (see page 135).

Sometimes we use energy in the form that we find it. Water mills and windmills use the mechanical energy of water or wind in motion to perform mechanical tasks, such as

grinding corn (see page 148). But often, we convert one form of energy into another that suits our needs. In a steam engine, the chemical energy of coal or other fuel is converted into mechanical energy. Burning the fuel changes the chemical energy into heat. This converts water to steam, which pushes pistons or turns a turbine. In a torch, chemical energy in the cells is converted into electricity, which the bulb then converts to light.

One of the main problems concerned with energy is the reduction of energy losses. In the case of a steam engine, heat energy is lost in the smoke and gases given off by the burning fuel. And the pipes carrying the steam also lose heat.

Below: Electricity is produced by the conversion of other forms of energy. In a hydroelectric scheme, water trapped behind a dam (1) is piped to a water turbine (2). The water turns the turbine, which is coupled to an electricity generator. Coal (3) is transported to conventional power stations, where it is burnt to heat water. The steam produced turns steam turbines coupled to generators (4). In a nuclear power station (5), heat produced by nuclear reactions is used to turn water to steam. This drives turbines, as in a conventional power station. We use electricity by converting it to other forms of energy. In the home, various devices convert electricity into other forms of energy. For example, light bulbs (6) produce light, electric fires (7) produce heat, motors (8) produce motion and bells (9) produce a sound.

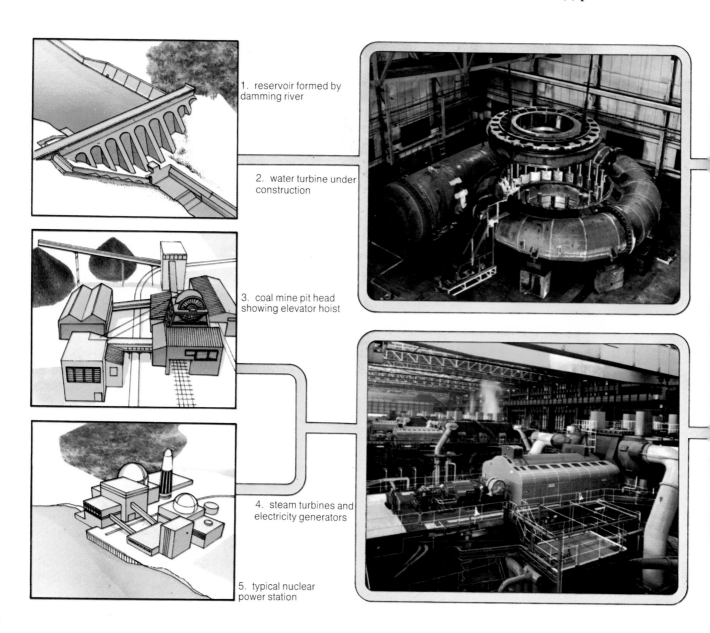

1. reservoir formed by damming river

2. water turbine under construction

3. coal mine pit head showing elevator hoist

4. steam turbines and electricity generators

5. typical nuclear power station

ALARM CLOCK

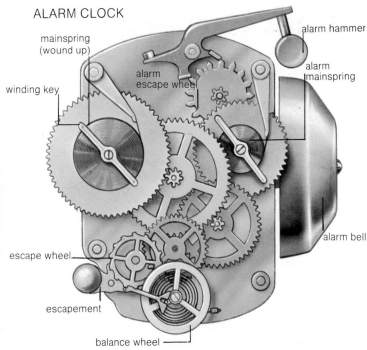

mainspring (wound up)

winding key

alarm escape wheel

alarm hammer

alarm mainspring

alarm bell

escape wheel

escapement

balance wheel

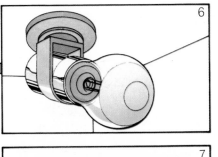

6

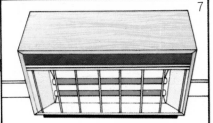

7

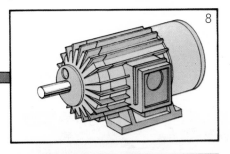

8

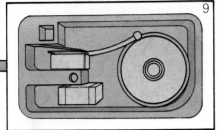

9

Above left: On sudden braking, a dummy's kinetic energy (energy of motion) shoots it through the car's windscreen.

Above right: We use energy to wind a mechanical clock. This energy is stored in the clock's mainspring as potential energy. As the spring slowly unwinds, it drives the mechanism to turn the hands and trigger the alarm. During this process, the potential energy is converted into kinetic energy. When the alarm goes off, some of the kinetic energy is transmitted to the air in the form of sound waves.

Right: Detonating explosives suddenly converts their chemical energy into heat, light, sound and the mechanical energy of the blast.

Further energy losses occur because of friction in the moving parts of the engine. Some of the mechanical energy produced is used up in overcoming this friction, which occurs wherever one surface moves against another. This wasted energy is converted into heat. Frictional losses are reduced by using special bearings and oil, graphite or other lubricants. But there is no way that friction can be completely eliminated. In a torch, a great proportion of energy is wasted. This is because an electric bulb produces much more heat than light.

Energy is expensive, and some supplies are short. So it is important to reduce losses as much as possible. This means increasing *efficiency* – the ratio of useful energy to total energy supplied. If an engine uses 100 joules (energy units) in the form of fuel to do 60 joules of mechanical work, then the engine is said to have an efficiency of 60 per cent. The other 40 joules of energy supplied are used up in heat and frictional losses. Thus all the energy supplied is accounted for. This is in accordance with the energy conservation law, which states that energy cannot be created or destroyed. Nuclear reactions produce heat energy by destroying mass (see page 152). But the conservation law still holds, as mass can be thought of as a special form of energy.

147

Alternative technology

At one time, water-wheels and windmills provided most of the energy in industry. Then, in the late 1700s, came the age of steam. Eventually, electric motors were introduced, and the use of steam engines in factories gradually declined. Nowadays, electrical power is widely used. But steam engines are still of great importance, because most of our electricity generators are turned by steam turbines.

Producing the vast amounts of steam required for modern power stations is now very expensive, as fuel costs have risen sharply in recent years. The main fuels are oil, coal and gas. These were formed millions of years ago, and no one knows for certain how much is left. Scientists predict that supplies of oil will run out in about 30 years. And the development of alternatives, such as nuclear power stations, has not been as rapid as had once been expected.

For these reasons, scientists have been taking a fresh look at ways of using the wind and water to provide us with energy. Other alternative energy sources under study include the Sun, heat from within the Earth, and gas made from dung. These sources will become increasingly important as our coal, oil and natural gas supplies gradually run out.

In many parts of the world, windmills of various traditional designs are still used for grinding corn, but the application of modern technology has resulted in several new designs. One type consists of a tall, vertical pole with two narrow metal strips forming arcs between the top and bottom. The strips rotate horizontally when the wind blows.

Many new ways have been found to utilise energy from the movement of water, although the traditional water-wheel is still used in some places. In hydroelectric schemes, a river is dammed, and the water made to flow through a pipe leading to a turbine. The water pushes on the turbine's curved blades, making them turn. Then it flows out through another pipe to continue its journey down to the sea. A generator, rotated

Above: In these modern windmills, the wheels are fixed to tail vanes. Wind pressure on the sides of the vanes swings them, so that the wheels are always kept facing into the wind. The wheels spin when the wind catches their many angled blades. Although generally called windmills, the machines shown here are not true mills – they are actually wind-driven water pumps.

Below: Some villages in China use a waste digester to produce methane gas. The gas is given off when waste matter undergoes a chemical process called fermentation. The gas produced is stored in a tank, from which it is piped to various appliances. When fermentation has ended, and no more gas is produced the waste material is removed from the digester and used to fertilize the land.

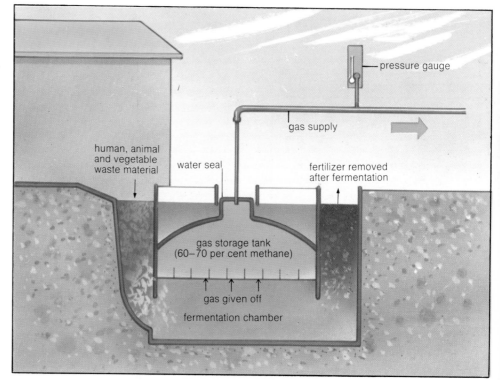

Above: A solar furnace uses the Sun's radiant energy to produce extremely high temperatures. This solar furnace is at Odeillo, in France. The huge concave mirror reflects the Sun's rays so that they converge to a focal point in the tower opposite. As the area of the mirror is large, it concentrates a great deal of heat energy at the focal point. Within minutes the furnace reaches a temperature of 3300°C.

Below: 'Nodding ducks', designed to harness the energy of waves. As the 'ducks' bob up and down, they operate a pump. This sends water to turn a turbine linked to an electricity generator.

Bottom: Geothermal energy is heat within the Earth. This New Zealand power station uses geothermal energy obtained from hot springs.

Above: The water-wheel was a most important source of power from Roman times until the development of efficient steam engines in the late 1700s. As with windmills, the rotating wheel can be used to turn many kinds of machinery. The water-wheel shown in this picture is at a mill in Arkansas, in the United States. It is an overshot wheel, being turned by water passing over it.

Above: As the cost of fuel continues to rise, houses with solar panels in the roof are becoming more common. Millions are in use in Japan, Israel and Australia. Radiation from the Sun heats the panels and the water that flows through them. The absorbed heat can be transferred to the domestic hot water system. So less fuel is used in bringing the supply up to the required temperature.

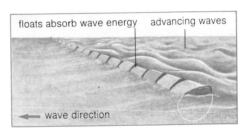

floats absorb wave energy   advancing waves

← wave direction

by the turbine, provides a cheap supply of electricity. Such schemes are efficient only in regions where the flow of water is reliable and fast.

Electricity can also be generated using the movement of sea water. One way is to use the rise and fall of the tides to make water flow through turbines. Alternatively, the energy of waves can be used to make special floats bob up and down. This action is used to pump water through turbines.

Solar energy – radiation from the Sun – can be used in many ways. Artificial satellites use banks of photoelectric cells to convert sunlight directly into electricity. Some modern houses have special roof panels in which flowing water is heated by the Sun. This heat is then transferred to the hot water tank of a central heating system, from which it can be released through radiators.

Power from petrol

The petrol engine is a form of *internal combustion engine*. This means that fuel burns inside it. Other such engines include the diesel engine and the rocket. A petrol engine works on the same basic principle as a cannon. In a cannon, exploding gunpowder forces a cannon-ball out of the barrel. In the petrol engine, a mixture of petrol vapour and air explodes, forcing a piston along a cylinder; but there the comparison ends. For the petrol engine is required to operate

continuously. So the piston has to be returned to its original position for the process to be repeated, and its back-and-forth movements have to be converted into smooth, rotary motion.

In a petrol engine, the following sequence of events takes place. The fuel and air are mixed in a device called a *carburettor*, and the mixture is drawn into a cylinder. A piston then moves up the cylinder. Some external force has to be applied in order for these initial stages to take place.

Petrol-powered lawn mowers are usually started by jerking a cord, whereas cars have an electric motor to start the engine turning. As the piston moves up, it compresses the fuel–air mixture in the cylinder. Then, as the piston nears the top of the cylinder, the mixture is ignited by means of an electric spark. This jumps between the two electrodes of a device called a *sparking plug,* which is screwed into the top of the cylinder. The gases expand explosively, driving the piston

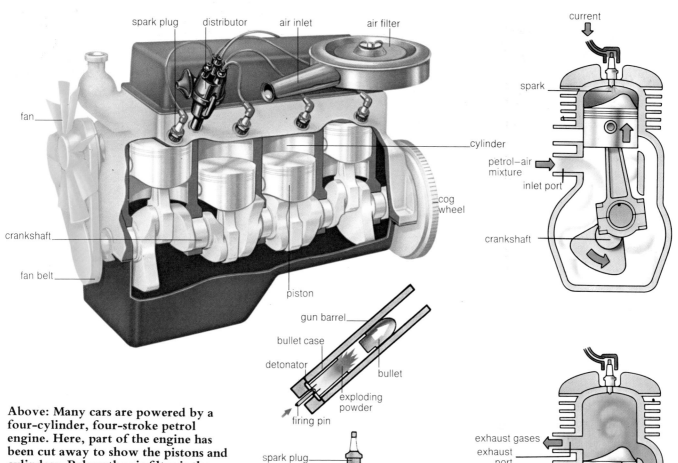

Above: Many cars are powered by a four-cylinder, four-stroke petrol engine. Here, part of the engine has been cut away to show the pistons and cylinders. Below the air filter is the carburettor (not shown), in which air and petrol vapour are combined. The explosive mixture goes to the cylinders, where it is ignited by sparks. The distributor sends pulses of electricity to each spark plug in turn, so that the cylinders fire one after another. Each time a cylinder fires, it forces the piston down, and this turns the crankshaft. The turning power produced is transmitted to the front or rear wheels via the large cog wheel. A fan belt links the crankshaft to a fan, which prevents the engine overheating.

Above: When a gun is fired, the explosion forces the bullet along the barrel. In the same way, an explosion forces the piston of an engine along its cylinder.

Above: In a two-stroke engine, compressed fuel is ignited while more fuel is drawn in. Then the exhaust gases are expelled and replaced by fresh fuel.

back down the cylinder. Then the waste gases are expelled, more fuel–air mixture is taken in, and the process begins again.

The thrust of the piston is used to turn a rod called the *crankshaft*. And a heavy flywheel fixed to the crankshaft keeps it turning after the piston has reached the end of its downward stroke. This continued movement pushes the piston back to its former position at the top of the cylinder. As the engine turns, it operates a switch so that the spark that ignites the fuel is produced at precisely the right moment in the cycle.

In some petrol engines, fuel is ignited each time the piston approaches the top of its cylinder. This system of operation is called the two-stroke cycle, as each ignition of fuel results in the piston moving down and then up again. Two-stroke engines are used in some small cars, motorcycles and lawn mowers. Although relatively cheap, two-stroke engines tend to waste fuel. So most cars have engines designed to work on the more efficient four-stroke cycle. Four piston movements follow the ignition of the fuel. These are known as the *power, exhaust, intake* and *compression* strokes. (The diagrams show what happens in each stroke.) Most petrol engines have several pistons in separate cylinders. The cylinders are fired in quick succession so that each piston in turn drives the crankshaft. This system results in smooth running.

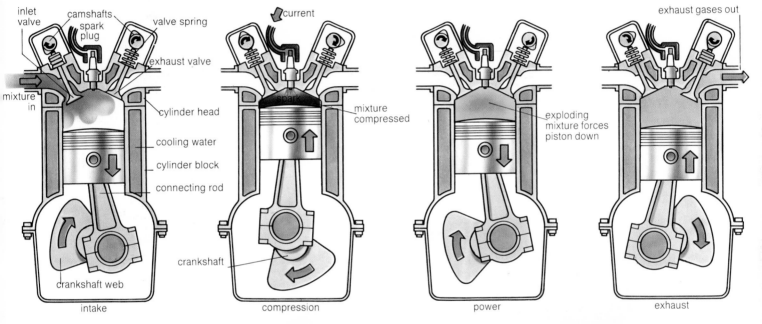

intake   compression   power   exhaust

Above: On starting a four-stroke engine, an electric motor turns the crankshaft. This starts the pistons moving up and down. On the *intake* **stroke of a piston, it moves down, and an inlet valve opens to let in some fuel. On the** *compression* **stroke, the valve closes and the piston moves up. It compresses the fuel at the top of the cylinder. A spark then ignites the fuel, causing an explosion, which forces the piston down again. During this** *power* **stroke, the piston turns the crankshaft. The final stage is the** *exhaust* **stroke, when the piston rises to force the waste gases out through the open exhaust valve. The four-stroke cycle repeats at high speed, with each piston in turn powering the crankshaft.**

Right: Racing motorcycles show the high power that can be produced by fairly small, light petrol engines. Some of them can reach speeds up to 300 kilometres per hour.

Power from the atom

Nuclear, or atomic, energy means energy obtained from the nucleus at the centre of an atom (see page 126). Under certain conditions, some of this energy may be released in a nuclear reaction. Chemical reactions involve changes in the electrons that orbit the nuclei of atoms, but, in nuclear reactions, changes occur within the nuclei. During a nuclear reaction, mass can be destroyed. In other words, the mass of the products formed may be less than the mass of the original substances. The lost mass is converted into energy, according to Einstein's mass–energy equation: $E = mc^2$. In this equation, E represents the energy in joules produced when a mass of m kilograms is destroyed. And the symbol c represents the speed of light in metres per second. Light travels extremely quickly, so c is large (about 300 million) and c^2 is enormous (about 90,000 million million). So, even if only a small mass is destroyed, the term mc^2 can still be very large. This means that a great deal of energy can be produced by destroying a small mass. For example, destroying a mass of 1 kilogram would produce sufficient energy to run a three-bar (3

kilowatt) electric fire for almost one million years.

We have all seen the results of nuclear reactions. For it is by means of such reactions that the Sun and other stars produce the vast amounts of light and other radiation that they emit. If they were just burning, they would soon go out.

Fission and fusion reactions

Nuclear energy may be produced by two types of nuclear reaction – fission and fusion. Fission reactions involve the splitting of heavy atomic nuclei to form lighter ones. This is sometimes referred to as 'splitting the atom'. In fusion reactions, light nuclei are fused together to make heavier ones.

Fuels suitable for fission reactions

Right: An enormous mushroom-shaped cloud forms as an experimental British atomic bomb is exploded at Maralinga, Australia.

Below left: In a nuclear reactor, the moderator slows down neutrons to a speed at which they react readily with the fuel. Control rods regulate the reaction speed. The heat given off is absorbed by the coolant and used to make steam.

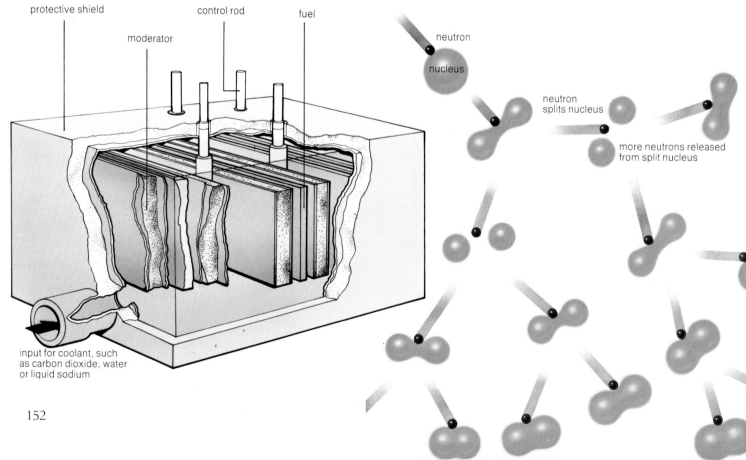

protective shield

moderator

control rod

fuel

neutron

nucleus

neutron splits nucleus

more neutrons released from split nucleus

input for coolant, such as carbon dioxide, water or liquid sodium

include the radioactive isotopes uranium-235 and plutonium-239 (see page 126). If the fuel is bombarded with neutrons, the atoms split in two and release more neutrons. Under suitable conditions, these can strike other atoms to cause further splitting and the release of even more neutrons. In this way, the reactions can spread throughout the fuel. This process is called a chain reaction. As mass is destroyed each time an atom is split, a great amount of energy is released.

Fission chain reactions are used to produce heat energy in nuclear power stations. The reaction rate is very carefully controlled. The heat produced is used to change water to steam, which then turns steam turbines linked to electricity generators.

If a chain reaction occurs rapidly, there is a devasting explosion caused by the sudden release of a large amount of energy. This principle is used in the atomic bomb.

The Sun produces its energy by means of fusion reactions, in which hydrogen atoms are converted into helium. A rapid reaction of this kind is used in the hydrogen bomb. To produce useful energy, the reaction must occur at a temperature of many millions of degrees Centigrade. This presents many technical problems that need to be solved before fusion reactions can be used in power stations. Fusion would be preferred to fission because the hydrogen fuel is plentiful. And, unlike the radioactive products from fission reactions, helium is harmless.

Above: A heavily shielded flask containing radioactive nuclear fuel.

Left: In a nuclear fission chain reaction, neutrons split the nuclei of fuel atoms to release nuclear energy. More neutrons are released, and these split other nuclei.

Below: A 500-megawatt nuclear power station at Trawsfynydd, Wales.

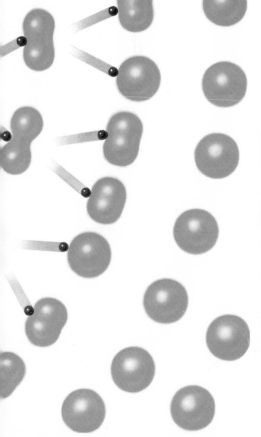

Iron and steel

Iron is a very useful metal. It can be made into heavy, strong structures such as bridges and machines. It can also be used to make equally strong, but smaller objects such as tools, and strong, flexible objects such as springs and wire.

But pure iron is not very hard. It is made much harder and tougher when it is mixed, or *alloyed,* with small amounts of carbon and other elements. Then, it is known as steel. All the objects mentioned above are usually made of steel.

Iron

Iron is found naturally, in the Earth's crust, in the form of *iron ores*. These are often near the surface, and are scraped up by giant excavating

Right and below: Iron is made by smelting it from iron ore. Smelting is carried out in a blast furnace, which towers 70 metres high. The furnace is fed, or charged, with iron ore mixed with other substances, at its narrow upper end. The charge melts in a fierce blast of hot air. It turns into hot gas, waste slag and molten iron. The hot gas is used to heat the air blast. The slag is removed at a slag notch.

Below right: The molten iron is tapped off at a tap hole.

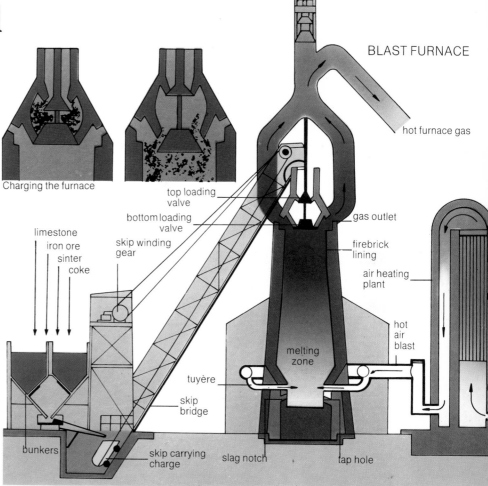

BLAST FURNACE

Charging the furnace

hot furnace gas

top loading valve

bottom loading valve

gas outlet

limestone
iron ore
sinter
coke

skip winding gear

firebrick lining

air heating plant

hot air blast

melting zone

tuyère

skip bridge

bunkers

skip carrying charge

slag notch

tap hole

154

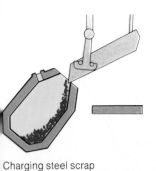
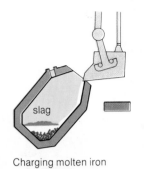
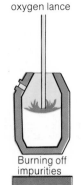
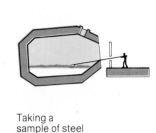

oxygen lance

Charging steel scrap

slag

Charging molten iron

Burning off impurities

Taking a sample of steel

Tapping off the steel

Tapping off the slag

Above: Steel is made by heating scrap steel, together with molten iron from the blast furnace. These are first charged into the steel-making furnace. All impurities are then burned off, or converted into slag, by oxygen. The oxygen is fed into the furnace through a long lance. The furnace is tilted sideways to pour off the molten steel and the slag.

Right: A steel-making furnace called a basic oxygen converter. The hood removes dangerous fumes.

Left: The steel-making furnace, shown in the tilted position, while it is being charged with molten iron.

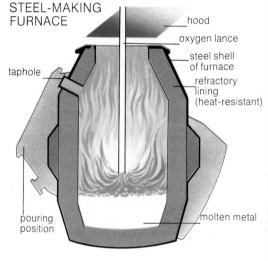

STEEL-MAKING FURNACE

hood

oxygen lance

steel shell of furnace

refractory lining (heat-resistant)

taphole

pouring position

molten metal

machines. They contain iron together with large amounts of such other elements as oxygen, carbon and sulphur. Iron is extracted from its ores in a process called *smelting*. This is carried out in a large tower-like building called a *blast furnace*. In the furnace, iron ores are heated to a very high temperature, together with coke (carbon) and limestone. A blast of air through the molten mass helps to remove the unwanted elements. Molten iron is run off at the bottom of the furnace. This iron, called *pig iron*, is then used to make steel.

Steel-making
Most of the world's steel is made in huge vessels called *basic oxygen converters*. Molten pig iron, together with scrap iron, is heated in the converter by blasts of oxygen. This also removes unwanted carbon, as well as such impurities as sulphur, phosphorus and silicon. Any remaining impurities are removed as a solid waste material, called *slag*. Molten steel is then poured or run off

from the furnace, cooled, and cast into steel slabs.

Most steel is used by industry as steel sheet. This is made by rolling steel slabs, while hot, in a giant machine. This sheet can be rolled again, but while cold, to make thinner sheet suitable for such purposes as making food cans.

The strength and hardness of different steels are controlled by the amount of carbon they contain. Mild steel, which is used for example to make bicycle frames, contains only 0.2 per cent carbon, while high-carbon steel, which is much harder and tougher, contains up to about 1.5 per cent carbon.

Special steels
Special steels, also known as *alloy steels*, contain small amounts of other elements, such as nickel, chromium, molybdenum and tungsten, which give the steel special properties. A familiar example is stainless steel, a corrosion-resistant alloy used for such objects as cutlery and razor blades.

Below: Most steel is used in the form of steel sheet. This is made from steel slabs by rolling them out, while very hot, through a giant rolling machine like the one shown here.

155

Alloys

Metals are noted for their strength and hardness. But many metals, when pure, are too soft, brittle or weak to be very useful.

On pages 154–5, we saw that pure iron is a rather soft metal, but that mixed with small amounts of other substances, it becomes the hard, tough alloy known as steel. In a similar way, other pure metals can be hardened and toughened by alloying them with other metals, or with non-metals.

For thousands of years, such metals as copper, zinc, tin, lead, gold and silver have been used to make alloys.

In our own century, many new alloys have been made using such metals as aluminium and titanium. These are much lighter in weight but just as strong as the heavy alloys.

Heavy alloys

Besides steel, and other iron alloys such as cast iron and special steels, heavy alloys have long included those based on copper.

The oldest copper alloy known to man was bronze, in which copper is alloyed with tin. Both pure copper and pure tin are soft metals, but bronze is hard and tough and so was used for armour, weapons and tools.

Another copper alloy is brass, in which copper is alloyed with zinc. In ancient times, brass, like silver and gold, was much used for coins. Both bronze and brass also have modern uses, for example in ships' propellers.

A more modern type of copper alloy is that containing nickel. Some copper-nickel alloys are very resistant to attack by acids and other corrosive chemicals. For this reason, these alloys are used in chemical equipment.

Nickel can also be alloyed with such metals as chromium and molybdenum, to make alloys that are so hard-wearing and heat-resistant that they can be used for the hottest parts of jet engines.

Lead is a heavy, soft metal which is alloyed with tin to make solder, used for joining metals together. Mixed with antimony, lead forms type metal, an alloy employed by printers.

Even heavier are such precious metals as platinum, osmium and

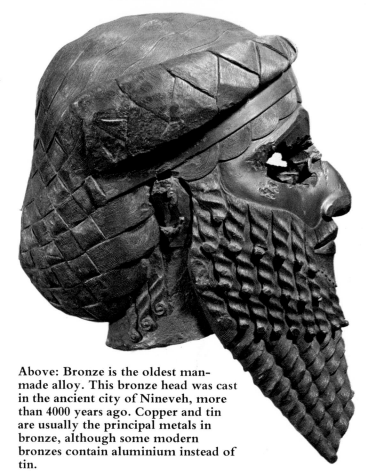

Above: Bronze is the oldest man-made alloy. This bronze head was cast in the ancient city of Nineveh, more than 4000 years ago. Copper and tin are usually the principal metals in bronze, although some modern bronzes contain aluminium instead of tin.

iridium. They are alloyed to make corrosion-resistant equipment and tips for pen nibs.

Heavy alloys may also contain small or large amounts of such metals as manganese, cobalt, vanadium, zirconium and tungsten. More rarely, special alloys contain such unusual metals as niobium and tantalum. All alloys are likely to contain small amounts of non-metals, such as carbon and silicon.

Lightweight alloys

The metal mainly used for lightweight alloys is aluminium. This is the commonest metal in the Earth's crust – commoner even than iron. But aluminium, because it is so difficult to extract from its ores, was not used widely until the early 1900s.

Aluminium alloys are now seen in every kitchen, in the form of pots and pans. Other major uses include aircraft construction and high-voltage cables for the electrical industry. Magnesium, another lightweight metal, is the other principal metal in aluminium alloys.

Other new lightweight alloys are those of titanium, another metal common in the Earth's crust.

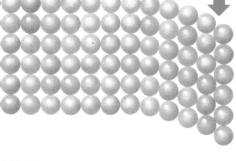
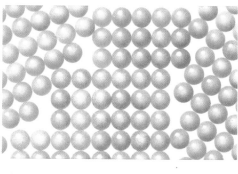

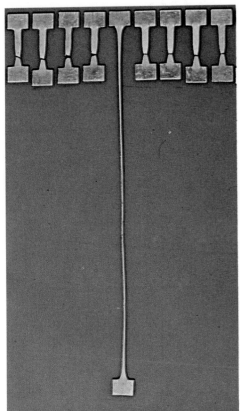

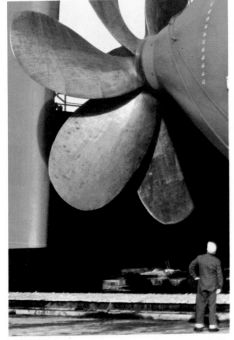

Above: This modern Japanese temple is roofed in shiny stainless steel. This iron alloy remains shiny because it does not rust easily. The roof looks blue because the polished steel surface reflects the colour of the sky.

Left: Why is an alloy stronger than a pure metal? The diagrams of metal atoms show the answer. A pure metal contains only one kind of atom, arranged in rows (top). A strong force can cause these rows to break up, or dislocate, leaving spaces where the metal is weak (centre). An alloy contains two or more kinds of atoms (bottom). All spaces are filled, so that the alloy does not weaken as easily as does the pure metal.

Below: Modern alloys are often made from metal powders. The pure metals are first ground up into powders. These are then ground together in a ball mill, which causes the particles of

different metals to weld, or alloy, together. The alloyed mixed powder is heated inside a steel can so that it fuses into a solid bar of alloy. This bar is then forced through the hole of a hard metal die, to make an alloy rod. The rod is first rolled, then heat-treated, to make a sheet of the alloy. This can then be formed into the object required, in this case, a blade for a gas turbine such as those fitted in jet engines.

Top right: Some alloys are very stretchable, or ductile. These alloy samples have all been stretched in a powerful machine. Most have broken, but one alloy, as you can see, is much more ductile than the others. It is a superplastic aluminium alloy and can stretch 18 times further than the other samples before breaking.

Right: A huge ship's propeller, made from a bronze alloy.

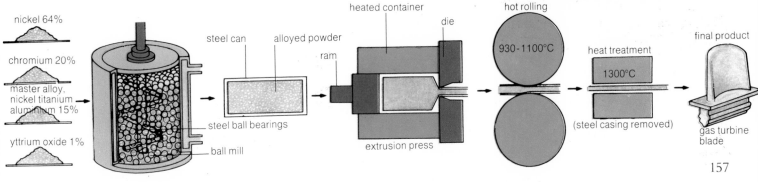

nickel 64%

chromium 20%

master alloy, nickel titanium aluminium 15%

yttrium oxide 1%

steel can

alloyed powder

ram

heated container

die

steel ball bearings

ball mill

extrusion press

hot rolling

930-1100°C

heat treatment

1300°C

(steel casing removed)

final product

gas turbine blade

Coal, oil and chemicals

Coal, petroleum oil and natural gas are all fuels that are found in the Earth's crust. Coal is extracted by mining, and oil and natural gas by drilling. We use these fuels for various heating purposes, for example in our homes. The fuels are called *fossil fuels* because they were formed, long ago, from living organisms, which became fossilized in the Earth's crust (see pages 34–7).

Coal, which was formed from various kinds of plants, consists mostly of the chemical element carbon, together with smaller amounts of other elements, including hydrogen.

Petroleum oil and natural gas, which were formed from much smaller living organisms, consist mainly of carbon and hydrogen. For this reason they are known as *Hydrocarbon fuels*.

How we use fuels

Large quantities of fossil fuels are supplied to giant power stations. There they are burned in order to generate electricity, which is then supplied to homes, offices, schools and so on, for heating, lighting and power.

Natural gas may be supplied directly to our homes for heating.

Oil, on the other hand, does not go straight from the oil wells to homes and factories. Crude oil, as it is called, is instead taken to oil refineries, where it is broken down into many different hydrocarbon products.

This breaking-down process is called *petroleum cracking*. Among the products obtained from crude oil by cracking are engine fuels such as petrol, diesel oil and aviation fuel. Other oils include heavy fuel oils and lubricating oils.

Besides these various oils, petroleum cracking produces still other very useful products, which are either

Left: Gases from petroleum distillation are compressed into liquids and stored in this kind of tank.

Right: Distillation columns are used to separate various liquids and gases from petroleum. These are then used as fuels and chemical raw materials.

Below left: The enormous machine in the centre of the picture is scraping away huge quantities of rock, in an open-cast coal mine.

Below right: The quality of petroleum products is controlled partly by analysis in the laboratory.

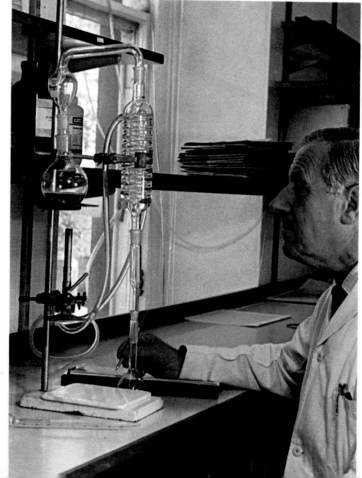

heavier or more lightweight. Among the heavier products are tarry and waxy substances; among the more lightweight are hydrocarbon gases, similar to natural gas.

Chemicals from fuels

These heavy or lightweight petroleum products are of the greatest economic importance. They are the raw materials needed by many other industries to make their own products.

For example, hydrocarbon gases are used on a huge scale to make the plastics products we see in every home. Petroleum products are also used to make synthetic rubber, medical drugs, explosives, fertilizers, insecticides and many types of industrial chemicals. Heavy tarry substances are also useful for road surfacing, and heavy waxy substances for waterproofing roofs.

Coal also supplies many raw materials for these purposes. In this case, coal is not burned as a fuel, but is distilled by heating without air. It then breaks down into a great number of useful raw materials. Besides the ones already named, these include organic chemicals which are the raw materials used to make dyes.

Below: All sorts of useful things are now made from plastics and synthetic rubber. The pictures show some familiar products manufactured from these man-made materials. The raw materials used to make plastics and synthetic rubber are of three main kinds: 1. hydrocarbons (chemical compounds which contain only the chemical elements hydrogen and carbon) which come from the distillation of petroleum, coal, and occasionally, wood (they include various hydrocarbon oils and gases); 2. mineral substances (such as salt, sulphur, limestone and fluorspar) which are mined or quarried; 3. gases (such as chlorine) which are obtained from petroleum, coal or chemicals.

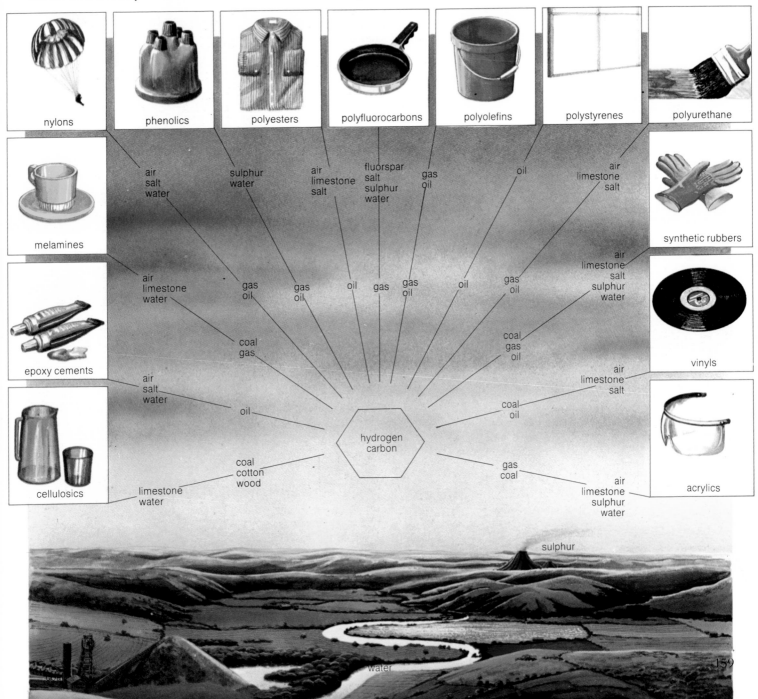

nylons — air, salt, water

phenolics — sulphur, water

polyesters — air, limestone, salt

polyfluorocarbons — fluorspar, salt, sulphur, water

polyolefins — gas, oil

polystyrenes — oil

polyurethane — air, limestone, salt

melamines — air, limestone, water

epoxy cements — air, limestone, water

cellulosics — air, salt, water

gas, oil — gas, oil — oil — gas — gas, oil — oil — gas, oil

coal, gas

oil

coal, cotton, wood

limestone, water

hydrogen carbon

synthetic rubbers — air, limestone, salt, sulphur, water

vinyls — coal, gas, oil

acrylics — air, limestone, salt / air, limestone, sulphur, water

coal, oil

gas, coal

sulphur

water

Paper-making

We use paper for many purposes. In the school and office, writing and typing paper and books are abundant. In the home, we also use wrapping paper, toilet paper, grease-proof paper, paper towels, napkins, handkerchiefs and perhaps even paper clothes.

In the supermarket, paper labels and wrappings are common, and so are boxes made from the thicker kind of paper called cardboard. Other kinds of thick paper are used in buildings, as linings for walls and roofs.

What is paper?

Paper is made from woody fibres which are matted and pressed together to make a thin, flat sheet. The fibres usually come from timber. Trees such as pines, firs and spruces may be grown especially for this purpose. Or, these and other trees are obtained from natural forests. To a lesser extent, fibres from other plants, such us grasses and reeds, are used to make special kinds of paper. More often, cotton rags and waste paper are used as additional raw materials.

From logs to paper

The general process for making paper is shown in the diagram. First of all, in a factory somewhere near the forest or plantation, logs are ground up and wetted to make wood pulp.

Below: The paper-making process. First, logs are cut into chips, which are then made into a chemical pulp (1) or are simply ground to a pulp with water (2). The wood pulp is formed into sheets, which are packed into bales (3) ready for delivery to the paper mill. Here, the bales are fed into another pulper (4) together with waste paper (5) and water. The pulp, or stock as it is then called, is treated in a

For the finest, strongest kinds of paper, such as writing paper, the pulp is made by digesting wood chips with various chemicals. For coarser, weaker kinds of paper, such as newsprint, wood chips are ground up with water.

The pulp is cleaned, dried and pressed into bales for transport to the paper mill.

At the paper mill the pulp is fed into a *stock preparer*, together with any additional raw material, such as cleaned waste paper, and water. Here, all coarser fibres are beaten until the pulp has the right consistency.

Fillers such as *china clay,* which make the paper smoother, are then added. So also are dyes, if the paper is to be coloured, and a substance called *size,* which makes it easier to write on.

The pulp mixture, now known as *stock,* is then fed into a paper-making machine, which may be more than 100 metres long. The wet stock is carried along on a moving, wire-mesh belt, through which water from the stock drains away.

The stock then passes through rollers which squeeze out more water and mat the woody fibres together. It then passes through more heated rollers, which remove the rest of the water, pressing and drying the stock into paper. This is rolled up at the dry end of the machine, ready for use.

stock preparer (6) which further separates the wood fibres. Next, various colours, fillers and binders are added in a mixer (7). The stock then passes on to the wet end of a long paper-making machine (8). Water is sucked out from the stock to make a damp web of paper, which is then squeezed and heat-dried through rollers (9), before being wound on to a large reel (10).

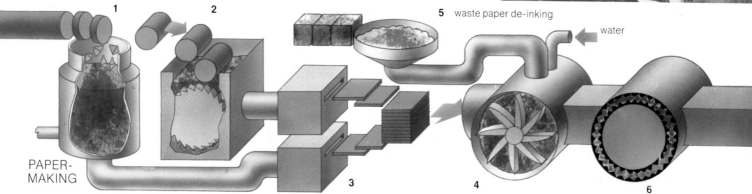

5 waste paper de-inking

water

PAPER-MAKING

1   2   3   4   6

Above left: Logs for paper-making are floated down a river from the forest to the sawmill.

Left: Before logs are chopped up and pulped to make paper, their bark is removed by a de-barking machine.

Above: Wood chips from the de-barked logs are here being fed into a chemical digester or pulper.

Above right: The wet end of the paper-making machine, carrying a damp web of paper.

Right: The dry end of the machine, carrying dried paper.

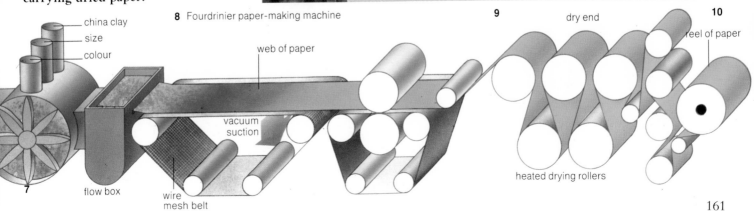

8 Fourdrinier paper-making machine   **9**   dry end   **10**

china clay
size
colour

web of paper

reel of paper

vacuum suction

heated drying rollers

7

flow box

wire mesh belt

The world of polymers

The word polymer is a modern, scientific one. Yet people have used polymers ever since they began to wear clothes. For example, the fibres of the cotton plant, which have long been woven into garments, are composed of a polymer called cellulose.

Cellulose, like many other substances in nature, is a chemical compound of carbon in which the carbon atoms are linked together to form long chains. The long fibres of cotton are given their strength by millions of these carbon–carbon links.

Man-made polymers

Cellulose is an example of a *natural* polymer. Nowadays, we also use many *synthetic,* or man-made polymers. The best known of these are plastics and synthetic rubber.

Right: Making polythene bottles.

Below right: Large amounts of polystyrene plastics are made from the much simpler compound styrene. This is mixed in a 'kettle' with a catalyst, which makes the styrene start to polymerize into polystyrene. Polymerization is completed in a much larger heated vessel. The solid plastic material is then chopped into granules, from which many polystyrene products are made.

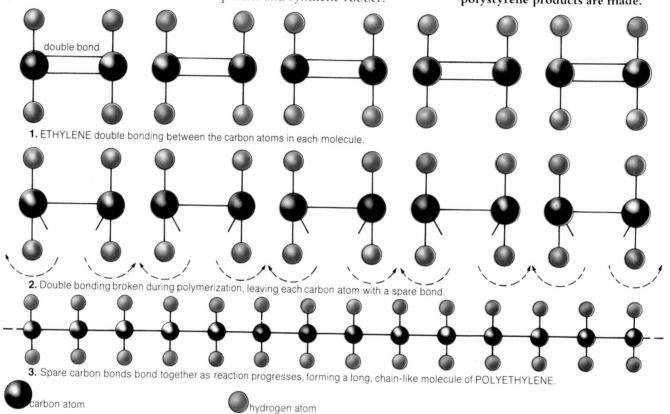

double bond

1. ETHYLENE double bonding between the carbon atoms in each molecule.

2. Double bonding broken during polymerization, leaving each carbon atom with a spare bond.

3. Spare carbon bonds bond together as reaction progresses, forming a long, chain-like molecule of POLYETHYLENE.

carbon atom   hydrogen atom

Above: The diagrams show how many small molecules of the gas ethylene bond together to make the solid plastic substance called polyethylene – polythene for short. This kind of chemical reaction is called polymerization. It is helped by another substance called a catalyst.

Below left: Extrusion is a process by which long rods and strips of polymers are made. Granules of a polymer are fed into the extruder. A screw carries the granules to a metal hole called a die. A heater softens the granules so that they can be forced, or extruded, through the die.

Below: Plastic objects such as buckets and records are made by compression moulding. The polymer is compressed between two halves of a mould. The heated upper half softens the polymer so that it can be moulded. The lower half of the mould cools and hardens the moulded object.

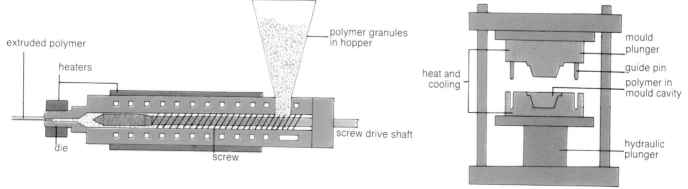

extruded polymer

heaters

polymer granules in hopper

die

screw drive shaft

screw

heat and cooling

mould plunger

guide pin

polymer in mould cavity

hydraulic plunger

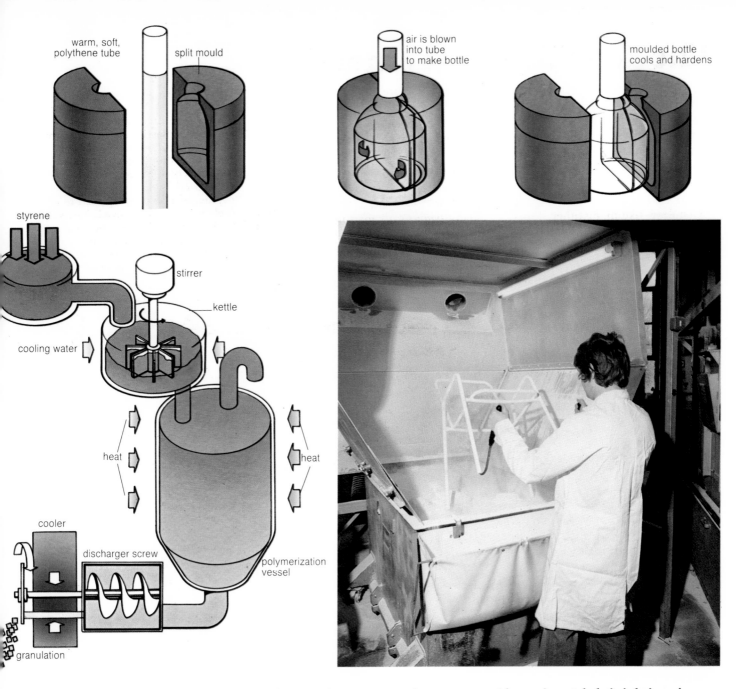

warm, soft, polythene tube

split mould

air is blown into tube to make bottle

moulded bottle cools and hardens

styrene

stirrer

kettle

cooling water

heat

heat

cooler

discharger screw

polymerization vessel

granulation

Above: A metal chair is being given a plastic coating. Inside the coating machine, a powdered polymer is kept air-borne. When the heated chair is dipped into this powder, the powder particles in contact with the metal melt to provide a smooth, even, plastic coating.

Like cellulose, plastics are made up of long-chain carbon molecules. So too are most types of synthetic rubber, although one type, silicone rubber, has long-chain molecules in which the links are between atoms of silicon and oxygen.

Whatever the type of polymer, it is made chemically by linking together many simpler, similar molecules called *monomers,* in a process called *polymerization.* (The word polymer means 'a multiple'.) By using different monomers scientists can produce polymers with special properties, such as strength, flexibility or hardness.

Wherever you happen to be, you will probably notice some kind of synthetic polymer. Even when you are

walking in the country, a glance at your own clothes will show you examples. Your raincoat will contain a plastic material, and the soles of your shoes are quite likely to be made of a synthetic rubber.

These are examples of flexible or springy synthetic polymers. Their long-chain molecules are able to slide back and forth along one another, to give them these useful properties.

Many other plastic objects and materials, however, are not flexible but rigid. Examples are plastic light switches and electric plugs, and plastic fillers that set very hard, such as those used to repair rust holes in car bodies.

In these kinds of plastics, the long-chain molecules cannot slide freely

along one another, because the chains are strongly linked together. Such polymers are said to be strongly *cross-linked.*

These cross-links are so strong that they cannot be broken without destroying the plastic material. Flexible plastics, when mildly heated, become softer, then melt. Cross-linked plastics remain hard, but blacken and decompose if strongly heated.

163

Fibres and fabrics

Fibres are used in the textile industry to make such familiar things as clothes, sheets and blankets, curtains and carpets. These and other textiles are made by weaving or knitting various kinds of yarn. A yarn is made by twisting together several strands of a fibre, in a process called spinning.

The spinning wheel was used for many centuries in the home, to spin woollen fibres into a thick yarn – the familiar ball or skein of wool. In the cotton industry, fibres from the cotton plant are spun by machine into another, thinner yarn – the familiar cotton thread.

Weaving is a method of making fabrics by interlacing two sets of yarn threads on a machine called a loom. One set of threads, called the *warp,* is stretched tightly along the loom. The other set, called the *weft,* is threaded, or woven, in and out of the warp threads, across the loom.

Sometimes weaving is done by hand, as on the carpet-making loom shown in the picture (page 165). In modern textile factories, it is done much faster, entirely by machine.

Knitting is a method of making fabrics that uses only one thread. In hand knitting, the thread is knitted with (usually) two long knitting needles. In the textile industry, knitted fabrics are produced much faster by large knitting machines.

Natural and man-made fibres

Nowadays, fabrics are woven or knitted from many different types of fibre. Some of these, such as wool and cotton, are *natural* fibres, that is, they come from natural sources (animals or plants). Other natural fibres include silk, a very fine fibre obtained from the cocoon of the silk moth. This is woven to make a fabric that is luxuriously smooth – in fact, silky. Linen is made from another natural fibre, obtained from the stem of the flax plant.

But many textiles today are woven partly or wholly from man-made, or *artificial,* fibres. These include fibres with such names as rayon, nylon, polyester and acrylic – names often found on the labels of clothes.

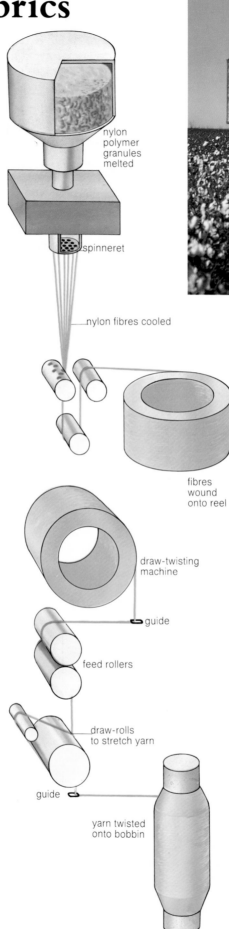

nylon polymer granules melted

spinneret

nylon fibres cooled

fibres wound onto reel

draw-twisting machine

guide

feed rollers

draw-rolls to stretch yarn

guide

yarn twisted onto bobbin

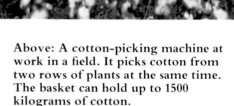

Above: A cotton-picking machine at work in a field. It picks cotton from two rows of plants at the same time. The basket can hold up to 1500 kilograms of cotton.

Left: How nylon yarn is made. Long nylon filaments are made by forcing melted nylon through the many small holes of a spinneret. The filaments are then cooled and hardened. When many filaments are twisted together, they make a yarn. This is done on a draw-twisting machine, and then the yarn is wound on to bobbins. Nylon yarn is as strong as steel wire.

Below: These large rolls supply yarn, or spun thread, to an automatic loom on which towelling is woven.

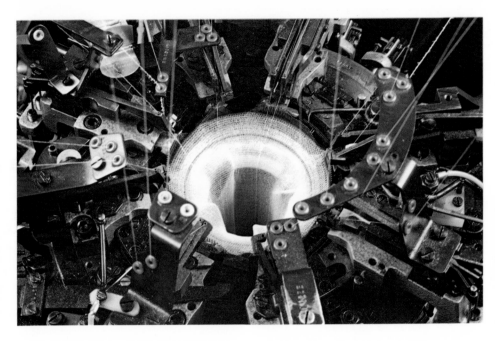

Above: This circular head is part of an automatic machine that knits nylon tights.

Right: Man-made fibres are here seen being spun into threads. The spinning machine is called a ring frame, from which the spun threads are drawn on to rollers.

Below: Weaving is carried out on looms. This type of carpet hand-loom has been used in the East for many centuries. In a modern factory, weaving is done by very fast, automatic machines.

Below right: A spinneret of the kind used in spinning nylon and other polymer filaments.

Man-made fibres are made from polymers (see pages 162–3). They are spun in a quite different way to most natural fibres, but in a similar way to that by which a spider spins its silken thread. The polymer material is forced through the many fine holes of a *spinneret* (see picture). Sometimes, as with nylon, the polymer is first melted, then it cools and solidifies into a thread as it comes out from the holes of the spinneret.

Other plastic materials are first dissolved in chemical solutions, which are then forced through a spinneret into other chemical solutions that solidify the threads.

Soap and detergents

Soap has been made at least since Roman times. A type of toilet soap used by the Roman nobility was made using animal fat together with wood ashes mixed with lime.

Wood ashes contain potash, and potash soaps, which are still used today, are the kind known as *soft soaps*. The soft soaps always make a good lather with water.

Hard soaps do not make such a good lather but they last longer than soft soaps. For this reason they were suitable for such purposes as scrubbing doorsteps and floors. Hard soaps are made in a similar way to soft soaps, but using soda instead of potash.

From the 18th century onwards, soap has been made on a larger scale in factories. In a soap factory, soap is made in enormous metal pans, known as *soap kettles*.

In a soap kettle, animal or vegetable fat is mixed with an alkali and water. For soft soap, the alkali is caustic potash. For hard soap, the alkali is caustic soda.

The mixture is then boiled, and brine, a solution of common salt, is added. This causes soap to separate from the mixture as a floating curd. After more boiling, all the fats remaining in the curd are *saponified,* or changed into soap. The purified curd can then be pressed into moulds to make bars of soap, or flaked to make soap flakes.

How soap works

The cleansing action of soap depends on the way that its molecules behave. Soap molecules have the long, rather tadpole-like shape shown in the diagrams.

The tails of these molecular tadpoles are repelled by water, but are attracted by oily or greasy substances. This causes them to attach to particles of greasy dirt, for example in clothes being washed. In contrast to the tails, the heads of the molecular tadpoles are attracted by water and repelled by oil or grease. They surround each dirt particle, so separating it from the article being washed.

The dirt particles, with their coating of soap molecules, float off and are seen as a soapy scum on the surface of the water.

Detergents

The word detergent means 'a cleansing substance'. So soap is one kind of detergent. However, the name detergent is usually reserved for the non-soapy types of powders and liquids that we use in washing machines and as washing-up liquids.

Compared with soap, detergents are recent inventions. They have only been widely used for about 30 years. Like soaps, detergents have long molecules in which the 'head' behaves differently from the 'tail'. But unlike soaps, detergents do not form scums.

Instead, when molecules of a detergent surround a dirt particle, both detergent and dirt remain suspended in froth. Unlike a soap scum, this froth is not likely to block up a washing machine.

The froth of early types of detergent could be a nuisance, as when it piled up on the surfaces of rivers, lakes and canals. But most modern detergents have a froth that breaks down quickly and disappears.

Above: A factory production line for a well-known washing-up liquid.

Left: An early soap advertisement for Sunlight soap.

Below: How a detergent or soap works. The molecules of these substances have a rather tadpole-like

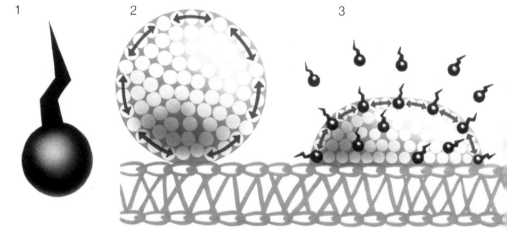

1   2   3

Right: Detergent foam can be a very unsightly pollutant when it piles up in rivers, as shown here. It may also be a danger to wildlife living in or near the rivers.

Below right: An oil spill is being dispersed by spraying it with a detergent. The detergent causes the oil to break up into tiny droplets, which eventually sink to the sea bed.

Below: Tea towels are stained with various substances, including tea, coffee, gravy and egg yolk. They will then be washed in different detergents to test the cleaning power of each detergent.

shape (1). Normally, water forms spherical droplets (2) but when detergents or soaps are added, the water drops are flattened and so have more wetting power (3). When detergents or soaps are added to oily or greasy dirt, their molecules surround the dirt particles (4), so making them much easier to remove.

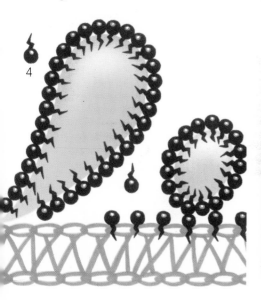

167

Dyes and paints

From ancient times, people have worn clothing coloured or patterned by dyes. These dyes were first obtained as natural substances from the bodies of animals and plants.

Traditional plant dyes include *saffron*, a yellow dye obtained from the crocus flower; *indigo*, a blue dye from the leaves of the Indigo plant; and *madder*, a red dye made from the root of the Madder plant. Another blue plant dye, used by ancient Britons to dye their bodies, was *woad*. This was made from the leaves of a plant belonging to the mustard family.

An ancient animal dye, famous for the colour it gave to royal Roman togas, was *Tyrian purple*. This was

Right: Man-made fibres such as polyesters, and natural fibres such as wool and cotton, are usually dyed before being knitted or woven. In this picture, man-made fibres are being fed automatically from a dyeing vat to a drier.

Below left: A motor car body is given its top coat of plastics-based gloss paint. This is being sprayed on top of the primer paint, which is dry.

Below right: Motor car paints must be able to withstand long exposure to sunlight, wind and moisture, without fading or cracking. Samples of various car paints are being tested here in a machine which speeds up these weathering effects.

obtained from the bodies of various types of snail. The Aztecs of ancient Mexico used a scarlet dye, *cochineal*, which they extracted from the bodies of certain insects.

Synthetic dyes

Natural dyes are still used in some places, but most types are now made chemically, or synthetically. The first synthetic dye, a blue–purple colour called *mauveine*, was made in 1856. It was soon followed by a whole range of coal tar, or aniline, dyes. One of these was the blue dye indigo, which

is now made synthetically, not extracted from plants.

Nowadays, dyers can choose from several thousand synthetic dyes, of many different colours. During the dyeing process, the dyes are chemically fixed to the cloth, or other material, so that they will not run out again when the material is washed.

The first paints

The very earliest paints were used by cave painters over 20,000 years ago. These were made from coloured mineral substances mixed with a kind

of 'glue', such as blood, animal fat or beeswax. The coloured substances, or *pigments*, were obtained from the earth or from ground up rocks. At first only a few colours were available; red and yellow from two different types of iron oxide, black from soot or charcoal, and white from chalk. Shades of brown and orange were made by mixing different amounts of red, brown and black. Later other coloured minerals were discovered and used as pigments.

The ancient Egyptians and Romans invented a wider range of paints.

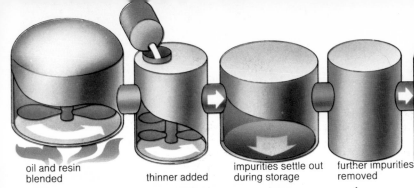

oil and resin blended

thinner added

impurities settle out during storage

further impurities removed

storage tank

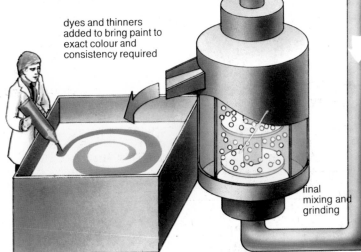

pigment and thinner added

sample from batch tested

dyes and thinners added to bring paint to exact colour and consistency required

final mixing and grinding

Below: Enamel paint flows smoothly from a ball mill in which its yellow pigment has been ground up together with the paint medium. After this milling process, no lumps of pigment remain in the paint.

Bottom: A lipstick is made by blending together waxes, oils, fats and a variety of coloured pigments. The picture shows a cosmetic scientist mixing these various substances, to make a new shade of lipstick. In the cosmetics factory, the new lipstick will be manufactured in large quantities by machinery. Only fine quality waxes, such as beeswax and carnauba wax, and oils, such as castor oil, are used. Also, the pigments and all the other materials must be very carefully chosen so that they are quite harmless even to the most sensitive skin.

Above and right: Paint is made from oils and resins, together with thinning liquids and colouring dyes or pigments. The diagrams show how a gloss paint is made. First, the paint medium, or binder, is made by blending together linseed oil and alkyd resin (a man-made polymer). This binder is thinned by white spirit and is then passed through several tanks in which all impurities settle out. In the final settling tank the binder is stored for as long as 5 months. In the next stage, pigments are added. This causes the paint to thicken, so more thinner is added. The paint is then thoroughly mixed in a ball mill, which ensures that all particles of pigment are wetted with the binder. Finally, to bring the paint to the exact colour and thickness required, more dyes and thinners are added.

Their coloured pigments included animal, vegetable, and mineral substances. As the *binding medium* – the liquid part of a paint that holds the pigments together – they used several types of glues and gums.

Modern paints
Modern paints still consist basically of a solid pigment, dispersed (or spread out) in a liquid medium. But modern paint makers use a far greater number of pigments and other substances to make a variety of paints suitable for different purposes.

Pigments now include chemical powders, such as metal oxides; finely ground metals, such as copper and aluminium; and synthetic dyes.

The liquid medium can be water, or a natural or synthetic oil or resin. Synthetic resins include polymers (see page 162). Paints containing large amounts of these polymer materials are very resistant to wear and to attack by corrosive chemicals.

Finally, varnishes and lacquers are paints that contain no pigment. They are transparent and have little or no colour.

The world of glass

Glass has been made by man since ancient times. The first glass objects, made by the Egyptians 4500 years ago, were beads. A thousand years later the Egyptians used a moulding process to make small glass bottles.

Even before this time, however, glass had existed on the Earth's surface. It was made there naturally, when lightning struck sandy soil, or when a volcano erupted. In either case, mineral substances were heated very strongly, so that they *fused,* or melted, to make the hard, transparent material we know as glass.

From this description, you can guess that glass can be made from a wide variety of minerals. Many oxides of metals and non-metals, for example, if heated strongly enough, will fuse to form types of glass.

The commonest of all these mineral oxides is *silica,* of which sand is largely composed. From the time of the ancient Egyptians onwards, glassmakers have made their glass by heating sand together with such other common mineral substances as soda and lime.

Glass is a liquid

We value glass for its remarkable properties. It is particularly suitable for windows because it is hard,

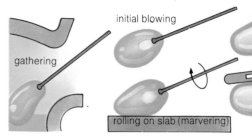

initial blowing

gathering

rolling on slab (marvering)

Below: Most glass containers are now made by a blow-moulding process. A lump of molten glass, called a gob, is first blown to make what is called a blank. This is then blown again to make a glass bottle. The whole process is carried out by automatic machines, and many bottles are made at the same time.

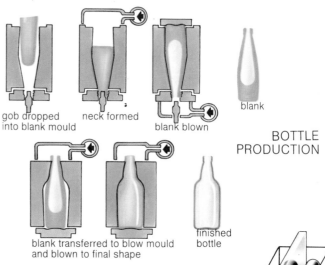

gob dropped into blank mould

neck formed

blank blown

blank

BOTTLE PRODUCTION

blank transferred to blow mould and blown to final shape

finished bottle

Below: The most modern method for making flat sheets of glass is the float glass process. On the left are shown the various substances that are needed to make the glass. These are melted together in a furnace. The molten glass is then floated out of the furnace on to a bath of molten tin, so that it forms a thin, very even sheet. The

molten tin is at a much lower temperature than the glass, so that the glass sheet cools and hardens.

Above left: The hardened sheet of float glass passes on rollers to where it can be cut up into sheets of the required size.

Right: In a rather older process, known as the sheet glass process, flat glass is made by dipping a metal 'bait' into molten glass, then raising this up so that the glass is drawn through water-cooled rollers, to make a glass sheet of the required thickness.

SHEET GLASS PROCESS

asbestos rollers

furnace

water-cooled edge rollers

molten glass

FLOAT GLASS PROCESS

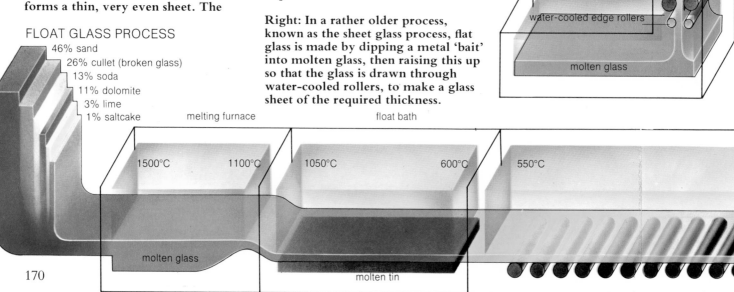

46% sand
26% cullet (broken glass)
13% soda
11% dolomite
3% lime
1% saltcake

melting furnace

float bath

1500°C   1100°C   1050°C   600°C   550°C

molten glass

molten tin

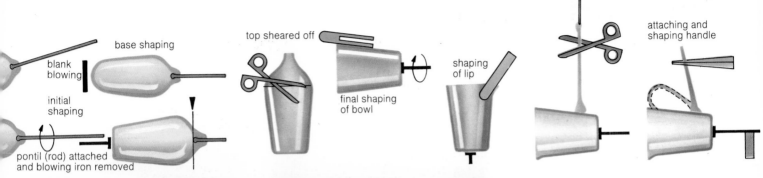

base shaping

blank
blowing

initial
shaping

top sheared off

final shaping
of bowl

shaping
of lip

attaching and
shaping handle

pontil (rod) attached
and blowing iron removed

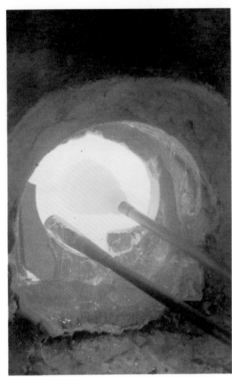

Above and above left: Glass-blowing by hand is a craft that has been practised for nearly 2000 years, since late Egyptian times. Nowadays it is used mainly for making glass objects of art quality. The pictures show how a simple glass jug is made by hand. This kind of work is carried out by skilled craftsmen.

Above: The end of the blowing iron, or tube, is placed in the glass furnace and twirled so that it gathers a quantity of molten glass.

Above centre: While the glass is still soft, it is blown to the required size and shape.

Above right: A stained glass window. Until the invention of plate glass in the 17th century, these were the only very large windows. They are made from many small pieces of glass 'stained' in various colours and held together inside a network of lead.

annealing lehr or cooling chamber

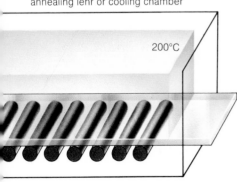

200°C

transparent, and lets in light without letting out too much heat. It is unaffected by rain, frost or corrosive chemicals in the air, so it can last a lifetime. On the other hand, it shatters rather dangerously when broken.

Many of these properties, particularly hardness, would seem to show that glass is a solid material. In fact, it is a liquid! Scientists call it a *supercooled* liquid, which means a liquid that has cooled without forming crystals. Like other liquids, glass flows, but the flow is so slow at room temperature that we do not notice it.

Special kinds of glass are now made which do not shatter dangerously when broken. The tough glass of a motor car windscreen, when it does break, fractures into many small, fairly blunt pieces. Glass ovenware, such as a casserole dish, is made of another type of special glass which can withstand

rapid heating and cooling without cracking or breaking.

Glass-making

The pictures show the three main processes now employed for making glass objects. In each process, glass is first melted in a furnace.

The oldest method is that of the craftsman glass-blower, who makes beautiful vessels such as goblets and vases. These vessels are often brilliantly coloured by adding further minerals or metals to the molten glass.

Most glass containers, such as bottles and lamp bulbs, are blown mechanically inside metal moulds.

Large sheets of glass are also made entirely by machinery. The latest process, shown in the pictures, is the float glass process, in which sheets of glass are floated and cooled on a bath of molten tin metal.

171

Preserving food

Man's ancestors, like his close relatives the great apes, hunted or gathered their food as they needed it. They had not yet invented methods of storing food for longer periods.

But all civilized peoples have needed to store and preserve food, as a reserve for times of shortage. In temperate countries, little grows during the cold winter months. Dry foods, such as grains of wheat and other cereals, can be stored for the winter simply by keeping them in a dry, clean place. On the other hand, without special treatment, meat and many vegetables will not keep long without going bad.

Food goes bad when it becomes infected with *bacteria* and the spores of *fungi*. These are *microscopic organisms* which are carried about in the air. When they land on moist foods, they are able to feed and grow on the foods, so causing decay.

Smoking, salting and pickling

Some ways of preserving food are age-old. These include various methods of *curing* food, or treating it in such a way that it cannot easily become infected with decay microbes.

Many prehistoric peoples undoubtedly had discovered that smoking and drying meat over a fire enabled it to keep. Meat treated in this way forms a hard, dry surface which, because of lack of moisture, prevents the growth of decay microbes.

Bacteria and fungi also dislike too much salt, so salting food is another way of preserving it.

Salting and smoking may improve the taste of many foods. Some food, like herrings, can be treated in either of these ways. Another old, but still popular, way of preserving food is by pickling it in vinegar, an acid which prevents microbial growth.

In Japan and some other far eastern countries, foods such as fish are dried and preserved by actually allowing certain fungi, or moulds, to grow on them. These moulds remove water from the food, so preventing attack by other microbes. Also (as with blue cheese) the moulds give the fish a special flavour. Other fermented

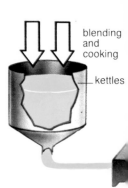

blending and cooking

kettles

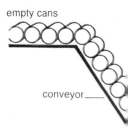

empty cans

conveyor

Above: A selection of cheeses from Holland. Cheese can be considered as a food in which the goodness of milk is preserved. It is made by curdling milk, then separating the curd from the thin liquid whey. In firm cheeses, such as Cheddar and Edam, the curd is pressed into moulds to make the cheese. It is then left for 3–6 months to 'ripen'. During this time, enzymes and bacteria are at work, enabling the flavour to develop.

Left: A fish-smoking kiln in Grimsby, England. When fish is smoked over a fire, the dried, sealed, outer layers of the fish form a protective coating.

foods, as they are called, include yoghurt and kumiss, which are types of fermented milk.

Modern methods

Eskimos have long stored and preserved their meat by keeping it frozen in snow. But in warmer countries, frozen-food storage began only with the invention of refrigerators. Most meat is now stored in this way, in large deep-freezers or in smaller household fridges.

In freeze-dried foods, all water is removed by a fast-freezing process. Vegetables will keep indefinitely in

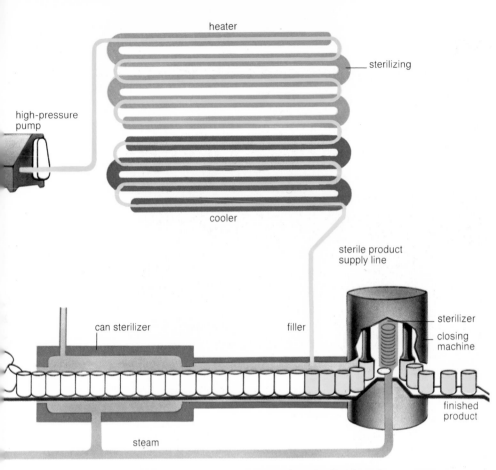

heater

sterilizing

high-pressure pump

cooler

sterile product supply line

can sterilizer

filler

sterilizer

closing machine

finished product

steam

Left: The diagram shows a modern process for canning liquid foods such as soups. First, the food is mixed in a 'kettle'. Then, it is pumped to a heater, which sterilizes the food – that is, kills any germs that may have been present in the food. Sterilized food flows on to a cooler, and then on to a moving line of metal cans, which are open ready to receive the food. The cans have also passed through a sterilizer and are quite free from germs. After being filled with food, the cans are carried on by a conveyor into a can-closing machine. This is also heated, to preserve sterility. The sealed, filled food cans are now ready to be labelled, stored, or despatched to shops and supermarkets.

Below: Cornflakes are made from maize, also known as sweet corn and corn on the cob. The maize is first cut into small pieces, which are cooked with salt and malt in a pressure cooker. In later parts of the process, the corn is steamed, rolled into flakes, and toasted to make the finished cornflakes you see here. These are then packaged to keep them fresh.

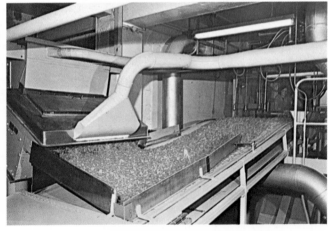

this form but when placed in water they soon become edible again.

Canning, invented in the early 19th century, preserves food by heating it to kill any decay microbes, then sealing it off, without air, inside a metal can. This prevents both the growth of microbes, and staleness caused by contact of the food with air.

If you read the label of a tin or jar of food, you will probably see that chemicals have been added. Some of these will be chemical preservatives, added to discourage microbe growth or to help the food keep its taste in some other way.

Above left: This machine makes potato crisps, which you can see emerging, fully cooked. First, potatoes are peeled, washed and sliced, all by machine. The slices are then washed again to remove starch, and dried. In this machine the dry slices are cooked in hot groundnut oil, then sprinkled with such flavours as cheese-and-onion, or salt-and-vinegar. The crisps will then be packaged in air-tight bags to keep them fresh.

Right: All these foods can be preserved by freezing. Frozen foods, stored well below freezing, last for a long time without going bad because spoilage microbes will not grow at such low temperatures.

The electric light

A source of light has always been very important to man. And the convenience of producing light simply by flicking a switch has proved to be one of the main benefits brought by the age of electricity. By the early 1800s, electric batteries had become readily available. As a result, many more scientists and inventors began to study the effects of electricity. Of particular interest was the fact that a strong electric current could make a wire glow red hot, or even white hot. Thus it was possible to produce light from electricity. But using a strong current meant that the batteries soon ran down. A thin wire needed less current to make it glow brightly, but the wire tended to burn out quite quickly. So many years elapsed before the incandescent (glowing) electric lamp became an economic and practical proposition.

An alternative way of producing light from electricity was to connect the supply to two carbon rods whose ends almost touched. A brilliant arc of light was produced between the rods but, again, a high current was needed. By the 1850s, electric arc street lighting had appeared in many towns. By this time, powerful electricity generators had been developed, so the production of a heavy current over a long period was no longer a problem. But it was the incandescent lamp that was to prove more suitable for use in the home.

Satisfactory incandescent lamps were developed independently in 1878–80 by Thomas Edison in the United States and Joseph Swan in England. Edison's first commercially produced lamps had a filament of carbonized paper, while Swan's used carbonized cotton. In both cases, the filament was enclosed in a glass bulb from which most of the air had been removed. With little oxygen in the bulb, the filament could glow brightly for many hours without burning out.

The modern incandescent electric light bulb has a filament of fine coiled tungsten wire. In an evacuated bulb, atoms of the filament would gradually break away and form a coating on the glass. So, to reduce this effect, the bulb

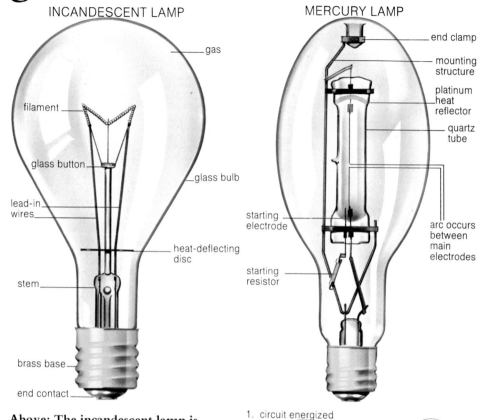

INCANDESCENT LAMP

gas

filament

glass button

glass bulb

lead-in wires

heat-deflecting disc

stem

brass base

end contact

MERCURY LAMP

end clamp

mounting structure

platinum heat reflector

quartz tube

starting electrode

arc occurs between main electrodes

starting resistor

Above: The incandescent lamp is simple in design and cheap to make.

Above right: When the mercury lamp is switched on, current flows through the resistor, starting electrode and lower main electrode. Heat is produced, causing the low-pressure mercury vapour to conduct electricity. When this occurs, the gas emits a bright, blue–green glow known as an arc discharge. Some mercury lamps have a fluorescent coating on the inside of the glass bulb. This converts ultra-violet radiation from the mercury vapour into light.

1. circuit energized

2a. pre-heat circuit heats cathode slowly

2b. rapid-start circuit heats cathode quickly

is usually filled with a mixture of argon and nitrogen gases. As in the early, evacuated bulbs, the absence of oxygen prevents the thin filament from burning out quickly.

Most domestic electric lamps are designed to last about 1000 hours. Their life could be extended by making them operate at a lower temperature, but this would make the light a reddish colour. Also, a larger proportion of the electricity consumed would be converted into heat instead of into light. As it is, a modern incandescent lamp converts only about ten per cent of the electricity into light. So it is not considered worth-

Above: Fluorescent tubes contain low-pressure mercury vapour, with a small amount of argon gas. The mercury vapour emits ultra-violet radiation when it is made to conduct an electric current. The electrons that make up the current collide with the mercury atoms. These become charged (ionized) and emit the radiation. The inside of the tube is coated with a chemical called a phosphor. This is an energy converter, absorbing ultra-violet radiation and emitting light. Pre-heat tubes are started by heating them momentarily. A current is passed through filaments at each end of the tube. Rapid-start tubes are heated continuously. A high voltage starts instant-start tubes.

Above: The lamps used for lighting highways include both incandescent and metal-vapour types. Mercury-vapour lamps give a blue-green glow, while sodium-vapour lamps emit orange light.

Right: Thousands of lights make night-time New York a colourful sight. Many of the so-called 'neon' lights in fact contain other gases.

Left: Most of the electricity supplied to a typical fluorescent lamp is first converted into ultra-violet radiation. The tube's phosphor coating then converts some of this to light. Although the fluorescent lamp is much more efficient than an incandescent lamp, only about 22 per cent of the electrical energy is converted finally into light. The rest is lost as heat.

Below left: Colourful display lighting, commonly used in advertising signs, is produced by using tubes filled with various gases or metal vapours.

while to further reduce efficiency in order to extend the life of a lamp.

Some incandescent lamps used for photography operate at extremely high temperatures. They are much more efficient than ordinary lamps and produce an intense white light. But the high operating temperature of these photographic lamps restricts their life to only 1 or 2 hours.

Vapour lamps, including fluorescent tubes, have greater efficiency, but also cost much more to manufacture.

However, they have a longer life than most incandescent lamps and are widely used in shops and offices, and also for street lighting.

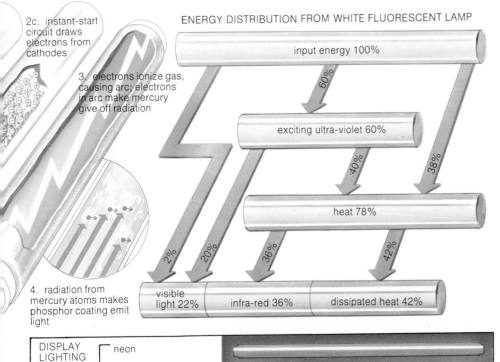

2c. instant-start circuit draws electrons from cathodes

3. electrons ionize gas, causing arc; electrons in arc make mercury give off radiation

4. radiation from mercury atoms makes phosphor coating emit light

ENERGY DISTRIBUTION FROM WHITE FLUORESCENT LAMP

input energy 100%

60%

exciting ultra-violet 60%

40%

38%

heat 78%

2%   20%   36%   42%

visible light 22%   infra-red 36%   dissipated heat 42%

DISPLAY LIGHTING TUBES		
GASES	neon	
	helium	
	nitrogen	
	carbon dioxide	
METAL VAPOURS	mercury	
	sodium	
	magnesium	

Electronics

In recent years, amazing advances have been made in the field of electronics. Complex circuits that once would have occupied a whole room can now be made no bigger than a thumb-nail. And costs have been greatly reduced too. A computer circuit costing £1000 in 1960 would have cost only £10 in 1965. By 1970, it would have been just £1. And now, the same circuit would cost less than a penny!

By the mid-1980s, it should be possible to build a cheap circuit containing one million components in an area measuring only 6 millimetres square. These tiny assemblies of components are called *integrated*

Below: The diode valve has two electrodes – a heated cathode and an anode. Heat causes electrons to leave the cathode. They travel to the positively charged anode. This electron flow forms an electric current. The diode allows current to flow in one direction only. In the triode, a small signal on the grid produces large variations in electron flow, thus producing an amplified (strengthened) signal.

circuits, or *microcircuits.* Some types can be programmed to carry out several functions and are called *microprocessors.*

Often the same microcircuit can be used in a wide range of equipment. And some equipment, for example computers, may use many identical microcircuits. The resultant high demand has enabled mass production techniques to be used. This is why standard microcircuits are now so cheap to produce.

Although most of the components in a piece of equipment may be contained in microcircuits, a few separate components are normally required too. These often cost much more than the microcircuits. And the assembly and marketing of the equipment may well cost most of all. However, the revolution in electronics is cutting these costs too. As in many branches of industry, electronically controlled automatic equipment is saving labour and reducing production costs. And modern electronic computers can assist in various stages from engineering design to marketing

and accounting (see page 184).

Electronics has applications in many other fields too. In hospitals, sensitive electronic equipment checks the patients' heartbeat and brain-wave patterns and enables X-ray photographs to be taken. On the roads, computer-controlled signals help to ease traffic flow. Radar equipment is used on land, sea and in the air for direction-finding, navigation and other purposes (see page 180). In the home, items such as washing machines are often controlled by microcircuits and they carry out a sequence of operations unattended. And pocket calculators are widely used in schools and offices.

The most fascinating aspect of electronics is that circuits can be designed to carry out almost any function. So it seems that in the future, electronic equipment will gradually take on more and more of the routine, boring tasks, both in industry and in the home. This should help the economy and enable us to lead more leisurely lives.

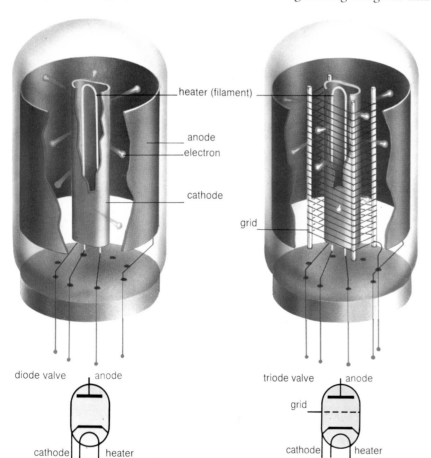

diode valve | anode

cathode | heater

triode valve | anode

grid

cathode | heater

heater (filament)

anode
electron

cathode

grid

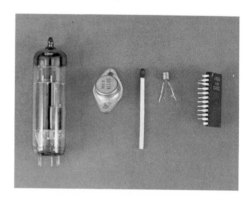

Above: A modern valve (left) compared in size with a matchstick, two transistors and an integrated circuit (right). The circuit contains the equivalent of thousands of transistors, built into a silicon chip.

Below: The internal structure of a transistor, with the crystal on the right.

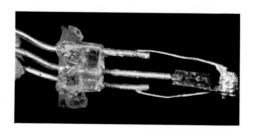

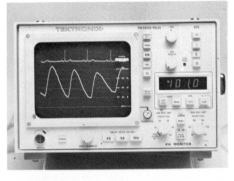

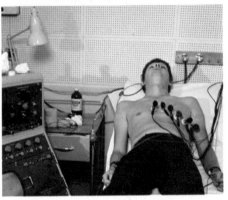

Above and above right: The tiny, square device on the tip of the index finger is a silicon chip. This thin slice of crystal contains a complex integrated circuit made up of about 5000 transistors. A magnified picture of the circuit is shown on the right. The circuit itself measures only about 2 millimetres square. Various parts of the circuit are connected to points around the edge of the square. The integrated circuit is normally contained in a plastic case with rows of protruding metal pins. These are wired to the circuit's connection points and are used to make connections with other components. Chips like this one are widely used in modern electronic devices.

Below left: Until a few years ago, most new electronic equipment consisted of numerous separate components soldered on to a circuit board. Copper strips below the board made connections between the various components. The circuit board shown here contains many transistors, capacitors (condensers) and resistors. Most of these circuit components could now be replaced by a single integrated circuit capable of carrying out the same functions. Such a circuit need be no more than a few millimetres square.

Below right: This integrated circuit measures only 5 millimetres square and is only $\frac{1}{4}$ millimetre thick.

Top: An example of the use of electronics in hospitals. This monitor shows a patient's heartbeat (upper trace) and blood pressure (lower trace). Pulse rate, blood pressure or blood temperature can be displayed in figures on the right.

Above: Signals picked up from a patient's heart are recorded on an electronic ECG machine.

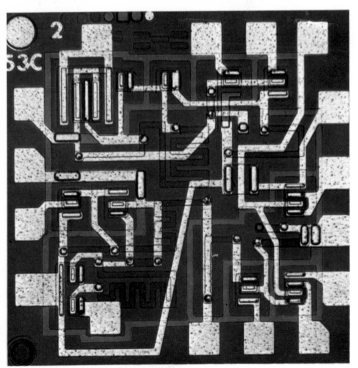

Radio

The story of radio began in 1887, when a German scientist called Heinrich Hertz discovered how to generate and detect radio waves. This led others to investigate the mysterious waves and, in 1896, the Italian Guglielmo Marconi patented the first practical system of wireless telegraphy. In 1901 Marconi managed to send a signal across the Atlantic.

Below: Sound signals are transmitted by using them to modulate (vary) radio waves. The radio waves are called the carrier, as they 'carry' the sound signals. The carrier can be modulated in various ways. The most common techniques are amplitude modulation (AM) and frequency modulation (FM). In amplitude modulation, the sound signal (1) is used to vary the amplitude (strength) of the carrier (2). The frequency of the modulated carrier (3) remains constant. In frequency modulation, the sound signal varies the frequency of the carrier (4), while its amplitude remains constant. Both AM and FM waves are used for radio broadcasts.

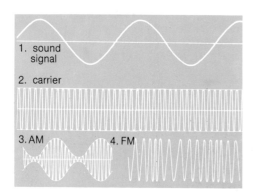

At first, radio was used only as a means of transmitting Morse code signals. Then, following the invention of the triode valve in 1906, it became possible to transmit actual sounds too. So messages could be spoken instead of having to be translated into Morse. Broadcast programmes of speech and music followed, and radio became a means of mass communication.

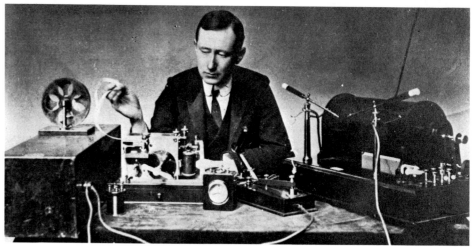

Above: The Italian Guglielmo Marconi, who developed wireless telegraphy equipment in the 1890s and early 1900s.

Below: In a transmitter, the oscillator produces a carrier signal. After amplification, this is modulated by sound signals from the studio. The modulated carrier is then amplified and fed to a transmitting aerial. This radiates the signals as radio waves. (This diagram shows AM waves.)

How radio works

The most important part of a radio transmitter is the *oscillator*. This generates a signal that can be radiated from an aerial as radio waves. To transmit Morse code, which is made up of dots and dashes, the oscillator is switched on and off so that the radio waves are transmitted in bursts. A short burst corresponds to a 'dot' in

Below: Radio waves induce extremely weak electric signals in the aerial of a receiver. Tuning circuits select the required signals, which are then amplified. A demodulator, or detector, extracts the sound signal from the radio frequency carrier. The sound signal is then amplified and fed to a loudspeaker, which reproduces it as sound. Electrical interference can spoil AM reception because it alters the amplitude of the waves, but it has little effect on FM.

Below: A sound broadcasting studio and its control room with tape and disc equipment. The window between the rooms is double-glazed to provide good sound insulation.

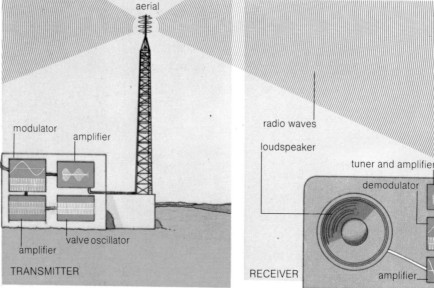

the code, and a long burst represents a 'dash'. To transmit sound, the sound is first converted to an electrical signal by means of a microphone. The sound signal is then used to *modulate* (vary) the signal produced by the oscillator. After modulation, the oscillator signal is radiated from the aerial as before, but in this case the radio waves are continuous. The oscillator signal is

thus made to carry the sound signal. For this reason, the signal from the oscillator is called the *carrier*.

A carrier can be modulated in several ways. The most common are amplitude modulation (AM) and frequency modulation (FM). An unmodulated carrier consists of waves generated at a frequency, or rate, of thousands or millions each second.

The amplitude, or strength, of the carrier is constant – that is, each wave is the same height as the next. In amplitude modulation, the amplitude of the carrier is made to vary according to the strength of the sound signal. At the receiver, these variations are detected and reconverted into a sound signal. This is then reproduced through a loudspeaker. Reception of amplitude-modulated signals is sometimes spoiled by electrical interference. This becomes superimposed on the transmitted carrier, causing unwanted amplitude modulation. The receiver cannot distinguish between wanted and unwanted amplitude modulation, and so converts the interference into hiss and crackles. In frequency modulation, the sound signal varies the carrier frequency. And the receiver detects only frequency changes. So the amplitude changes caused by interference are not detected and have no noticeable effect.

CHARACTERISTICS OF RADIO WAVES

exosphere (to 8000 km)

satellite

560 km

ionosphere

very high, ultra high, super high and extra high frequencies

super high frequencies

super high frequency of 4 to 8 gigahertz

330 km

280 km

short waves (night)

short waves (day)

200 km

medium waves

long waves

100 km

stratosphere

troposphere

50 km

Above: In the upper atmosphere are layers of charged particles forming the ionosphere. These layers reflect some radio waves, enabling them to be picked up over a wider area. Extremely short waves penetrate the ionosphere and can be used for satellite communication.

Above: This low-power TV and VHF radio transmitter ensures good reception in a valley shielded from the main transmitter.

179

Radar

Radar is a means of 'seeing' by radio. It enables the direction and range of distant objects to be determined accurately, even in fog or at night. The name 'radar' comes from the words 'RAdio Detection And Ranging'.

Radar depends on two basic principles discovered early this century. Radio signals can be reflected. And the direction from which they come can be determined accurately. In 1901, Marconi transmitted radio signals across the Atlantic. This long-distance communication around the curvature of the Earth was thought to be possible because of a reflecting layer in the upper atmosphere. The theory was that signals from the transmitting station in England reached the receiver in Newfoundland by bouncing from this layer. In the 1920s, the presence of a reflecting layer in the atmosphere was confirmed by experiment. Pulses of radio waves were sent towards the sky to see how long it took for them to bounce back again. Knowing the speed at which the signals travelled, it was then possible to work out the distance of the reflecting layer above the Earth. (We now call this layer the *ionosphere,* and know that it extends from a height of about 50 kilometres to 400 kilometres.)

In the early days of radio, it was found that receiving aerials could be made with extremely directional properties. In other words, they needed to be turned directly towards a transmitter in order to pick up its signal. Directional aerials were used in World War I (1914–18) to determine the positions of enemy shipping. This was done simply by scanning a directional aerial across the seas until it

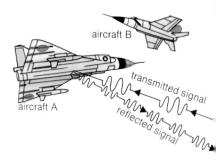

Right: This diagram shows the basic components of a typical radar system. The transmit/receive cell is an automatic switch. It operates at high speed, connecting the antenna (aerial) to the transmitter and receiver alternately. The antenna radiates a burst of radio waves each time it is connected to the transmitter. The aircraft reflect these signals back to the antenna. When the receiver is switched to the antenna, it amplifies the signals for display on a plan position indicator or range screen.

plan position indicator   range display

range marks   range

prompt action to be taken to avoid any risk of collision. Near land, the coastline can be seen on the radar screen because it too reflects pulses of radar signals.

Below: An early radar-controlled searchlight. In this experimental model, the rear aerial was used to transmit the radar signals. Reflections from aircraft were picked up by the four front aerials. Electric motors, controlled by the reflected signals, kept the searchlight pointing at the aircraft as they moved across the sky. This model was one of the first automatic tracking devices.

Below right: A ship's radar system enables it to avoid collisions when visibility is bad. A rotating antenna (aerial) sends out pulses of radar signals in all directions. Any other ships in the area reflect the pulses back to the antenna. The reflected pulses are amplified and displayed as spots of light on a plan position indicator. The range and bearing of any nearby vessel can be seen at a glance. This enables

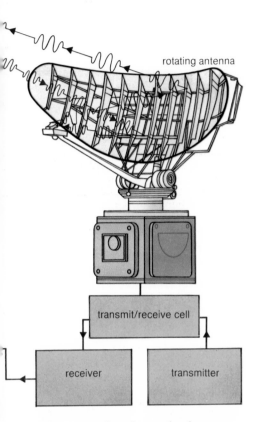

rotating antenna

transmit/receive cell

receiver

transmitter

Below: Overlapping radar beams are emitted from O. Targets along OP reflect the beams equally. Unequal reflections from targets along OABT enable their directions to be found.

picked up a ship's radio signals. This technique, called *radiolocation*, only gave an indication of direction, not range (distance). But it proved extremely useful in detecting movements of enemy warships. The actual location of a transmitter could be found only if bearings were taken from two receiving systems at different locations.

Radar was first developed in Britain in the 1930s to give early warning of the approach of enemy aircraft. Like the ionosphere, an aircraft would reflect pulses of radio waves. So its distance from the radar station could be found by timing the signals. And, if a directional aerial was used to receive the signals, then the exact location of the aircraft could be found.

A convenient way of measuring the time between transmitted and reflected signals is to display them on the

Below: The plan position indicator displays a map of the area covered by the radar system. The centre of the map represents the position of the radar antenna. Objects reflecting radar signals show up as patches of light on the screen. Compass bearings marked around the screen show the direction of any object. The distance of the object from the antenna is indicated by a series of range circles.

cathode-ray tube of an oscilloscope. This can show the transmitted pulse, a gap and then the pulse received back from the aircraft, or other reflecting target. By means of a suitable scale, the length of the gap between the pulses can be read directly in terms of the distance between the radar station and the target. But other display systems can give much more information than this. The *plan position indicator*, for example, shows a map centred on the radar station. A rotating aerial sends out pulses in all directions. The reflected signals are displayed as spots of light, correctly positioned on the map to represent the reflecting objects.

Peace-time uses for radar include air and sea navigation, air traffic control, vehicle speed measurement, the detection of storms and the study of planets and comets.

Below: Modern warships are equipped with radar systems for purposes of navigation, defence and attack. Here engineers are testing a radar-operated gunfire control system on board the USS *California*. This is one of the US Navy's nuclear guided missile frigates. The screen of a plan position indicator can be seen in the middle of the central control console. The radar antenna is on top of the ship.

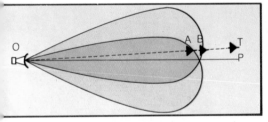

Left: A radar tower and antenna used by an airport's air traffic control. The antenna is often called a scanner, as it turns continually to probe different parts of the sky. It measures about 12 metres across. Aircraft hundreds of kilometres away can be detected by means of radar.

Television

Work on television design started in the 1870s, soon after two telegraph engineers accidentally discovered the *photoelectric effect*. Variations in the light falling on metallic selenium was found to alter its resistance to the flow of electric current. So light values could be converted into electric signals. A signal representing brightness would be formed for each part of a picture. The signals would then be sent along wires to some distant point and there converted back into light in order to reconstruct the picture. Although the principle was quite sound, it was impossible to put into practice at the time. The main problem was that the signals produced were too weak, and no amplifying device was available at that time to strengthen them.

Gradually the problems were solved. Amplification became possible in 1906, when Lee de Forest invented the triode valve. And by the early 1920s, practical television systems had been developed. At the same time, radio broadcasting was becoming established. So it was a relatively small step to devise techniques for transmitting and receiving vision signals by radio, instead of by wires.

In a modern black-and-white television camera, a special cathode-ray tube, called an *image orthicon*, forms the video (picture) signal. A lens focuses the scene on to a light-sensitive layer at the front of the tube. The light falling on this layer makes it emit a pattern of electrons corresponding to the image brightness. These electrons strike a plate called the target and remove electrons from it. Thus the brightness of each part of the image is converted into an electronic pattern on the target. Regions with few remaining electrons correspond to bright parts of the image. And unchanged regions represent dark parts of the image. A narrow beam of electrons scans the target in a series of parallel lines. At any point where there is a lack of electrons, this is made up by absorbing electrons from the beam. The beam then returns to the other end of the tube, varying in strength according to the number of electrons

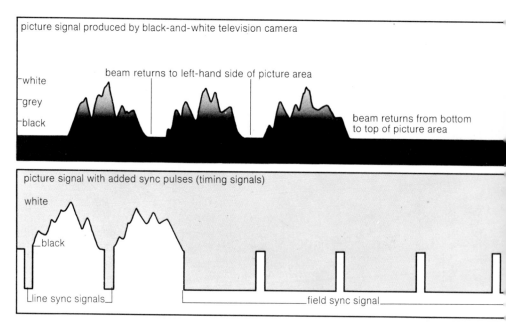

left at the target. The electrons eventually strike a plate called the *anode* and flow out of the tube as an electric current. This forms the video signal. At any instant, its strength represents the brightness of one small part of the image on the front of the camera tube.

Sound and vision are transmitted together. In the receiver, the video signal is displayed on a picture tube – another form of cathode-ray tube.

Above: The picture signal represents the brightness along each line of the image. Sync signals are added before transmission. The receiver's television aerial picks up the transmission. The field-sync signal makes the television set start reconstructing the picture from the top of the screen. The line-sync signals control the time at which each new line is started.

This has a screen coated with a chemical that glows when struck by electrons. An electron beam traces out a series of lines across the screen. And the strength of the beam is controlled by the video signal. Thus the glow produced at each point varies according to the strength of the video signal, and a reproduction of the original scene is formed, bit by bit. This occurs so rapidly that, to the eye, the picture appears complete.

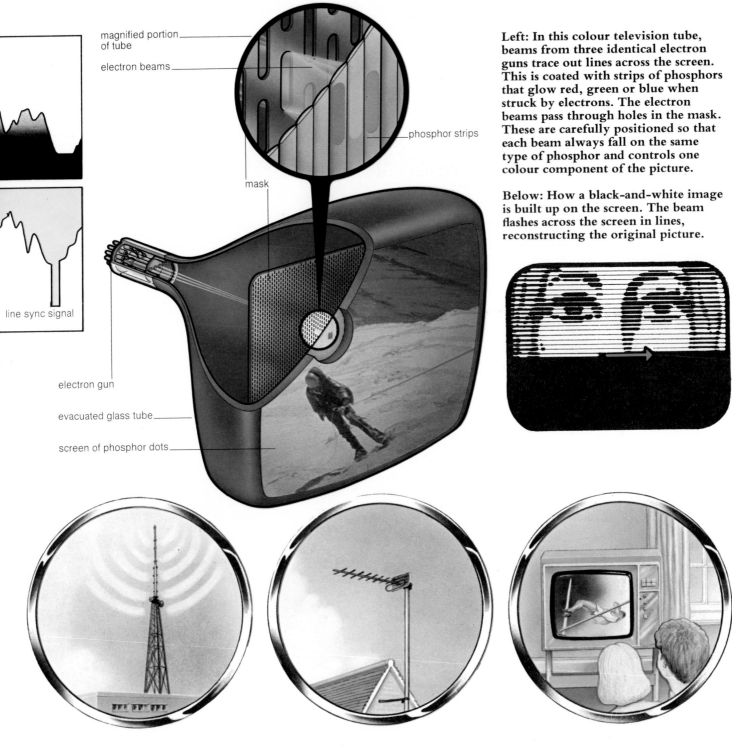

magnified portion of tube

electron beams

phosphor strips

mask

line sync signal

electron gun

evacuated glass tube

screen of phosphor dots

Left: In this colour television tube, beams from three identical electron guns trace out lines across the screen. This is coated with strips of phosphors that glow red, green or blue when struck by electrons. The electron beams pass through holes in the mask. These are carefully positioned so that each beam always fall on the same type of phosphor and controls one colour component of the picture.

Below: How a black-and-white image is built up on the screen. The beam flashes across the screen in lines, reconstructing the original picture.

Above left: A television studio during the recording of a play. The microphone, hung from a long boom, is kept close to the actors when they are talking. Care is taken to prevent the microphone appearing in the picture. Several cameras are used to provide different views. The pictures and sound are recorded on a videotape machine.

Above: Television transmitting aerials are mounted on tall masts so the signals reach a large area.

Above: Best reception of television signals is obtained by using an outside aerial. And, in some areas, the signals are so weak that an outside aerial is essential. It should be mounted as high as possible and kept away from any sources of electrical interference. After installation, it should be connected by a cable to the set and rotated until the best possible picture is obtained. The aerial shown is highly directional, and must be carefully positioned to get a clear picture on the television screen.

Above: In the television receiver, tuning circuits select the required signal, which is then amplified. The sound and vision signals are separated. And the vision signal is separated into picture and sync components. Deflection circuits, controlled by the sync signals, make electron beams trace out lines across the screen (as shown in the picture above). The picture signal varies the brightness and colour along each line. In this way, a complete image of the studio scene is built up on the screen.

183

Computer technology

The rapid advances being made in many branches of science and technology owe much to the computer. Man would not have got to the Moon without the help of computers. For many complex calculations have to be made during a space flight, and unaided human operators are just not quick enough. However, it would be a mistake to think of computers as mere calculators. Another important function is the simulation of physical processes. For example, a computer can be used to train pilots by simulating the movements of an aircraft. This allows pilots to gain flight experience without even leaving the ground. A screen shows a view similar to that seen from an actual aircraft. As the pilot operates aircraft-type controls connected to the computer, the view changes accordingly. Any number of takeoffs, landings and emergency situations can be simulated without risk, and without interfering with an airport's normal traffic.

Analog and digital techniques

The most useful computers consist of complex electronic equipment. But many simple devices can be used as computers too. And they illustrate clearly the difference between the two main kinds of computer – analog and digital. All analog computers use variable quantities to represent other variable quantities. The ordinary mercury thermometer, for example, is a simple analog computer. For the mercury column rises or falls in an *analogous* (similar) way to the surrounding temperature. Whereas analog computers depend on the *measurement* of variable quantities, digital computers calculate by *counting* fixed quantities. For example, a child counting on his fingers is using his hands as a simple digital computer. Each finger represents one unit. An early digital computer still widely used in some countries is the abacus, or bead frame.

Electronic analog computers are useful for solving problems in engineering design. For example, to investigate the stability of a ship in rough seas, voltages would be used to represent such factors as the waves and the ship's load. These voltages would form the inputs to the computer. The computer output could be a diagram of the ship displayed on a screen. Specially designed circuits in the computer would produce appropriate changes in the output in response to changes at any input. As a result, the ship on the screen would respond to the voltage representing the waves, in exactly the same way that the real ship would respond to real waves.

Most electronic computers are of the digital type and they carry out simple calculations at high speed. All information used is converted into coded pulses. These can be stored as magnetic pulses on tape or as holes punched in cards, and converted into electrical pulses when required. A *program* of coded instructions controls the way the computer deals with the information fed in. The computer may record its results on tape or print them out automatically.

Below: A piece of punched computer tape. The information stored on punched tape can be used as the input to a computer (bottom). The control unit organizes the computation carried out by the arithmetic logic unit according to a program of instructions. Stores hold data until it is required.

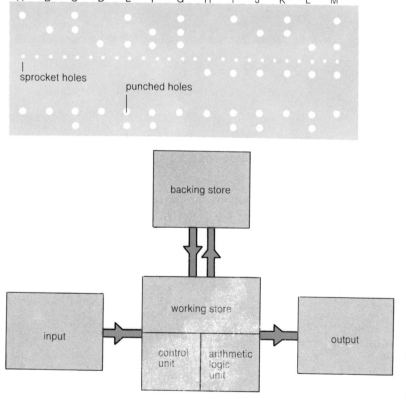

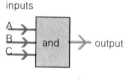

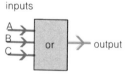

inputs			out-
A	B	C	put
0	0	0	0
0	0	1	0
0	1	0	0
0	1	1	0
1	0	0	0
1	0	1	0
1	1	0	0
1	1	1	1

inputs			output	
A	B	C	or	ex or
0	0	0	0	0
0	0	1	1	1
0	1	0	1	1
0	1	1	1	0
1	0	0	1	1
1	0	1	1	0
1	1	0	1	0
1	1	1	1	0

input	output
0	1
1	0

Above: These logic circuits are used in digital computers. They give an output: when all *and* inputs are on; when any *or* input is on; or when the *not* input is not on.

Left: These tables correspond with the computer logic circuits next to them. They are called truth tables and show how the outputs of the circuits vary according to the input signals applied. The 0s and 1s represent the absence and presence of signals respectively. These two states are referred to as off and on.

The table for the *and* circuit shows that its output is 1 only when A and B and C are 1. Any other input combination results in 0 at the output.

The middle table shows the output for the *or* circuit, and also the output for an *exclusive or* circuit. When A or B or C or any combination of them is 1, then the *or* output is 1. But the *exclusive or* circuit has an output of 1 only when A or B or C is 1, and not when more than one of the inputs is 1.

The bottom truth table shows that the output from the *not* circuit is the opposite of its input.

All computers contain complex combinations of *and*, *or* and *not* circuits, together with other kinds of logic circuit. These are the basic units that enable the computer to carry out calculations and work out problems.

Above: In industry, computers are widely used to check or control various processes. Here a computer is providing information on the oxygen flow and operating temperature of a converter used to make steel. The information appears on a screen mounted in the converter's control desk. The use of computers in industry increases efficiency and reduces costs.

Below left: A row of tape machines used as part of a computer system. Information is stored on the tapes as patterns of magnetized dots.

Below: A visual display unit, used for obtaining information stored in a computer. The operator can request information by pressing buttons on the keyboard. Answers are displayed almost immediately.

Telephone calls

When telephones were first made available, all the exchanges were manually operated. To telephone someone, you had to ask a switch-board operator to make the necessary connection. But, as the number of subscribers increased, the need for automatic exchanges became apparent. Today, most calls are made by dialling, or by pressing numbered buttons. Equipment at the telephone exchanges automatically connects a caller's telephone to the number required.

Originally, all connections between exchanges were made by means of wires – one pair for each conversation. Over the years, more and more cables were laid to cope with the ever increasing number of calls. And various techniques were developed to enable several calls to be sent along a single pair of wires. But wires are not the only means of transmitting signals from one exchange to another. Many calls are now transmitted by radio

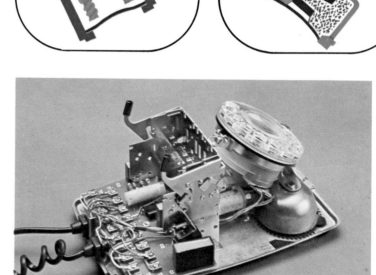

handset

caller's phone

earpiece

microphone

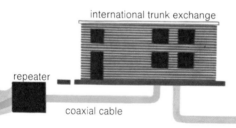

international trunk exchange

repeater

coaxial cable

submarine coaxial cable

fibre-optic link

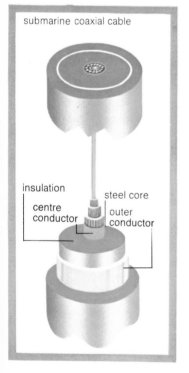

submarine coaxial cable

insulation

centre conductor

steel core

outer conductor

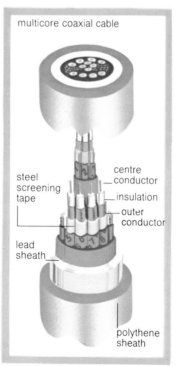

multicore coaxial cable

steel screening tape

centre conductor

insulation

outer conductor

lead sheath

polythene sheath

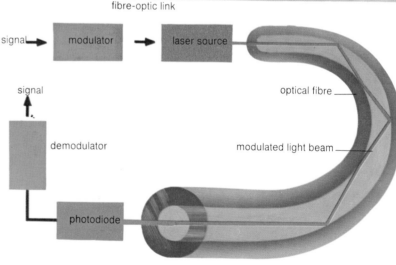

signal → modulator → laser source

optical fibre

signal

demodulator

modulated light beam

photodiode

Left: Details of submarine coaxial cable and the multicore coaxial cable used on land. These cables can carry thousands of telephone calls simultaneously. This is done by superimposing the calls on carrier waves, like those used in radio transmissions.

186

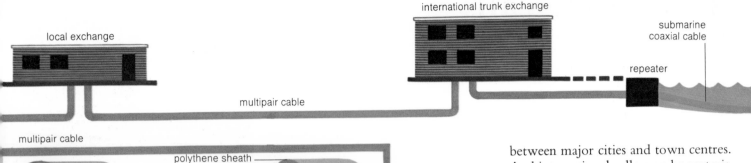

local exchange

multipair cable

international trunk exchange

submarine coaxial cable

repeater

multipair cable

polythene sheath

cable pairs

lead sheath

between major cities and town centres. And international calls may be sent via a satellite hovering many thousands of kilometres above the Earth.

Fibre optics

Another very important technique is fibre optics – the use of hair-like glass fibres to transmit light from one place to another. The fibres are designed in such a way that light passing in at one end travels to the other, no matter how much the fibre is bent. Fibre optics are important in telephone communications because light can be used as a carrier of speech signals, just as radio waves are used as carriers (see page 178). So telephone signals can be impressed on a light beam and transmitted along a glass fibre. In fact, millions of calls can be carried on a beam of laser light travelling along a single fibre no more than one-tenth of a millimetre thick. Of course, a laser beam can be used for communication without the need for fibre optics. But such a system can be used only between points within sight of one another. A fibre-optic cable allows light to be guided along any route just as easily as an ordinary cable guides electricity.

The automatic exchange

When a caller lifts his telephone handset, a switch in the exchange connects his line to a series of selectors called Strowger switches. Then the dialling tone is automatically connected across the line, indicating that the equipment is ready to accept the call. Dialling a digit sends pulses of electricity to operate the first switch. This connects the caller to a second switch, which moves when the second digit is dialled. In this way, the caller is routed through to a final switch. If all goes well, this connects the caller to the required number, and ringing commences.

Left: A modern telephone with the case removed to show the circuits, cradle-switch mechanism and the bell gongs.

Above left: A telephone handset, with sectional diagrams of the microphone and earpiece. In the microphone, sound waves vary the resistance of some carbon granules. A current flowing through the granules is thus made to vary like the sound waves. In the earpiece, sound signals from the other end of the line pass through an electromagnet. The varying current causes similar variations in magnetism. This makes a thin metal diaphragm near the electromagnet vibrate and reproduce the original sound.

Above: Part of a route by which a telephone call is made to a person overseas. Details of the multipair cable, which can carry 4800 wires, are shown in the box.

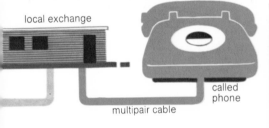

local exchange

called phone

multipair cable

Left and above: A continuation of the long-distance telephone circuit shown at the top of the page. Repeater stations placed along the line boost the signals to prevent deterioration in quality becoming excessive. Between the international and local exchanges, the signals are carried on a fibre optic link. This consists of a glass fibre that guides light along it. A laser beam directed at one end of the fibre will emerge from the other end, no matter how much the fibre is bent. The beam simply bounces from the walls of the fibre and remains inside, as shown in the detailed diagram. The beam is modulated by the signal. At the far end, a photodiode and demodulator re-form the electric signal. Each fibre carries millions of calls.

Right: In a telephone exchange, wires from thousands of subscribers are connected to tag blocks. From there, they are linked to selectors and other equipment.

Lasers

Lasers produce pure light. It can be intense enough to cut through steel, or delicate enough to weld tissues in eye operations. Laser light is also used in precision measuring instruments and in communications systems. A single beam of the light can carry millions of telephone calls (see pages 186–7). And life-like three-dimensional images can be produced by special photographic techniques using laser light. This relatively new branch of technology is called *holography*.

Light is a form of energy that is transmitted as electromagnetic waves (see page 135). The length of a light wave determines the colour sensation it produces in the eye. A laser beam consists of light of one wavelength only, and thus has a characteristic colour. Ordinary white light is a mixture of light of different wavelengths. A coloured beam can be produced simply by passing white light through a colour filter. But, although the light might look identical in colour to a laser beam, it would differ in one important way. For a laser beam consists of what is called *coherent* light – all the waves rise and fall together. In a coloured beam produced by filtering ordinary white light, the waves would not be in step with one another. Such light is said to be *incoherent*.

The coherent light produced by a laser has quite different properties from incoherent light. Laser light is emitted as an almost parallel beam and can travel great distances without widening very much. This enables a laser beam to be directed with great accuracy on to a distant target. The beam might be used instead of radar to determine the range (distance) of an object. Or, if powerful enough, the beam could even be used to destroy the object. Experimental 'death-ray' laser beams have been used to bring down target aircraft at distances of over 3 kilometres. But the range cannot be extended much beyond this because atmospheric effects tend to distort the high-energy beam.

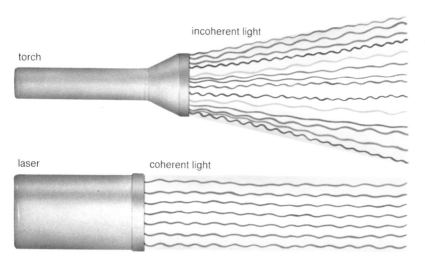

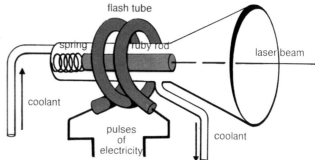

Above and below: A ruby laser consists basically of a coiled flash tube and a ruby rod. Light from the flash tube makes the ruby emit particles of light energy called photons. These are reflected back and forth between two mirrors, finally emerging as a laser beam.

Above: The diagrams show the differences between a torch beam and the light emitted by a laser. The torch beam is whitish. Like sunlight, it contains light of various frequencies. The laser beam has a characteristic colour determined by the substance used to produce the beam. All the waves in a laser beam have the same frequency. And they are emitted in phase (step) with one another in a parallel beam of what is called coherent light.

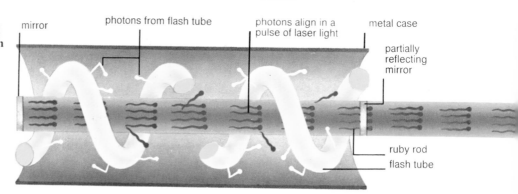

Left: The coherent light from a laser can be used to photograph and reproduce objects in three dimensions. This technique is called holography. The photographic record does not resemble the object. It is made up of abstract patterns, formed when laser light reflected by the object is mixed with an undisturbed beam. The image, in this case a telephone, is reproduced by illuminating the hologram with laser light.

Above: Beams of laser light can be used to produce interesting lighting displays. Here a laser beam is used to project an image.

Below: A powerful beam from a carbon dioxide laser quickly cuts through sheet metal. As a cutting tool, the laser is unique as it does not make contact with the material. The laser is also used for drilling and welding.

However, the accuracy with which a laser beam can be projected has proved extremely useful at short distances. In surgery, the retina of the eye can be repaired by welding it with a flash of laser light lasting only one-thousandth of a second. And, in dentistry, laser beams are now being used for burning away decayed parts of teeth. In industry, too, lasers are used for many precision operations. A fine beam of laser light can make tiny holes in extremely hard substances, such as diamond and steel. And the heat of a laser beam can be used for welding together metal parts quickly and accurately, and also for cutting through metal sheet.

To the general public, holography has proved to be the most interesting application of laser light. The solid-looking images produced are unlike those produced by conventional three-dimensional photography, which show only the view as seen by the camera. With a holographic image, changing your position gives you a different view, just as if you were looking at a real object.

Fighting fires

Fires, when uncontrolled, endanger or even destroy life and property. Dangerous fires usually start accidentally, as when someone fails to put out a lighted match or cigarette. Sometimes, however, someone will deliberately set fire to property, a crime known as *arson*. During wars and rebellions, much damage may also be done by fire.

Early fire brigades

The earliest well-organized bands of fire-fighters, or fire brigades, were those of the ancient Romans. Roman firemen used many items of equipment that are still familiar today. These included water pumps and hoses for dousing fires, ladders for reaching up to burning areas, and pickaxes for clearing away and demolishing fire-damaged structures.

After the fall of the Roman empire, the craft of organized fire-fighting was lost for well over 1000 years. As late as 1666, a great fire destroyed most of the City of London, largely because there was no efficient fire-fighting service.

After this time, fire brigades began to be formed in many towns and cities. In the 18th century, the first fire engines appeared. These were carts drawn by firemen or horses, bearing pumps, hoses and supplies of water.

In the early 19th century, steam-powered pumps were used, and later the fire engines themselves were driven by steam. The much speedier fire engines of today are powered by diesel engines. Their powerful pumps can spray water for hundreds of metres and their rescue ladders can reach several storeys high.

Suits, sprays and sprinklers

All firemen normally wear protective clothing, including the famous metal helmet. To enter a blazing building, a fireman will put on an asbestos suit which protects him completely against the flames, and he will carry his own air supply.

Hand-held fire extinguishers are now found in most buildings. These spray either water for dousing the fire, or a chemical foam or powder for

Above: Fighting a large fire in a London hospital. Two firemen are perched atop two turntable ladders, which can reach 45 metres high. A third, telescopic ladder reaches up to one of the highest windows of the hospital, in order to rescue people who may be trapped by the fire. The fire-fighting vehicles here include those carrying the ladders, fire engines with pumps, and control vehicles.

smothering the flames or starving them of oxygen.

All large buildings are now also required to have fire escapes leading outside to ground floor level, and fire alarms to warn the public and the fire brigade. Many buildings also have an automatic sprinkler system which begins to spray water when the inside temperature reaches a certain level.

In streets and buildings, water for fire-fighting is provided through fire hydrants, to which hoses may be connected. For forest fires, water has to be taken to the fire, or pumped from a nearby lake. Forest fires are also fought by localizing them. Foresters fell lines of trees to make gaps that the fire cannot bridge.

Below: For tackling very hot fires, such as this burning oil, firemen need to wear very special clothing. The fire-fighting suits shown here cover the whole body. They are made of special heat-resistant materials and will not burn, so that the firemen can get very close to the fire, or even walk through it unharmed. Special breathing apparatus may be used when dangerous fumes are present.

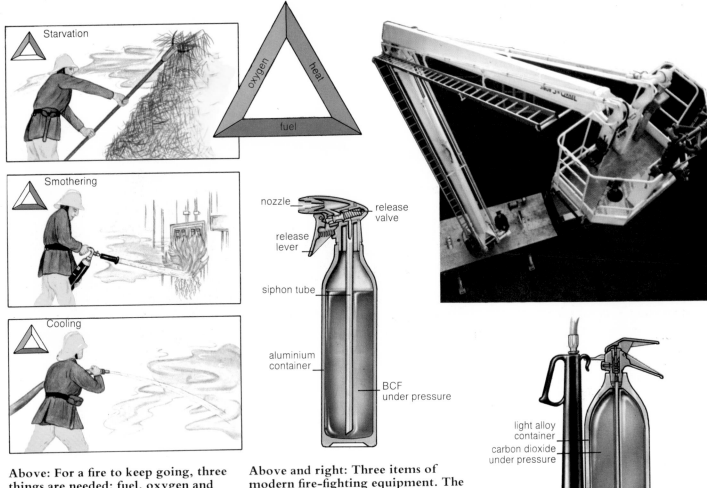

Starvation

Smothering

Cooling

oxygen · heat · fuel

nozzle
release valve
release lever
siphon tube
aluminium container
BCF under pressure

light alloy container
carbon dioxide under pressure
distributor horn

Above: For a fire to keep going, three things are needed: fuel, oxygen and heat. In the top picture, the fireman is starving the fire by removing its straw fuel. In the centre picture, he is keeping out oxygen by smothering the fire with foam. And in the bottom picture, he is cooling the fire with water. To fight a large fire, two or even all three of these methods might be employed.

Above and right: Three items of modern fire-fighting equipment. The platform ladder can raise several firemen very quickly, by hydraulic (liquid) pressure. Hand-held fire extinguishers include those that squirt fire-smothering substances. Carbon dioxide, one such substance, is a non-flammable gas, and BCF is a non-flammable liquid. Both substances are kept under pressure in extinguishers.

Above: When an aeroplane crashes, its highly flammable aviation fuel is very likely to spill and burst into flames. To tackle these fierce fires, crash trucks, similar to the one shown here, are kept at the ready on every airfield. This one sprays foam, to smother fires.

Submarines

The first underwater ship, or submarine, was built more than 250 years ago. Its inventor, the Dutchman Cornelis van Drebbel, demonstrated his submarine before King James I by rowing it for some distance under the surface of the River Thames.

This first submarine sank underwater when attached leather bags were filled with water, so making the craft heavier than water. When water was squeezed out from these bags, the submerged craft became *buoyant,* or lighter than water, and rose to the surface again.

All later submarines were able to dive and surface in a similar way, by filling and emptying *ballast tanks* built into their hulls.

Among the earliest of propeller-driven submarines was that used in 1776, during the American War of Independence, to make an underwater attack on a British ship. However, neither this submarine nor others built at this time were very safe or useful craft. Their hand-turned propellers pushed them along only very slowly, their angle of descent could not be controlled and they could not be steered accurately at the required depth.

Modern submarines

During the last 100 years, much more efficient submarines have been built. These have all been cigar-shaped, and most were made of steel.

Driven by propellers and steered by adjustable rudders, these craft could move swiftly and accurately underwater. As fighting ships, some could carry as many as 24 torpedoes, usually to be fired at enemy ships sighted through a periscope while the submarine was still underwater.

In any modern submarine, the crew enter and leave by the *conning tower,* a water-tight structure which contains radio and radar antennas for navigation. Beneath this is the *control deck,* from which the engine, rudders, armament and air supplies are controlled. Air is supplied by pumps and valves, not only to the ballast tanks but also to all the living spaces inside the submarine.

Many fighting submarines are powered by diesel engines, but since 1955 the largest have been nuclear powered. Carrying their long-range nuclear missiles, these powerful vessels can remain submerged for months at a time, and have voyaged right around the world without surfacing.

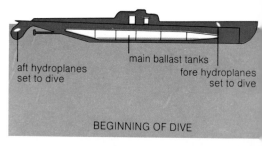

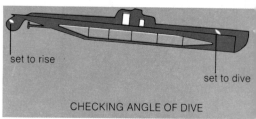

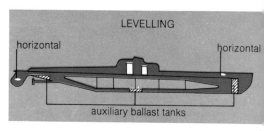

Above: Three diagrams showing how a submarine dives. First, the fins, or hydroplanes, are set to the dive position (top diagram). Then, the main ballast tanks are flooded (centre), so that the craft becomes heavier than water and sinks. At the required depth, the craft is levelled off by partially flooding and emptying smaller ballast tanks (bottom).

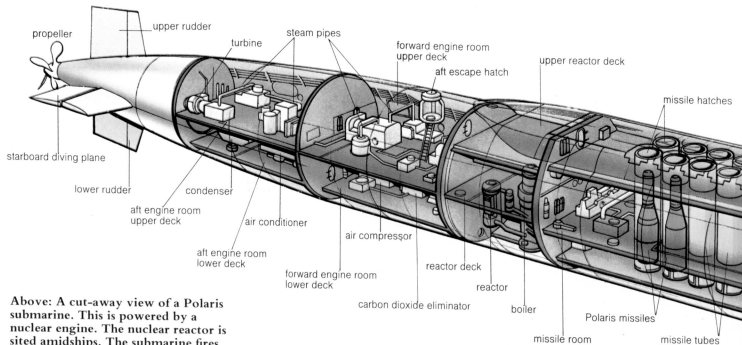

Above: A cut-away view of a Polaris submarine. This is powered by a nuclear engine. The nuclear reactor is sited amidships. The submarine fires both conventional underwater torpedoes and Polaris intercontinental missiles carrying nuclear warheads.

192

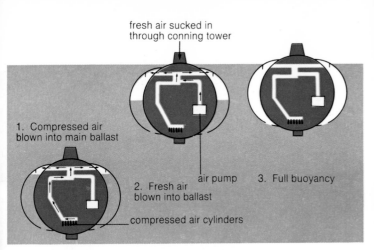

fresh air sucked in through conning tower

1. Compressed air blown into main ballast

air pump

2. Fresh air blown into ballast

3. Full buoyancy

compressed air cylinders

Above: How a submarine is brought to the surface. First, it is steered towards the surface using the hydroplanes. Compressed air (from cylinders) is then blown into the main ballast tanks, forcing some of the water out. This makes the craft more lightweight than water, or buoyant. As the conning tower leaves the water, fresh air is sucked in through it, to make the submarine fully buoyant.

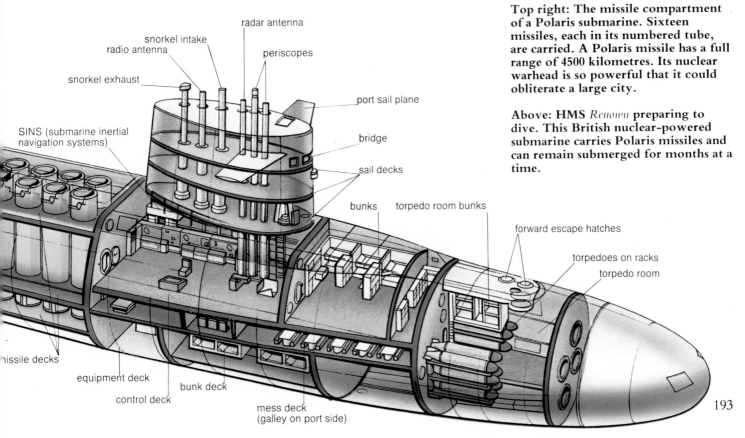

radar antenna

snorkel intake

radio antenna

periscopes

snorkel exhaust

port sail plane

SINS (submarine inertial navigation systems)

bridge

sail decks

bunks

torpedo room bunks

forward escape hatches

torpedoes on racks

torpedo room

missile decks

equipment deck

bunk deck

control deck

mess deck (galley on port side)

Top right: The missile compartment of a Polaris submarine. Sixteen missiles, each in its numbered tube, are carried. A Polaris missile has a full range of 4500 kilometres. Its nuclear warhead is so powerful that it could obliterate a large city.

Above: HMS *Renown* preparing to dive. This British nuclear-powered submarine carries Polaris missiles and can remain submerged for months at a time.

Jumbo jet

If you go on a holiday, or other visit to a far-away place, you will probably travel there and back in a large jet airliner. The largest of all is the Boeing 747, or Jumbo jet.

Since starting operation in 1970, these giant aircraft have carried a vast number of passengers to destinations all over the world. In 1979 alone, nearly three million passengers travelled by Jumbo each month.

Such a huge aircraft is certainly an impressive sight, perhaps most of all as you first approach it from the airport building, before climbing on board. The Jumbo then towers above your head to a height of more than 19 metres. Its wingspan is 60 metres and its total length is more than 70 metres. Fully loaded at takeoff, a Jumbo may weigh as much as 400 tonnes.

Inside, you will take your seat together with hundreds of other passengers. Some Jumbos can accommodate up to 500 people, but on a typical flight there would be some empty seats and probably only about 300 passengers.

The seats are arranged in rows, nine or ten seats abreast, with two aisles separating the rows. Most of your fellow passengers will be travelling economy class, but up to 48 people may pay extra to travel first class.

To get a Jumbo off the ground requires a great deal of lift and thrust. This is provided by four powerful turbofan engines (see page 197), two on each wing. After takeoff the plane

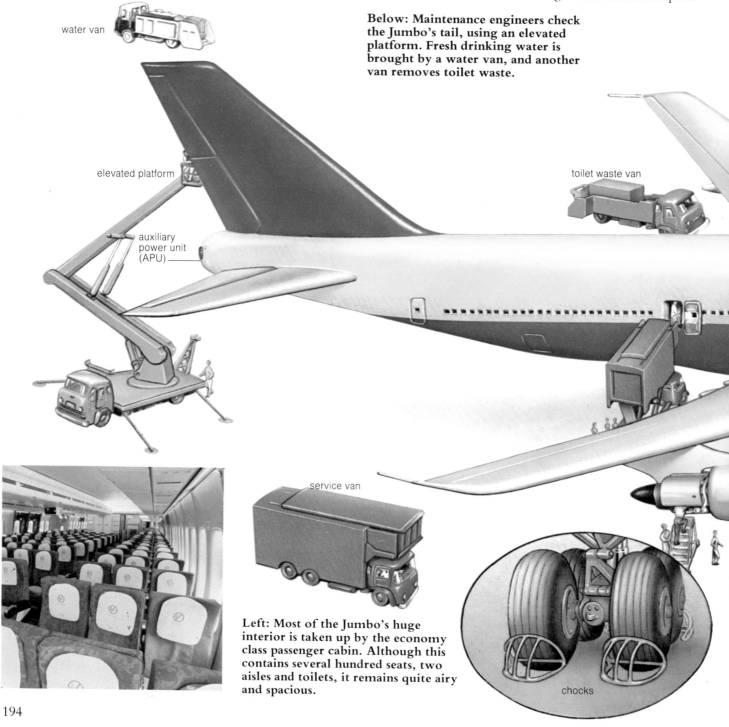

water van

elevated platform

auxiliary power unit (APU)

Below: Maintenance engineers check the Jumbo's tail, using an elevated platform. Fresh drinking water is brought by a water van, and another van removes toilet waste.

toilet waste van

service van

Left: Most of the Jumbo's huge interior is taken up by the economy class passenger cabin. Although this contains several hundred seats, two aisles and toilets, it remains quite airy and spacious.

chocks

ascends to a cruising height of nearly 14,000 metres and travels at a cruising speed of about 520 knots (970 kilometres per hour). The interior of the plane is, of course, pressurized so that you feel comfortable at such a great height. Outside, you would soon die because there is not enough oxygen to enable you to breathe.

Once airborne, you can settle back in your seat to gaze at the cloudscape, or perhaps watch a film if one is being shown. Or, you can go to sleep, but

Below: To freshen and cool the cabins, an air conditioning van may arrive to pump fresh air into the Jumbo.

you may soon be woken again by the arrival of food!

Jumbo turn-around

Jumbos cost a great deal of money and must be kept in operation for as much of the time as possible, during their active lifetime. The picture shows the many servicing operations that must be carried out between one flight and another. The total time taken for these operations is called the turn-around time. For a giant jet such as a Jumbo,

Below: Passengers may alight and disembark by mobile steps. But sometimes an enclosed passageway, or mobile jetty, is brought up to the plane's doors.

the turn-around time is about 3 hours. For some smaller jets it can be less than an hour.

After the plane has touched down at the end of a long journey, the crew leave for home or an hotel for a rest. Before a new crew arrives for the next journey, the plane must be spruced up, refuelled and checked over very thoroughly by maintenance engineers.

Refuelling takes about an hour, during which time up to 175,000 litres of aviation fuel are loaded into fuel tanks in the wings. The flight crew members, when they arrive, check the aircraft's instruments, while the cabin crew sees that all the emergency equipment, such as oxygen masks, is in good order. Baggage and other freight is loaded into the giant hold, passengers climb on board, and the Jumbo is once again ready for takeoff.

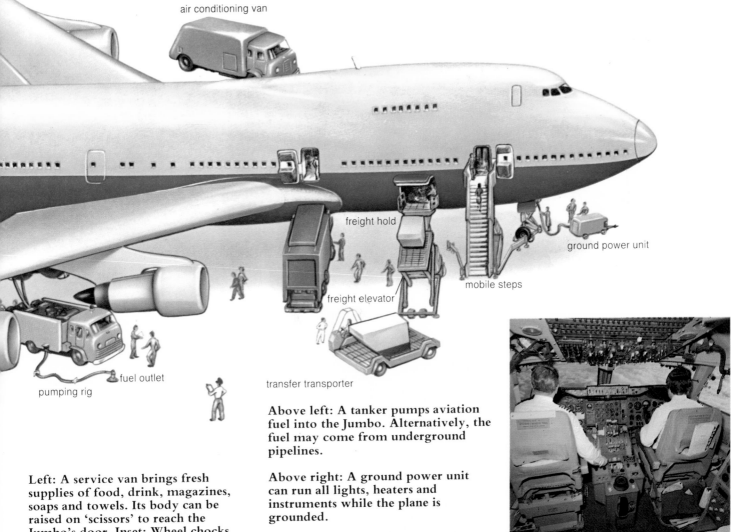

air conditioning van

freight hold

ground power unit

freight elevator

mobile steps

transfer transporter

fuel outlet

pumping rig

Above left: A tanker pumps aviation fuel into the Jumbo. Alternatively, the fuel may come from underground pipelines.

Above right: A ground power unit can run all lights, heaters and instruments while the plane is grounded.

Right: Inside the Jumbo's cockpit.

Left: A service van brings fresh supplies of food, drink, magazines, soaps and towels. Its body can be raised on 'scissors' to reach the Jumbo's door. Inset: Wheel chocks prevent the plane from moving.

195

Helicopters

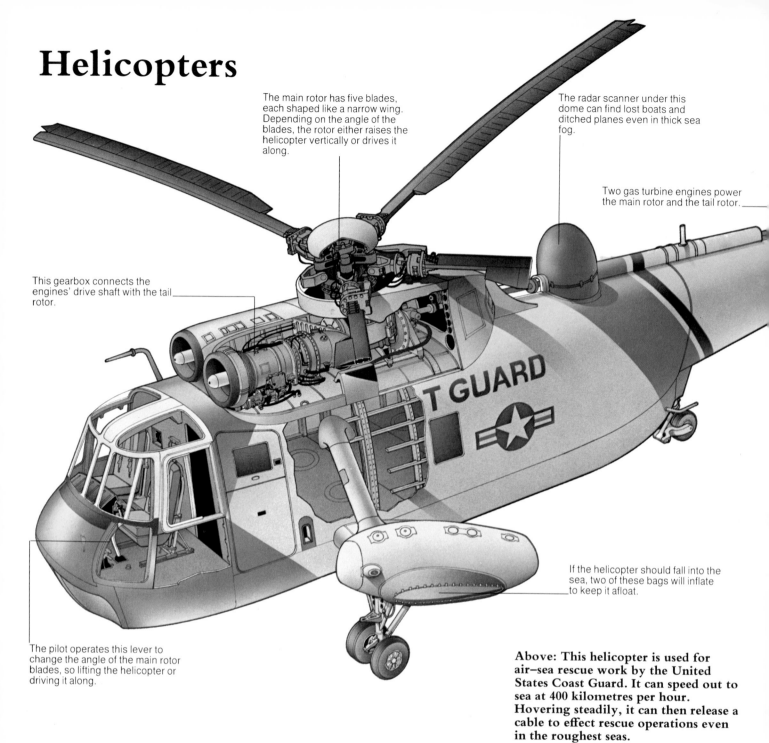

The main rotor has five blades, each shaped like a narrow wing. Depending on the angle of the blades, the rotor either raises the helicopter vertically or drives it along.

The radar scanner under this dome can find lost boats and ditched planes even in thick sea fog.

Two gas turbine engines power the main rotor and the tail rotor.

This gearbox connects the engines' drive shaft with the tail rotor.

If the helicopter should fall into the sea, two of these bags will inflate to keep it afloat.

The pilot operates this lever to change the angle of the main rotor blades, so lifting the helicopter or driving it along.

Above: This helicopter is used for air–sea rescue work by the United States Coast Guard. It can speed out to sea at 400 kilometres per hour. Hovering steadily, it can then release a cable to effect rescue operations even in the roughest seas.

Rotating wings

Almost certainly, you will have seen a helicopter fly across the sky. If you have ever visited an airport or heliport, you will also have seen how this type of aircraft takes off and lands vertically, without using a runway.

A helicopter can rise vertically into the air because its long, horizontal, rotating blades can lift it directly upwards. Helicopters have from two to seven of these blades, which together are called the *rotor*.

Other types of aircraft, as they move along, obtain lift from their

wings – this is what keeps them in the air. Each of a helicopter's rotor blades is really a thin, rotating type of wing. In fact, the name helicopter means 'rotating wing aircraft'.

Acrobats of the air

Helicopters are the most acrobatic of aircraft. They can hover quite still, or fly backwards, forwards or sideways. The pilot controls all these movements from his cockpit.

To ascend, he moves a lever that causes all the horizontal blades of the rotor to change the angle at which

they are tilted sideways, so that they 'bite' more air. This lifts the helicopter directly upwards.

By moving the lever the other way, he changes the angle of the blades so that they bite less air and so provide less lift. The helicopter then begins to descend.

By carefully balancing the lever in a midway position, he can cause the helicopter neither to ascend nor descend – that is, to hover.

To make a helicopter fly along in a horizontal direction, the pilot changes the blade angle in a different way.

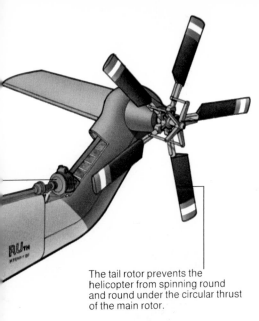

The tail rotor prevents the helicopter from spinning round and round under the circular thrust of the main rotor.

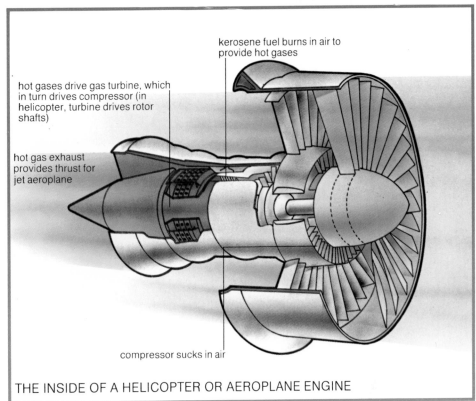

kerosene fuel burns in air to provide hot gases

hot gases drive gas turbine, which in turn drives compressor (in helicopter, turbine drives rotor shafts)

hot gas exhaust provides thrust for jet aeroplane

compressor sucks in air

THE INSIDE OF A HELICOPTER OR AEROPLANE ENGINE

Right: Engines containing gas turbines are used both in winged aircraft and in some helicopters, such as the one shown here. In jet aircraft, they drive the plane along by the thrust of their exhaust gases. In the helicopter, they turn the rotors, so providing both lift and thrust.

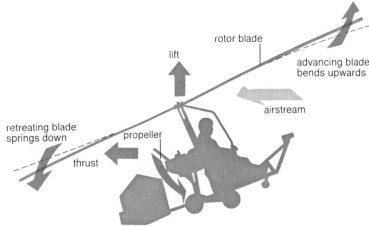

rotor blade

lift

advancing blade bends upwards

airstream

retreating blade springs down

propeller

thrust

Think of the rotating blades as forming a disc. Then if the blades in one half of the disc are angled to bite more air than those in the other half of the disc, the disc will be tilted.

When the pilot tilts the rotor blades in this way, the helicopter is thrust along in a horizontal direction, while still remaining airborne. By tilting different sides of the disc, the pilot flies his helicopter forwards, backwards or sideways.

The long rotor blades also produce a strong twisting force on the helicopter. To prevent this force

twisting the aircraft round and round in the air, another, much smaller rotor is mounted in the tail.

This tail rotor rotates vertically. It produces a twisting force which equals that of the main rotor, but which acts in the opposite direction. The twisting forces therefore cancel each other out.

Helicopters are extremely useful machines. For example, they carry passengers between city centres and airports, and vital supples to oil rigs. They are also important in dangerous rescue operations, where no other craft is able to help.

Above: An autogyro is very like a helicopter. Both machines have rotor blades, which provide lift, but the autogyro has a vertical propeller for driving it along. In this small autogyro, the propeller can be seen turning behind the pilot. Because of the immediate forward thrust of the propeller, the autogyro, unlike the helicopter, needs a runway. But because the autogyro's rotor provides such strong lift, the runway need only be a very short one.

Above left: The Wallis autogyro is a small pusher-propeller autogyro, similar to the one shown in the diagram.

Hovercraft

For short, fast journeys by sea, many people now choose to travel by hovercraft. Although this type of vehicle looks rather like a boat, it is really an aircraft.

It rides, or hovers, on a cushion of air, which keeps it clear of the surface. Air Cushion Vehicles, or ACVs, as these vehicles are also called, can travel over both water and fairly level ground, although they cannot climb steep hills.

Over water, a hovercraft can move faster than most boats, because it does not have to overcome the *drag,* or resistance, of the water. Large hovercraft that ferry passengers and road vehicles between England and France have a maximum speed of about 80 knots (150 kilometres per hour). This compares very favourably with the top speed of an ocean liner, which is about 35 knots (65 kilometres per hour).

How a hovercraft hovers

The hovercraft was invented in 1953 by a British engineer, Christopher Cockerell. In his first experiments, he blew air into a vessel resembling an upturned boat, so that the boat lifted from the ground under the pressure of the air. Air was prevented from leaking by a ring of high-pressure air jets, which were directed downwards around the lower edges of the vessel, to form an air curtain.

Cockerell soon discovered that this system needed too much air power to be really efficient. He improved it greatly by replacing the curtain of high-pressure air jets with a flexible rubber skirt which extended right around the vessel.

When air was blown into the vessel, most of it was kept in by the skirt. A quite moderate amount of air, from a fan or blower, was now sufficient to lift the hovercraft from the surface.

A further improvement was the addition of an inner skirt, so that the air now passed between this and the

Right: A hovercraft rides on a cushion of air, provided by large fans. Some air escapes from beneath the skirt, but enough always remains to allow the hovercraft to slide along easily.

Below: The US Navy employed many hovercraft like this one, in the Mekong Delta during the Vietnam War. These vehicles are ideally suited for travel in marshy areas, where boats and wheeled vehicles quickly get bogged down.

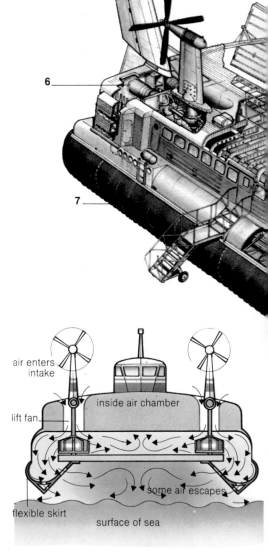

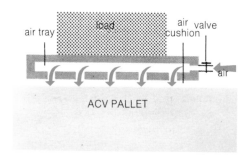

198

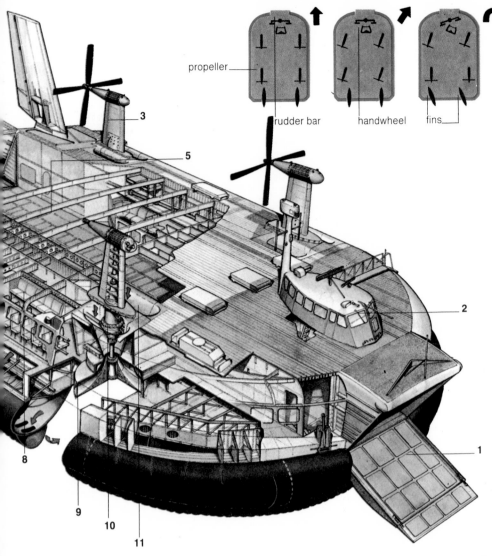

propeller

rudder bar   handwheel   fins

Above left: Three diagrams showing how the SR-N4 hovercraft is steered. The pilot controls the rudder bar and handwheel, which turn the large rear fins and the propellers and their pylons.

Left: Main parts of the British SR-N4 hovercraft:
1, car ramp (one at each end)
2, pilot's control cabin, set high on the craft to give a good view
3, propeller pylons, which can be swivelled to change the craft's direction at average speed
4, steering fins, used for steering at high speeds
5, car deck, taking up most of the space inside the hovercraft
6, gas turbine engines, which drive the propellers and fans (the exhaust gases help to push the hovercraft along)
7, the tough, flexible rubber skirt, which surrounds the craft
8, one of the main passenger cabins
9, an air cushion fan, which blows air into the cushion under the craft
10, the gearbox, which turns the fan and propeller
11, the air intake for the fan

Below: The SR-N4 hovercraft, its ramp lifted and closed, is ready to begin its regular journey across the English Channel. The craft weighs about 160 tonnes and can travel at speeds up to 150 kilometres per hour.

Below left: Hovercraft are also called Air Cushion Vehicles, or ACVs, because they travel on a cushion of air. Other types of ACVs include conveyors for moving heavy loads, such as the one being used to lift this aeroplane. The diagram below shows how the ACV pallet conveyor works. As in the other hovercraft shown on these pages, once the air cushion has been formed, there is little resistance to forward movement, so that even very heavy loads can be moved about easily.

outer skirt. The shape of the craft now resembled a smaller upturned boat inside a larger one.

Hovercraft today

Several kinds of hovercraft are in use today. Those with flexible skirts are *amphibious*, that is, they are able to travel equally well over land, sea, or marshy areas. Other hovercraft, intended only for travel at sea or along

rivers, are built with a rigid side-wall instead of a flexible skirt. The side-wall dips for a short way under the water, so keeping in the air cushion.

Amphibious, seagoing hovercraft are usually powered by engines driving large propellers. Both flexible skirted and rigid side-wall hovercraft can also be pushed along by air jets. Hovercraft are steered both by rudders and by air jets which face sideways.

To slow down and stop, a hovercraft reverses its propellers or jets. This method of braking is a much slower one than the wheel-brakes of a motor car, so that hovercraft come to a halt only gradually.

The hovercraft principle is now used to lift and transport heavy weights. Also, experimental hovertrains are built to run smoothly on a cushion of air.

Building roads

Those of us who live in developed countries take road travel for granted. Our town and country roads have hard, smooth surfaces, suitable for all kinds of vehicles. At night, the roads of towns are well lit for safety.

The beginnings of road-building
Before the mid-19th century, many of our roads were uneven, unlit dirt tracks. In winter they could turn into quagmires in which carts and coaches easily got bogged down.

The ancient Romans built long, straight roads for the movement of their armies. These had a paved surface made from flat stones laid side by side on earth that had been well flattened. A Roman road, although it lasted well, was rather like a wall laid on its side. It must have provided a very bumpy ride!

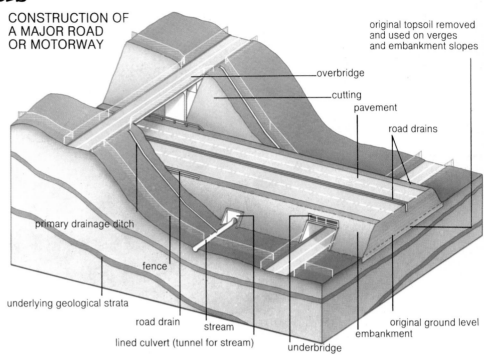

CONSTRUCTION OF
A MAJOR ROAD
OR MOTORWAY

- original topsoil removed and used on verges and embankment slopes
- overbridge
- cutting
- pavement
- road drains
- primary drainage ditch
- fence
- underlying geological strata
- road drain
- stream
- lined culvert (tunnel for stream)
- underbridge
- original ground level
- embankment

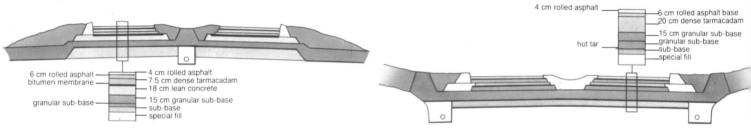

- 6 cm rolled asphalt
- bitumen membrane
- granular sub-base
- 4 cm rolled asphalt
- 7.5 cm dense tarmacadam
- 18 cm lean concrete
- 15 cm granular sub-base
- sub-base
- special fill

- 4 cm rolled asphalt
- hot tar
- 6 cm rolled asphalt base
- 20 cm dense tarmacadam
- 15 cm granular sub-base
- granular sub-base
- sub-base
- special fill

Top right: A sectioned landscape showing how a major road or motorway is constructed. It is crossed overhead by a minor road bridge, and underneath by another roadway for vehicles or pedestrians.

Above left: This cross-section of a road shows one type of construction used for a road that passes over areas of fairly well-drained land. The thickness of some of the layers may be varied to suit local traffic conditions.

Above: This cross-section shows the type of construction used when the road is passing over ground which often becomes flooded. This is a more flexible type of construction than that shown on the left.

Above: Surfacing a major road with asphalt. The large machine first lays down a hot, plastic ribbon of asphalt. It then sprays this ribbon with stone chippings coated with black, tarry bitumen, and rolls the chippings into the asphalt surface.

Below, far left: Bulldozers and scrapers cut a path for a new road.

Below centre: A huge machine lays stone chippings on a major road base.

Below: A motorway interchange near Manchester, England.

Modern roads

These began with the discovery of road-surfacing materials such as tar and bitumen. These materials, which are easily melted, are spread to make a smooth, hard surface.

When a new road is to be built, surveyors first plan its line or route. Then heavy machines move in to cut the road. Bulldozers clear away trees, rocks and even buildings that lie in the path of the road. If the road passes through hilly country, larger quantities of earth and rock are blasted away with explosives, to make road cuttings and large embankments.

In very hilly or mountainous areas, road tunnels are excavated. Most large modern roads are crossed by many bridges, which may also be built at this stage. Sometimes, as with flyovers, the road itself is raised above the ground on concrete pillars.

At ground level, large scraper machines remove topsoil to make the road bed. *Culverts,* or drainage channels, are then laid to keep the new road from flooding and its embankments from collapsing. Into the road bed is packed a hard foundation material, such as crushed rock or gravel. When this has been laid, the road is ready for surfacing.

A black-top surface is one made of bitumen together with stone chippings. The bitumen is melted, laid down and rolled flat by machines.

Other major roads are given a concrete surface. This is laid down often by a single machine, at a rate of about 2 metres per minute. Whatever the road surface, it is always laid with a *camber.* That is, it is curved so that water drains off at the roadside.

A road is completed by the laying of cat's-eyes and the painting of white lines, which indicate its traffic lanes.

Trains for tomorrow

Many trains of today carry passengers at high speed between one city and another. Among the fastest of all passenger trains are the French Mistral express and the Japanese Tokaido express. Both these super-express trains have travelled at speeds of well over 240 kilometres per hour. The British Advanced Passenger Train (APT) is another super-express, also designed to carry passengers at high speeds in complete safety. Because of its special suspension, it can travel around bends at speeds up to 200 kilometres per hour without passengers feeling discomfort.

The powerful locomotives that pull super-expresses are of three main kinds. They all have electric motors which drive the wheels.

The Mistral and Tokaido expresses, for example, both have an all-electric locomotive. Their huge electric motors are fed with electric current from an overhead power line. Electricity passes from this power line to the electric motors through a sort of metal cradle, called a *pantograph*. This projects from the roof of the locomotive and keeps in constant contact with the power line as the train speeds along.

The second type of super-locomotive, used on many modern high-speed trains, really has two engines. One is the electric motor that drives the wheels. The other is a diesel engine, which drives a generator, which drives the electric motor. So this type needs diesel fuel but no power line.

The third type of super-locomotive also has an electric motor driven by a generator. But the generator is driven by a gas turbine, which uses a fuel such as diesel oil. So far, this type has been used mainly on experimental trains, including the British APT.

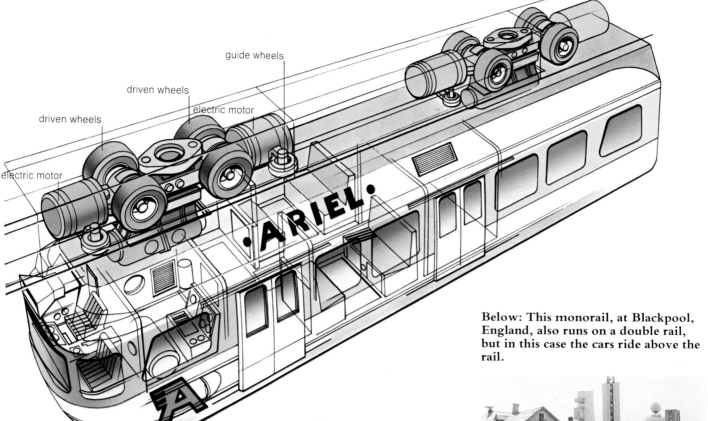

guide wheels

driven wheels

driven wheels

electric motor

electric motor

ARIEL

Below: This monorail, at Blackpool, England, also runs on a double rail, but in this case the cars ride above the rail.

Above: A French monorail. The rail car is slung beneath its rail. It runs on eight wheels, which are placed on two bogies having four wheels each. The wheels of each bogie are powered by an electric motor.

Right: The wheels of the rail car actually run on a double rail. This is formed as two parts of a single split steel box, shown in this end-on view of the rail car.

split steel box

guide rail

supporting rail

.31

Monorails and hovertrains

Many local trains and underground railway trains run on electricity that is supplied by a metal rail. This electrified rail lies close by the double-rail track on which the train wheels move.

A more recent type of electric-rail train is the monorail. These need only a single rail (or two or more rails placed very close together). The train may either travel on top of the rail, or be suspended from it (as shown in the diagrams).

Some of the fastest of all the experimental trains are monorails. One

very fast French experimental monorail is driven along its rail not by an electric motor but by a powerful jet engine like the ones that are used on jet aircraft.

The Japanese experimental monorail shown in the picture below does have an electric motor, but this is of a new, powerful type called a linear induction motor.

This train, as you can see, is kept clear of its monorail by wheels. Another type of monorail with a linear motor is kept clear of the track not with wheels, but by a cushion of air. This train is called a hovertrain, because it hovers above the track (see also Hovercraft, pages 198–9).

Hovertrains may be among the super-expresses of the future, travelling at 600 kilometres per hour or more!

Below: The British Rail APT has a top speed of more than 200 kilometres per hour. Here, it is seen cornering at high speed. Because of the self-levelling suspension, passengers feel no discomfort.

Below: This experimental monorail, in Japan, is powered by a special type of electric motor, called a linear induction motor. Such a monorail can move very fast, because there is no frictional resistance between the rail and the rail car. This model runs on wheels, which do generate some resistance. But linear induction monorails of the future will move along, like hovercraft, on a cushion of air, and so attain great speeds.

Above: A signal box at London Bridge station, British Rail Southern Region. This controls all train movements for British Rail's busiest 250 kilometres of track. Train movements are computer-controlled and the precise movements and identities of all trains are shown on the electronic track diagram at the top of the picture. This type of signal box will become increasingly important in the future.

How rockets work

Of all the propulsion engines man has ever built, the rocket is unique. It was invented long before the others, originally as a weapon. Records show that the Chinese used the rocket in a battle in 1232, and it may have been invented some 200 years earlier. The reason why the rocket came so long before other engines is that it works on an extremely simple principle. However, despite its simplicity, the rocket has proved to be of continuing importance. For it is the only engine capable of propelling a vehicle through space.

In a simple rocket, burning fuel produces large volumes of gas. This is forced from a hole at the back, causing the rocket to move forward. The principle of rocket propulsion is explained by Sir Isaac Newton's Third Law of Motion: for every action, there is an equal and opposite reaction. The rocket exerts a backward force (action) on the gas. So the gas exerts an equal, but forward force (reaction) on the rocket. In other words, it is the gas pushing on the rocket that makes it move.

Jet engines work in a similar way to rockets, but with one important difference. Jets suck in air from the atmosphere and use the oxygen it contains for burning the fuel. But rockets are completely self-contained and carry their own oxygen supply. This can take many forms. In solid-fuel rockets, one of the chemicals in the fuel mixture contains oxygen. For example, the small rockets used centuries ago as missiles were filled with gunpowder – a mixture of sulphur, charcoal and potassium

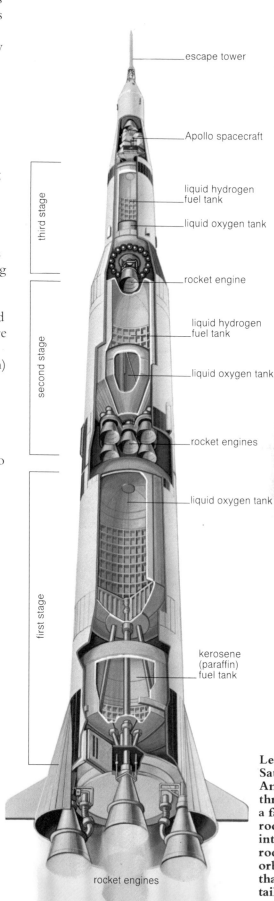

escape tower

Apollo spacecraft

liquid hydrogen fuel tank

liquid oxygen tank

third stage

rocket engine

liquid hydrogen fuel tank

second stage

liquid oxygen tank

rocket engines

liquid oxygen tank

first stage

kerosene (paraffin) fuel tank

rocket engines

second stage fires

first stage jettisoned

lift off

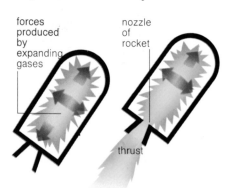

forces produced by expanding gases

nozzle of rocket

thrust

Above: A rocket is propelled by gases expelled through the nozzle.

Left: A cut-away view of the giant Saturn 5 space rocket, used for the American Apollo Moon missions. The three-stage rocket is 111 metres long – a fantastic size compared with the rockets used for man's first journeys into space. For example, the Atlas rocket that launched John Glenn into orbit in 1962 was only a little longer than the distance across the Saturn 5's tail fins.

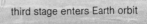

third stage enters Earth orbit

third stage fires

second stage jettisoned

escape tower jettisoned

Left and above: The sequence of events that takes place when a Saturn 5 rocket is used to launch a spacecraft. At lift-off, the five powerful engines of the first stage blast the rocket into the sky. The outer engines can be tilted to control direction. Fuel and liquid oxygen is used up at the rate of 15 tonnes per second during lift-off. After $2\frac{1}{2}$ minutes, the first stage separates and the second stage fires. This occurs at a height of 61 kilometres. The escape tower is then jettisoned. Nine minutes after lift-off, stage two separates and the third stage fires. Three minutes later, the third stage enters Earth orbit at a height of 185 kilometres. By this time, it has been accelerated to a speed of just over 28,000 kilometres per hour.

nitrate. In this case, the nitrate provided the oxygen necessary for combustion. Today, many rockets are powered by a mixture of liquid hydrogen and liquid oxygen.

When a space rocket is launched, the thrust produced by the exhaust gases causes lift-off and acceleration. But the Earth's gravitational attraction tends to pull the rocket back. The only way the rocket can break free from the gravitational field is by travelling faster than a certain critical velocity called the *escape velocity*. This is about 11 kilometres per second for a rocket leaving the Earth. Unfortunately, a simple rocket can never attain a velocity above about 6 kilometres per second. A higher velocity can be achieved only if the mass of the vehicle is reduced in some way. In practice, the problem is overcome by using a *multistage* rocket. The large first-stage rocket accelerates the vehicle to a certain velocity. Then, when its fuel is used up, this stage is separated from the rest of the vehicle and allowed to drop away. The remainder of the craft is further accelerated by a second-stage rocket engine. This is dumped after use, and a third-stage rocket then takes over. In this way, the mass of the vehicle is progressively reduced, enabling it to reach escape velocity and break free from the Earth's pull.

Above: A floodlit American Saturn 5 rocket on its launch pad at Cape Canaveral, on the Atlantic coast of Florida. The transporter that carries the rocket and its huge steel servicing tower from the rocket assembly building to the launch pad measures 40 metres long by 35 metres wide. It is the largest land machine ever built. The rocket is disconnected from the tower just before the launch.

Above: An American Titan/Centaur rocket at lift-off. The length of the rocket is about 49 metres – just under half that of the Saturn 5 launcher. It consists of a pair of solid-fuel boosters, a Titan 3 rocket and a Centaur final stage. The boosters produce more than one million kilograms of thrust at lift-off. This type of rocket was used to launch the Viking probes.

Man-made satellites

Gravitational forces help to keep the universe in order. In our part of the universe, the Sun's gravitational attraction holds the planets in orbit around it. The planets are, therefore, said to be the Sun's satellites, a term derived from a Latin word meaning 'companion'. The Earth's only natural satellite is the Moon. But, since 1957, man has made thousands of artificial satellites and placed them in orbit around the Earth.

Some artificial satellites are used for scientific research, while others provide routine services, such as communications links and weather information. Satellites also have military applications, and they have now replaced the high-flying spy aircraft once used to observe foreign terrain. Pictures taken by a satellite and transmitted back to Earth can show clearly any military manoeuvres taking place in other countries. Such information would be so useful in the event of war that 'killer' satellites have now been developed. These would be used to destroy enemy spy and communications satellites. In fact, some satellites have already been destroyed. This sometimes happens when it is suspected that a satellite described as non-military is being used for spying purposes.

Like the Moon, artificial satellites reflect sunlight and can be seen clearly in the night sky. Being small, they appear as tiny specks of light and may, at first, be mistaken for stars. But most satellites appear to move relative to the stars, although their apparent speed varies considerably. Some take only a few minutes to move right across the sky, whereas others have to be observed carefully in order to detect their relatively slow movement.

Satellites are placed in orbit by multistage rockets. The shape of an orbit is determined by the satellite's speed, height and direction when the last rocket engines were cut off. This is the instant known as *orbit injection*. Although the orbit can be circular, it usually takes a slightly flattened, elliptical form. The highest point in an orbit is called the *apogee,* and the lowest point is the *perigee.*

Right: The Russian satellite Sputnik 2 was launched in November 1957. It carried a dog called Laika, which became the first living creature to orbit the Earth. Laika died in space, for a means of returning a satellite safely to Earth had not then been developed.

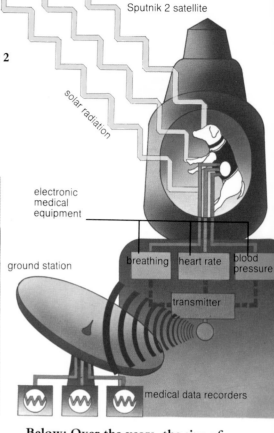

Sputnik 2 satellite

solar radiation

electronic medical equipment

ground station

breathing | heart rate | blood pressure

transmitter

medical data recorders

Above: The Russian dog Belka was among the first living creatures to return safely to the ground after orbiting the Earth.

Below: A satellite at a constant height of 1686 kilometres takes only 2 hours to orbit the Earth.

Below: Over the years, the size of communications satellites has increased dramatically. On the right of this picture is a model of the tiny Early Bird satellite (Intelsat I), which was launched in 1965. On the left is Intelsat IVA, which was put into orbit exactly 10 years later.

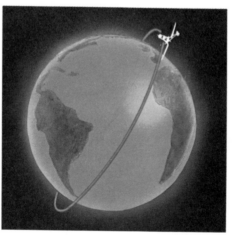

Why does a satellite stay in orbit? If it was not for the force of gravity pulling the satellite towards the Earth, it would tend to fly off into space. In the same way, if you tie an object to a piece of string and swing it around, the object would fly off if the string broke. The tension in the string acts in the same way as the Earth's gravitational force.

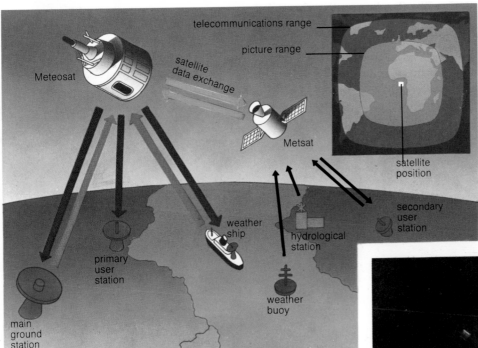

telecommunications range

picture range

satellite
data exchange

Meteosat

Metsat

satellite
position

weather
ship

hydrological
station

secondary
user
station

primary
user
station

weather
buoy

main
ground
station

Left: Meteosat hovers above the coast of west Africa, making weather observations. The satellite can also receive weather information from other satellites and ground stations. This data is transmitted to various users.

Below left: The Echo II satellite was a large balloon with an aluminium coating. This was used to bounce radio signals between ground stations.

Below: The ATS-6 satellite hovers in the sky over East Africa, relaying educational and health broadcasts from an Indian ground station to the entire Indian continent.

A satellite that is in orbit close to the Earth will be travelling faster than a similar satellite in an orbit a long distance away from the Earth. In the same way, an object twirled around on a short piece of string tends to move faster than a similar object on a long piece of string. If the satellite is in a circular orbit, it moves at a constant speed determined by its height. At a height of 35,900 kilometres, the speed will be such that the satellite makes one orbit in 24 hours. This is the time the Earth takes to rotate once on its axis. So, if the orbit is above the equator, and the satellite moves in the direction of the Earth's spin, then the satellite will appear to hover motionless. Such a satellite is said to be in *geostationary* orbit. Many geostationary satellites are used for bouncing radio, television and telephone signals from one continent to another. Unlike most satellites, which periodically pass over the horizon, geostationary satellites can provide *continuous* communications.

Other kinds of satellites in orbit above the Earth's atmosphere are used for research in astronomy.

Journeys into space

The space age started in October 1957, with the launching of the first Russian satellite, Sputnik 1. Progress in the new technology was rapid, with the United States and Russia competing in what became known as the 'space race'. The result was that within 12 years man had landed on the Moon, our nearest neighbour in space.

Man's landing on the Moon was the climax of a long space programme. Over the years, launching and re-entry techniques were perfected. And astronauts orbiting the Earth gradually acquired the necessary experience of working, eating and sleeping in space. These pictures show the sequence of operations that had to be carried out during man's longest-ever voyage of exploration. Astronauts Armstrong and Aldrin became the first two men to set foot on the Moon in July 1969. They brought back samples of Moon rock.

Sputnik 1 was a small aluminium sphere fitted with a few scientific instruments and a radio transmitter to send back data to Earth. Although less than 60 centimetres across, this first man-made moon aroused great public interest. All around the world, people watched to see the tiny, bright speck move across the night sky.

The next month saw another great achievement for the Russians when they successfully launched a larger satellite carrying a dog called Laika. This was the first animal to orbit the Earth. Medical instruments attached to the dog were connected to a radio transmitter so that their readings could be sent back to Earth. This enabled

2. After the first- and second-stage rockets have burnt out, the third stage takes the craft into orbit.

4. The CSM latches to the Lunar Module, and the joined craft leave the third stage behind.

1. The Saturn 5 rocket's powerful first-stage engines launch Apollo 11 on its Moon mission.

3. After leaving Earth orbit, the Command and Service Module (CSM) separates from the third stage.

5. After three days, the rocket on the Service Module is fired to reduce speed and enter Moon orbit.

6. The CSM remains in orbit, while the lunar Module carries two astronauts to the lunar surface.

Left: Astronaut James Irwin salutes the American flag during his Moon walk on the Apollo 15 mission. A rod is used to hold out the flag, as there is no wind on the Moon. In the centre is the Lunar Module, with a Lunar Rover on the right.

doctors to see how the dog stood up to the stress of takeoff and then to the weightless conditions in space. It was essential to obtain this information if man was to venture into space too.

Meanwhile, scientists in the United States were preparing to launch their first satellite. Named Explorer 1, this was launched in January 1958. It was

even smaller than Sputnik 1, but it enabled a most important scientific discovery to be made. Instruments in the satellite revealed the presence of a layer of charged particles around the Earth. This is now known as the inner Van Allen belt.

Having achieved satisfactory launching techniques, the next step

was to try to bring satellites safely back to Earth. For this would pave the way for *manned* space flight. The Russians concentrated on parachuting to the ground, while the Americans preferred to splash down in the sea.

By 1961, Russia was ready to stage the first manned orbital flight. On April 12, travelling in Vostok 1, Yuri Gagarin made one complete orbit around the Earth. Then rockets on the Vostock were fired to start the descent, and parachutes were used to reduce the spacecraft's speed through the atmosphere. Finally, Gagarin jumped out to make an ordinary parachute landing. America's first man in orbit was John Glenn, who made three orbits in his Friendship 7 spacecraft in February 1962.

7. **The Lunar Module fires its rocket towards the surface to reduce speed as it lands.**

10. **The Service Module is dumped near the Earth, and the Command Module starts the descent, base first.**

While experimental spacecraft were being flown around the Earth, others were being sent to the Moon. As early as January 1959, the Russian Luna 1 had flown within 7500 kilometres of the lunar surface. And, during the 1960s, manned Moon flights were being planned. In May 1969, two American astronauts circled the Moon in a controlled craft less than 14 kilometres above the surface. And, two months later, man took his first historic steps on the Moon.

8. **After exploration, the Lunar Module takes off, leaving its base section behind on the Moon.**

11. **The Command Module completes its descent by parachuting into the sea near waiting recovery vessels.**

Someday, man may travel to other planets in the solar system. But the many problems associated with living in space must first be overcome.

9. **The astronauts rejoin the CSM in lunar orbit and then blast off towards the Earth.**

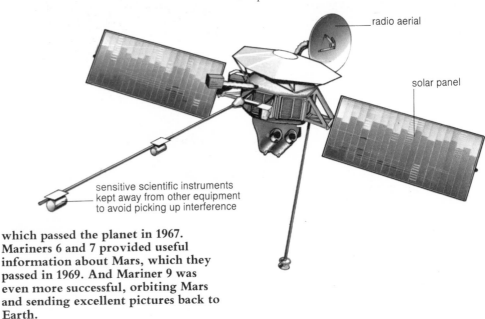

radio aerial

solar panel

sensitive scientific instruments
kept away from other equipment
to avoid picking up interference

Right: One of the series of American Mariner space probes that has provided us with much important information about the closer planets. Mariner 2 passed Venus in 1962, and Mariner 4 flew by Mars in 1965. Venus was again the target for Mariner 5,

which passed the planet in 1967. Mariners 6 and 7 provided useful information about Mars, which they passed in 1969. And Mariner 9 was even more successful, orbiting Mars and sending excellent pictures back to Earth.

Living in space

In the spring and summer of 1979, two Russian cosmonauts spent a record-breaking 6 months in space. After some 3000 orbits of the Earth in their space laboratory, Valery Ryumin and Vladimir Lyakhov returned. Then doctors began a series of tests to see what effects the journey had had on the bodies of the cosmonauts.

One effect was immediately obvious: walking on the Earth proved almost impossible for the men after such a prolonged period in space. Having spent so long in weightless conditions, their bodies were unable to cope with the effects of gravity. Suddenly, everything seemed extremely heavy, and even a simple task like moving their legs required considerable effort.

Another problem was that the two cosmonauts had lost their sense of balance. For the delicate balance-control mechanisms in their ears had been idle throughout the trip and needed time to recover.

Finding ways to combat the ill effects of space travel is important if man is ever to make long journeys to distant planets. For it is no use spending billions of pounds on a manned space mission if the crew are likely to become unfit for work. Various kinds of machine can be used to exercise the muscles, but it is impossible to ensure that every muscle in the body is kept in trim by this method. So spacecraft of the future may be provided with *artificial gravity* in an attempt to simulate conditions on the Earth.

Artificial gravity can be produced in a spacecraft simply by using a blast from a rocket to start the craft spinning. For convenience, the vehicle

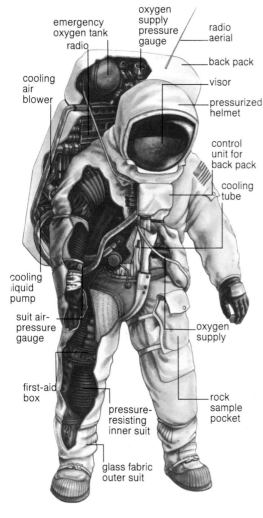

Above: American Apollo astronauts wore space-suits like this on their journeys to the Moon. It would be tiring to carry so much equipment on the Earth. But it weighs less on the Moon, which has a relatively small gravitational pull.

Labels on diagram:
emergency oxygen tank radio
oxygen supply pressure gauge
radio aerial
back pack
visor
pressurized helmet
cooling air blower
control unit for back pack
cooling tube
cooling liquid pump
suit air-pressure gauge
oxygen supply
first-aid box
rock sample pocket
pressure-resisting inner suit
glass fabric outer suit

Left: An aircraft flies in an arc to simulate the weightless conditions of space during a training programme. As in an orbiting satellite, the Earth's gravitational attraction is balanced by an equal centrifugal force in the opposite direction.

Right: If the Earth's population does not stop growing, future generations may live in space colonies. This artist's impression shows two such colonies, each more than 30 kilometres long. The mirrors reflect sunlight into the colonies.

Right: An astronaut floats in the weightless conditions of space.

210

could be made in the form of a large wheel, as depicted in many science fiction stories. The outward force produced by the spin would tend to make the contents of the spacecraft fall towards the rim of the wheel. So this would form the floor of the vehicle while it was in space. Walking along this curving floor would provide a strange sensation. There would always be a steep slope ahead. But it would be as easy to walk along as level ground on the Earth. Two people on opposite sides of the craft would be upside-down relative to each other, but both of them would feel that they were standing upright.

In weightless conditions, everything in a spacecraft tends to hover, so great care has to be taken with food, water, waste and other materials, to prevent them from contaminating the air. Besides irritating the occupants of the vehicle, such substances could cause damage to equipment. The provision of artificial gravity would solve this problem too.

Other stars, like our Sun, may have planets around them too. But manned space flight to these stars presents enormous problems. The nearest one, Proxima Centauri, would take thousands of years to reach by means of an ordinary rocket. One way to overcome this problem would be to slow down the rate at which the travellers age, by causing hibernation in some way. Alternatively, a colony of travellers could be sent so that their descendants would eventually reach the chosen planet. However, it will probably prove easier to increase the speed of travel several thousand times by developing nuclear-powered starships.

Glossary

The glossary gives a short explanation of some important, and perhaps difficult, words used in this book. These words appear in **bold type**. Words printed in *italics* are explained elsewhere in the glossary.

Adapted: (of an animal or plant) suited to a particular way of life or environment by means of physical or other characteristics. For example, a mole, with its large front digging limbs, poor vision and short hair, is adapted to burrowing.

Aerial: an electrical conductor used to radiate (give out) or to pick up *radio waves*. *Radar* aerials are generally called antennas. (In the United States, this term is used for all aerials.)

Algae: a group of plants that have no roots, stem or leaves, and that live in water or damp places. It includes a variety of plants from single-celled *organisms* to giant seaweeds.

Alloy: a mixture of a metal with one or more other metals or non-metals. Alloys generally have more useful properties than the pure metals from which they are made.

Amphibian: an animal that lives on land and in water, or any one of the group of animals that includes frogs, toads, newts and salamanders. Some members of this group spend all their time in water (see pages 68–9).

Ancestor: any individual from whom an animal or person is descended.

Antibody: a substance produced by the body, which circulates in the blood and fights infections, such as those caused by invading *bacteria*. Chemically, antibodies are types of *proteins*.

Atmosphere: the blanket of air surrounding the Earth (see pages 10–11 for a description of the layers of the atmosphere).

Atom: the smallest part of an *element* that can take part in a chemical change. Atoms consist of particles called *protons*, *neutrons* and *electrons*. These vary in number from one element to another (see pages 126–7).

Bacteria: microscopic, single-celled forms of life. Many cause disease but many others, living in water and soil, are vital to nature. These include the bacteria which cause decay.

Blood capillaries: tiny blood vessels in the body which connect the network of arteries and arterioles with that of the veins and venules (see pages 100–101).

Bloodstream: the blood flowing through the *blood vessels* of the body.

Blood vessels: tubes which extend throughout the body, carrying blood to all parts. Arteries and veins are the largest blood vessels; arterioles and venules are smaller; and the *blood capillaries* are the smallest of all (see pages 100–101).

Camouflage: disguise, by means of shape, colours or patterns that allow an animal to blend in with its surroundings and avoid being seen.

Carbon dioxide: a colourless gas present as about 0.03 per cent of the Earth's *atmosphere*.

Carnivore: a flesh-eater, or a member of the order (group) of mammals called Carnivora; this includes not only flesh-eaters, such as cats, but also bears and raccoons, which eat all types of food.

Cell: the basic unit of life, consisting of cytoplasm, nucleus, plasma membrane and (in plants) a cell wall (see pages 40–41). See also *electric cell*, which has a different meaning.

Chain reaction: a process that produces *energy* in nuclear bombs and power stations. The reaction is started by firing *neutrons* at a suitable fuel. The reactions that follow produce even more neutrons which continue the process (see pages 152–3).

Charge: an electrical property possessed by *protons* (which are positively charged) and *electrons* (which are negatively charged). Uncharged objects have equal numbers of protons and electrons. A body becomes charged if this balance is upset. Bodies with like charges repel one another, while bodies with opposite charges attract each other (see pages 128–9).

Chlorophyll: the *pigment* in plants that gives them their green colour (see also *photosynthesis* and pages 48–9).

Circuit: a path through which an *electric current* can flow. Many circuits consist of complex arrangements of components, such as resistors and *transistors*, wired to a battery or other source of power.

Compound: a chemical combination of two or more *elements*. Water, for example, is a compound of hydrogen and oxygen (see page 127).

Condensation: a change of state to a denser form, such as when a gas (or vapour) changes into a liquid (see pages 14–15 for a description of how water vapour is condensed to form clouds).

Conifer: Any one of the group of trees that includes pines, spruces, firs, cedars and larches. They all produce their seeds in cones and have long, needle-like leaves. Most are tall pyramid-shaped trees (see pages 44–5).

Continent: a huge land mass, including nearby islands. The seven continents, in order of size, are Asia, Africa, North America, South America, Europe, Oceania (Australasia) and Antarctica.

Continental shelf: the gently-sloping sea bed around the *continents*. It ends where the continental slope begins.

Crystal: a three-dimensional body whose shape is determined by the arrangement of the *atoms* within it. Nearly all minerals have distinctive crystal forms.

Digest: to break down food materials (using *enzymes* produced by the body) so that they can be absorbed by the body.

Earthquake: a sudden tremor in the *Earth's crust* (see pages 18–19).

Earth's crust: the thin, solid outer shell of the Earth, which rests on the denser mantle (see page 8).

Electric cell: a device in which a chemical reaction produces an *electric current*. A battery is made up of several cells connected together.

Electric current: a flow of *electrons*. The strength of an electric current is measured in amperes.

Electric generator: a machine for converting mechanical *energy* (energy of motion) into electricity. Some bicycles use a dynamo as a form of generator. Huge generators are used in power stations.

Electrode: an electrical conductor used to convey *electrons* to or from a substance or another electrode. In an *electric cell*, electrons enter and leave the electrolyte by means of the electrodes.

Electromagnet: a coil of wire wound around a core of soft iron. Passing an *electric current* through the coil temporarily magnetizes the iron.

Electromagnetic wave: a form of *energy* that can travel through space at the speed of light. Such waves include *radio waves*, infra-red (heat) radiation, light, ultra-violet radiation, X-rays, gamma rays and cosmic rays (see page 135).

Electron: a negatively charged particle that orbits the nucleus of an *atom*. In an electrical conductor, electrons can pass from one *orbit* to another to form an *electric current* (see page 128).

Element: one of the 106 simple substances (92 natural and 14 man-made) from which all matter is made. An element cannot be split into simpler substances. Each of its atoms has the same number of *protons* (see pages 126–7).

Embryo: an unborn baby during its first three months of development inside its mother's womb.

Energy: the capacity for doing work. Energy can take many forms, such as heat, mechanical, electrical, chemical, nuclear and radiant energy. Radiant energy travels through space as *electromagnetic waves*.

Enzyme: a *protein* made in the body, which causes a chemical reaction to take place. The body needs many enzymes for all its different chemical reactions.

Equator: an imaginary line around the Earth, representing 0° latitude, which is exactly half-way between the north and south *poles*.

Erosion: the process by which natural forces, such as weathering, running water, the action of bodies of ice and sea waves, wear away the land.

Evaporation: a change of state – opposite to *condensation* – such as when a liquid becomes a gas or vapour. Evaporation occurs when water is heated and changed into invisible water vapour.

Evolution: the gradual development of plants and animals, whereby higher life forms have arisen out of lower forms, over millions of years.

Extinct: no longer living or active. An animal *species* becomes extinct when the last member of the species dies. An extinct *volcano* is one which has not erupted for over 25,000 years.

Fault: a crack in the *Earth's crust* along which rocks have moved.

Fertilization: the joining together of a male sex *cell* and a female sex cell. The resulting cell develops into a young animal or plant.

Fibre optics: fine, transparent fibres, and their use to guide beams of light along any required path. In telecommunications, the fibres are used to convey light beams carrying numerous sound or vision signals (see pages 186–7).

Filler: a substance, usually a powder, added to industrial material to make it more bulky. For example, powdered chalk and clay are sometimes added during the manufacture of rubber.

Fission: see *nuclear fission*.

Foetus: an unborn baby during the last six months of development inside its mother's womb (see pages 116–7 for how an unborn baby develops).

Fold: an upward or downward bend in formerly level *rock strata*, which was caused by lateral (sideways) pressure (see pages 22–3 for a description of fold mountains).

Force: that which can alter a body's state of motion or rest. A force applied to a body initially at rest will cause it to accelerate. The force of *gravity* causes a body to accelerate towards the ground when dropped.

Fossil: any evidence of ancient life found in rocks (see pages 38–9 for a description of the main kinds of fossils).

Fossil fuel: coal, petroleum oil or natural gas. These fuels were all formed in the Earth's crust as the fossil remains of once-living *organisms* (see pages 34–7).

Frequency: the rate at which waves occur. The unit of frequency is the hertz, which is equal to one cycle (complete wave) per second.

Friction: a force that tends to resist the motion of one surface over another. The moving parts of machines are oiled to overcome friction. Brakes on cars use friction to slow the wheels.

Fungi: a group of plants that reproduce by means of spores and do not contain *chlorophyll*. Familiar fungi include moulds and toadstools (see pages 50–51).

Fusion: see *nuclear fusion*.

Generator: see *electric generator*.

Glacier: a body of ice formed from compressed snow in mountains, which flows downhill along the valleys.

Gland: an *organ* in the body, or in a plant, that makes a special substance and then releases it. Some glands in the body, such as sweat glands and milk glands, release their substances outside the body. Other glands release their substances into the *bloodstream*.

Gravity: a force of attraction that exists between any two masses of matter. For example, the Earth's gravity attracts objects towards it and is responsible for their weight.

213

Glossary

Harmonics: multiples of a main (fundamental) *frequency* at which waves are produced. The different harmonics of various musical instruments help to give them their characteristic sounds (see pages 142–3).

Holography: a technique by which *laser* light is used to photograph objects and reproduce them in three dimensions. The images are recorded as complex patterns. These are formed by the addition and cancellation of waves in two beams of light, one of which is reflected from the object (see pages 188–9).

Hormones: substances made by *glands* in the body and released into the *bloodstream*, where they act as chemical messengers (as described on pages 106–7).

Ice sheet: a vast, thick body of ice, such as those that blanket Greenland and Antarctica. Smaller ice sheets are called ice caps.

Igneous rock: any rock formed when *magma* solidifies, either underground or on the surface.

Infection: invasion of the body by harmful *microbes*.

Invertebrate: an animal without a backbone, for example insects, shellfish and worms.

Isotopes: *atoms* of the same *element* that contain different numbers of *neutrons* in their nuclei. Isotopes are distinguished from one another by their atomic number (the total number of neutrons and *protons* in each atom). Carbon-12, for example, is much more common than carbon-13.

Labour: the mother's part in the birth of her baby (for the various stages of labour, see pages 118–9).

Laser: a device used to produce extremely pure, concentrated light, with all its waves in step with one another. This is called coherent light. The word laser is made up from the initials of a phrase describing how it works: Light Amplification by Stimulated Emission of Radiation (see pages 188–9).

Latitude: the angular distance of a place north or south of the *equator*, measured from the centre of the Earth. Lines of latitude are imaginary lines around the Earth that are parallel to the equator, which is 0° latitude.

Lava: molten rock (*magma*), which erupts on to the Earth's surface through *volcanoes*.

Long-shore drift: the process by which sand and pebbles are moved along beaches in a zig-zag direction, because waves push these materials up beaches at an oblique angle, while the backwash pulls them back at right angles to the shore.

Magma: molten rock formed by great heat and pressure at considerable depths below the Earth's surface.

Mammal: an animal with hair that suckles its young. There are three kinds of mammals: monotremes, which lay eggs; marsupials, which give birth to undeveloped young that are then kept in a pouch (see pages 78–9); and placental mammals, which retain their young inside a womb until they are quite well developed – the young are nourished in the womb by a *placenta*.

Marsupial: see *mammal*.

Mass: a measure of the amount of matter in a body. On the Earth, a mass of one kilogram would weigh one kilogram. On the Moon, its weight would be less, as the Moon's weaker *gravity* would not exert such a strong pull on it. But its mass would be the same, because it would still contain the same amount of matter.

Mating: the act by which male and female animals bring together their sex *cells* prior to *fertilization*.

Membrane: a thin, soft, sheet of *tissue* which covers or lines *organs* and other parts in the body.

Metamorphic rock: an *igneous* or *sedimentary* rock that has been changed by heat, pressure or by chemical action inside the *Earth's crust*. For example, limestone is changed into marble, and shale into slate.

Metamorphosis: a rapid change of form. In animals the change is from a larval form, for example a tadpole or caterpillar, to a completely different adult form, such as a frog or butterfly.

Meteor: a shooting star, consisting of lumps of rock that usually burn up when they enter the *atmosphere*. Lumps of rock that do reach the Earth's surface are called meteorites.

Microbe: a form of life that is microscopic in size. Microbes include viruses, *bacteria*, *protozoa* and various *algae* and *fungi*.

Microcircuit: a miniature electronic *circuit*, usually containing thousands of *transistors*. These are assembled on a chip of silicon measuring only a few millimetres square.

Microscopic organism: see *Microbe*.

Migration: the movement of a population of animals from one area to another and back again. Animals generally migrate in autumn from their summer breeding area to a warmer area, in which they spend the winter. They then return to their breeding area in spring.

Mineral: an inorganic (lifeless) substance that has a definite chemical composition and particular properties. Some minerals are native (pure) *elements*, but most are chemical combinations of two or more elements. Rocks are made up of minerals.

Molecule: normally, a combination of *atoms*. A molecule of the *element* hydrogen, for example, consists of two hydrogen atoms. A molecule of a *compound*, such as water, contains atoms of different elements – in this case, hydrogen and oxygen. Certain rare gases occur as single atoms. These are described as monatomic molecules.

Mollusc: any one of the group of animals that includes shellfish, snails, slugs, squids and octopuses.

Morse code: a signalling code invented by Samuel Morse in 1837. In the code, various combinations of dots and dashes – short and long signals –

represent letters and numbers. The signals are usually sent as bursts of *radio waves* or as flashes of light.

Navigate: to find the way from one place to another; to find one's position and work out which way to travel.

Nerve: a *cell* with a long fibre along which electrical messages pass in the body. Cell fibres extend to and from the brain, spinal cord and most other parts of the body.

Neutron: a particle found in the nuclei of all *atoms*, except hydrogen. Unlike the *proton*, the neutron has no electric *charge*.

Nourishment: substances needed by the body for its health and growth. Food and *oxygen*, carried in the *bloodstream*, are nourishment for *cells* and *tissues*.

Nuclear fission: a reaction in which the nucleus of an atom is split, with the release of nuclear *energy*. Fission reactions are used in nuclear power stations and atomic bombs (see pages 152–3).

Nuclear fusion: a reaction in which atomic nuclei are joined, with the release of nuclear *energy*. The Sun and the hydrogen bomb produce their energy by means of fusion reactions (see pages 152–3).

Orbit: the path of one body around another. *Electrons* move in an orbit around the nucleus of an *atom*. The *planets* orbit around the Sun.

Ore: a *mineral* substance from which one or more useful metals or non-metals are extracted.

Organ: a part of an animal or plant body composed of special tissues, which performs a particular function. Two examples in the body are the heart, which pumps blood, and the skin, which is the body's outermost protective covering.

Organelle: small structure in the cytoplasm of a *cell* that has a particular function (see pages 40–41).

Organism: any individual animal or plant.

Oxygen: an odourless, invisible gas that makes up about 20 per cent of the Earth's *atmosphere*. Oxygen is essential to all living *organisms* in the process of *respiration*, and is produced by green plants during *photosynthesis*.

Parasite: an *organism* that lives on another (its host), depending on it for food and/or water. The host does not benefit, and some parasites eventually destroy their hosts.

Photosynthesis: the process in which plants make their own food (in the form of sugar) from water and *carbon dioxide*. Two essential aids to this process are *chlorophyll* and light. *Oxygen* is released during photosynthesis.

Pigment: a colouring substance. Two examples are a pigment which colours a paint, and the colouring pigment of an animal's fur or eyes.

Placenta: an organ which develops inside a pregnant woman, and passes *nourishment* from her bloodstream to that of her unborn child.

Planet: a heavenly body that rotates around a star, such as the Sun.

Plates: large, rigid blocks of the *Earth's crust* that are slowly moving, carrying the land masses which rest on them around the globe (see pages 16–17 for a description of plate tectonics and continental drift).

Poles: two points on the Earth's surface at the ends of the Earth's axis are the geographical poles. They are at latitudes 90° north and 90° south. Because of Earth magnetism there are also two magnetic poles, which are near the geographical poles.

Pollination: the act of transferring pollen from an anther to a stigma (see pages 46–7).

Polymer: a substance consisting of giant chemical *molecules*, each of which is made up of many small sub-units linked together. Natural polymers include cellulose (cotton); and man-made polymers include plastics.

Power: the rate at which work is done, or *energy* used up. When energy is used at the rate of 1 joule per second, the power consumed is 1 watt.

Predator: an animal that hunts, kills and eats other animals (its *prey*).

Preservative: a substance that prevents decay or other forms of deterioration. Preservatives are often added to packaged foods.

Prey: see *predator*.

Primate: any one of the group of animals that includes monkeys, apes and Man.

Proteins: chemical compounds with very large *molecules*, which are very important in the body. Muscle or red meat, and hair, are composed mostly of proteins. The vital molecules called *enzymes* are other forms of proteins.

Proton: a particle found in the nuclei of all *atoms*. It has a positive electric *charge*, equal in strength to the negative charge on an *electron*.

Protozoa: microscopic, single-cell forms of life. They are larger than *bacteria* and, unlike *algae*, do not have the green *pigment, chlorophyll*.

Puberty: the time of life when a girl develops into a woman, or a boy into a man.

Radar: the technique of transmitting bursts of *radio waves* and observing any reflections obtained. This may be done to locate aircraft, ships or objects that reflect radio waves. The word radar stands for RAdio Detection And Ranging (see pages 180–81).

Radioactivity: the property of certain unstable *atoms* to emit radiation spontaneously and form atoms of other *elements*. The *isotope* radium-226, for example, emits two *protons* and two *neutrons*. This process, called decay, converts it to the isotope radon-222.

Radio-waves: *electromagnetic waves* used to carry sound and vision signals for purposes of communication and entertainment. Like other types of electromagnetic waves, radio waves travel through space at the speed of light (see pages 178–9).

Glossary

Raw material: a natural substance used in industry to make products. For example, cotton is a raw material for making clothing, and crude oil is a raw material for making petrol.

Reptile: any one of the group of animals that includes snakes, lizards, crocodiles and turtles.

Respiration: the process in which an *organism* takes in *oxygen* and uses it to 'burn' food chemicals, which release energy. *Carbon dioxide* is formed during the process and is released.

Richter scale: a scale used to measure the intensity of *earthquakes*. The scale runs from 1 to 9 and each successive number represents a ten-fold increase in the magnitude (strength) over the previous number. For example, people hardly notice an earthquake with a 2-point magnitude. But a 7-point magnitude earthquake is severe, being 100,000 times more powerful.

Rock strata: distinctive layers of rock, usually *sedimentary rocks*, which range in thickness between several metres and a few millimetres.

Sediment: material that settles at the bottom of a liquid, such as the fine mud, sand and gravel that has been worn from the land and carried into the sea by rivers, or the remains of sea *organisms* that settle on sea beds.

Sedimentary rocks: rocks formed mostly from layers of sediment which settle on sea and lake beds. Some sedimentary rocks, such as coal, consist mainly of organic matter. Others are formed by chemical action, such as rock salt, which is left behind when seas dry up.

Sense organs: the *organs* of sight, hearing, touch, taste and smell, all of which tell the brain about what is happening outside the body.

Solar energy: *energy* produced by nuclear reactions that take place in the Sun. This is radiated as light and various other forms of *electromagnetic waves* (see pages 134–5).

Solar system: the Sun, together with the nine planets, their satellites (moons), asteroids, comets and meteors, which rotate around the Sun.

Sonar: the technique of detecting the position of objects by producing very high-frequency sound waves and listening to the echoes.

Species: the smallest group used in the classification of animals and plants. Members of the same species can successfully breed only with each other. The Latin name of a species has two parts, for example *Panthera leo* (the Lion) and *Panthera tigris* (the Tiger). *Panthera* is the genus name: *leo* and *tigris* define the two species.

Spectrum: a band of *electromagnetic waves* of different *frequencies*. The spectrum of white light, for example, consists of rays of different colours (see pages 134–5).

Stomata: tiny pores on the undersides of the leaves of flowering plants (see pages 48–9). When open, they allow *oxygen* and *carbon dioxide* to pass in and out of the leaves (see *photosynthesis* and *respiration*) and water to pass out (see *transpiration*).

Supercooled liquid: a liquid that has been cooled below its freezing point without becoming solid. Only liquids completely free from dust or other particles can be supercooled.

Synthetic material: a man-made material, such as a plastic or a synthetic rubber.

Temperate regions: the middle latitudes of the world, where there are no extremes of cold or heat, and where the year is normally divided into distinctive seasons.

Tissues: substances made up of many *cells*, which make up the various *organs* and other parts of the body. Examples are bone, blood, mucous *membrane* and glandular tissue.

Transistor: a crystal of silicon or germanium, specially treated so that it can be used to amplify (strengthen) electrical signals (see pages 176–7).

Transpiration: the loss of water by evaporation from the *stomata* of the leaves of a plant (see pages 48–9).

Tropical regions: the part of the world between the Tropic of Cancer (*latitude* 23½° north) and the Tropic of Capricorn (23½° south), where it is generally hot all the year round.

Turbine: a wheel with blades turned by a flow of liquid or gas. Most power stations use steam turbines to drive their *generators*. Hydroelectric power stations use water turbines (see page 146).

Ultrasonic: a term applied to waves having a *frequency* higher than that of sound – that is, above about 20,000 hertz. Ultrasonic drills work by vibrating rapidly rather than turning, and can cut square holes.

Vacuum: an empty space which does not even contain air.

Vertebrate: an animal with a backbone, for example fishes, amphibians, reptiles, birds and mammals.

Vitamins: substances contained in some foods, which are vital for health, but which the body needs only in very small amounts.

Volcano: a hole in the Earth's crust where *magma* rises to the surface; also the mountain formed by the erupted magma (see pages 20–21).

Voltage: a measurement, in volts, of electromotive force. This is the electrical 'pressure' that makes a *current* flow around a *circuit*. The potential difference – the difference in electrical pressure between any two points – is also expressed as a voltage.

Water vapour: invisible moisture in the air, created by *evaporation* and *transpiration*.

Wavelength: the physical length of a wave, measured in metres. Waves emitted at high *frequency* have a relatively short wavelength. This is because they follow closely, one after another.

Weather: the day-to-day condition of the air. The typical weather of a place, based on average weather conditions measured over a long period, is known as the climate.

Index

A

Index

Index